Wendy Rober...........................lecturer and journalist,
was recently Arts Council Writer in Residence in a
women's prison. *THE LONG JOURNEY HOME* is her
seventeenth novel in a list which includes contemporary,
historical and children's novels. She lives in the north of
England.

# The Long Journey Home

Wendy Robertson

**headline**

First published in 2002
by HEADLINE BOOK PUBLISHING

First published in paperback in 2003
by HEADLINE BOOK PUBLISHING

10 9 8 7 6 5 4 3 2

ISBN 0 7472 6601 8

Typeset in Times by Avon Dataset Ltd, Bidford-on-Avon, Warks

Printed and bound in Great Britain by
Clays Ltd, St Ives plc

HEADLINE BOOK PUBLISHING
A division of Hodder Headline
338 Euston Road
London NW1 3BH

www.headline.co.uk
www.hodderheadline.com

To the late Jean S., who told me the Raffles tale that inspired this story. In writing the novel I also pay tribute to the women of all races who find themselves stranded on the fault-lines of countries at war. Their grit, endurance and grace often go unremarked but to me these women are heroines.

# Acknowledgements

The events and characters in this novel are pure fiction, but in bringing them to life I have been helped by conversations, correspondence with, and materials from, a range of people. These include Anne Gibbon and her mother, Margaret Blyth, who escaped together on one of the last ships from Singapore, and Jeremy Atkinson, whose father was a quiet hero of the last days. I talked to John Fenton, who was there with the RAF after the liberation, and Peter Lee of Singapore showed me his beloved island. I would also like to thank Avril Joy for her friendly support during the Singapore research, during which we found ourselves unwittingly, albeit temporarily, resident in the red-light district.

# Glossary

*amah* – generic term for maidservant, so a wash-*amah* is a laundry woman

*barang* – luggage

brownout – Singapore version of the British blackout

*kampong* – village

*chi-chak* – small house lizard

*chungkol* – spade

*godown* – quayside warehouse

*jaga* – Sikh watchman. Many houses and businesses had these

*kebun* – gardener

*Kempai Tai* – Japanese secret police

*kongsi* – group of friends, probably from the same district in China

*padang* – open green space, square

*sambal* – relish made from vegetables and fruit

*sola topee* – pith sun helmet

*stengah* – cooling drink, popular with men. Also a derogatory term for a Eurasian – half and half, like the drink

*susah* – carry-on, row

*syce* – groom/driver

*tong* – stoneware jar

*trompahs* – wooden-soled home-made mules

*tuan besar* – great gentleman, big boss

*tutup* – soft collarless jacket

# Prologue

I have this dream. It comes back to me from time to time. It came in the night as I huddled in an alleyway near the big liquor *godown*. It came in those broken nights in the camp on the slatted platform they called a bed.

In this dream I'm sitting on a wall by the great priory gates. My legs can't reach the pavement so I must be four or five years old. We must be 'home' on leave in London and visiting my nana in the North. My real home, though, is Singapore, where I was born. I know this even inside the dream.

Someone has lifted me on to the high wall to keep me out of their way. A voice is saying something about me being a dratted nuisance yet again. Then I can see the burly broadcloth back of my nana receding towards the market. This market is the grey Durham market I would expect. But I can see acrobats and puppets and bright dancers like those in the Great World; a swaying kite in the form of a fat bright mandarin. If they are true, then the smell is wrong. Where's the stench of spices and fragrant flowers, human sweat and open drains? Instead, my nose wrinkles at the smell of cold and cabbages. Potato chips fried in animal fat. And the prickle of burning tar.

In this dream, imprisoned as I am on the high wall, I have to content myself with watching passers-by. This is when I see the boy, blond-haired, narrow-faced, nodding his head as he juggles three white tennis balls that flutter from his hands like butterflies, over his head, behind his back, higher and higher in the air.

Now in my dream I fly from the wall to his side and the balls have multiplied from three to six, to eight, to twelve, to twenty-four. They're flying between us, and through the spinning whirl of balls I can see him laughing, his blue eyes shining like ships' portholes.

Now he's caught me; throws me into the air as though I, too, am a ball. Now I'm flying through the air again and again, high, back on to my place of imprisonment on the wall and he is nowhere to be seen.

That is the dream.

Mind you, I think I do have what I know are real memories of this same pale boy. We were on leave from Singapore again, visiting Nana in her tall house opposite the Grammar School in Priorton, the Durham town that was her home. Feargal was there, a baby then, like a coiled pink shell on my mother's shoulder. Crying, always crying, piercing to the bone of my head.

Nana's house was larger than the rest in that road, having two front bays and a warren of rooms upstairs. I don't know how many months we were there. We'd come up from our London home to be away from the bombing. It was the very beginning of the war in Europe. My father was only present then in his letters, which crackled like dry leaves. They came from that 'land of milk and honey' which was Singapore, and flaunted lists of mangoes, pomegranates, pineapples, bananas, bougainvillaea, oleander and moonflowers with faces as large as plates.

The crackling letters made me feel sad. They made me think of the dry certainty of pure heat in that far place where I was born.

In that Durham house with two bays the air between my mother and grandma would spit and spark like Chinese crackers. There'd be pneumatic sighs from my mother and clashing pans from my nana. The baby always wailed. In the fractured space between them I grew naughtier and naughtier. I think it got to be a habit.

A year later on the long veranda, my mother and father talked about those rows. My mother took a gurgling sip of her gin *pahit*. 'My mother has no idea,' she said.

'She means it all for the best, Lesley.' My father had this deep soft voice he used with my mother, always talking through a smile.

I remember then he touched her neck and my own neck shivered with embarrassment. (Their passion excluded out-siders, especially children.)

But to get back to that early time in the house in Durham, England. On this particular day there is something about the way my mother dresses. Always very elegant, she is more so today. There is something about the paint she puts on her face, the heavy scent she wears. These things make me feel warm towards her, excited by her.

I sit beside her at the dressing table as she presses and powders her face, prinks and curls her hair.

'There, darling, what do you think of Mummy?' She looks at her reflection, fine brows arched.

For once she's gentle with me, soft. There is a tender hand on my shoulder, a murmured suggestion that today we're going to a castle, no less! Just me and her. 'Feargal will stay with Nana. Just you and I will go to the castle.'

She shows me her special invitation from Lord Chase, on thin shiny cardboard. It seems that we're buying Spitfires for the War Effort, to beat the Germans. Just me and her.

That is, just me and her and a thousand others. We arrive to find a Spitfire aeroplane parked just inside the castle gates. There are big red fire buckets placed all round it. The coins people throw in chink on to the pile below. They do this, then press through the gate in droves. My mother stops to look up into the eyes of an officer with a big peaked cap.

This is my chance to slip round the corner, along a narrow path and through a gate into a kind of citadel enclosed by four long brick walls. Row on row of cabbages, cauliflowers, leeks and wayward beans grow there. Apples and plums climb up walls trying to escape the marauding potatoes.

In one corner of the citadel a boy is throwing a ball up against the wall: throwing with one hand, catching with the other. Throwing with one hand, catching with the other.

He must know I'm here but he ignores me. I make my way down one of the narrow paths, passing my hands over the tops of cabbages. My fingertips itch. In the corner of the garden stand two old apple trees, stubby and gnarled. On their branches the blossoms have just folded and tightened themselves into buds.

I climb the low branches of one of these trees and lie along a branch like a tiger. I've seen tigers and I know how they lie. My father's friend shot one off the Bukit Timah road. I heard him tell the story. I close my eyes, knowing the walls protect me and my mother will never find me. I can smell green, and can hear a single bee buzzing.

Through veiled eyes I see the boy coming nearer and nearer, throwing the ball ahead of him to lead him forward. He stops beside me.

'It's private here,' he says. 'You shouldn't be in this place.'

I survey him from the top of his blond head to the heels of his brogue shoes. He's very big. I've not worked out yet when people stop being boys and girls and become grown-up. This boy is somewhere in that shady place in between.

'We paid. We put money in the box. My mother did.'

'That money's for out there. This is in here. This is private.' He's staring at me very intensely. I feel that soon he'll throw that ball at me like it was a stone. I have to do something to stop him.

'We were bombed out,' I offer. 'In London. Our street was flattened.'

The hand with the ball drops to his side. 'Your house was bombed?' he says. His voice is like Mr Attwood's, our doctor back at home in Singapore – kind of drawly and soft, echoing somewhere in his nose and cheeks.

'No.' I have to admit this. 'But the house next door was. So we decided to skedaddle.'

He starts to bounce the ball off the wall. 'So, who's *we*?'

'My mother and my baby brother. And me.'

'Is your father in the forces, then?'

'No. He's out in Singapore. He manages the office of a firm which Ships Rubber for the War Effort.' I've heard my mother say these words in this same defensive tone. I'm not quite sure what they mean, but they do the trick.

'Oh. Well.' He puts down the ball and crouches down, his back against the wall, still watching me closely. 'Are you from Singapore?'

'Yes. I was born there. We're on leave so my mother can have the baby. First in London and now here. She's had him now. His name's Feargal. We're going back to Singapore soon. My mother says it's safer there and there's no rationing. They have fruit there. And sweets. It's safer. I belong there.'

'I'd have picked you for a foreigner. Suited to it. Dark-skinned, don't you know?'

'No, I don't know. It's rude to talk about people's skin. My mother says so.' I change tack, as I've seen her do many times, when *skin* is mentioned. 'So is your father at the war, then?'

'Yes,' he says. 'North Africa. And I'll go in two years, when I'm eighteen. The Durham Light Infantry.'

'Do you want to kill people?' I'm curious. 'They kill people, soldiers.'

'You have to. My father killed Huns in the Great War. We practise it at school. Officer training.'

'Oh.' I am tired of all this talking, having to say sensible things to this man-boy. I jump down from my branch. The tree shudders, rustles, and settles itself. 'Well,' I say, echoing my mother's voice. 'We're getting out of it. All the killing.'

'How's that?'

'We're going to Singapore on a big ship. Out of the range of the bombs.' I pick my way back down the path. 'No bombs there. No rationing. Lovely flowers. And fruit. I remember them. And my father says so in his letters.' I'm back at the gate, a place of safety.

'Hey!' His voice rings down to me the length of the garden.

'What?' I yell.

'Have I seen you somewhere before?'

He has. On another leave. In the marketplace. He was the juggler. But I don't want to let him know he's right. He's too clever by half. 'Don't be silly,' I say. 'How could you?'

Of course, when I get back to the priory gates my mother's frantic; she's been charging about in the crowd looking for me. 'What is it about you, Sylvie? Stupid girl. Always running away.' She grabs my arm and smacks my bottom all the way to the gate and I set up this great howling. The crowd parting before us looks on in approval.

# Chapter One

## The Sambucks at Home

*Monday, 8 December 1941*

Lesley Sambuck lay back in the long wicker chair, breathing very slowly, allowing the hot air to cool as it entered her body. The fan paddled the air, creating its own oven-warm breeze. The shimmering light, dancing under the pearly cloud cover, made her view of the town, stretching out beyond the garden, swell and retract with her pulse.

Lesley's glance dropped to the rolling lawn. She wasn't satisfied with what she saw. Despite Bo's dedicated work with the *kebuns*, the problem of the lumpy hills in the lawn hadn't been solved. Lesley liked things in straight lines.

Wong Mee walked on silent feet across the veranda, tray in hand. Lesley took the new glass greedily from him before he could place it in its wicker holder.

She settled back again. One of the dips in the lawn almost hid the gaggle of children near the gate, who clustered round the slender, linen-clad figure of Virginia Chen. Lesley stood up and took a step towards the edge of the veranda, shading her eyes against the brassy glare. How she wished it were evening so that the darkness would allow the offshore breeze to filter up the hill to cool the wide verandas of Hibiscus Lodge.

'Whatever will we do with that girl, Bo?' she said.

'She's just boisterous, Lesley. A little girl, that's all.' Bo, lounging in the other long chair, kept his eyes glued to the *Straits Times*.

'Little? Nine years old is hardly little.' Lesley eased the collar of her dress. She'd have to go in and change it in a minute, for one almost identical. She'd never been able to bear the sense of her own sweat seeping through the cloth. If her dresses were only slightly marked she could instruct the wash-*amah* to refrain from giving them her usual destructive pounding. This only worked if the clothes were virtually clean when the woman took them away.

They were sitting in the deep shadow of their veranda, waiting to catch any breeze that would honour them with its presence. 'I should have left her at home. My mother . . .' Lesley's thin, elocuted voice cut the air like a sharp-edged reed.

'Her place is here, with us, Lesley. I told you not to talk of the child leaving,' Bo, his voice suddenly very sharp, clipped in a military fashion, rapped out. 'She should be here.' He was used to his wife's plaintive arguments over the girl and gave no quarter.

Lesley retreated to regroup. Before her, on the long lawn, her son, Feargal, whose birthday they were celebrating, was playing sedately, batting a ball to and fro with his *amah*, Ah

So. The nursemaid, immaculate in her wide black silk trousers and white blouse, moved at a speed that belied her natural dignity.

The boisterous Sylvia, more usually called Sylvie, was some distance away, almost lost to sight by the undulating lawns. She was turning very effective cartwheels and ignoring the young party guests. With every turn she showed her long brown legs and flashed white knickers.

Lesley could bear it no longer. 'Miss Chen,' she called, 'would you kindly go and organise some game which does not involve Sylvie being upside down half the time?'

Virginia Chen emerged from the cluster of children and glided across to where Sylvie was. Her linen dress accented her slender figure. Lesley reflected resentfully that Virginia could wear a dress all day without showing a mark.

'It's in the blood,' she murmured.

'What was that, dear?' Bo looked at her over his paper, having just read yet again that although the Japanese were rattling their samurai swords on the mainland to the north, there was no chance, no chance at all, that Singapore would be threatened. It was armed. Impregnable. 'What is it now?'

'Virginia Chen never perspires,' she said. 'All normal people perspire in this awful climate.'

He nodded. 'They tend not to – the Eurasians. But it's not an awful climate, Les. It's just different.'

'Mm. As I was saying, it's in the blood.' She looked at her husband, immaculate in his soft cotton jacket and sarong. He, like many of the Europeans, resorted to a version of local dress to relax in. 'Come to think of it, you don't perspire.'

'It's the tennis, old girl. My old man always advocated it. Two hours' hard tennis a day. Thins the blood. You should take it up.'

Lesley watched now as Virginia Chen drew all the children around her, rising from the crowd of young faces like a flower stamen. She had Feargal by the hand. Ah So was standing by the hedge with two other *amahs*. These women were her friends, part of her *kongsi*. They too had come originally from Guangzhou province to escape the mother-in-law-driven oppression of a Chinese marriage. At Feargal Sambuck's party they watched over their European charges with proprietorial affection.

It just took a few minutes to get a game of rounders into some kind of shape. Sylvie cracked a great hit into the bougainvillaea and was flying round the wooden markers, her skirt tucked into her knickers.

'She'll have to go,' announced Lesley. 'Go to school. She can stay with my mother in Durham and go to my old school. It would quieten her down. They certainly kept me in order at The Mount.'

'Sylvie's not the same as you, Les. She's very different.' Bo clicked his finger and Wong Mee silently glided in to fill his glass. A half-glass of whisky topped up with soda – the perfect *stengah*.

Lesley flushed. 'I can't think why you say this. Sylvie's my daughter – our daughter. How can she be different?'

Sylvie had been born exactly one year after Lesley came out to Singapore and exactly ten months after Bo and Lesley had been married. The child was a perfect stranger, with her golden skin and black hair. 'Well, sweetheart, she's nothing like you. A chip off another old block,' he said now, savouring his *stengah*. 'Bit of a throwback, old Sylvie,' he went on. He wasn't looking at Lesley but she could feel his keen attention all the same. She flooded with resentment at him, with his hearty certainties, his teasing. There had been some joke at a party once about a man in his old regiment who'd been threateningly dark. 'What we need is pedigrees. Like the gee-gees. Ten generations. Save coming up with a touch of the tarbrush in the wrong place, what?'

She'd joined in his laughter. Bo's family had been in India for sixty years. He must know something about all that. But now Lesley felt resentful. 'She's your daughter, Bo. She is just about out of control.'

'Wouldn't say that, old thing. Turned a very fine cartwheel myself at that age.' He rattled the paper. 'Old Shenton Thomas says we're safe as houses down here on the island. Those bombs last night – just a chance unloading of some idiot Jap pilot.'

Lesley sipped her drink. 'The Governor should know about that if anyone would. So many soldiers in the town now. Can't turn a corner without bumping into one.'

'There you are,' said Bo. 'Safe as houses.'

The sweating was getting too much again. Lesley returned to the cooler depths of the veranda and the sanctuary of her long wicker chair. 'That's a comfort.' She paused. 'I thought at least my mother would be safe in Durham. But it's so dangerous back there in England. Think how those planes flattened Coventry. Now they are bombing the Tyne.' She shuddered.

'Just now you were wanting to send Sylvie there. Rationing, bombing – send her there and if she doesn't die of starvation she'll be blown to bits.'

'Don't exaggerate, Bo dear. Ma's safe as houses up in Durham. No aeroplane factories there.'

'Jolly nice cathedral, though, for them to blow up. Happened in Coventry. It can happen in Durham.'

'Bo! Don't.' A hard ball came whooshing through the hanging bougainvillaea and rattled on the boards just beside her chair. Shouts and squeals from young throats cut the soft air like fine reeds. Bo picked up the ball and threw it back. Lesley went to the edge of the veranda to see Miss Chen, with a wriggling Sylvie held firmly by the hand, marching back towards the game.

'That child!' said Lesley.

'Throwback,' said Bo. He sat down again and pulled up the drawbridge of his newspaper with rustling finality. 'Can't argue with the blood.'

Lesley stared at the children running and shrieking at the behest of the cool Virginia Chen. At the other side of the lawn the *amahs* now sat with younger children on their knees or at their feet. They twittered among themselves like a flock of birds.

This predilection of the Chinese and Malays to speak their own language among themselves had annoyed Lesley from the first. Bo laughed at her, told her it was *their* country and she should take some lessons. He'd done that himself straight away when he'd arrived here from Ceylon in '31. Easy as pie, he'd said. And he did rattle away at them all with disturbing ease.

*Easy as pie*. Bo had a cool way of boasting that did not make it seem like a boast.

Lesley had been instantly defeated by the complications of Chinese. She'd tried more lessons in Malay but the kind, patient teacher made her mind feel like cotton wool, her tongue feel like a log in her mouth. In the end, parrot fashion, she'd learned just a few essential words that everyone used: *amah* for a Chinese maidservant, *ayah* if she were Indian or Malay. *Barang* meant luggage. *Stengah* was Bo's favourite drink. *Bukit* meant hill. This one was easy. Bo played golf at the course at Bukit Timah – Timah Hill – three times a week. She usually joined him there to meet friends on the terrace at six thirty. They'd sit over long drinks and listen to the band that played there every evening from six to eight thirty. The brief sunset, sometimes blood red as the ball of the sun set into the shimmering pink and purple of the lake there, was one of the sights of Singapore.

Then there was *jaga*, which meant watchman or guard – usually Sikh; *cumshaw*, which meant tip; *prahus* and *sampans*, those crowds of stinking native boats in the harbour. And just a few more.

Although she knew these words Lesley avoided saying any of them. They felt clumsy in her mouth. If she needed to say anything in the streets or in the shops, Virginia Chen, who spoke all their dratted languages, was usually on hand. In the house, Lesley tried, without much success, to insist that the servants spoke only English, even among themselves.

This need to be outside and above what was going on

around her set in with Lesley early in her life. Her father, ex-army, latterly a much-feared primary school headmaster, had insisted on what he called 'the King's English', and was not above getting out his leather strap if she brought home the quaint South Durham words she heard at school. He shuddered with distaste when she spoke in that local fashion. So those home-grown musical vowels came to make her shudder too. This created some difficulty because her own mother spoke in this way. She learned to shudder at this alongside her father.

She suffered the same effect now when she heard these Malay and Chinese words on Sylvie's lips. She knew perfectly well that sometimes Sylvie would deliberately tease her by saying those dratted foreign words. Though there was no leather strap she'd slapped Sylvie more than once for using them.

'Mother, Mother.' The subject of Lesley's recent reverie was standing before her, sweat on her upper lip, dress tucked into her pants, demanding her attention.

'What is it, Sylvie?' Lesley touched her own neck again. The collar of her dress was soaking.

'One of the boys here says a bomb dropped on Robinson's last night. That was what we heard – those bangs and crashes down in the town. Will we be able to shop there now? Will they drop a bomb on us up here? Like in England?' The sherry-coloured eyes looked directly into Lesley's, demanding, as always, a direct answer.

'Yes, a bomb did drop on Robinson's. And no, one will not drop on us. We are perfectly safe. Now go and play. Fifteen minutes. Then you'll have to change out of your dress. We have guests arriving at two.' She turned to Ah So, who had walked softly up to the veranda with a tearful Feargal in her arms.

'What is it, Ah So?' Lesley's voice as always was sharp when dealing with her servants. It was the only way.

'Feargal fall down and hit his head, *mem*.' Ah So surveyed her calmly. 'Needs calm down.'

Feargal looked up at his mother from the safety of Ah So's narrow hip, unshed tears still in his eyes.

'Give him a cool drink and sponge him down. This heat is just too much for him. And while you are inside, Ah So, lay out Miss Sylvie's green gingham frock. The one she's wearing will not survive the rounders.'

Sylvie was still looking at her.

'Go and finish your game, Sylvie,' Lesley said, turning back towards her long chair.

'But the Japanese, Mother. They'll bomb here too. John Hoxton says so.'

'Sabre rattling.' Bo's gruff voice emerged from the curtain of his newspaper. 'Samurai sabres. Don't worry, poppet.'

'Go and play, for goodness' sake, girl,' said Lesley, standing up. 'I have to change.' She turned her back on Sylvie and walked along the veranda to her bedroom.

Bo went back to his newspaper. 'Go and turn a few cartwheels, Sylvie, there's a good girl.'

By the time Lesley, showered and changed, had come back along the veranda, Sylvie was on the front lawn bouncing a ball.

Bo smiled faintly at his wife. 'Lovely as ever, Les. You look a treat.' He threw the newspaper down on the wooden floor at the side of his chair. 'I've been thinking. Perhaps the girl *should* go, Les. You and the boy as well. Things are warming up here, no matter what these fools of journalists say.'

'You don't want me to go? Me?' This was hard to believe.

Bo was a bustler, a cool businessman, a hard man with his staff, a man who enjoyed the company of other men. But he loved his home and he loved Lesley. He'd been touchingly delighted when she and the children came back out last year, after their home leave. To celebrate their homecoming he'd had Wong Mee fill the bungalow with flowers and ordered Tang Peng to cook up a feast of seafood and sweet cakes.

Unfortunately that first night she thought she would faint from the scent of Wong Mee's flowers. Bo had to wake the 'boy' out of his bed to clear the bedroom before she could get any sleep.

Now Lesley stood up, glancing at her watch. Two o'clock precisely. 'Here we go,' she said. She called out to Sylvie to go to the *amah* and get her to help her change her frock.

The Hoxtons' Riley was purring up the drive, closely followed by the Carricks' Ford and the Allisons' Citroën. Lesley glanced back to the shady space under the flame trees to where Wong Mee was supervising his brothers, who were putting the finishing touches to Tang Peng's spread. This feast, in the children's honour, included sausages decanted from tins delivered from the Cold Store. But the bulk of it was rice, seafood and exotic pickles – adult fare. A child's party was a good enough excuse for the parents to get together yet again.

Later, tiffin, the midday meal, duly consumed, and the men out on the lawn giving galumphing drunken piggybacks to delighted children, Lesley sat on the veranda, downing iced lime juice with her women guests. Virginia Chen sat slightly to one side, Feargal on her knee. She read *The Tale of Peter Rabbit* to him in a low voice. Feargal kept his eyes on her face, nodding at every word.

Vera Hoxton laughed at the antics of the men. 'Look at them. Big kids, every one of them. Not a care in the world.'

Hilary Carrick scowled. 'The world crumbling around them and they're playing like big kids.'

'Bit of an exaggeration, Hil,' said Fee Allison. 'A stray bomb on Chinatown, that's all.'

'Robinson's new restaurant . . .' said Hilary. 'Blown to bits.'

'So,' said Lesley, 'we can find a new place to eat.'

'The whole thing makes me shudder,' said Hilary. 'Those dreadful little men creeping down Malaya, ready to pounce.'

'Safe as houses,' said Vera. 'Singapore's crawling with soldiers, bristling with guns. Two big ships in the harbour.'

Lesley laughed. 'Bo calls it sabre rattling. We're a different kettle of fish than those Chinese in Nanking. They'll find that to their cost.' She was suddenly aware of Virginia Chen staring at her over Feargal's head, the story forgotten. 'Will you go and get Sylvie, Miss Chen?' she said abruptly. 'She's turning cartwheels again.'

# Chapter Two

## Pearl Harbor

'What's wrong with cartwheels?' Sylvie's voice was muffled by the clean dress, which Ah So was pulling over her head. Her head emerged and she turned round to let the *amah* button up the back and buckle the belt. 'Why can't I do cartwheels?'

Ah So pulled the skirt straight and patted Sylvie on the face, smiling her approval.

Virginia, who was supervising the dressing, laughed at her. 'Because, Miss Indignant, it makes you see the world upside down.' She spoke English with the slightest of lilts, sharp as a china plate. 'And that can't be right. The world must be the right way up.'

'I like it upside down. In fact, what I like most is going up on my hands against the big flame tree. And staying there.'

'Why do you like that?'

'Because it feels like I'm the queen of that upside down world. I can say what I like, do what I like.' Sylvie stood very still while her *amah* put a brush through her smooth black hair. 'In fact, sometimes I swear. A lot.'

'Sylvie!'

'It's just a whisper. I say "bloody".'

'Your mother would be very cross.'

'I whisper it, Miss Chen. No one can hear.'

'It's a sin of the heart. You must not do this.'

'What does that mean? Sin of the heart?'

'If you do a bad thing and no one in the world can see, it stains your heart and you have less heart to love the people you love.'

Sylvie was now immaculate. Ah So put her hands in her sleeves and said something to Virginia.

'What are you saying?' said Sylvie. 'What is she saying, Miss Chen?'

Virginia hesitated.

'You can't tell a lie,' said Sylvie. 'It's a sin of the heart. Tell me what she said.'

'She asks me to ask madam your mother if she may wear a black blouse instead of her white blouse.'

Sylvie frowned. All the *amahs* wore white blouses and black trousers. It was as much a uniform as that of the soldiers and sailors now filling the streets. 'I think she looks nice in her white blouse. I like her in her white blouse. She always wears it.' She took Ah So's arm. 'You look nice with your nice blouse. Black would be like a funeral.' She nodded and smiled at her. She thought of her Great-auntie May's funeral back in Priorton, which had been full of people in musty black, lurching around like crows. 'Why does she not like her white blouse?'

Virginia glanced at Ah So, who was looking at her with a rare crease of anxiety on her face. 'She thinks the white blouse will attract the attention of the Japanese pilots.'

'That's silly!' said Sylvie. 'They can't see from the planes. Really silly.'

'It is not silly,' said Virginia. 'It is fear. She knows the Japanese do not like the Chinese. They hate the Chinese.'

'Because they stole Nanking and Hong Kong?' They'd been through all this before, in their lessons, those unsupervised by Sylvie's mother.

'Yes. And if they steal Singapore it will be a very bad day for the Chinese.'

'And will they steal Singapore?'

'I don't know. I thought not. But . . .' Virginia frowned. 'But we will be all right now, Sylvie, because the Americans will join in the war.'

'Why? Why do they join the war?'

'Because when the Japanese were bombing Robinson's last night, they also bombed a big harbour with American ships, a long way away. So now the Americans will join the war.'

'And the Japanese won't steal Singapore?'

'I don't know this, Sylvie. To be honest I don't know this. I don't know this at all.'

Later that night Lesley, having spent ten minutes hearing Sylvie read her good-night stories, moved to Virginia Chen's door. She knocked, waited for Virginia's voice, then went in. Virginia was sitting at a table writing in the light of the lamp. Above her head the electric fan stirred the still air.

She stood up. 'Mrs Sambuck,' she said, 'can I do something for you?' She was wearing a Chinese silk dressing gown with wide embroidered sleeves and her hair was tied severely back from her face, making her cheekbones more prominent, her eyes narrower.

'You were talking to Sylvie,' began Lesley.

'That is my job, Mrs Sambuck.' There was no trace of irony in her voice. 'Talking to her, reading to her, teaching her.'

'You told her the Japanese had bombed the American navy.'

'Yes. I am afraid it just slipped out.'

'I am surprised at you, Miss Chen. Feeding lies into the mind of an innocent child.'

'They were not lies, Mrs Sambuck. I was talking with Mrs Hoxton's driver, whose cousin drives for the Governor. They have it on government radio. Many ships of the American navy in Hawaii. A great bombing raid. This is the truth.'

'Well, then . . .' Lesley did not quite know what to say. 'You must not speak of these things to Sylvie. She is very impressionable. Overexcitable.'

'Very well, Mrs Sambuck.' Virginia stood very quietly.

As Lesley turned, her eye fell on Virginia's notebook. 'You keep a diary, Miss Chen?'

Virginia moved so her notebook was out of Lesley's eyeline. 'Not so much a diary, Mrs Sambuck, more a daybook, in the Victorian sense.'

Lesley moved to peer more closely in the book. 'You write in English?'

Virginia placed a hand squarely on the open page. 'Of course I do. After all, it is my language.' She paused. 'I could, of course, write it in Mandarin, or in French. But I prefer English, which I learned at my mother's knee.'

Not for the first time, Lesley was floored by this flaunting of intelligence. She herself had gone to a girls' school where, above all, the pupils were taught manners and domestic management. To be faced by a young woman who'd matriculated and spoke three languages fluently, and two others quite well, was disconcerting. Lesley's secret comfort was that at least this cleverness was constrained by one inevitable fact. As a Eurasian, Miss Chen would never be more than a governess, a secretary or a shop girl in Singapore. Could be worse. The high-class whorehouses in the city were full of Eurasians.

Lesley backed out of the room. 'Take care, Miss Chen. One day you might cut yourself with that razor-sharp mind of yours. And for goodness' sake be discreet with Sylvie. She doesn't need to know the terrible things you hear on your Chinese tom-toms.'

'Very well, Mrs Sambuck.' The young woman gave her a very level look, then, very deliberately, sat down and took up her pen. 'Although if you will recall, tom-toms are played in Africa, not Singapore.'

On the other side of the door Lesley stood very still, almost choking with dislike for Virginia Chen. Bo had turned up with the creature one day after Lesley had complained that the *amah* was spoiling Sylvie, who was becoming a veritable savage. She had already disposed of a temporary tutor who couldn't cope with the child.

Bo, in his practical way, had gone to an agency in town and snapped up Virginia Chen, who had the highest qualifications. Bo, having been born in India and worked in the East all his life, had no problems with half-castes. He laughed at Lesley's fears and told her to be careful or she might come across as rather too much of an unsophisticated English provincial.

Lesley was calm by the time she'd walked through the bungalow into the large bedroom she shared with Bo. Beyond the French doors of their bedroom the night ticked and shirred with life. The fireflies danced in the dark of the veranda; the tick-chah of the *chi-chak* punctuated the rustling tropical night.

'According to Virginia Chen,' she said, getting into bed, 'the Japs have bombed the American fleet in Hawaii.'

Bo sat up straight. 'What?'

'You heard what I said.'

'How does she know?'

'Drivers,' said Lesley briefly.

'I see.' The Chinese grapevine was the most reliable source of real information on the island. He reached for her lazily and drew her to him. 'If that's the case, Les, it's the best news I've heard in weeks.'

Virginia Chen: Her Book
There are times when I must remind myself that I am truly lucky to have obtained this post. Mr Sambuck was charming indeed when we first met. He is rather a large, muscular man, rusty coloured in the English way. His

skin is tanned golden brown and his cheeks burn like fire. His hair is bleached to straw. His pale eyes look straight at you in the way we don't like, although I have learned this is not considered bad manners among the English. (Mrs Sambuck is very lacking in manners. I have guessed that she comes from a rather lower station than Mr Sambuck who, despite staring at you, is, in other ways, quite appropriate.)

At my interview – in his dusty quayside office – Mr Sambuck laughed a little at the list of my qualifications. He asked me if I really wanted to teach an eight-year-old whippersnapper who's already caused two tutors to run away howling. I said that I had some thoughts on a teaching career and this was an opportunity to try that out.

Mrs Lesley Sambuck is like so many of the *mems* in one way but unlike them in others. Unlike most of them she is elegant, restrained, not decorating herself like a Christmas tree at the drop of an old hat. Like them, though, she has a great sense of her own consequence without much reason for it. At least the husbands actually do something – they manage their rubber plants, run their *godowns*, police our city, run our hospitals, our administration. They leave the Chinese to run their businesses, to make their own way. But these women are here as part of their *barang*. Camp followers. I read of such in Wellington's army during the Napoleonic wars. They are partners for dance and for bed: decorative ornaments, audiences for bad jokes.

Their qualification is to be untainted and shriek their English.

It's true, I suppose, that this purely decorative function has changed in the last few months. They must do something for the city. They have this odd phrase: 'doing their bit'. So they type lists for the military, roll bandages and count stores in the hospitals and other essential things. Mrs Sambuck, though, is not even burdened by this, having such a small child. Feargal is, of course, taken care of by Ah So and Cookie so he does not disturb the painting of the nails or the consumption of gin *pahit*.

She and Mr Sambuck seem very much in love. There is no denying it. There is little room for anyone else. Especially not Sylvie. I cannot understand how much Mrs Sambuck seems to dislike Sylvie, who is her own daughter. She is very sharp with her, often with no cause. Sometimes very *severe*. Not infrequently Sylvie will run off, away from the tirade. Then Amah and I have to go off with John in the car looking for her. She is never too far and I can't find the heart to chastise her, though this is what Mrs Sambuck instructs. She has been sufficiently chastised.

I do have a feeling that Mrs Sambuck is afraid of those of us who are not European. She gets fidgety if we talk with each other in Chinese or Malay, and shouts, 'English, did I not say English?' like a madwoman. If she ventures to the market she clings to me like a limpet and demands 'Translation! Translation!' As if the stallholders are plotting against her while they are just seeing to their business.

She has little time for the children. Feargal, perhaps, being giggling and helpless, holds some appeal. However, the girl, each time she looks at her it is to criticise and complain.

But there is, as I have said, one saving grace. Her passion for Mr Sambuck lights up the room when they are together. It seems to me that this is no 'fishing marriage' – where desperate Englishwomen come out on 'fishing trips' to catch a man equally desperate for any legitimate partner to bring comfort to their lives. These two really love each other in a way that is almost too vulgar to witness.

But the reason why I stay here, despite the woman, is my little Sylvie Sambuck. She is a four-foot-tall nine-year-old stick of dynamite. Her face is sharp, fine-featured, closed and watchful. She is tanned like her father without the red cheeks. Her hair is thick and fine, very dark. She might be an attractive child were it not for that frown with which she greets most experiences.

Mr and Mrs Sambuck, in their golden love circle, have little time for this child. Her father pets her now and then but in general they leave her to her own devices. Then her mother punishes her for some newly noticed infringement. It is not surprising that, when I got to her, she was bad-tempered and rude most of the time.

Yet there is something about Sylvie which appeals to me. Some echo in her that resounds in me. After early necessary accommodations we have become attuned to each other. These days she frowns much less.

My grandmother was not happy that I would have to live here in the *tuan*'s house. 'They will use you like an *amah*,' she said. 'What good is all that education then?' She is a businesswoman of the old school and knows her worth.

'I will be using that education in teaching the child,' I said. 'And I will only be a mile from our house here in Beach Road. I will have a room to myself as big as a church, overlooking the whole city.'

'You must stay separate from them, Jin Kee,' she said to me, 'or they will nibble you in the night and I will not recognise the girl who comes back to me in Beach Road.'

But my grandmother could not deny that the pay was good for little work. She has sound business sense, and knew I would make a contribution to the family coffers. In the end she agreed, but told me to watch my soul.

My soul is in no danger of nibbling from anyone except the winsome, frowning Sylvie. And she is too busy with her own soul to be aware of that.

# Chapter Three

## Flying Kites

If Sylvie was sure of one thing it was the fact that her parents loved each other like life. In the house her mother was always at her father's side. She rose at seven to breakfast with him on the veranda before he went to his office on Collyer Quay. Sylvie would watch from her window as the two of them took an early morning stroll in the garden right down to the hibiscus hedge. Then they would saunter along by the flame trees and back through the flowerbeds planted with giant phlox, then back to the steps to see if any new moonflower had blossomed overnight.

John Singh, the *syce*, would bring round the car. Her mother would kiss her father and hold his briefcase as he got into the back of the car. Then she would hand it to him through the window. She would stand and watch as John brummed the engine and set the car on its way.

Her mother always made sure she returned promptly from her inevitable morning jaunt into town. She had to be there when Bo returned from the office. They'd talk while he changed into the more comfortable sarong and *tutup*. Then they would have tiffin together on the west veranda, so much cooler in the afternoon. After that they would retire to the long chairs to chat and snooze, sharing their 'lie-off' – their afternoon siesta – as they'd shared most other things in their lives since they first met.

In the old days, after his tiffin and his rest, Sylvie's father would put on fresh clothes and return to the office for a couple of hours. But in recent months he'd been donning military uniform and leather belt and going off for his afternoon training as a Volunteer. Sylvie had heard her mother grumbling that there must be no need for this. The place was crawling with soldiers – a hundred thousand, didn't he say? – and they were still pouring in off the ships. Why distract important commercial people in this way? Didn't Britain need all the tin and rubber from the *godowns* to make their tanks and keep them running?

While Bo was training to defend his city, Lesley had a proper siesta before embarking on her own late afternoon. This consisted of checking on Sylvie's lessons, and usually berating Virginia Chen about her daughter's lack of progress. She gave educational pointers to Virginia Chen, using tales of her own proper English education at The Mount.

On the afternoon after Feargal's party, Sylvie stumbled disgracefully through her reading practice. In fact, she was making amazing progress with her reading, but when her mother put her through her paces she balked at all the fences. Lesley endured her stumbling performance with a frozen face, then asked Virginia Chen if they could have a private word and led the way to her sitting room. When she had reprimands to dole out she always made sure that she was at her desk, just inside the veranda of the east sitting room.

Lesley gestured to a chair and Virginia sat down, knees close together.

'What on earth are you doing with the girl, Miss Chen?' Lesley burst out. 'She's even worse now than when you came. Adherence to standards, Miss Chen, is the key.' Her voice rang through the open doors of the bungalow. 'Perhaps it is difficult for you to imagine a proper English school, Miss Chen.'

Virginia kept her eyes on the edge of the table. 'I was at the best girls' school in the city, the Methodist Girls' School, Mrs Sambuck. And at a French university. It was in my references.'

'Precisely,' said Lesley, bored now with the conversation. 'Now, will you send in Cookie? Those rolls at tiffin were like leather.'

'Mrs Sambuck?'

'Yes?'

'I promised to take Sylvie kite flying this afternoon. There will be quite a breeze down on the esplanade. You can see the tops of the waves. It is suitable.'

'Sylvie doesn't have a kite.'

'We can go to Orchard Road. I know a trader there.'

'Of course you do.' Lesley flapped her hand, shooing her away like a recalcitrant puppy. 'Go! Go! Please make sure Sylvie has on her gloves and her hat, and Feargal is properly occupied with Ah So. And send Tang Peng, for goodness' sake. Those rolls were quite disgraceful.'

Whatever the reason, whatever the excuse, Sylvie loved going into town with Virginia Chen. On the way there, over the toiling back of the rickshaw man you could look down towards the sea. Nearer the town you started to weave your way through the heaving mass of people, the impatient cars and the bullock carts. The delicate scents of the frangipani and the garden orchids mingled down here with the intense sweet-sour scents of the port. This quickened Sylvie's pulse, brought a flush of excitement to her cheeks.

She always dragged Virginia Chen to the paper toy maker, a woman with wise eyes and hair pulled back so tightly that her forehead was a golden wrinkled cliff. On the stand in front of her, paper birds and moving men, butterflies and insects rustled in the breeze of passing crowds. Virginia had told Sylvie more than once that the little toys were really made for people's coffins, but this did not lessen her desire to have one for herself.

Today they lingered by the fortune-teller, who beckoned them with narrow fingers. Then they bought cookies from a hawker's basket. Sylvie had to take off her gloves to eat hers, which was a sweet concoction of rice, ginger and coconut.

'Perhaps we will have peach tea,' said Virginia. 'I know another place.' She hailed another rickshaw and they bowled right through the town and down on to Beach Road, past the sprawling Raffles Hotel. Eventually they stopped outside a narrow shophouse. 'We will go in there, in this place.'

Sylvie looked blankly at the shopfront. It was guarded on

one side by a set of camphor-wood boxes set with mother-of-pearl, on the other side by a spider-legged cabinet displaying a line of blue ginger vases.

Sylvie made her way round a brass bucket of small carpets standing upright like flowers.

At the back of the shop, almost dwarfed by bulky brass-handled cabinets, stood a heavy-shouldered man in a long black coat. Beside him at a table sat a smaller, more fragile creature, whose eyes were netted in fine wrinkles.

Virginia bowed very low, first to one, then to the other. 'Here is my Uncle Wo,' she said.

The large man bowed stiffly from the waist, his eyes closing as his head came down. 'Good afternoon.' It was a large voice even for such a large man.

'And here is Uncle Chu.' The other man hauled himself up from the table. He nodded so many times that Sylvie thought his head might fall off. But he kept his eyes on her and his mouth smiled a merry smile. 'Afternoon!' he said, in a voice much deeper than his brother's.

'Now, dear uncles,' said Virginia Chen, 'here is my young friend, Sylvie Sambuck.' She said the words first in Hokkien, her family's dialect, then in English.

Sylvie bowed very low indeed. 'How do you do?' she said.

Virginia led the way up two flights of dark wooden stairs into a room with two windows, which looked out at the street. The sheer clutter of furniture and pictures reminded Sylvie of her nana's house in Priorton. In the shade between the windows, on a high chair with padded arms, sat an old woman. Her face was long, made longer by a bony forehead and

sparse black, pulled-back hair. Her expression was questioning and sharp. She wore a loose, high-necked black gown
with gold thread trimming the edges of the sleeves.

Virginia Chen bowed, stepped forward, kissed a hand frail
as a leaf, then murmured something to her. Then she turned
to Sylvie. 'Sylvie, this is my grandmother.'

Sylvie's mind was tumbling. 'Like mine,' she said. 'I have
a grandmother at home, in England. This room is like hers.'

'What do you say, Sylvie?'

Sylvie cast out an arm as though she were scattering seed.
'Like my nana. This room is like my nana's in England.'

Virginia Chen raised her eyebrows. 'So where are your
manners, Sylvie? Will you say hello to my grandmother?'

Sylvie looked at the face that was so gravely surveying
hers. She couldn't think of what to say. 'What can I say?' she
said, looking at Virginia Chen.

'Just say "Good afternoon".'

Sylvie ducked her head and half curtsied. 'Good afternoon,
Grandmother. I am Sylvie.'

There was a spurt of laughter like a rusty key turning in a
lock. The frail hand came towards her and she found herself
kissing it just as Virginia Chen had. 'Sit down, little missee.
Sit down.' The voice was creaky, rusty like the laughter.

Sylvie sat on a stool at the grandmother's feet and Virginia
sat by the narrow window where a wayward flash of sunlight
illuminated her sleek hair and the soft gold of her skin.

The old woman clapped her hands and a slender boy came
in with a wicker tray with delicate china and a plate of small
coconut cakes like miniature haystacks. He carried it softly in

his large hands, left it on a carved table beside the grand-mother, then departed without even glancing in Sylvie's direction.

Then Virginia Chen talked with her grandmother – Sylvie heard the word 'America' in the scatter of Hokkien – and Sylvie could look more closely at the cluttered room. Worn wall hangings; a heavy carved bureau with photographs; a carved metal stand in the form of a dragon with a round man's hat hanging from it; a stove with filigree ironwork; a bookcase stacked with English books on the far wall. On a table in the corner sat a gramophone with a wide black trumpet. In pride of place, on a mount of fine lace, hung a portrait of a soldier, with brass buttons and a swagger stick, in a uniform not unlike that worn by soldiers who were teeming into the city today.

Virginia Chen caught her glance. 'You want to know who he is? That gentleman there?'

Sylvie nodded.

'He is my grandfather, James Arbuthnot. He worked for the architects who built the new Raffles Hotel in 1913. He managed the quantities. Bricks and sand and marble. Things like that.'

'He looks like a soldier, not a builder.'

'He was, afterwards. After he did this work on the build-ings. He went to fight for Britain in the Great War.'

'Did he come back? Here to Singapore?'

'No.' Virginia glanced at her grandmother. 'He was killed in a very great battle. My grandmother has a medal which the King sent her. In a box.'

'He was Grandmother's husband?'

'No. But he loved her very much.'

Sylvie knew about that. The way her father loved her mother. It was about touching and private talk. It was about glances exchanged when you came into the room to disturb them.

Virginia took a photograph from the shelf. 'And this is *my* mother and father. *They* were married, at least.'

This was a full-blown wedding picture with two flower girls and a cake ten tiers high. The bride was beautiful, clearly Virginia's mother. The groom was very tall and elegant with golden, wavy locks.

'My father was partly French, partly Chinese. He worked out of Cochin China, an agent for silks. His father and grandfather lived up there in that country. My father said it was very beautiful. His grandfather on the other side, Mr Chen, was Chinese, brother to the grandfather of Simon, who brought the cakes. So Simon, unlike me, is completely Chinese.'

Sylvie frowned at the complications. 'It looks like a very grand wedding,' she said at last, for want of anything else to say.

The grandmother tapped on the tray with a folded fan. 'Now eat, Sylvie Sambuck. Eat up your cake,' the voice cracked out.

'Your mother is like a princess, Miss Chen. She is very beautiful.'

'So was my grandmother. See.' Virginia Chen took another picture from the shelf. Here was a girl with a fine crown

37

head-dress of brocade and flowers, a gold brocade tunic and skirt. A closed fan swung from her hand. Sylvie glanced at the grandmother, then back at the beautiful girl in the portrait. Her heart swooped downwards. She'd thought before about dying, at her Durham great-aunt's funeral. But here she was *seeing* ageing, just *how* you got old. To get as old as the woman before her from the young beauty in the photograph – that seemed much sadder than death.

Beside the girl who was now the grandmother was the soldier from the other portrait. This time his blond curls were crammed under a round cap with a gold brooch on the front. He had a high-necked dark blue brocade jacket with velvet toggles, and some kind of silk sarong. Like the girl, he wore velvet slippers. Only the blond hair and creamy skin told you he wasn't Chinese.

'She looks like a princess too,' said Sylvie.

'These were their wedding clothes.'

'But you said they weren't married.'

'No. They were never married.'

They sat a little while longer. With Virginia as interpreter the grandmother asked Sylvie about her own health, and that of her mother and father. She asked about her grandmother and grandfather and Sylvie told her that *her* grandfather had died a long time ago, but not her grandmother. 'She's called Nana. She's very funny. She makes me laugh. I had another grandma and grandda in India but they both died.'

'How does the grandmother do this? Make you laugh?'

Sylvie glanced at Virginia Chen. 'She would take out her

teeth and make a face. Like this.' Sylvie made an ugly, gurning face. 'My mother really, really does not like it. She says it is very *common*.'

The grandmother and Virginia Chen laughed heartily, their voices pealing together like bells.

'My mother stopped my nana doing this,' said Sylvie. 'They had a big, big argument. My nana threw a teapot at my mother.'

The grandmother dabbed her eyes with a lace handker-chief. 'I am very sure, little Sylvie, that your grandmother, and your grandfather, will keep watch over you in these hard times.' As Virginia Chen translated the words the grandmother closed her eyes and for a second seemed to sag in the chair.

Virginia Chen stood up. 'We must leave Grandmother. She is tired. Now, say thank you, Sylvie.'

Sylvie stood up and bowed her head again over the old woman's hand. A hand came up, touched her head and said something to Virginia in Hokkien. When they got out into the sunshine, Sylvie squinted up and asked Virginia what had been said.

'She said you must come from these parts. You have eyes the colour of wine and very dark hair.'

Sylvie laughed. 'Well, she's wrong, isn't she? I come from Priorton, County Durham, England. That's what my mother says. Even though I was born here.'

In the market they bought a kite in the shape of an old Chinese mandarin with deep sleeves. The man from whom they bought it told his son to go with them to the esplanade to help them to fly it.

Beside the sea the boy held the string while Sylvie ran with the kite. Then he shouted to her to let it go. He released the string and started to unwind it from the crossed sticks.

The nodding mandarin rose majestically into the silver-grey sky. It floated over the esplanade, bobbing and swooping there for many minutes like some presiding god. As Sylvie watched, it seemed the splashing of the tides and the rocking of the boats ceased for a moment to pay homage to this god.

Then the wind changed and the kite came down on a part of the sea wall. The kite boy, running to get it, was beaten by two dogs, who got there first and started to fight over it. It was many minutes before the kite boy could wrest it from them. He held his hands towards Sylvie and in them the kite was now a clutch of torn paper and broken sticks.

'No-o!' Sylvie started to scream and stamp. Virginia Chen clasped her shoulders and held on to her tightly as the kite boy hurried towards them. Sylvie burst into tears and broke free of Virginia Chen. She screamed at the dogs, throwing her gloves, then her shoes at them. They picked these up and started to snarl and tussle over them.

Virginia caught Sylvie and held her hard by the hands. She whispered in her ear until she calmed down and then took her, whimpering, into her arms. The kite boy went to retrieve the shoes and gloves which, when they came back, were in a bedraggled state. Taking one look at them, Sylvie started to howl again. 'She'll beat me for this. She'll surely beat me for this.'

Lesley had a narrow cane, which was brought out very occasionally when Sylvie had her violent paddies. It was supposed to bring Sylvie to order but really all it did was make Lesley feel better.

Sylvie could smell camellias in Virginia Chen's clothes; in her hair.

'No. No,' said Virginia Chen. 'We will go now to Robinson's and buy exactly the same shoes and gloves. And no one will know any different. I promise you.'

Sylvie's eyes opened very wide. 'You'll pay? Yourself?'

Virginia grinned. 'What do you think I am, Sylvie, a pauper? Like my grandmother I am a businesswoman and know how to salt away my gold. But also like my grandmother I know when to open my purse. Come on now! We go to Robinson's!'

And this they did. Robinson's did not dignify their bomb damage with closure. So Sylvie returned home in as pristine a condition as that in which she had left. As she helped her out of her rickshaw, Virginia whispered in her ear, 'Now, this is all a secret – the grandmother and the new shoes and gloves. All of it. You promise me, Sylvie?'

So later that night, when her mother came in to see her on her return from dancing and dining out at the Tanglin Club, Sylvie was able to answer her when she asked if she'd enjoyed the kite flying.

'Yes. It was really lovely. Like an old mandarin. It bobbed high in the air. But dogs came and got it and broke it.' Tears came to the surface again.

Warmed by a congenial evening and four gin slings, Lesley put a hand on her daughter's head. 'Not to worry, darling. The man will soon mend it.' She had other things on her mind.

There'd been talk at the club of Japanese landings at Kota Bharu in Malaya. Incredible as it seemed, those little men had started the long march that could lead to Singapore. The bombing on the town had signalled that for sure. Everyone said so.

'Lesley.' Bo's voice boomed through the house.

'Coming, darling!' Her mother tripped out of the room. In the light from the door, Sylvie could see fronds from her feather boa hover in the air for a moment, then drift to the ground.

She turned over. The lie was not such a lie really. Just a not-telling. But she would have liked to talk to her mother about the little old woman; how her sitting room was cluttered and stuffed with photographs, how Virginia's father was a French Chinaman and . . .

She dreamed that she was a princess dressed in gold braid and there were a lot of soldiers and sailors marching across the *padang* and all of them had to salute her as they marched past. If they did not do so they were very severely punished.

# Chapter Four

## Breakfasts

The next morning, quite unusually, Lesley joined the children and Virginia on the veranda for breakfast. Ah So sat on a low stool beside Feargal. When he paused for breath, she popped food into his mouth as assiduously as a mother bird with her chick.

Lesley sat slightly to one side with tea and orange juice on a tray, staring out over the garden, which glowed in the limpid early morning light. The wisteria tumbled in an arabesque over the special frame built by Bo's Javanese *kebun*. The beds of giant phlox, brighter-coloured and shorter-stemmed than those in Lesley's mother's English garden, accentuated the curve of the drive, before the bougainvillaea surged forward to tumble across it. Beside the gate the moonflowers as big as dinner plates were sprouting from their stubby cactus-like leaves. Bo had commented as he went to work that there were ten now. There must have been a full moon. Even from eighty yards away, their scent pervaded the breakfast table.

'Miss Chen,' said Lesley, 'I was wondering how sensible it was to spend money on a kite, then allow it to be ruined.' Her voice was raw from so much cigarette smoke. Her head ached with the aftermath of too much gin.

'It wasn't on purpose, Mummy,' said Sylvie. 'It was an accident. The naughty dogs grabbed it in their mouths. They tussled with it.'

'Perhaps you should not have gone to the esplanade, dear. Dogs, rats – this city is infested with them.'

Virginia Chen pushed a bowl of chopped pineapple and mangoes, oranges and pawpaws in front of Sylvie, who started to pick at them, starting with the mangoes. 'The kite was only fifty cents, Mrs Sambuck. I will pay for it myself.'

Lesley stared at her glumly, then turned her gaze on Sylvie, who had finished the mango bits and was starting on the pineapple. 'Don't shovel that in, child. So much you take for granted! In England now you'd be lucky to get an apple. You'd really do badly there – everything rationed, no little treats. No little treats at all.' She twisted in her seat and raised her voice. 'Boy!' she said.

Wong Mee moved quietly on to the veranda. '*Mem?*' he said.

'Aspirin and water.'

'Yes, *mem.*'

Lesley took an immaculate silver cigarette case from the pocket of her silk dressing gown and was just about to shout again when Wong Mee came back with a wicker tray on which stood a glass and a china dish with three aspirins. She waved her cigarette at him and he went to a side cabinet, took out a heavy jade lighter and flicked a flame for her to light her cigarette. Then her eye left him and he withdrew. No 'thank you'. Mrs Sambuck was not known for politeness.

The children's breakfast, usually a chattering, jolly affair, was blighted by Lesley's glum presence. Sylvie fought the desire to laugh out loud at the pantomime of the cigarette. She wanted to leap over the rails of the veranda and do cartwheels on the lawn. She contented herself with slurping and chewing at her juicy fruit. Lesley looked at her sharply and was building up to say something when Virginia Chen spoke.

'There is a silk merchant,' she said. 'Mr Lee, the silk merchant, is returning to Hainan and is selling his stock.'

Sylvie watched her mother draw hard on her cigarette and puff slightly to let the air out. 'Thinks we're done for, I suppose. Wise man.' The smoke streamed out of her mouth with the words.

'It seems he is selling all his stocks. He has lovely Swatow, Foochow and Pekin lace. Shanghai silk. Bargain prices. All the European ladies are sending for him.'

Lesley stared at her, then threw her cigarette into the bougainvillaea. For a second the air was filled with the scent of dying tobacco. 'Why not? I could have it packed and shipped. It'd create quite a stir back home.'

'We're going home, Mother? Back to England?' Sylvie stopped slurping. Her eyes, bold as any puppy's, bored into her mother.

Lesley stared at her. She and Bo had argued into the night. Oh yes, he agreed now that she should go! Things were getting bad. You could smell it in the air. But he must come too. She tried to insist on it. But this Bo would not do. All this civil defence, this Volunteer stuff had got into his head. 'They'll need us here, sweetheart. We can hold on until more planes arrive; keep the little men off.'

'But I can't cope without you, Bo. I couldn't cope with dreary old England without you. If you stay, I stay.'

He'd turned his back on her then and she'd lain in the jungle-dark, thinking of grey England, the narrow streets of Priorton and her mother's cold house.

Now she said to Sylvie, 'Daddy's going to P & O today to get our passes. They say there are great queues of people there, waiting for tickets. Everyone's going home so I guess we must as well.'

Feargal started to whimper and Ah So shushed him and stroked his cheek. She watched the *mem* from under her lashes. They would go. All the *mems* and the *tuans* would go now. It was whispered everywhere. The women in her *kongsi* said so. No places for the *amahs*, who had taken care of the beloved children since birth; places only on the boats for the Europeans. No one else. It was whispered. Everywhere.

Lesley stood up. 'So. Perhaps we should see your Mr Lee and his silks, Miss Chen. I have to meet Mrs Hoxton for shopping this morning. Then tiffin. Tell him to come at four o'clock this afternoon.'

'I will send Tang Peng's brother with a note.'

At the back of the house across a dusty quadrangle was a narrow house where the cookie, Tang Peng, lived with his wife, children and his younger brother. Other relatives visited them from the *kampong*, from time to time. The brother had a battered bicycle, which he used for errands.

'Four o'clock.'

Lesley was already drifting towards her bedroom door. 'That's what I said, Miss Chen.' She paused. 'Perhaps, Sylvie, you should do some extra reading today? You are so far behind. And perhaps some writing about the dogs and the kite? I don't know what the English schools will think of you when we get there. So far behind. Inferior teaching, of course.'

The door swung behind her and everyone on the veranda relaxed. Sylvie returned to her fruit. Only the pawpaws to go now. 'Do I have to write that stuff,' she said, her mouth full, 'when I'm getting on the boat tomorrow or the next day?'

'So we are instructed. We must do as we're told, Sylvie.'

'It makes my hand hurt, writing. And my finger. This one.' She held out the offending digit.

'I have an idea. When I tell Tang Peng's brother to go to the silk merchant, I will tell him also to order a taxi for us for one o'clock. Before that, you will read twelve pages to me from *The King of the Golden River* and you can write the story of the dogs and the kite. We will talk it and you can write it.'

'What is the taxi for?'

'We will go to the Great World and see the puppet theatre.' The Great World was a space where the ordinary people of Singapore indulged their delight in entertainment and spectacle. Raffish and unrespectable, it nevertheless had charm.

'So who will go?'

'You and I. We will see if Ah So and the little Feargal will come. Then back here for four o'clock for Mr Lee and his silks.'

In the end Feargal went to sleep and Ah So stayed to watch over him. Virginia and Sylvie went to the Great World on their own.

# Chapter Five

## Granddaughters

Sylvie clutched Virginia Chen's hand as they pushed their way through the crowd at the gateway to the Great World. Soldiers in tartan bonnets queued up to have their fortunes told by a man who used a bird to peck out their fates, which were now predictable. Large red-faced boys in swept-back hats whooped their way towards the funfair. Indians in pale uniforms made their stately way through the narrow alleyways.

Sailors, some with taxi dancers on their arms, waited at photographers' booths. The Japanese signs hanging outside these had been crossed out, and they were manned now by Chinese photographers. The Japanese, famous in old Singapore as photographers, had been deported as undesirable aliens, or had fled to the safe shores of Japan. A grave-faced scholar was writing a script being dictated by a neatly dressed Malay. Further on, in the high wrestling ring, an enormously tall man with a topknot was holding another flailing man at shoulder height, preparing to crash him to the ground.

Hawkers crouched beside their baskets or bent over their smoking cauldrons. They sold everything from conker-coloured flattened duck to delicate cakes and cut fruit. Sylvie's nose twitched and her stomach became hungry at the syrupy, fruity, sweet-sour smell that came in waves down the alley.

She dragged Virginia Chen back to the animal enclosure and stamped her foot until Virginia Chen agreed to take her in. Inside, the elephants walked and kneeled in their ring at the merest touch of the keeper's whip. The tigers lay full of melancholy in the corner of their netted compound. But it was the lions that attracted Sylvie. They walked around their enclosure marking their contempt for the watchers with every slinky stride, every swish of their tails.

Sylvie stood very still, watching a younger lion, whose markings seemed to move and change in the dense air of the Great World. His head turned slightly towards Sylvie and his deep gaze went through and over her. 'Isn't he marvellous? It must be wonderful to be a lion. I love the lions best of all, Miss Chen.'

'Then this is your city, Sylvie.'

'My city?'

'*Singa Pura* means City of the Lion in the old language, in the language of the first people.'

'Is that Chinese?'

'No. No. The Chinese are newcomers here, like the British and the Dutch. The first people were Malay. Like the men who work in your father's *godown*.'

The rolling noise of the vast crowd stilled for a second and people looked at each other. Once, back home in Priorton,

Sylvie's nana had shuddered. Sylvie had asked, 'What is it, Nana? What's the matter?'

'Someone walked over my grave, pet. That's all.'

Now here it was, that tension, that sudden stillness. It made Sylvie shudder. She whispered, 'What is it, Miss Chen?'

Virginia put a hand on Sylvie's mouth. 'Ssh.'

Into the silence came a muttering, a strangled shouting from the crowd as across the silver grey of the sky three aeroplanes with red spots on them flew in formation. They flew quite low. Sylvie gulped. Then the aeroplanes turned and moved towards the western horizon and the crowd hummed to life again.

'Will they bomb us?' said Sylvie.

'Not this time.' The voice was deep and rolled with a Devon burr.

They turned round. Just behind Virginia, in a well-brushed naval officer's uniform, was a tall man with the regular features and bright eyes put together in a way called handsome. Sylvie saw Virginia Chen blush. She had never seen her blush. Not ever.

Virginia pulled herself together. 'Just letting us see their muscles, Sylvie. They think they are warriors.' Her tone was contemptuous. They turned to continue on their way.

'Our fliers will shoot them down, though, won't they?' Sylvie looked up at Virginia Chen.

'They would if they were here, Sylvie. But it seems they're not quite here yet.' Virginia pulled Sylvie to her.

'But they will come?' she said. 'Our fliers?'

'So they tell us.'

Virginia took Sylvie by the hand and they walked on. She stopped at the entrance of a narrow black-draped booth and tipped some coins into the hand of the old woman who sat there on a low stool.

When they squeezed through the narrow space by the door, Sylvie wrinkled her nose. She was used to the salt-spice-flesh-fish-flower-laden, faintly rotting smell of Singapore. But here in the packed booth it was intensified a dozenfold. Before them was a brilliantly lit screen. Fluttering to and fro on the screen were shadows depicting – Sylvie guessed – some story about a king and queen and some kind of crucifixion, then a battle. The crowd shouted out hoarsely in support of their hero.

Virginia whispered into Sylvie's ear, 'The old king had a wife whom he came to hate, so he impaled her in the marketplace. Her father was so angry that he conspired with the Javanese to beat the king. There was a great battle and the fighting was so fierce that it was said that this is why the soil of Singapore is blood red, even now.'

'Nice to know that.' They turned at the sound of a voice behind them: the handsome naval officer grinned down at them.

'You followed us,' said Sylvie, scowling.

'Afraid so, m'dear. This city is full of faces and it's so hard to find a friendly one.' He cocked his head on one side and looked at Virginia Chen. 'I felt in that second with the planes overhead that we recognised each other. These are strange times. We all know it.'

Sylvie could feel the strain in Virginia beside her. 'We were going behind the screen to see the puppet man.' She tugged Virginia's sleeve. The people were tumbling past them to get out of the booth. 'Miss Chen says we can go and talk to him.'

'Can I come?' the officer pleaded. 'Miss Chen? Do you have a name? You must have a name. I *have* to know your name.'

Virginia Chen stood there, staring at him, a slight frown on her smooth brow.

'She's called Virginia,' said Sylvie. She watched the officer very closely but he did not take his gaze from Virginia Chen.

'Can I come with you, Miss Virginia Chen?' He said the words quite softly. Sylvie could hardly hear. He took Virginia's hand in his. 'I'm called Albert Taft.'

Virginia Chen pulled her hand away. 'Very well,' she said finally, in a cool tone that made even Sylvie shiver. 'But you must not get in the way.'

'I promise.' He put a hand on his breast pocket, just above his heart. 'I won't get in the way. You can trust me. I'm a West Country man. They've been trusting us since Drake.'

Virginia Chen took Sylvie's hand and led the way.

Behind the screen a neat old man was sitting on a low stool, adjusting what looked like bats on bamboos, then sticking them into a pineapple, which was wedged on to a stick before him. Behind him was the giant paraffin lamp, which cast the bright lights for the shadow puppets. Sylvie imagined her own shape making a shadow for the people on the benches.

Virginia Chen bowed over her hands to greet the puppeteer. She pulled forward Sylvie, who mimicked Virginia's bow.

Then, for no reason she could fathom, Sylvie dropped on her knees. The old man put a hand on her head.

'Sylvie,' said Virginia. 'This is Mr Yap Pak. He is a very honoured man, whose father and grandfather were performers. They took their puppets to the *kampongs* to tell their stories. Now he stays in the Great World and the *kampongs* come to him. And the travellers from the ships.'

'You must ask him if his puppets tell the story of Singa Pura, Miss Chen. The story you told me.'

Virginia spoke rapidly to the old man.

He nodded and pulled out one bundle of his sticks from the pineapple and spread it out for her. Now you could see that it was made of leather so fine it was like parchment; it was a creature with a lion's head and a waving fish's tail. The man's narrow shoulders and whipcord arms moved and his hands manipulated the fine wires. The tail swished as the lion's head rose up to growl.

Sylvie clapped her hands. 'Mr Puppeteer, he is wonderful.'

The man nodded gravely. Then he said something to Virginia, reached under his stool and brought out a bundle of sticks.

'Mr Yap Pak says would you like this? It is his old Singa Pura. The one he used for many years. He was saving it for his granddaughter but she was killed when the bombs dropped the night before last. She was nine years, like you.'

Sylvie blinked at the tears that suddenly came to her eyes. 'Can I have him? Does he say I can have him?'

'Mr Yap Pak says you must take care of him. He says he will bring you luck in a hard life.'

Sylvie stood up and touched the ragged leather with her fingertips. 'He is lovely. I would like him.' Very carefully she took the puppet from the old man and bowed very low. She looked at Virginia. 'Tell him I like him always and I am very sorry for his granddaughter.'

The old man hauled himself to his feet and put his hand on her head for a second. She could feel it resting there very softly. Then more words crackled out of the old man and he was fluttering his hands at them, shooing them away. The navy man, who was standing quietly in the doorway, turned to lead the way out.

The public area of the booth was filling again as they went back through the entrance. The officer dropped two dollars in the old woman's basket as they passed.

'Why did you do that?' said Virginia Chen sharply when they were in the road. 'It was too much.'

Sylvie could tell she felt more comfortable now with this navy man. She was no longer blushing.

'Because I felt bad about the old man's granddaughter. My brother's kid died in the bombing in Portsmouth. It doesn't seem right, children being killed like that.'

'Many innocents are killed in war. Hundreds of thousands of Chinese innocents in Nanking not so long ago.' Virginia thought of Mrs Sambuck's off-hand remark to her friends. 'There will be more here . . . here in this city.'

'That was your war with the Japs, of course,' he said thoughtfully.

'*My* war?'

'Well, your people.'

'My people! Perhaps you mean *some* of my people. My other people, the French of Cochin China, were only recently at war with the Japanese. And now my English part is doing battle with them.'

Sylvie could feel the tension of the quarrel between them, but could also feel that other tension. The tension that happened after a quarrel between her mother and father. Those fights ended with her parents in each other's arms and the shooing of Sylvie out of the room. She felt very gloomy about the way these two were staring at each other. She pulled at Virginia Chen's arm. 'Tell him to go away, Miss Chen. It's just us. You said it was just us.'

Virginia walked on a few paces with the navy man and talked to him. She put one hand on his arm and he tried to put his hand on hers and she wrenched it away. Then he shook her hand, said something to her, shook it again, then marched off, pushing his way through the crowd.

Sylvie relaxed. Now they were rid of the man they could enjoy their day. 'What did you say to him?'

'Well, Sylvie, I had to say I'd go to the pictures with him tonight. The Cathay. *Gone with the Wind*.'

'That's Vivien Leigh. I wanted to see that. She's called Scarlett O'Hara. I read it in the paper. I can come with you.'

'They will not let you. You're too young for such films.'

'You're going tonight?'

'Yes.'

'But who'll take care of me? Those two will be going out. They're always out. Even when there's bombs, I'll be in danger. The Japanese marauders will get me.'

'Don't say "those two" like that, Sylvie. They know you are safe. There is Ah So. She will watch over you. And the *jaga* will be at the gate. He'll guard you with his life. That is his job.'

'But—'

'No buts. Now we have to go home. Mr Lee will be there with his silks at four o'clock.'

In the taxi Virginia Chen was very silent. Sylvie leaned against her shoulder. 'He was very handsome. Like a prince in a story. Did he fall in love with you?'

Virginia Chen put an arm round Sylvie and pulled her close. 'You say such silly things sometimes, Sylvie.' For a second the scent of camellias filled the narrow dusty space in the back of the taxi.


Lesley woke refreshed from her afternoon lie-off. She lay there very still for a moment. The mosquito net veiled the room, making it misty and distant. She noted with approval that the silent-footed Ah So had put away her shopping, taken her used clothes away and put out a fresh linen dress, brassiere, and knickers on the rattan couch before the veranda windows.

Not for the first time Lesley relished her own common sense about clothes. Unlike many of the memsahibs who fussed eternally about clothes and scanned the London magazines to find the latest fashions for their little dressmakers to copy, she'd solved the problem of what to wear at a stroke. In the daytime she wore the linen dresses of the same design: close-fitted, boat-necked, belted and flaring to mid-calf. She'd had the design made up in seven pale rainbow shades. For the evening she got her dressmaker to make her seven identical long, strapless, silk dresses with little matching boleros touched up with sequins and brilliants.

Bo, who'd have thought her beautiful in rags, applauded her cunning in avoiding the petty rivalries over dress, which were rife among the bored women of the island. His salary as an accountant to a rubber agent was not overgenerous and he had a habit of speculating with his spare money, which did not always pay off. He once applauded what he called 'her canny Northern spirit', which offended Lesley so much he had to promise not to say it again.

Ah So, sensing the *mem*'s movement, was suddenly in the room. She placed a tray with a tall jug of lime juice and a glass on the rattan table on the bedroom veranda. Lesley got out of bed, padded out to the veranda and sat down to light a cigarette. The ice cracked and split as Ah So poured the lime juice over it.

'Where's Feargal?' said Lesley, through a yawn.

'Feargal sleep,' said Ah So, her hands now folded neatly before her. She had changed her white blouse for a black one. 'I wake soon.'

'And Miss Sylvie?'

'Missie Sylvie is at Great World with Miss Chen. She telephones to say come back at four and Mr Lee the silk man comes at four thirty.'

Lesley's mouth hardened. 'The Great World! Miss Chen should not take Miss Sylvie there. It's running with dogs and rats. And there are the very lowest grade of soldier and sailor crawling all over the town.' Earlier that day she and Vera

Hoxton had had to endure their insolent stares as they got into their car after lunch at Raffles. One of the sailors made a remark about there being a war on and 'you'd never know it in this bloody town the way people go on having a bloody good time.' Lesley had been forced then to point to a Royal Navy notice on the wall that said 'Out of bounds to other ranks.' But still they stared and she was pleased when the car roared off, spewing black fumes into their sour faces.

That had not been the only disturbance of the day. The new air-conditioned basement restaurant at Robinson's (where she and Vera had planned to have lunch) had been damaged by bombs, so they'd had to resort to Raffles. And there was an unusual bustle there as well, with an undermanager fussing with workmen on the issue of the brownout in the big ballroom.

And when she went to Maynards the chemist, to get in a stock of medications for their journey, that place too was crawling with workmen, who were boarding up its shattered windows. There was actually some mention of looters! And they were even digging up the *padang* outside Government House. When Vera said, in all seriousness, 'I think something really is up, Lesley,' Lesley had laughed hysterically for minutes before, hiccoughing, she could calm herself down over her gin sling in the Long Bar.

Ah So was still waiting, hands folded.

'That will do, Ah So.' Lesley waved her hand.

Ah So receded from the veranda into the room and all Lesley could hear was the flutter of activity as she busied herself tying back the nets and putting fresh sheets on the bed. Then the *amah* went away, presumably to wake up Feargal. Lesley sipped her lime juice and pressed a cigarette into its holder.

The afternoon was thick with heat, permeated by a faint oven breeze, which always threatened rain at the monsoon. Outside beyond the hibiscus hedge, the city shimmered in the light, trembling on the lip of the sea beyond. Dominating the gaggle of boats were the two great navy ships, which had just arrived for their protection, the *Prince of Wales* and the *Repulse*. When the ships arrived, Bo had said, they'd have nothing to worry about, nothing at all. These ships were a sure sign of Churchill's intentions. The Old Man would not let Singapore go. You could be sure of that.

She looked at her gold watch. Those two would be back soon. She'd have to talk to Virginia Chen about this escapade to the Great World. That young woman continued to overstep the mark. Her sense of her own consequence was too trying.

Lesley was already sweating. She decided to use Bo's shower. He used this when he came in from work, decrying their rather neat bathroom as a 'woman's place'. 'The cold water's never cold in there. What you need, darling, is the good old *tong*.' His shower, a brick room off the bedroom veranda, had a concrete floor with a drain in it. In the corner was the *tong* full of water, with a kind of pan to ladle out the water. Uniquely, this water was always quite cool – something about the earthenware. She flinched as the cool water crashed against her hot skin, again and again, making her breathe harder and harder. There was pleasure in it.

When she came out she was entirely refreshed and not so worried. The cold water had shocked her brain into action. Now she was looking forward to seeing this Mr Lee and his silks. Perhaps they would have to be stockpiled until after the war, but they would be a bargain, that was for sure. Mr Lee, fleeing like a rat to Hainan, deserved no less, no more.

As it was, Mr Lee, then Virginia and Sylvie arrived in successive taxis. While Virginia Chen watched Wong Mee as he helped the rather stout Mr Lee and his thin boy with his bags and boxes, Ah So took Sylvie to the bedroom, where she changed her into her clean clothes, and kneeled down to buckle her sandals.

When Sylvie came back, Mr Lee had already begun to lay out the silks and lace on the dining table. He placed them on the mahogany with great reverence: each type of fabric had its own particular place in the rainbow. Then at the end, like the froth on the top of a wave, he placed the lace, in shades of white and cream, finely wrought. Then he stood at the end, hands folded, to wait for Lesley's decision. He did not sell; he simply stood.

The room was hot and quiet. From the garden they could hear Feargal say, 'Faster, faster!' as a panting Ah So pushed him on his toy tractor. Sylvie stood at her mother's elbow as she fingered the fabric, which shimmered in the heavily shaded light of the dining room. Lesley picked out some cream, some deep fuchsia and some lime green, and enquired the price. When Mr Lee told her she put back the bolt of fabric. 'This is too much, Mr Lee. You have to take all this back to Hainan. The costs of shipping are very high. Much better to sell it here.'

'This is true, *mem*. But to sell too low would dishonour my trade and profession. It is better that I throw them overboard into the South China Seas. On my way home to Hainan.'

Lesley took another step away from the table. 'Then you must throw it overboard, Mr Lee.'

'Oh, Mother, don't make Mr Lee drown the silks. Poor silks. In the water.' Sylvie picked up the fabric Lesley had put down.

Mr Lee's glance flicked towards the child, then back to Lesley. 'I will allow fifty cents less on each length because the child shows her appreciation of such fine cloth.'

Lesley hesitated a moment. In truth, the price was ridiculously low. 'Very well. I'll have these and perhaps a length of the gold.'

Mr Lee cut the material and then carefully wrapped each length in white tissue and put them neatly on a side table. His assistant – his son or his grandson perhaps – quietly packed the rest of the fabric in the trunk they had brought with them. Sylvie helped the boy, fingering the bolts of cloth as they lay like a captured rainbow in its recesses.

Lesley took out her pen to sign the chit. Mr Lee was already shaking his head. 'I regret, *mem*, I must ask for payment. No chits. No longer.'

Lesley dropped her pen. In Singapore you signed a chit for everything, right down to single drinks in a bar. 'What?' she said, poise lost for once.

'My ship will embark for the mainland tomorrow, *mem*. Chits will not suffice. I cannot call them in from Hainan. Impossible.'

Lesley glanced at the fabric so carefully wrapped on the small table. 'Wait!' she said, and stalked out.

Sylvie helped with the last bolt of fabric and watched as the boy buckled the leather straps. The trunk itself was a wonderful item of some kind of snakeskin. She fingered its ridged surface.

Lesley bustled back in, a handful of banknotes in her hand. She counted the notes carefully and the money vanished into Mr Lee's sleeve. Then he bowed to her. 'Thank you, *mem*.' He nodded to the boy to go for the driver to help with the trunk, then he leaned over the trunk and opened a section of the lid. Out of that he brought a garment. It was a white silk coat with a high collar, flared at the hem. Sylvie clapped her hands and smiled till her cheeks hurt. Mr Lee floated it in front of her. 'This for the young lady, *mem*,' he said.

Lesley clutched her remaining notes. 'I do not think so, Mr Lee.'

'The coat is a gift, *mem*.' Virginia Chen was the only one who detected a note of contempt in his voice. 'It is a gift to the child to wish her a lucky voyage.' Then he said something in Mandarin to Virginia Chen, who took the coat from him and gave it to Sylvie to try on. It fit very well. Even the sleeves were right.

Lesley started, 'We can't—'

Virginia Chen said, 'Mr Lee said he made it for his granddaughter as a special gift. She was killed in the first

63

bombing. You must take it, Mrs Sambuck.' Virginia Chen was very firm, as she was with Sylvie when she wouldn't do her work.

*Two granddaughters*, thought Sylvie. Earlier the puppet man's granddaughter, now the silk man's granddaughter. Three with Miss Chen, who is the old woman's granddaughter. Four with herself. She thought of her nana with her upholstered bosom which, if you pressed it with your head, cracked like soft armour. 'Please,' she said very quietly.

'Yes. Very well. That's most gracious of you, Mr Lee.' Lesley bowed her own head. 'I'm sorry about your grand-daughter. These are hard times.'

'Indeed.' Mr Lee's face was impassive. He bowed to Lesley, then bowed to Sylvie who, awkward in her bulky coat, bowed back. Then he rapped an order to the driver and the boy and preceded them from the room.

'If I didn't know better,' said Lesley, 'I'd say that's quite an arrogant man.'

'He is a highly regarded merchant, Mrs Sambuck,' said Virginia Chen. 'He is used to respect.'

'And that thing about the chit? What was that about?'

'None of the Chinese merchants is taking chits now, Mrs Sambuck. Cash only. They say now for certain the Japanese will take Singapore. That is why there are no chits.'

Lesley laughed. 'Don't be so silly, Miss Chen. Where's your patriotism?' She paused. 'I suppose it's different for you, of course. Think of the Blitz. Think of Dunkirk. *We* don't give up that easy.' She turned to Sylvie. 'Will you remove that ridiculous garment, Sylvie? You look like the abominable snowman.'

Sylvie drifted away, visiting every mirror in the house to look at herself before going to her bedroom and slipping out of the wonderful garment. Behind her Virginia Chen was explaining to Lesley that she would be going out tonight. Yes, she did know Mrs Sambuck was going out with Mr Sambuck, but perhaps Ah So and her sister would be there for the children?

Sometimes Virginia Chen had a way of saying something that stopped Lesley in her tracks. She rarely asked permission to do anything. She was immensely polite but she knew her rights.

Upstairs, Sylvie laid the coat on the bed beside the dark bundle of sticks that was her Singa Pura puppet. She picked it up, separated the sticks, opened it up and held it, fragile and battered, to the light. The stretched leather exhaled the scents of the Chinese market and the puppeteer's dusty storeroom. She took it to the veranda and held it up to the sunset. The leather was so fine that the light of the sun shone through. At first it looked like some kind of bat. Then she squeezed her eyes and could see the lion king with his great crown and fishtail flowing behind him. She put her fingers through two of the holes. They would have to be mended. Miss Chen would have to fix that.

She put on her pyjamas and over them she put on the white silk coat. Then she went to sit on her veranda and watch the sun as it dropped through streaked pink and magenta cloud into the rosy ocean, and the night came down like a black cloth over a birdcage.

# Chapter Six

## A Night Out

The Cathay Cinema, tucked into the bottom of Singapore's tallest building, was crowded with customers keen to enjoy the dark charms of Vivien Leigh in *Gone with the Wind*. Two-thirds of the customers were in uniform: among them members of the Singapore Volunteers, British Army, Australian Army, Indian Army and Royal Navy. RAF uniforms were thin on the ground. Soldiers and citizens muttered in the streets and on the verandas about this matter. The more informed gossips knew that the lack of air cover was also a bone of contention between the military and civilian high-ups in Singapore and their masters in London. Those in London had other things on their minds. For them the war in the Middle East was much more important than this alleged threat from the Japanese. Even so, they continued to protest that they were pouring soldiers into the city from every part of the Empire. This was undeniable. But they were short of aircraft. Singapore would have to wait its turn.

The officer, Albert Taft, was waiting outside the Cathay when Virginia Chen's taxi drew up. She was wearing a near full-length cheong sam in a medium blue silk, which matched her eyes.

'I say, you do look nice,' said Albert. Calm and confident by nature, he was pleased he'd made his own luck in this city where men now vastly outnumbered women. Unless you wanted to go to the brothels of Lavender Road or Smith Street to hire one for an hour, or to the Great World Cabaret to buy tickets for a taxi dancer, women were an impossible luxury, out of bounds for most of the military who were desperate to enjoy these last hours.

And this girl, well, she was quite something.

Men in the cinema queue, some known to Albert, shouted and whistled at the handsome couple (he in his whites, she at her most Chinese in her cheong sam), as they made their way up the stairs.

The programme started with a hearty and prolonged rendition of the National Anthem, with every line, every word roared with a desperate and needy patriotism. The familiar words were bellowed out by men who only recently had been singing it in their school assembly. In that close, hot space, the roar generated an optimism, a certainty, that a war was to be won. In this atmosphere uncertainties seemed unpatriotic.

The battle scenes in the film were clapped and halloo'd. The tempers and tantrums of the beautiful Scarlett O'Hara were greeted with whistles. Miss Leigh was a pin-up. No denying that.

The film was very long indeed and when they got outside again, Albert's immaculate whites were crumpled and his young face was gleaming with sweat. 'What now? Is there a good restaurant?' He took her arm. 'I'll take you to the best restaurant. We'll go to Raffles. Dinner and dance with the best.'

Virginia laughed. 'They won't be happy at me with you in Raffles.'

'Why not? You'll be the most beautiful woman there.'

'Believe me, they won't like it.'

'Bloody silly, if you ask me. Excuse my language.'

'We will go to the Coconut Grove. That is better. More fun.'

'Will the band play there?'

'Oh yes. It will play there.'

Albert hailed a taxi and jumped in beside her, making sure that they sat close, thigh to thigh, in the back. She didn't move away from him, but there was absolutely no response on her part. He could see he'd have his work cut out here if he wanted to make the most of his short time on this island.

Raffles Hotel, like the Cathay Cinema, was doing good business. Here the masters of local commerce – the *tuans besar* – joined the higher echelons of the military in flying the flag, demonstrating 'business as usual' in their own inimitable way. But unfortunately, even here, the war was poking its long talons. The dancing room, in fact a great veranda, was usually open to the night to catch the slightest breeze from the sea. But now they were at war any light was the light of betrayal.

As the brownout was only partially complete, the lights had to be kept very dim. Still, the determined regulars intended to have fun and defy the Japanese; they'd read of London carrying on as normal even in the Blitz. They would do no less.

Lesley and Bo Sambuck made a four table with their friends, the Hoxtons. While they settled, Lesley told Vera Hoxton about Mr Lee and his bargain silk and lace.

'So will you ship them?'

'I suppose so. Bo says we must go. How awful to think of going.'

'John's got our tickets. Practically pushing me on to the boat. I can't bear to think what will happen.'

Bo put his finger up like a schoolmaster. 'Now, dear girls. No defeatist talk! Let's have our dinner and enjoy the dancing.'

Lesley and Bo were one of the few couples who actually got up to dance. As they performed their immaculately executed slow foxtrot, Bo murmured in her ear, 'D'you remember that night you showed me how to do this? A bit quicker then, what?' Here in Singapore, all dances, even the slow foxtrot, were performed in an even slower fashion or they made you sweat, which simply wouldn't do.

Lesley and Bo had met at a dance given by Lord Chase for his daughter, Suzanne, in 1931. Bo had been on leave from Ceylon where Suzanne's brother, Gerald, was in the colonial service. Bo had followed Lesley round all evening until she'd agreed to dance with him. He'd said he couldn't dance, so she'd taught him the slow foxtrot.

He'd called on her the next day to win her mother's heart so he could get to hers. They were engaged within a month and he went to take up a new post in Singapore. Two months later she followed him and they were married in St Andrew's Cathedral.

They'd loved to dance together ever since. Here in Singapore, they danced most nights at Raffles or at the Tanglin Club. Sometimes they danced at home to the wind-up gramophone. They always loved to be close.

That first night he'd asked to drive her home but she wouldn't let him, not sure what he would think of her modest house near the Grammar School where her mother, the very respectable but rather common-speaking widow of a junior school headmaster, ruled the roost.

But after the dance, he followed her to find where she lived. It was years later that Lesley realised that he had had to make haste. His leave was half over. Later a woman in Singapore told Lesley these colonial boys were always in a hurry.

Now, in the middle of the dance at Raffles in the dim light they bumped into their friends the Carricks. Lesley started to laugh but Hilary Carrick burst into tears and was led away by Len.

'This is hopeless, darling, like dancing on someone's grave,' said Bo, leading Lesley back to their table. 'Let's get out of here.'

He was putting her silk wrap round her shoulders when Len Carrick called across, 'We're off to the Coconut Grove. Could have a bit more life than this mausoleum. Fancy a trip?'

\* \* \*

The Coconut Grove was a small, open-air restaurant on a promontory surrounded on three sides by the sea. The pretty lights strung through the trees, which normally made it such a fairy-tale place, were not lit these days. The candles on the tables were unlit too. But a yellow moon relieved the darkness, and the dancing, eating and talking proceeded as though there were no brownout at all. The waiter found Bo and his party a table under the overhanging roof and they settled there to view the crowd and watch the fun.

Of course, more than half the crowd were in uniform. In the corner a table full of noisy Australians, sharing the company of one very pretty European woman, seemed to be having a good time.

Lesley's eye fixed on a handsome young couple who were dipping their way through the tango, becoming visible then vanishing on the moonlit dance floor.

'Do you see what I see?' said Bo.

'She's a stunner,' said John Hoxton. 'Could be an Italian if she didn't wear that Chink dress. They have no sense, these *stengahs*.'

'My God!' said Lesley. 'How could she? Don't you see, Bo?'

Vera Hoxton looked at her sharply.

'She's your children's governess, isn't she?' said Hilary.

'Jolly clever young woman,' said Bo. 'Speaks five languages. Daughter of an Indo-French *tuan besar* from Indochina. Name of Chen.'

'Too embarrassing,' said Lesley glumly. 'How could she?'

\*  \*  \*

Out on the dance floor, as Albert pulled Virginia close after one dramatic sweep she caught sight of the group at the table. She hesitated, then took Albert's hand and walked across to the veranda. The men at the table stood up. Lesley stared despondently at the fan in her hand. The men shook Albert heartily by the hand and asked him about his ship. After more than a few minutes' hesitation, Bo asked him to sit down.

Albert felt Virginia's foot on his in the darkness. 'No, thank you, sir. I have to see Miss Chen . . . er . . . home. And I have to get back to my ship. Cinderella and all that.'

'What it is to be young,' sighed Len, stretching back in his chair. 'Young and beautiful.'

'Len! Don't be silly!' His wife scowled at him.

'We should have gone to the Tanglin,' said Lesley. 'They don't allow that sort of thing there.'

'Wonder which ship he's on,' said Bo. 'The *Prince of Wales*? They say the Admiral's flown over to Manila, so he can't be worried about the Nips. Got it in hand.'

The taxi stopped at the gate of Hibiscus Lodge. Albert walked with Virginia up the long drive towards the house. At the bottom of the steps he picked one of the moonflowers and twirled it in his hand so the perfume thickened in the air. They walked along the veranda and sat on the long chairs. Virginia kicked off her shoes and they fell with a clatter on to the boards. Albert leaned across and took her hand. She let it lie there.

'What do you think,' he said in his soft West Country drawl, 'about this theory of falling in love at first sight?'

His hand tightened on hers but she had no time to agree or protest because Sylvie came out on to the balcony yawning. Albert released Virginia's hand, smiled at Sylvie and greeted her warmly. She climbed into the chair with Virginia and snuggled in. Around them the whirr of the cicadas, the yelping murmur of birds in the high canopy, the click of the tick-tack lizard joined together and filled the night.

Ah So came and stood by the door yawning. Her face, above her black blouse and trousers, seemed to be floating in the dark. 'Missie best in bed,' she said. Virginia smiled and shook her head and the *amah* melted back into the house.

Albert stretched out his legs in the chair and started to talk. He told her about his home in Devon, about his father who was a fisherman and his three brothers who were in the army, and how much he loved the navy. He talked of how many hundreds of men his ship had saved at Dunkirk. 'They stood in lines up to their necks in water, waiting to get on. Such patience.'

'You will be doing this too, here, in the next week or so,' said Virginia. 'Helping them get away.'

Sylvie liked this, when adults let you stay and listen.

Albert laughed. 'But they'll not be up to their necks in water. The Japs won't take Singapore.'

'We are going on a boat,' announced Sylvie. 'My father has the tickets. He says we must go or the Japanese will get us. But he won't go, as he must fight the Japanese.'

Albert looked at Virginia. 'You too? Are you going?'

She shook her head. 'There has been an order. European women and children only. No Chinese. No Malay. No Indian. No Eurasian. So much for us all being in it together.'

'That's jolly unfair.'

She shrugged. 'This is my country. My people came here from China just after Mr Raffles. I would not wish to leave my country.'

'It's my country too,' said Sylvie. 'I was born here anyway. So I don't have to go either.'

'It's better that you go,' said Albert grimly. He seemed not so young now. 'And Virginia too. It's not fair you can't go.'

Any further discussion was pre-empted by the noisy arrival of the Sambuck car along the drive.

Virginia stood up, her shoes in her hand. 'You should go, Albert.'

He took up his cap in his hands. 'Well!' he said awkwardly. She didn't move towards him. 'Well, then. I should go. I meant what I said just now. Love and all that. About tomorrow . . . I don't know what . . .'

Virginia moved now to kiss his cheek. 'No one knows about tomorrow, Albert. Now go.'

Bo nodded at the figure of the young officer striding down the drive. 'Seemed like a good enough feller.'

'Oh, Bo,' said Lesley, waiting for John Singh to open the door, 'you really don't know anything, do you?'

She was furious when she saw Sylvie was out of bed and started to yell at her. Sylvie slipped along the veranda to her bedroom, closely followed by Virginia.

Lesley called her back. 'Miss Chen?'

Virginia returned on quiet feet. 'Yes, Mrs Sambuck?'

'I really think you should be very careful whom you see, Miss Chen. And where you go.'

Virginia looked her in the eye. 'Who I see and where I go is my business, and my business alone, Mrs Sambuck.' She picked up her shoes then and walked away, the boards of the veranda creaking slightly under her bare feet.

'Cheek! Cheek!' spluttered Lesley. 'How dare she? Tomorrow you must dismiss her, Bo. I'm telling you. Get rid of her.'

Bo put an arm round his wife and led her towards their bedroom. 'Don't go on, old dear. You'll only be here one more day and you'll need Miss Chen to help to organise the children, and the packing.' He closed the door behind them. 'The important thing is, darling, tomorrow you will leave and I'll be alone. All by myself.' He took off her silk wrap and folded it neatly. Then he began to unhook the back of her long silk gown. 'I've never seen you looking lovelier and now it seems I'm to lose you. Think of that. We have so little time, sweetheart. So little time . . .'

Virginia Chen: Her Book

The men streaming in and out of this city – and there have been many – are inevitably interested in female company (that is if you except one alley behind Lavender Street where women who are really men reign with queen-like splendour).

This eagerness for female company is not a recent thing brought on by the present emergency. Through the years my great-grandmother, my grandmother, my mother have always been the subjects for leering and proposition in Chinatown where company was always a commodity that could be bought, alongside the gold and diamonds and rice. (Until very recently you could buy slaves – little girls and boys brought in from the provinces of China for sale as servants.)

The female company that could not be bought could often be flattered, cajoled, lured with the enticements of love and long-term security, as marriage was not usually an option.

In consequence, there are many like me (half Indo-Chinese French, quarter English, quarter pure Chinese – Sylvie has made me think of this, and goodness knows what else). What nonsense is this thing about labels. As I grew and talked about things to my grandmother and my teachers I discovered advantage in this. I am not tied to any tradition, any history. I can choose to be myself.

I have arguments about this with my cousin Simon Chen, who says to me that the obvious place for my loyalty must be with the Chinese. In some ways he thinks I should be ashamed of the bits of me that aren't Chinese. Surely my Chinese self must be the most potent, most significant part of myself? Simon talks with many people now who call for a Singapore free of the British, run by its own people. Some of them see this conflict with Japan, problematic as it is, as an opportunity.

One outcome of all this is that, old as I am at twenty-seven, I have tended to avoid the close company of men. There was that affair with Jean Babtiste, which taught me about the realms of love within me. Then when he scurried back to France I learned also the mistake of involvement with married men, no matter how they profess their great love.

The Chinese are not interested in me because I am such a mixture. The Europeans are interested only in what they see as exotic and are compelled by the thrill of the illegitimate.

Ah So, like her so many *amah* friends, has disavowed the prison of marriage and takes others' children for her own. Perhaps she is wise.

This man Albert Taft does seem different from all the others, I know, even on so short an acquaintance. He is honest and forthright and peculiarly innocent. These are difficult times for all of us. My guard was down. We did kiss in the taxi and that stirred me more than made me comfortable. But these are strange times and he seems such a good, honest man.

It is certain, though, that I will never see him again. These are not the days to find a soul mate.

# Chapter Seven

## The White Coat

The next morning Sylvie and Feargal had breakfast on the veranda with Virginia. Their father looked in on them before he set off, very late, for the office. 'Your mother's resting on, Sylvie. Don't disturb her. Perhaps Miss Chen would help you to pack a small case? That would help your mother. We will all have to do our bit. You need to be ready for the ship tomorrow.' He hugged Sylvie then and she could feel the pressure of his lips on her hair.

After breakfast Ah So took Feargal to play bat and ball under the long shadow cast by the hibiscus hedge. Wong Mee moved about quietly clearing the breakfast things away.

'Now,' said Virginia, 'you must do your reading and your writing and we will trace on the map the route of your boat. Then you can learn the names of the ports.' She brought the books and the rolled-up map, and spread the world map on the cleared breakfast table.

'Let's do the map first,' said Sylvie.

'Sylvie!'

'Look, Miss Chen, will it make one jot, one iota, of difference whether I do my lessons this morning or not?'

'*Iota*?' Virginia Chen stood still for a second, then shrugged her shoulders. She ran a hand over the map. 'See. Here we are. I don't quite know which route you'll take, but you will probably go to Bombay ... then perhaps Durban ... then Capetown and on to Liverpool.'

'The other side of the world, isn't it, Liverpool?' said Sylvie. 'What a long way that is. It took us ages to get there when we went on leave. Months. It's a very long way. And there are submarines.' She ran her finger along the glossy blue that was the sea, making her finger the big ship that would take them home. The red, she knew, was the British Empire, on which the sun never set. 'I don't want to go,' she announced. 'I want to stay here.'

Virginia laughed. 'Of course you must go. Your mother and Feargal are going. You must go too.'

'Why can't you come?'

'Because this is my home. Singapore is my place.'

'Well, it's mine too. I was born here.'

'But it's dangerous, Sylvie. There is great danger now from the North.'

'There's danger in England. The cities are being blitzed. There's no food. My mother said.'

'It is your country, Sylvie. It is your mother's country. Your mother country.' She rolled up the map crossly. 'You do not belong here.'

Sylvie was very still. She pressed her lips together to stop them trembling. 'I don't want to go. But I quite like it when my nana's there!' She paused, wondering why she liked her nana. 'She holds you close and calls you "pet", and makes you strawberry pancakes.'

'She makes them herself?'

'Oh, yes.' There was no Cookie there. No *amah*. No Virginia Chen. Her lips started to tremble again. 'She smells of soap and . . . and mothballs.'

Virginia reflected that the Chinese thought the English smelled of corpses. No thought to pass on to a child on such a day. 'Now!' she said brightly. 'No lessons then! What should we do?'

'I want you to do my hair for me. I want you to do it like yours, all smooth. And I want you to take a photograph of me in my white mandarin coat.'

'Right, then, come on, young lady. We will dress you for *Chu Chin Chow*!' She held out her hand. Sylvie took it and they walked along the veranda into Virginia's bedroom. They had a fine time with Virginia's pins and combs and sweet-smelling oil. Virginia pulled Sylvie's hair back and up very tightly, so that her cheekbones flattened out and her dark eyes lengthened. She rubbed Pond's cream on her face and made it shine. Then Sylvie ran to her own bedroom to get the white coat and her little camera.

They went out away from the shade of the house to take the photograph in the sun. Ah So and Feargal came to watch the fun and Ah So went into the house to get Virginia's purple fan. Virginia took Sylvie's picture with her hands in the wide sleeves of the coat, then holding the fan to her eyes, and then out to the side. She was photographed with Feargal and with Ah So. Then Ah So, having had instruction, took a photo of Sylvie with Virginia Chen, and then of them both with Feargal.

'Sylvie! Sylvie! Come here at once!' Her mother's voice shrieked from the house. 'Miss Chen, bring Sylvie here. Amah, bring Feargal. This minute! This minute!'

They trailed up the long lawn, each absorbing the fact that they were in trouble. Lesley was at the door in her long silk dressing gown. Her hair was loose about her shoulders. She caught hold of Sylvie, gripping her arm painfully. Sylvie wriggled but could not escape.

'What on earth do you think you're doing, tricked out like a native?' Lesley started pulling at Sylvie's hair, making her howl. She slapped her face. 'What muck have you got on your hair, your face? You bad girl!' She started to slap her about the head. She looked with loathing at Virginia. 'I imagine you're satisfied now, miss. Making her into some half-caste like yourself. You wicked woman!' She dragged the screaming Sylvie away into the house.

Virginia glanced at Ah So, who shrugged and picked up Feargal, who was whimpering. 'Feargal need his elevenses, I think,' she said.

Virginia went to her room and sat on the bed, listening to Sylvie's screams.

Lesley had pulled off the silk coat and dragged Sylvie into Bo's bathhouse. Holding her by one arm, she dipped into the large *tong* and splashed pan after pan of cool water over the screaming and gasping Sylvie. Finally, she tired herself out and her grasp slackened. Sylvie wriggled free. She ran through the house and threw herself into Virginia's arms.

'I hate her! She is a cow! I hate her! Why did she do that?' Her face was red from her mother's slaps and she was trembling.

Virginia took a large towel and wrapped Sylvie in it. Then she sat beside her, took out the last pins from her hair and calmed it with her fingers. 'Ssh. Ssh,' she said. 'It's nothing, Sylvie. Nothing at all. Your mother is tired. She is worried about going on the ship.' She got her brush from the dressing table and brushed Sylvie's hair smooth, into its usual long bob. She took her hand. 'Come, and we will find you some nice, clean, dry clothes. Me also. You have me all wet.'

As they walked through the house, Virginia Chen picked up the white silk coat and folded it over her arm. Ah So came in and took the wet clothes. The house was quiet. All seemed right again. Mrs Sambuck would emerge beautifully dressed and coiffed and act as though nothing had happened. They had been through this before.

'Now,' said Virginia, 'what about this packing?' She found a small case and placed it on the bed. 'What first?'

'My white coat.'

Virginia folded it gently in tissue and laid it flat on the bottom of the case. 'What next?'

'*The King of the Golden River* and my writing book. I'll do my lessons on the ship and think of you.'

Virginia smiled. 'Now, what else? We must be practical. Knickers. Two vests. Two dresses. A spare pair of sandals. Socks, do you think? It might be chilly at night on that ship. A woolly jumper? And now for the Lady Sylvie. That lovely pearl necklace your father gave you for your birthday. Your best straw hat. What else?' Dumbly, Sylvie handed her the crumpled lion puppet. Tenderly, Virginia wrapped him in tissue and laid him on the top. Then she clicked the case shut.

'There now, ready to go anywhere.' She smoothed Sylvie's fringe. 'Why don't we go on the veranda and have a game of dominoes? It's far too hot outside to run about out there.'

When they got on to the veranda, Lesley was already there on a long chair, a clinking glass of lime juice at her side. She was reading the *Illustrated London News* of September 1941. She looked up.

Virginia and Sylvie froze like thieves caught in the act. 'We thought we would play dominoes,' said Virginia. She held up the box.

'Is that so?' Lesley looked at her for a long minute. 'Well first, if you will be so kind, Miss Chen, would you fetch Cookie, as I want to make changes regarding dinner?'

Virginia went off and Sylvie went to the far end of the veranda to set up the dominoes on a low table. She kept her back to her mother.

Lesley called, 'Sylvie?'

Carefully Sylvie placed the dominoes, one by one, wrong side up, on the table. Above her, the fan turned and re-turned in the stifling air.

'There's no need to sulk, child.' Sylvie could hear the chink of ice on glass. 'You must learn that it's inappropriate to put your trust in certain people. Quite inappropriate, the way you are so influenced by Miss Chen. Just remember, Miss Chen is a servant, just like Amah and the garden boys. It's inappropriate. You'll learn how inappropriate it is.'

A minute later, Tang Peng, expecting another reprimand, came puffing in, followed by Virginia. When she reached the low table, Sylvie was already putting the dominoes back into their carved wooden box.

'What's this?' said Virginia with forced gravity. 'No dominoes?'

'I've changed my mind. Is it all right if we play catch down by the hibiscus hedge? I don't want to play here at the house.' As they walked across the lawn she said in a light, carefree voice, 'I hate her, you know. I absolutely do hate her.' Then she threw the ball a really long way and Virginia Chen had to run hard to get it before it rolled under the hedge.

# Chapter Eight

## An Abnormal Day

That afternoon followed the absolute pattern set by the Sambucks in their lives in Singapore. Bo came home at one from the office for tiffin, leaping up the steps and handing his *sola topee* to one garden boy and his stick to another. He had a shower and changed into his sarong and his cotton *tutup*, then joined his family for his favourite 'Chinese chow'. Tang Peng, knowing this was near the end of things, had made the *tuan*'s favourites: four kinds of seafood in sharp and sweet sauces, a big stoneware bowl of rice and his favourite *sambals*. He had been making this for Tuan Sambuck long before the intrusive and volatile *mem* came on the scene.

As they chatted at the table, Bo avoided mentioning the meeting he'd had in the office about the fate of the agency should the war actually reach Singapore. Better to keep things light around the table. He picked up his chopsticks and noticed that his daughter was picking at her food. 'Now then, sobersides, who has spilled your milk?'

Sylvie dug into her shrimps and rice with her chopsticks and kept her eyes on her hands.

'She was a very silly girl today, Daddy,' said Lesley, 'weren't you, darling?'

'No I wasn't.'

'Yes you were.'

'No I wasn't.'

Bo put down his chopsticks. 'Ladies, ladies! This just reminds me of a school playground.' The lazy thread went from his voice, to be replaced by soldierly authority. 'Now, young Sylvie, what have you done?'

'I was dressing up. And *she* smacked me on the face and dragged me and threw water over me in your bathhouse.'

'Your daughter, Bo, was dressing up as a native. A Chink.' Lesley glanced at Virginia, who was steadily eating her meal. 'She had filthy grease on her hair and brown grease on her face.'

'It wasn't brown grease on my face. It was Pond's cream. Just Pond's cream.'

'Anyway, she made a guy of herself and was punished. That was all.'

Sylvie stood up. 'I didn't.'

Lesley raised her eyebrows.

'I didn't. It was you who made a guy of yourself. Screaming like a parrot.'

Bo stared at her. 'Go to your room, Sylvie,' he said coldly. 'Miss Chen, will you see that she goes there and stays there?'

He watched them leave and turned to Lesley, who had

picked up her china spoon. She could not cope with chopsticks. 'What was that about?'

'Nothing. Miss Chen had her togged up as a Chink and I washed it all off. The woman eggs her on.'

'She said it was Pond's cream.'

'She was lying.'

Bo took up his chopsticks yet again. 'Perhaps it's a good thing you're all going home after all.'

'Yes. I suppose it is.' She put down her spoon. 'There's something about Sylvie, Bo – so dark, and that temper. Where can it come from?'

'Not from my family, honey. White as the driven snow.'

'But ... India, Bo. I hate to say this, but in three generations—'

'As I say, white as the driven snow. My grandfather would have called you out in a duel for making such a dastardly allegation.' He smiled at her. 'Don't get worked up, sweetheart. Old Sylvie's just a bit of an odd bod, that's all.' He called for the boy to clear and stood up, yawning. 'I'll just go for my lie-off, then what say we go down to the club for a game of tennis? I said to Len that we probably would. No Volunteers this afternoon. I have leave because it's your last day. The whole town's in turmoil, but today's turnout's cancelled for me. I'm supposed to be helping the *mem* to pack.'

'It's done.'

'I saw the cases. I don't know that they'll take all those, pussy. Luggage is still piled on the docks from the last embarkation.'

'I'm only taking absolute essentials. Just essentials.'

'Well, then! A game of tennis! That'll blow the cobwebs away.'

'Yes.' She stirred in her chair. 'I'd like that.'

'Our last game of tennis, after all.'

'Yes. We'll beat their socks off.'

'That's the spirit!' He walked round to their bedroom veranda, climbed into a long chair, and fell fast asleep.

In the end Len and Hilary didn't turn up at the club, and Bo and Lesley played a desultory game of singles. Bo thrashed Lesley, even though he wasn't trying. The club was half empty. They sat over their gin *pahits*, staring into space. The barman watched them mildly, repolishing a line of glasses, which were already gleaming.

Hilary and Len finally turned up, full of apologies, and they sat talking for a little while. But there seemed, finally, nothing to say. In the end Bo went to the telephone and rang ahead for Cookie to have their dinner ready, and they came home early.

Sylvie had already eaten. She never joined her parents for dinner as it was always late, sometimes as late as ten thirty before they ate their evening meal. She visited Virginia in her room. Virginia was lying on her bed reading. She nodded across to her crammed bookcase.

'Choose a book, Sylvie. Come and read.'

'Don't want to.' She sat down on the floor with her back to the bed and started to fiddle with her leather puppet. She'd unpacked it and brought it along to discuss with Virginia how they might mend the holes.

From the other end of the house came the click of silver on

china, the murmur of her parents' voices, the pick and drone of music on the radio. 'They're early,' she said.

Virginia put down her book. 'What is it, Sylvie?'

'I wondered what we could do about these holes, Miss Chen.' Out of the pocket of her dressing gown she pulled a brown leather glove. 'I thought we might, kind of, patch it, with this.'

Virginia Chen laughed. 'That's a perfectly good glove, Sylvie.'

'And it will be perfectly no use to me because I've a pair of gloves in my case and these will be perfectly well left behind.'

Virginia nodded. 'Well, then. Let's go and ask Ah So if she can do it. She's a wizard with a needle.'

They moved softly along the browned-out veranda. The *amah* was sitting in a rattan chair on the corner outside Feargal's room. She stood up from the shadows and glided softly towards them. They were just whispering to her about the glove and the puppet when there was a scream from the dining room.

Virginia put a hand on Sylvie's shoulder. 'You wait here. I will go.' Still, Sylvie was at her heels.

Bo looked up. He had his arm round Lesley. 'It's all right, Miss Chen.' He leaned behind him to turn off the crackling radio.

'Is Mrs Sambuck well?' asked Virginia.

'What is it, Daddy?' said Sylvie, coming from behind. She wondered whether it was all her bad feelings and wishes that had made her mother ill. 'Is she dead?'

'No.' Wong Mee was hurrying in with a glass of cold water on a tray. 'She's had a shock.' Bo looked at Virginia Chen and Sylvie, who now stared at him with almost threatening query.

'It was on the wireless. I am afraid the Japanese have sunk the *Prince of Wales* and the *Repulse*, the great ships which came to defend us. We're defenceless now. They can bomb us when they like. It's all over, Miss Chen. We're unprotected. It is unthinkable but it's happening.'

He lifted Lesley to the couch and Virginia sat beside her, feeding her sips of water. Bo called back Wong Mee and started stamping around the house, hauling precious things from the cupboards: china and crystal, ancient photographs and ornaments. From his study he got a steel box where (Sylvie knew) he kept his paper money from going mouldy in the hot, damp air. These they made into a higgledy-piggledy pile on the veranda.

Sylvie followed him. 'What are you doing? Will these come on the ship with us? All this stuff?'

'No. No. There'll be no room on the ship. We'll put them in a safe place before daylight. God knows what will happen now. We need to keep some things safe. God knows where we'll be next week.' He started to mutter under his breath and Sylvie couldn't understand what he was saying.

Lesley struggled upright, throwing off Virginia Chen's ministering hands. Just then the siren went, weighing on the air like a dying man's shriek. They looked at each other. 'Under the table!' said Bo.

Ah So walked in with a whimpering Feargal in her arms, Tang Peng behind them. Bo pushed them all, including Ah So, Cookie and Wong Mee, under the dining table, then raced round the house pulling mattresses off beds to pile on top. Under the table, Sylvie found herself between her mother's knees, clasped tight in her mother's arms. How strange it was to feel so protected by someone who, an hour ago, you wished were dead. She could feel her mother flinch as Virginia and Ah So slipped under the table.

'Come here, Feargal.' Lesley held her arms out wider and the *amah* tipped a sleepy Feargal into them. When Bo dipped his head under the table, he was wearing his tin helmet and his leather Volunteer belt, complete with pistol. As he did so, they could hear booming and crashing in the town below. Lesley screamed. Virginia Chen put her hands over Feargal's ears. Sylvie loosened herself from her mother's grasp and leaned on Virginia Chen.

Virginia Chen: Her Book
I waited until they were all asleep, Feargal muttering, Mrs Sambuck expelling bubbling snores, her mouth open. I disengaged my hand from Sylvie's and set out down the long Hibiscus Lodge drive for the town. I ran all the way.

The sky was as light as daytime with all the flames. The streets were gagged up with fire engines and ambulances; military vehicles taking the dead; soldiers throwing bodies like sacks. The dust underfoot was muddy with the bloody water from the hoses. On the corner of my grandmother's street stood a woman with no clothes, shrieking.

In her room at the shophouse my grandmother was sitting with her back to the window, fanning herself vigorously with her oldest fan, the one with the silver filigree. The gramophone was blaring one of her favourites: 'The Soldiers of the King' by some military band with many trumpets and drums.

I bawl to her suggesting she should, perhaps, go downstairs and find a safer place. 'No!' she shouts. 'I do not hear so they will not hurt me.' I sit down, helpless and ignorant as she always makes me feel. 'How is that child?' she bawls. 'She is safe,' I say. 'Good!' she shouts. 'Good child. Go back to her. Keep her safe.' And she closes her eyes, still flapping her fan under her chin.

When Bo came back, dusty and dirty, at three o'clock in the morning, his family were still huddled there under the table. Feargal, uncomfortable in Lesley's clasp, had crept back into his *amah*'s arms and was fast asleep. Sylvie was stretched out with her back to her mother and Lesley herself was sitting, hollow-eyed, with her knees drawn up to her chin. Bo pulled off the mattresses.

'Come on, come out. Didn't you hear the all clear?'

They shook themselves like dogs and crawled out, blinking in the white dawn light.

'I thought they would come back,' mumbled Lesley. 'I was sure they would come back.'

Bo peered under the table. 'Where's Miss Chen?'

'She went. When the all clear sounded. Something about her grandmother. I told her that she must stay here, that her place was with us. You really must dismiss her, Bo.' Lesley was rubbing her hands down her frock, trying in vain to smooth out the creases.

Bo frowned. 'Large sections of Chinatown are blown to smithereens, Les. We were digging bodies out. The streets are an open cemetery. Perhaps there'll be no grandmother there for her to find.'

Sylvie grasped Bo's forearm. 'The old nana, Miss Chen's grandma? Is she dead? She was a nice old lady.'

'Have you been there? Did she take you in those hovels? That's it, Bo! Something—' Lesley's voice rose yet another pitch.

'Really, Lesley, get a grip,' snapped Bo. He put a hand on Sylvie's shoulder. 'We don't know, Sylvie. Miss Chen's gone to find her so she should be all right.' The eyes he raised to his wife were weary with the sights he had seen. 'Now, Lesley,' he said quite gently, 'you go and put on your nightie and go to bed. You too, Sylvie. Amah will see to Feargal. I'm going to have a shower, then go down to the office to close it up.' He pulled his wife to him. 'And at four o'clock this afternoon, you're getting on that ship and going to South Africa.'

'South Africa?'

'You have to go where the ship happens to be going. First stop South Africa, if you want to go west. Then on to England if they can dodge the U boats. Otherwise just stay there. It will be safe enough there. There are so few ships. Not everyone will get off. You have to get off. I'll sort you out some banker's drafts and some gold. And I've got letters of introduction for you. They'll take care of you, I promise you. I promise. This is no place for you, Les, or these offspring of ours.'

\* \* \*

Sylvie went to her room, pulled on shorts, a linen blouse and her Dutch clogs. Then she pulled a pillow down in the bed under the single sheet. They would think it was her. She tucked in the mosquito net all round, slipped into the garden from her own veranda and sidled down to the front, where her father's car was parked. She lifted the boot lid, lowered herself in and pulled the cover down over her. She took off her yellow belt and put it over the closure mechanism, so she wouldn't be trapped inside. It was very hot in there and became hotter and hotter as the minutes ticked by. She began to pour with sweat. Then she could hear her father clattering down the steps, throwing over his shoulder instructions to Wong Mee about the digging of a hole.

Sylvie wondered where John Singh was, then decided that he must have gone off to see his family, like Miss Chen.

Less than ten minutes later they drew up outside her father's office on Collyer Quay. She waited for the car to lift on its springs as he got out and then two minutes later she raised the boot lid and rolled out into the dusty road, hot, sweaty and gasping for breath. It was a relief to get out of the dizzying heat of the car into the very slightly fresher air of the early morning.

As she stood still in the road, the stench hit her. She was used to Singapore's own smell, which, on the day they returned to Singapore from leave in England, had made her feel comfortable, at ease. But this smell was different. There was the stench of burning rubber from the *godowns*, which had been set alight, and another smell, powerful and strange, which made the bile rise in her throat.

She set off at a run towards Beach Road. Already at this early hour the dock area was crowded. Looking back behind her, she realised that the crowd was really a long, straggly queue of dusty, exhausted-looking people. Cars and trucks were parked all along the quay, abandoned at strange angles as people drove as near to the queue as they could, then took their chances. Cars had been driven into the dock, one on top of another.

As she pushed and shoved to force her way through, Sylvie realised that she was pushing against only European bodies. Apart from a silent *amah* waiting here and there, all the faces were white. There were hundreds of them. The queue was very long. There were soldiers in wide hats pushing people aside to move up nearer to the boats. She saw a woman shoved roughly to the ground, her howling toddler with her. Other women closed protectively round the woman and stared resentfully at the backs of the soldiers, who were now making their way easily through a crowd that was opening up in front of them like the Red Sea before the Israelites.

Free of the crowd at last, Sylvie made her way through to the city. Great holes had been blasted out of the street like ragged tooth extractions. Gaggles of individuals, in and out of uniform, were pulling away at wood and plaster, digging at the debris to get at the people who were trapped. A few individuals were wailing and crying, but some were just standing and staring at the wreckage as though they could see through the tangle of wood and plaster to their friends and relatives inside. Up one alleyway she finally saw the cause of the stench: two unclaimed bodies covered now in busy excited flies. In her head Sylvie could see the nana's shophouse crashed to the ground in splinters. But then when she turned the corner, the house was still there, though in front of it was some kind of crater. The two uncles and the boy who had brought the tea were still there, lolling at the back of the curio shop. They looked at her blankly when she came up to them.

She took a breath. 'I was here the other day,' she said. The one called Uncle Chu opened his eyes more widely as though to take in who this strange small person was.

'I lookee Miss Chen,' she said desperately. 'Miss Virginia Chen. I lookee Missee Chen. Virginia Chen.'

At last the tea boy smiled, showing a row of white, gleaming teeth. 'You wish to see Virginia?' he said, in a near-perfect English accent, just like Virginia's. 'Well, we'll just have to see if she's here, won't we?'

He turned and she followed him up the two flights of stairs again to Madame Chen's parlour. Virginia was there, drinking tea with her grandmother out of fine china cups. Sylvie looked around at the unchanged room. It was hard to think that outside in the street there were great holes, wailing people and dead bodies.

She rushed into speech. 'My father came home and you were gone. He said Beach Road had been bombed and I worried about the nana. Then I worried about you.'

The old woman said something to Virginia, who said to Sylvie, 'Grandmother says you should have some tea, as you look hot and very dusty. Will you sit with me?' She patted the space beside her on the carved wooden settle. 'Thank you, Simon,' she said to the boy from the shop. 'You met my cousin, Simon?' she said to Sylvie. 'Simon Chen. This boy is having a very easy time these days. His school's been turned into a hospital so he's forgotten how to study.'

Simon put out a hand to shake Sylvie's. 'Raffles Institute. I'd rather be back at school than dealing with this lot.' He jerked his head towards the window and, as he did, his gleaming hair rose like black rain and settled again. 'Or fighting the Japanese fools.'

'I don't go to school,' said Sylvie, hanging on to his hand. 'I wish I did.'

He wriggled his hand free. 'I know. My cousin Jin Kee teaches you. She says you are very lazy and backward with your reading.'

'Simon!' commanded Virginia. 'Go and mind the shop. The looters will have our bowls and cupboards before you can blink an eye.' She handed Sylvie a small, handleless cup. 'Now then, drink this and we will have to see about getting you home.'

'He called you Jin Kee,' said Sylvie.

'You would call it a pet name. Inside the family. Simon likes it because it is more Chinese. Jin Kee Chen. He likes all things Chinese, unlike some people on this island.' She poured Sylvie some tea. 'You really shouldn't have come, Sylvie.'

'We're supposed to be getting the boat this afternoon, but the queue's a mile long. We'll never get on a boat.'

'We will go and tell your mother and father they must join the queue now.'

The grandmother leaned forward and said something to Virginia, who smiled and turned to Sylvie. 'My grandmother says she is grateful for your care in coming here and that you will always have a home under her roof.'

Sylvie blushed. Then she nodded very hard towards the old woman and said, 'Thank you,' in a very loud voice, hoping that its very loudness would sound Chinese.

From somewhere distant came the thump of guns and Sylvie dropped her tea. The tea bled over the floor, standing proud of its glittering surface. The cup did not break, but rolled into the corner with a ringing sound. Tears came into Sylvie's eyes.

'Don't worry,' said Virginia. She kneeled down to mop up the spill with the small napkin that lay over the tray.

The old woman banged three times on the floor with her stick. When the boy Simon put his head round the door, she rapped out an order.

'What's she saying?' Sylvie looked at Virginia with wide eyes.

'He has gone to get a car we keep in the warehouse. In storage now, because only the Europeans seem to get petrol rations these days. But there will be enough to get up to Hibiscus Lodge. I think you will need to join that queue at the docks very soon. Now you must say goodbye to Grandmother.'

Sylvie stood before the old woman and bowed her head. You did this in church when you prayed, so it must at least show respect.

The old woman said something. 'Kneel down, Sylvie,' said Virginia.

Sylvie looked at Virginia and did as she was told.

The grandmother said something else.

'The grandmother says that her wish will keep you safe. That your ancestors will keep you safe. She also says that you share her ancestors.'

'What does that mean?'

Virginia shrugged her shoulders. 'She is very wise. Perhaps it means that all human beings are in danger now.'

Simon Chen drove his way expertly between potholes and past clusters of soldiers who were sitting at corners or on pavements, looking dirty and resentful. One soldier hit the top of the car with a rifle and shouted something about 'Chinks'.

As they bumped along, Sylvie asked what 'looters' were. Virginia pointed to gaping holes in the front and the sides of shops. 'The Japanese drop the bombs and scoundrels of every race go in and steal.'

'Even soldiers!'

'Especially soldiers.'

'Miss Chen?'

'Yes?'

'I think I will call you Jin Kee.'

Virginia laughed. 'Here we are.' The car was swinging up the drive of Hibiscus Lodge. Everything was astoundingly normal. The gardeners had already replaced the green turf on the great hole Tuan Sambuck had them dig to hide all his big tin trunks. They had now moved on to the more routine gardening, moving slowly from flowerbed to flowerbed, watering as they went. The door boys were on the steps as usual, waiting to help with hats or canes or the opening of car doors. One of them rushed forward now and opened the door.

Simon put the car into gear and saluted them in a soldierly fashion. 'Bye, Auntie Jin Kee. See you later. Bye, Sylvie Sambuck. I don't suppose I'll see you any more. You'll go to school in England and become a good scholar, then a little *mem* like your mother.'

'I'll come back,' said Sylvie earnestly. 'I will come back.'

He laughed loudly at this, his white teeth gleaming. 'I would say that will be unlikely. All will be changed.' The wheels of the car ground into the gravel, throwing up the dust as he turned the circle. He passed Bo's big car in the gateway.

Bo jumped out of the car. 'What's this?' he said. 'Who was that?'

'I have been to see that my grandmother was safe and my cousin drove me back up the hill,' said Virginia smoothly. 'Sylvie was watching out for me.'

'There's a great queue of people at the docks,' Sylvie rushed in, then faltered. 'Virginia told me,' she said.

'Yes,' said Virginia. 'There are cars everywhere and no order in the queue. Some people have been queuing for hours.'

'Yes, yes. Don't you think I know this?' Bo gave the boys his stick and hat and leaped up the steps. 'I've come for all of you. We should go there now or God knows whether we'll get you on that boat at all.'

From down in the city another explosion crumped into the hot morning air. Sylvie jumped and tears again came unbidden into her eyes. She looked at her father, tall and ruddy, his eyes creased with unfamiliar anxiety. He was solid and familiar and the world was crumbling around them. Those dead bodies with the flies. The terrible vacancy where there had been houses. The big holes in the road.

'Will you be coming with us on the boat, Daddy?'

He shook his head. 'There's no chance of that, darling. War footing. I'm under orders. Perhaps I'll come soon – when things sort themselves out here.'

Virginia put a hand on Sylvie's shoulders. 'Come on, Sylvie, we will go over the things in your case, just once more. You might have forgotten something. We'll make sure you have money in your own little purse.'

'I'll put my puppet back in.'

'Now that's a good idea. You can make stories for other children on the boat. We'll see if Amah's mended the holes.'

Bo charged through the house, hurrying Lesley with her packing, giving Feargal one last aeroplane swing, checking that the boys had done a proper job of burying his boxes by the hibiscus hedge.

Within the hour, they had locked the gate of Hibiscus Lodge behind them and were on their way in a laden car, down to the harbour. A grim-faced Virginia and weeping Ah So were to come with them to see them off, to keep the children calm.

Lesley went through all this like a wooden doll. She did as she was told, went where she was told. But right through the rattling and jolting and swerving round the potholes, she sat rigid and looked at no one except Bo. She was like a drowning woman with only one hope of safety. Beside that, her children were nothing. Feargal, nestling in his *amah*'s arms, had no idea of this. Sylvie watched her mother from inside her own fear. She was just about to part from Virginia Chen; she felt absolutely and utterly alone.

# Chapter Nine

## Embarkation

The Sambucks stood in the queue that was milling about and surging in a worried mass in the general area of the dockside boarding ramp, which led on to the *Felix Roussel*. Around them were families, every member carrying his or her own box or bags. Even small children had rucksacks, bulging with beloved possessions. One or two families had prams or trolleys piled with cases. Here and there a rickshaw boy kept pace with the queue, his rickshaw piled with luggage, and the *mem* who fed him with money like a person at the English seaside feeding pennies in a slot machine.

The crowd pressed together, fearful of losing their places, only parting when an official-looking person in uniform came along saying, 'Excuse me, excuse me' in such a way that they could only fall back. One group had sub-machine guns, and staggered and grunted as they walked. People gave these soldiers a wide berth, muttering and accusing only when the group was out of earshot. One part of the quayside was strewn with discarded luggage, much of it open and rifled.

Bo had obtained a small trolley from the harbour office and had piled the family's luggage on it. 'Well, darling, I'll go forward and see what's what.'

Lesley clung to his arm. 'Don't go. Don't leave us.'

'I must. I need to see what it's like down there; how long you'll have to stand here in this heat.'

She clung to his arm. 'I'll come with you. Don't leave me.'

He took her hand and placed it by her side. 'They'll think we're jumping the queue, sweetheart,' he said quietly. 'They'll lynch you. Just let me see. Please, darling.'

When he came back his face was grim. 'They won't let you take all this luggage on board. One case, that's what they're saying. And food. You should take food on. They will be massively overloaded. They'll be hard put to feed everyone. Have you got food?'

Sylvie watched as her mother and Miss Chen scrabbled around in the cases and crammed things into one large case. Lesley took Sylvie's case and pressed in an extra towel. 'I don't know what rubbish you've got in here, Sylvie.'

'It's my stuff! Don't touch it,' shrieked Sylvie. 'Don't touch it or I'll kill you.'

'Leave it, old thing,' said Bo. 'There's enough panic round here already. Don't put Sylvie into a state.'

The hours ticked by. Feargal started to whimper and tears were falling down Ah So's face. When they were six from the front they watched as a child was dragged, kicking and screaming, from its *amah*.

'Come across here, old man,' said Bo, looking down at Feargal's serious face. 'Come and hold your mummy's hand because I want her to take great care of you. Amah will carry your bag to the gangway. Then on the ship you must carry it like a big boy.'

Feargal smiled up at his father. 'Amah carry my bag all the way on to the big ship.'

Bo shook his head. 'Sorry, old boy. Amah has to take care of her family, her sister and mummy in the little house behind ours.'

Feargal scowled. 'Amah has no little boys of her own. She take care of me for all of the time.'

'Tell the woman to go!' The words burst from Lesley like pellets from a gun. She grabbed Feargal by the arm. 'Bo! Will you tell her to go? And tell Miss Chen to go. We don't need them any more.'

The queue heaved forward again and scattered as a squad of soldiers, this time Scottish, by their tartan caps, forced their way through. Bo grasped Sylvie's shoulder and looked across her head at Virginia. 'Such a pity we can't take you and Ah So with us, Miss Chen. But . . .'

'The orders were "European woman and children only". I know this.' She looked him directly in the eye. 'I have heard this. That you will leave us to their tender mercies.'

His voice was steady. 'I'd put you on board if I could, Miss Chen. Believe me.'

'Singapore is my country, Mr Sambuck. I would not go. It is my country. It was my father's country and my grandfather's country.'

Sylvie pulled away from her father and almost banged into Virginia Chen. 'It's my country too. I was born here.' She clung to Virginia Chen's arm. 'I belong here. I will stay. Miss Chen is my friend. I hate you.'

'Don't be ridiculous,' her mother screamed. 'Bo, send that woman away.'

Bo unclasped Sylvie's fingers. 'Please, Miss Chen,' he said. 'This is all so difficult.' He took Sylvie's bag from her. 'Come on, Sylvie! Stop these games.'

Virginia Chen took Ah So's arm, stood back against the wall and allowed the surging crowd, with its shouts and cries, its wailing children, to go past them. Bo kept Sylvie clasped closely in one hand, her case under another arm and, acting as a shield against the crowd behind, he pushed Lesley and Feargal before him. Sylvie stared back, trying to keep Virginia Chen in sight until finally she was lost in the surge of bodies.

Sylvie pulled against her father. 'I want to go. I want to go with Miss Chen. This is my place.'

Her father yanked her forward. 'Nearly there, nearly there,' he kept saying. 'You'll all be aboard soon.' Now they were alongside the looming ship and could see crowds of anxious faces on its rails, through its portholes. They could hear the growl of engines, the squeal of hysterical voices, the alarm of single shots; the distant rumble of aeroplanes.

Just ahead of them was a very pretty woman with a close straw hat and a baby in her arms. The man beside her, mild-faced and bespectacled, was carrying four cases, two jammed under his arms, two in his hands. A ripple of panic flowed down the queue of people as it stretched and settled again like a snake. In the town, the bomb alert was sounding once more and the thrum of planes became louder.

Sylvie looked up and counted the planes. Twenty-seven. Nine and nine and nine. 'Come on! Come on!' They were near to the front of the queue now. Military men stood behind desks at a kiosk. Like the gangplank it was guarded by soldiers with machine guns. There were explosions further down the quay as a smaller boat cracked, then exploded in a show of lights, and bodies were propelled into the air and splashed down into the water.

Then, as they watched, the pretty woman in front of them collapsed to the ground, a great gash in her head. The baby cried. The man dropped his cases, kneeled down and picked up his child, still clasped in the woman's lifeless arms. 'No. No. This can't be.' His voice came out in a terrible scream. 'Judith . . . Judith . . .'.

Sylvie stared at the pulse of dark, sticky blood, pumping into the dust, at the wide, lifeless eyes. She'd seen those stinking bodies with flies, but they had been a day old. This was how it started. A falling down and pulsing blood.

Bo let go of Sylvie's arm and pushed her case back into her hands. He dragged the man to his feet. The crowd surged on around him. Bo wrapped the man's arms more tightly round his baby. 'Get on, man! Get your baby away. She'd want it. I know this.'

'But . . . I can't. She's my wife.'

'*My* wife is going on the ship. There she is. Follow her. I will take care of *your* wife, I promise, as though she were my own.' The crowd surged forward and the man was through the gate on the gangplank, walking backwards, staring wide-eyed at the wife whom he had just left to a foreign grave.

The crowd surged again. Sylvie stood back against the wall, clutching her case, letting the people go forward in front of her just as they had in front of Miss Chen. She watched as her father passed on through the gate and pushed her mother on to the gangway with the man with the crying baby in his arms. Bo looked back and couldn't see Sylvie.

'Where's that child?' wailed Lesley.

'Sylvie? She must have gone on to the boat,' said Bo. 'She's already gone ahead. I pushed her onward. She must be on board. Go! Go and find her.' Lesley turned back once more and he kissed her, then pushed her hard. 'Go! Go!' he said.

'Sir!' said one of the soldiers. 'You're blocking the way.'

Bo stepped back and the next family vanished into the black hole at the top of the gangplank. And the next. He scanned the rail for ten minutes but he couldn't see Lesley. The ship had swallowed her up. She'd be finding Sylvie and getting a place to sleep. The ship was supposed to take eight hundred passengers but, he was told by the man at the kiosk, they were allowing two thousand on. One thing was sure: they'd be safer in Bombay than they would have been here. And Lesley had money to get her to South Africa, and on to Britain, should she get a safe passage.

He watched the soldiers pull up the gangplank and stood there scanning the rails for Lesley. She'd be safe now, he was sure of it. They would all be. All three of them.

Now he turned his attention to the poor dead woman, but there were soldiers there, wrapping her in some kind of tarpaulin. A clergyman of some kind had pushed through the crowd and was watching them, his face craggy with despair.

Bo closed his eyes and thought of his lovely Lesley and his son, Feargal. And Sylvie, of course. All safe now. He sighed, put back his shoulders and stepped out in a lively fashion up in the narrow alley beside the company *godown* to retrieve his car. He'd call at his office to do the final things that were waiting for him there, then report to his unit to put himself in their hands; ask what he would do. Surely there was something they could all do if they put their minds to it, even at this late hour.

The talk in the queue had been that the Japanese had crossed the peninsula and were on their way, pushing the Australians and Indians aside like flies. How strange this seemed. Wasn't the town full of soldiers, some drunk and competing with these women and children to get away? He wondered why they weren't rushing to the front line to stop Yamashita's onrush. There must be some strategy behind it all, some last-ditch saving of the city. But he couldn't for the life of him imagine what it was.

Virginia Chen: Her Book
I must confess to a feeling of anger as Ah So and I stood with our back to the dusty wall and let the crowd surge past us, carrying as it did Sylvie and the Sambucks with it. Part of my anger was seeing these people – once compact, phlegmatic, self-contained Europeans

– pressing forward like a flock of fleeing pigeons. Some moved in a solid way, trudging forward in a deadly fashion; some cried and panicked, pushed and screamed. We were even treated to the sight of soldiers pressing their way with rifles: these men who had come to defend our city.

I reflect that these fluttering, pouting, fleeing pigeons were the people we had been tuned to respect; to acknowledge their capabilities, their greater right to overlordship in our land.

It was in the newspaper. The Governor said he would take care of all the people on the island. None of those at risk would be left to the mercy of the Japanese. Then, there was another announcement, from a British Government envoy, to say that there would be places only for the Europeans; that we were indeed to be left to the mercy of the Japanese.

I am most angry with myself for believing the myths of respect that they have fed us. It occurs to me that I have been on the wrong side in my arguments with Simon.

And what about Miss Sylvie Sambuck, my protégée, my own little pigeon? I wonder how she will fare under the tender mercies of Mrs Sambuck? She's in for some beatings, that's for sure.

# Chapter Ten

## The Chrysalis

Sylvie watched numbly from a distance as the barrier came down. The soldiers stood to attention in front of the gangway, rifles drawn to repel further boarders. She scanned the crowd for her father. He would be pleased to see she'd stayed to keep him company, she felt sure. Perhaps she could go to the army with him. She couldn't see him. He was not by the rails where she'd last seen him. Perhaps he'd got on to the ship with Mother and Feargal. Perhaps he'd gone to South Africa.

She was hot and her head was swirling. She felt as though the throb of the ship's engine was coursing through her. She closed her eyes, then she slid down the wall until she was nearly crouching on the dusty, littered ground. They were gone. They must have both gone.

She crouched there and watched while the engine of the *Felix Roussel* took on more power. At last the ship pulled away from the dock. Sylvie could see the rails more clearly now. There were many desperate white faces. But there was no sign of them: no Mother, no Feargal. No one.

But she was not alone. Scrubbing the tears from her eyes with a dirty hand she stood up, grabbed her case and began to work her way against the tide of people on the crowded quayside. She would look for Virginia Chen and Ah So. They would take care of her.

They were nowhere to be seen. The panicking men and women in the queue, fully absorbed in their own misery and difficulty, ignored the dark-haired child in the green frock as she picked her way through them. They were not bothered that she scrutinised their faces one by one. She looked and looked, but her father, and Virginia, and Ah So had vanished.

She began to wonder what had happened to the man and his baby. Her father said he would take care of the woman. Sylvie made her way back to the place where the woman had been killed but there was only a pool of blackening blood. Someone had moved the woman; taken her to hospital. Perhaps it was her father who'd done that. Hadn't he said that he would take care of her?

She came upon the little trolley with their own abandoned cases. They were comforting to see – a box with her father's name on it and battered luggage with old travel markings. She would take care of it. With this she belonged to somebody – well, something. It had the smell of safety. She pushed the trolley before her through the milling crowds. People were still arriving in cars, even rickshaws. One family's goods were hauled on a bullock cart. She felt like shouting at them to go away because the ship was on its way out of the harbour. But perhaps there was another ship. She tried to speak to a woman who looked like Mrs Hoxton, and then a thin man who looked like a man from her father's office. They looked at her blankly and brushed past her as though she were a puppy impeding their path.

In this fashion she made her way back up through Change Alley towards the town, pushing her heavy trolley. Even now this alley buzzed. Some of the stalls were open, buying and selling stuff abandoned by the Europeans.

Pushing the trolley was a help to Sylvie. It was a hard thing to do and it stopped her thinking too much. An empty rickshaw creaked past her, then stopped. The wiry driver stood up silently between its shafts, his head turned round beneath the shadow of his shady hat. He smiled a broken-toothed smile. 'I take missee?'

She remembered her purse in the little side compartment of her case. 'How much to go to Leonie Hill Drive?' she said.

The man's head dipped over her pile of luggage. 'One dollar, missee,' he said.

'One dollar?' She'd made that journey from her father's office a dozen times for a fraction of that. 'That's very expensive.'

He shook his head sadly. 'Very hard times, missee. Not happee.'

She nodded her head. The times were certainly bad. 'Well. Can you help me to load these?' She loaded the small boxes, leaving the heavy ones for him. Then she waited, looking in despair from the man, back to the laden rickshaw.

'It all looks very heavy,' she said.

'I very strong, missee. Very happee carry.'

'Well . . .'

'Jump on, missee.'

She looked again at the pile, then back to his narrow frame, his whipcord legs and arms. She could not see his eyes under the wide brim of his hat.

'One dollar make very strong, missee. Very happee. Jump on now.'

So she clambered on top and directed him first to her father's office, which was not far away. It was closed and padlocked and the *jaga* would not let her in. He pretended not to understand her when she spoke. So she stumped away and directed the rickshaw man to Hibiscus Lodge on Leonie Hill Drive.

When they got there those gates were also padlocked. The house was shuttered and silent. She told the rickshaw man to wait, then she climbed over the gate. The garden was peaceful in the fading evening light, the flowerbeds only faintly showing their colour. The insects buzzed in the still air. The moonflower had two new blossoms and their sweet scent tickled her nose.

The house was padlocked too. The shutters had heavy new locks. Her footsteps made a hollow sound on the veranda as she tried each door. Someone had pulled all the blinds, so that the wide, shady places she had played in since she was born were dingy and threatening and smelled of overused spices.

She went then round the back to the huts where Ah So and Tang Peng lived, where he did his cooking and the wash-*amah* sorted her clothes. These little huts too were padlocked, and looked as though they'd been shut away for days rather than hours. She remembered now her father's instructions, repeated by Virginia, that Ah So should go to her *kongsi* and the others go back to Chinatown, to the protection of their own families. That would be safer than these suburban roads.

Sylvie sat on the step of the veranda and looked back out over the town. She could see dense smoke rising from the *godowns* and she could smell the burning rubber. There were flames like candles lighting the sky in the direction of Chinatown. And above it all was the darkening blue sky and two red streaks of sunset. Again the tears started. Again she wiped them away with a dirty hand. She stood up. She'd better get a move on. Very soon it would be pitch-dark.

The house, her own home for all of her life, now seemed threatening and strange. It was no place for her. No place at all.

She padded down the gravel drive and climbed back over the gate. She wouldn't have been surprised if the rickshaw man had gone off with all her bags and boxes. But he was there, sitting on his haunches, smoking a skinny cigarette. He balanced the rickshaw and she clambered aboard. 'Now Beach Road,' she said.

'Many houses blow down, missee,' he said.

'Not all of it. My friend Miss Chen lives in number nineteen. Long time after Raffles Hotel. That not blow down.'

She felt the load move and settle to a steady rhythm in time with his plodding steps. She looked at his narrow corded back and the wide cone of his hat. She closed her eyes and tried to remember what he looked like from the front. She could only remember the broken-toothed smile. She couldn't think whether it was a young strong face like Simon Chen's, or an old face like the old nana's.

She closed her eyes even tighter to stop more tears. She tried to think of her mother's face, then her father's, then Feargal's. She wondered if, in the boxes she had here, there were any photographs. She wondered whether her father had, despite his plans, gone on board the ship with her mother. He hadn't been hit and killed like the woman with the baby or she would have seen him bleeding on the quay. His body would have lain there, like that of the pretty woman.

But he hadn't been on the quayside. Perhaps those rampaging soldiers with the big hats had knocked him into the dock and he was drowned. That would not be impossible. Nothing, now, was impossible.

But no, she decided that it was better to think that he was here somewhere in the town, using his pistol to kill some of the dratted Japanese.

Her eyes blinked wide open. The rickshaw almost tipped over sideways as it swerved to skirt the bomb-holes and three Chinese men in some kind of uniform still digging for bodies. They squeezed past an army truck that was being used to load up dead bodies, piled up like skinny bales of straw under the canvas.

The rickshaw stopped very neatly in front of the shophouse at number nineteen. Simon Chen, who was lounging in the shop with his uncle, came out to the front.

'Will you help me with these boxes?' said Sylvie. The boy

stood very still, scowling at her. She stamped her foot. 'Help me!'

'What are you doing?' he said finally. 'You went with the others. On the ship. Jin Kee told us.'

The rickshaw man lifted the boxes down. Sylvie dug in her purse and found one dollar fifty cents and gave it to the man, who tucked it in his waistband. 'I very happee,' he said. Then he balanced his rickshaw and drew away.

'I've come to see Miss Chen.' Sylvie's voice was almost failing her now. 'I've come to see Miss Chen,' she whispered. 'I want to see your Jin Kee.' The tears fell down her cheeks unchecked.

Simon Chen looked up and down the street, which was thick with people and smoke; noisy with the calls of rescuers digging in the ruins of a shophouse of Mr and Mrs Wu. They'd traded in basketware and lacquerware, once very popular with sailors, who'd taken them home and hung them over their fireplaces in Rochdale and Blundellsands.

Simon Chen took Sylvie's arm and pulled her inside. She pulled back. 'My boxes,' she said. 'I must have my boxes.'

'I'll get them,' he said. 'You go up and see the grandmother.'

She found her own way upstairs. The stairs seemed narrower and steeper than before, the green painted ceiling with its flowers seemed higher than the sky. She stood outside the grandmother's door. From inside the room came the tinny sound of music; the wailing thump of jazz and blown instruments. Now it was overlaid by the wail of sirens, immediately followed by the crump of bombs and the firework whoosh of conflagration. Sylvie began to cry. She battered the door. 'Miss Chen!' she cried. 'Jin Kee! Where are you?'

It was not Virginia Chen who came to the door, but the diminutive grandmother, who peered down at her in the gloom of the landing, her dark eyes gleaming within the folds of her cheeks.

Sylvie swallowed her tears and made her face hard. 'Nana, I want to see Miss Chen. I couldn't get on to the ship and I went to the house and it was locked up and there was no one there, not even Amah. And my mother left all this stuff on the quayside . . .'

A hand, dry and crisp as a leather sleeve, was clamped on her mouth and she was grabbed by the shoulder and planted on the carved bench by the window. Then she was released.

'Nana, I—'

A finger placed firmly on her lips stopped her speaking. 'Sss,' said Nana. 'Sss.' She went to the door and shouted something and then came back beside Sylvie on the bench by the window. Then she beat her big stick hard on the floor several times.

In this day of bustle and chaos, Sylvie had felt tearful but not really frightened. There was just this sense of hurry, this rush to do the right thing, to stay on her island and to be with her father and with Miss Chen. Now she felt fear. She was sitting in this strange room with its dark reds and greens, its gleam of gold. The horn of the gramophone was blaring some larruping sounds of a clarinet, and beside her an old mad

Chinese woman was beating the wooden floor with a stick for all she was worth. Now Sylvie felt fear looping through her like a spider on a web.

Simon Chen slipped in through the dark doorway and Sylvie breathed a sigh of relief. 'Tell her I mean no harm. I think she is angry with me.' The grandmother rose, straight-backed, from the bench and went to sit on her own chair with its footstool.

Simon Chen listened to his grandmother, then turned to Sylvie. 'My grandmother says why are you here? The Japanese are baying at the gates and will kill all the *angmoh kwai*, that's for sure. People say this.'

'*Angmoh kwai*? What's that?'

'Red-faced devils. We call the Europeans this because they have red faces and hair.'

'I don't have red hair. Or a red face.'

'It is a metaphor.' He scowled at her. 'Have you never heard of a figure of speech?'

'No, I haven't,' said Sylvie humbly.

'Ah yes. You have not been to school. Well, my grand-mother says you should be gone on a ship. You have put yourself in danger.' He frowned again. 'We are in danger ourselves. They slaughtered hundreds of thousands of us in Nanking. They will do the same here.'

'I missed the boat,' said Sylvie, rather more interested in her own fate than that of the whole Chinese population. 'A woman was killed by a shell splinter on the harbour and there was her baby with blood on it, and then the crowd pushed and pushed and my mother went up the gangway and my father

118

vanished and the soldiers shut off the gangway and there was a lot of screaming. So I thought I should stay on my own island and find my father.'

Simon whistled a long, schoolboy whistle. 'So you should go and seek your father. He will take care of you.'

Sylvie glanced at the horn of the gramophone, which was still blaring its music.

'My grandmother likes the music,' shouted Simon Lee. 'She says it drowns the sounds of war.'

'I went to my house,' shouted Sylvie. 'All padlocked. No one. They are all gone. So I came for Miss Chen. I came for Jin Kee.'

He stared at her. 'Jin Kee went to the hospital to see if she could help. There are lots of injured soldiers there – Indian, Malay, English. And they've sent a lot of the Australian nurses packing on the last ships. So people like Virginia must help.'

'That's not fair, the nurses going.'

'The Japanese did awful things to the *angmoh kwai* nurses in Hong Kong. So they say. It is not safe.'

Sylvie sat back in her chair, exhausted by the music, the shouting and the strangeness of everything.

Simon turned to the grandmother and spoke at length. The old woman listened carefully, then said something. Simon turned to Sylvie. 'My grandmother says you are to lie on the bench and rest. You sleep, then my cousin will be here. She will come soon.' He took a cushion and a folded cloth from a chair. He placed the cushion at the end of the bench. 'Lie,' he ordered.

Sylvie put her head on the cushion. He drew the cloth over

her and tucked it around her. Then he took a mosquito net and covered her entirely with it, tucking it around her head so she could see the room, and the grandmother, and Simon Chen, through a mist. 'I am a chrysalis,' she said. 'Is that a metaphor?'

'Sleep!' he ordered. Then he went to the gramophone and changed the record. Now it was softer music, with rising, surging strings like the breath of the wind. This must, she thought, closing her eyes, be what it is like to be a chrysalis. She'd seen them on the bougainvillaea at Hibiscus Lodge. The chrysalis was as big as your finger. The butterfly would be as big as your hand. The butterflies in her nana's garden in Priorton were tiny. She turned over and put one hand under her cheek. The Priorton butterflies were as small as the hand of that baby at the harbour. Tiny. Not like the butterflies in Singapore.

Virginia Chen: Her Book
All I can offer at the hospital is a willing heart, willing hands and that bit of first-aid training I did in August. Nevertheless I am welcomed. They have lost so many nurses, ordered directly to the boats. It seems the Japanese have done some terrible things to nurses. They have done some terrible things to the Chinese, of course.

I am given the appropriately menial tasks of washing and feeding. It is not easy, as the beds are crowded into the space. There are even makeshift beds on the floors and in the corridors. Some boys are still on the stretchers that brought them in. Some of them mutter about their commanders and the mistakes that have been made but many are too depressed to speak.

One man actually smiles at me through the mud and blood. 'You're a sight for sore eyes, Nurse. So bloody – pardon my French – clean and fresh.' No point in explaining that I am not a nurse, so I put the tin cup to his mouth so he can drink. Both of his arms are heavily strapped and the blood is seeping through.

I did not stay clean and fresh very long. Gradually my apron became covered with blood and dirt as I held the men to help them drink and eat a little, and cleaned the worst of the mud from their faces.

There was no time to think, which was a blessing.

# Chapter Eleven

## Refuge

Sylvie dreamed that her mother and Ah So were pushing her down the lawn towards the hibiscus hedge. They were rolling her in a length of Mr Lee's white silk. Her arms were pinned to her side and what had been fun was now restricting, frightening. She struggled and struggled, and fell down into the deep hole the *kebun* had been digging to hide her father's treasures. In the hole of darkness above her floated a lion kite with a fish's tail.

She stretched her eyes wide into blackness. The lionfish melted away. Of course, she'd been dreaming, so that was all right. The worst part of the dream had been where a woman was killed on the quay, her baby in her arms. All that sticky blood.

A dream. She wriggled. How hard her bed was. She struggled free from her covering sheet and pulled the mosquito net from her face.

No. This wasn't her room. The smells were wrong. She

blinked and lay there, trying to sort out the dreams from the non-dreams. Ah yes. She knew where she was. The carved bench by the window. She sat up. Here she was. In the gloom she could make out the grandmother's chair, which was quite empty, apart from a wrinkled, embroidered cloth draped across one arm.

Someone had taken off her shoes. She turned and lifted the painted window shutter. The street outside was quiet, apart from an occasional shriek and a dull rumbling, like heavy wagons going over wooden tracks. These must be guns, she thought. Japanese guns. There were soldiers in the street but they were slumped in a doorway, not making a lot of noise. They looked dirty and tired. When the time came, though, they'd shoot at the Japanese. They would all be all right. Saved. Even Simon Chen, though he was Chinese.

In her head she tried to conjure up a picture of a Japanese soldier. He was probably taller than her father. And broad. And he would have these staring eyes. And he would have a sword in one hand and a gun in the other. She shuddered. She crept to the door, opened it and listened. The house was infused with a close, sticky silence, an absence of presence. She wanted to shout at everyone to wake up, wake up, but she resisted the urge. What would she say when they came?

Then she heard a door open, very quietly, downstairs. It clicked shut. Then there was a rustle and the steady tread of feet on steep, creaking stairs. Sylvie thought it must be a Japanese soldier, creeping into the shophouse at the dead of night while everyone was asleep. Then he would kill everyone

123

with his long sword. The old nana, Simon Chen, Miss Chen. And Sylvie too. That was quite likely, Sylvie thought.

The steps came nearer, but she stood her ground. She'd face this Japanese so that he would not get his sword into the old nana or into Virginia.

A light from some kind of torch pointed the way for a figure that was steadily making its way up the narrow stairs.

Sylvie held her breath, then gasped her relief when she saw who it was. She flung herself into Virginia Chen's arms and then drew back in distaste. 'Miss . . . Jin Kee . . . you smell like a pig.' Her glance dropped. 'There's blood . . .'

Virginia Chen held her by the shoulders. 'Sylvie.'

'I was sleeping.'

'I know. Simon came to the hospital to tell me. But there was too much going on there for me to come right away. He said you were safe.' She pushed Sylvie into the room. 'Go in there, Sylvie, turn up the lamp. Close the shutters. I will come back to you.'

In no time she was back, her hair brushed down and a silk dressing gown tied tightly round her waist. She came to sit beside Sylvie on the carved bench. 'Now then, Sylvie!'

'Tell me about the hospital.'

'I can't do that. It was too terrible, Sylvie. Those poor men. Some were dying. Others were not just injured, but desolate.'

'Desolate?'

'Very downhearted. Despairing.'

'Simon Chen says the Japanese will come in and kill all the *angmoh kwai*, the red-faced devils.'

'You are not to use that word. It's very rude. Simon was very bad to tell you this.'

'He says they will kill the Chinese as well, like they did in Nanking and in Hong Kong.'

'Simon Chen may be very clever, he may be top of his class at the Raffles Institute, but he does not know everything.'

'So they won't do that?'

Virginia watched her thoughtfully. 'It is now your turn to tell me how I come home and find you here when I thought you would be safe by now, sailing the high seas to Bombay.'

Sylvie told her about standing back. 'I didn't want to go. I told you.'

Virginia Chen shook her head.

'They were swept away from me. I stood back. They didn't miss me. I saved all the *barang* that my mother had to leave on the dock,' said Sylvie. 'Simon Chen put it in the back of the shop. I'll sell that so I have money to live. I thought of that.'

Virginia Chen smiled faintly. 'No, Sylvie. We will find your father and we will put you on another ship.'

Sylvie was silent for a moment. 'I should stay, I think. I should definitely stay. I'm like you. I was born here. This is my land. I should stay.'

'It is not your land, Sylvie.'

'I was born here, like you, I tell you.'

'But you are English.'

'You're Chinese – well, a bit Chinese – and this isn't China.'

Virginia tried another tack. 'But your poor mother will worry . . .'

'My mother has Feargal to take care of. And I am "an infernal nuisance" to her. You've heard her say that many a time. I'll stay here with you.'

Virginia let out a long sigh. 'Oh, Sylvie. We will talk of this tomorrow. I am so tired.'

She took Sylvie by the hand. 'Come on now. You can finish your sleep in my bed. Then, in the morning, you can get up, have a good wash and we will decide just what we are to do with you.'

# Chapter Twelve

## Jin Kee

Sylvie had been watching Virginia Chen from the moment she opened her eyes. This, somehow, was a different Virginia Chen. She looked the same. She went about in the same graceful style as always. But she was different. Here in this house she was a very important figure. At Hibiscus Lodge, she'd been quiet, watchful, not really like Ah So, but like her in some ways. But here she was a central figure and it showed. She was Jin Kee, a leading member of this family.

They had breakfast at a lacquer table that had been put up in the grandmother's parlour. Around the table sat the grandmother on her high throne and the two uncles. Uncle Chu had brought in the breakfast in a basket, from a hawker in the street.

As Sylvie sat drinking her tea it seemed that an argument bubbled up round the table. The uncles stayed silent unless you counted the slight slurping as they raised their bowls of tea to their withered lips.

The quarrellers were Simon Chen and Virginia. Sylvie became aware that *she* was the subject of the quarrels. Simon Chen cast glances and nodded towards her at various parts of his argument.

'What is he saying, Miss Chen? What's he saying, Jin Kee?' Sylvie said at last, invading the torrent of talk. 'It's about me. He doesn't like me, I can tell.'

The row subsided.

Virginia Chen shrugged. 'It is difficult to say this, Sylvie, because, of course, you are welcome in this house.' She shot a cold look at her cousin. 'It would be impolite to think otherwise. Simon says this also. However, he is concerned because of those dogs of Japanese at the gates of this city. They will be vengeful towards the Chinese. They hate the Chinese. The Chinese fought them fiercely in defence of their homeland. The Chinese have the courage to match the Nippon and they do not like it. So, if we give shelter to an English girl, one of the vanquished, they will have no mercy.'

'The English are not vanquished. We rule the waves. It says so in the song.'

Simon Chen laughed and then went quiet as words rapped out like viper's poison from the old grandmother.

Virginia Chen glanced at her grandmother, who, she knew, had been following the English very well. 'No more, I think, Sylvie. The English, they are too busy defending themselves against the Germans in the North to worry about the dangers this far East. We seem a long way away for Mr Churchill or for the King.'

Now Sylvie knew she was alone. She bit her bottom lip until it hurt, to stop any tears wandering into her eyes. The faces around her were the faces of strangers. Even Virginia Chen looked at her coldly. Her mother and her little brother were bobbing out there on the sea. Her father had vanished, probably dead on the docks like that woman with the baby. The European soldiers had viewed with blank eyes her progress through the broken streets on her rickshaw. Not one of them asked her why she was there. She truly was alone.

'Wait!' she said. 'All of you, wait here!' She ran upstairs, rubbing renegade tears from her eyes. She raked through her case till she found the white mandarin jacket from Mr Lee. She stripped off to her vest and knickers and pulled it on. She buttoned it up and tried to smooth out the creases with frantic fingers. Then she took some of Virginia's scented oil and combed it through her hair. She brushed the hair back from her face and clipped it hard and high with Virginia's kirby-grips. She used some of the oil on her face, polishing it until it gleamed.

At last she looked hard in the mirror and was satisfied. Then she raced downstairs and presented herself at the table. Uncle Chu and the grandmother only betrayed emotion by a slight raising of the eyebrows. Uncle Wo chuckled. Simon Chen grinned openly.

Virginia Chen said, 'Sylvie, what is this? What are you doing?'

'I'm not English, I'm like you. I am, Jin Kee. This is my city.' She was aware of Simon Chen behind her, rattling out a translation for his grandmother and uncles. She heard the flutter of polite laughter. She was a joke to them.

Then Uncle Wo said something and they all laughed heartily. Sylvie went bright red. 'What did he say?' she demanded. 'Tell me, Jin Kee. Tell me!'

Simon said, 'Uncle Wo says that it is only the ugly round eyes and the long nose which spoil the whole effect.'

'Simon Chen!' said Virginia, only slightly reproving, a smile hovering on her lips.

Tears came to Sylvie's eyes. Then Uncle Chu said something more grave, which did not evoke laughter, and the grandmother nodded.

'But honourable Uncle Chu says that your eyes are as ugly as Jin Kee's here. She also has ugly round eyes and a long nose so perhaps you could be her little sister. Your grandfather also could be a French *tuan besar*.'

Virginia Chen smiled at this. 'I am unfortunate in that I have the ugly round eyes of my French foreign devil grandfather.' She took Sylvie's face between her hands. Sylvie shuddered at the sheer comfort of her touch. 'There is something in this, Sylvie. This perhaps was why your mother was so angry with you.' She turned to Simon Chen. 'I will have her as my sister. Then we will take care of her.'

The grandmother said something.

Sylvie looked into the old face where the skin was so tightly stretched over the bones they might have been gilded. She examined the severe line that was the mouth. 'What did she say? What did the nana say?'

'She says that it is agreed. That you will be the little sister and you must wear the cheong sam and tie your hair back,' translated Simon Chen. 'She also says you will not be the only little half-stranger in the city. In the streets you must not talk any English. And she says you must always remember to call Jin Kee by her name, not Miss Chen.'

Virginia laughed. 'Do you know what people like your mother call people like me, Sylvie? *Stengahs* – like the thing they drink when they come off the golf course. Long drink, half whisky, half water. Half red-faced devil, half Chinese.'

Sylvie frowned. 'That's very rude, Miss Chen . . . Jin Kee.'

'So it is, little sister. But we learn to laugh.'

'Anyway, I think you have beautiful eyes.'

It was only later, when she and Virginia Chen were picking their way through the streets and down past the blasted front of Government House, that Sylvie thought of something: how, in the end, Simon Chen had stopped translating for the grandmother. The old woman knew what was being said. She didn't need a translation at all.

They passed three soldiers, one with sergeant's stripes, begrimed, sweating and in their underpants, who were washing their shorts in water gushing out of a blasted pipe. They rubbed at the cloth slowly and disconsolately as though it was the very last thing they wanted to do. Only in these last two days had Sylvie seen any white man less than immaculate. Her own father changed his clothes three times every day. Her mother changed more. It was so easy to be clean. Although her mother complained that the wash-*amah* ruined her clothes, she came every day in her rickshaw with its large basket and she charged very little.

The soldiers glanced at the neatly dressed half-caste and the child with its black trousers and light top, its pigtailed hair under its small straw cone. The sergeant stood up and looked at the sky, watching for the next Japanese twenty-seven formation and wondering, as he had all this last wretched week, where the hell the RAF was. It was all right to talk about North Africa or the bloody Greeks but this was no fucking joke, stuck here, sitting ducks all of the time.

Near the hospital Virginia Chen and Sylvie came upon Albert Taft, immaculate in navy tropical kit. They saw him in the distance, lounging at the gates of the hospital. Now and then he would jump on to a wall to keep clear of the trucks, carts and body wagons that were streaming through the hospital gates.

Virginia Chen looked at him with disbelief. He jumped down from the wall and dusted his hands, rubbing one against the other.

'Virginia Chen,' he said. 'My love-at-first-sight.'

'What on earth are you doing here?' she said.

He took her hand. 'I came to say goodbye to you and to remind you that in a fair world we would be together from this day on. That from the first second I saw you, I saw our future. But I'm under orders to leave. All the last navy personnel are ordered to leave now. I have a berth at eight o'clock.' He looked at his watch. 'I'll have to race.' He reached into his breast pocket and pulled out a folded piece of paper. 'This is my name and number, and my address in England. I want you to know who I am and where I'm from. Our future together will start here. I would take you with me now but the

132

Japs are bombing ships out of the water so there is a chance . . .'

She took the paper. 'So what would you like me to do? With this?'

'Write to me, will you? Write me long letters to tell me how you are and what's happening to you. I'll get them one day. Shouldn't be too long. When London can get their eyes off Europe and focus on the East proper, they'll sort this lot out. Then you come to me there in my village. That's our future. I'm telling you now.'

'We've only met once, Albert – one and a half times,' she protested.

He shook his head. 'It's war, Virginia Chen. Once means ten times in war. Everything is more.' His glance dropped to Sylvie, holding Virginia tightly by her other hand. 'So who's this?'

'This is my sister, Syl Vee Chen,' said Virginia Chen calmly.

Albert's large, capable hand engulfed Sylvie's. 'Pleased to meet Virginia's sister,' he said. 'Any time, you come and see me as well, in my village.'

As she shook his hand Sylvie kept her eyes down under the shade of her hat. She held her breath. Surely he would recognise her. Perhaps he would grab her up and take her off. Perhaps he knew her from last time. But no. People see what they think they see. Albert did think she was Virginia's sister.

Virginia gave him a push. 'Now go.' Her glance went past him to the cluttered hospital compound and the lines of stretchers. 'You are wasting time. Go.'

'You will write to me? And come when this is over?'

She looked at him, neat and whole in his smart uniform, and thought of the poor broken boys she had seen yesterday in the hospital. She thought of him on the Sambucks' veranda. How very dear to her he had seemed at that time. It was an easy promise to give. 'When this is over? All right, Albert. And I will write to you sometimes. I promise.'

He gave them a salute, then marched away. Sylvie and Virginia pushed their way to the wide hospital entrance.

'I thought you'd have told him to take me,' said Sylvie, not knowing whether to be pleased or sad about this. 'I was afraid. I didn't want to go with him.'

Virginia's mind was on the more important tasks. 'I wouldn't want to risk that,' she said. 'It's true what Albert said. The Japanese are bombing the refugee boats. All this is whispered. You would have been no safer than you are here with me. Perhaps it's the best thing for you that you did not get on that ship.'

Sylvie pulled her to a stop. 'My mother's ship? Have they bombed her ship? Hers and Feargal's?'

'Oh no,' said Virginia, walking along. 'They say the *Felix Roussel* got away.' She didn't know the truth of this, but it was unnecessary to trouble the child.

They wove their way unhindered through crowded corridors littered with stretchers. They stepped carefully over heaps of bloody, discarded bandages. When they reached Virginia's ward, Virginia made Sylvie sit outside while she went to the nurses' station to ask for her tasks and to explain the presence of the child and that she'd be no trouble. She had been told quite firmly by her cousin Simon Chen that he would not be responsible for the girl; that she must take her with her.

'Sit there and say nothing,' she ordered Sylvie, 'till I come and get you.'

There was no panic in the hospital. The nurses and doctors who were left just worked with dogged determination on the bodies of the men who'd been driven back from the peninsula on to the island in the ravaging retreat.

Virginia arrived on her ward to find her tasks were again to be the cleaning, dressing, feeding and watering of the patients. Three priests in different tropical garb were moving through the men, comforting, feeding, occasionally assisting with dressings. Too often they were called on to administer skeleton versions of last rites to anyone who wished for the transient relief of eternal certainty.

Once Virginia got her tasks she gathered up Sylvie to help her. In the harassed chaos of the day no one took much notice of the little Eurasian child shadowing the Eurasian nurse, helping, lifting, carrying where requested.

Within forty-eight hours of seeing the woman killed on the dock, Sylvie had seen five men die, had fed seven dying men with water, and observed others whose wounds ranged from a shot-off leg to a blasted skull. She tried to keep her mind blank, just doing what Virginia told her and trying not to look into the shamed and wretched eyes of the men.

Twice, a bomb alert sounded, followed by the crack of guns and the crump of bombs. Once it was so near that the walls shook. In that few seconds everyone stopped what they were doing, like statues in a play. Then the building settled and the doctors, nurses and all their helpers got on with their tasks.

An hour later they were transfixed by a sustained rattle of gunfire and piercing screams. A woman doctor hurried down the ward speaking in low tones to all the staff. She reached Virginia. 'The Japanese are in the grounds,' she whispered. 'Hide yourself. For God's sake, hide that child.'

Virginia thrust a cup into the shaky hand of the silver-haired boy she had been feeding. 'I am sorry, really sorry, David. We will be back soon.'

He pushed at her weakly with the back of his hand. 'Go, you stupid girl, go. And take that kid with you.'

Virginia and Sylvie made for the opposite end of the building to the tumult and the noise. People were moving in all directions around them. On the long central corridor they passed patients in makeshift truckle beds. They went up a short flight of stairs, turned left and came to a dead end. Up against each dead end of this corridor were two high steel cabinets with grilles in the top half. Virginia wrenched one open, pulled out the blankets from the top shelf and pushed them into the bottom of the cabinet. Awkwardly, she lifted Sylvie on to the shelf and covered everything except her face with a red blanket.

Downstairs the cacophony of gunfire and shrieks intensified. Screams penetrated the stairwells, stained the walls.

'Now stay there,' said Virginia grimly, 'and don't move a muscle till I come for you.'

'Where will you go?' There was no worry about moving

muscles. Sylvie's face muscles were so stiff she could hardly get the words out. 'Where?'

'Another cupboard, other end of the corridor.' Virginia was already banging the door shut. Sylvie strained to hear Virginia's footsteps among the more distant screams and shouts. Then all she could hear were the muffled sounds of crying and crashing and the occasional crack of a gun.

Sylvie lay very still, her hands clenched for many minutes. She thought of her tall, handsome father and wondered where he was. She thought of her mother bobbing on the sea to Africa. She thought of Simon Chen, with his brave, bold eyes, and the grandmother with her gilded face and her trim, smooth hair.

Then she could hear running footsteps, rough shouts and screams. She could hear someone scrambling up the stairs, the heavy flap of boots. Then her ears were bruised with a loud scream, which culminated in a moan, then thuds and bangs. Silence. After that a low growl and, incredibly, laughter. After that she could hear flapping footsteps accompanied by a kind of clanking. She thought of a cowboy movie she'd once seen at the Cathay Cinema, where the baddies came in, their spurs clanking on the barroom floor.

She opened her eyes slightly to look through her lashes, then through the crack in the red blanket and the downward slant of the steel slats.

She could see dusty boots but no spurs, dun-coloured trousers and a leather belt; a hand holding the stock of a gun. She could hear the headless creature muttering, calling to some other and getting a kind of response. Then from somewhere came the high, piercing sound of a whistle, blown three times. Now the muttering faded away. There were further clumping footsteps, some kind of exchange and a dull thump, as though someone had kicked a cushion. After a while there were only more distant sounds, the distant shots.

Sylvie breathed slowly again through her mouth. They hadn't opened her cupboard. She had not heard them opening the other cupboard at the end of the corridor. They had not found Virginia Chen either.

She had to lie still. She knew she must stay still. Virginia Chen said stay until she came and she would do that. She thought about Virginia Chen and how life at Hibiscus Lodge had changed since she came. Before that, there had been her beloved *amah*, Ah Choy, whom her mother had dismissed despite her father's protests before their last trip home, because 'Sylvie is no longer a baby'. Then there'd been the young man tutor who'd been brought in to brush up Sylvie's brain so she would be fit for some English school. But he'd only been interested in tutoring her between tennis games with her mother. He'd then succumbed to a bout of malaria after a hunting trip up country. He had been after tigers.

After that Virginia Chen had come to Hibiscus Lodge. She was undeniably clever. After an initial tussle she and Virginia had made a deal: two hours of hard work and then they would have fun. The fun might be a trip to Robinson's for ice cream, the beach for kite flying, or the Great World for the round-abouts and the things like puppets.

That was how Sylvie made such progress, leaping through her reading and arithmetic books with ease in spite of her mother's criticism. That was why, despite her mother's plaintive pleas to her father, Virginia had stayed and stayed.

Sylvie started to sweat. The blanket was degenerating to a sticky sludge. There was some creeping creature crawling down her forehead on to her nose. Now she was aware of a big difference outside the cupboard. The noise had gone entirely. The distant cracks and shots had stopped, the screams had faded. Apart from that, nothing. She lost consciousness. She didn't know for how long. She came to once or twice but didn't move, remembering the fear that brought her here but not quite the reason to fear.

Then she woke again as dawn light filtered through the door and the sweat on her brow froze as she heard footsteps in the corridor outside. She tried to stop breathing in case the breathing would give her away. The sweat in her eyes stopped her seeing through the slats. The footsteps kept coming, very steadily.

The door was wrenched open and a scream rose unbidden from deep inside her into the hot air. 'Ssh, Sylvie, ssh,' said Virginia Chen. 'Do be quiet. It seems they have gone but . . .' She lifted Sylvie down, then touched her face with a cool hand. 'I thought you might have gone. It has been hours. I saw . . .' She didn't want to tell the child what she had seen. 'You are fine, so do not shout!' She bent down and looked directly into Sylvie's eyes. 'Now, Sylvie. At the top of the stairs is a poor man whom those dogs have killed. He must have got this far before they caught him. Now remember, nothing can hurt him again. Remember this! Nothing more can hurt this man. He is with Jesus, or his ancestors. I want you to pass him but not look. Don't look. You promise me?'

As they made their way down the stairs they could hear low moaning from the ward below. The waves of sticky heat had the gamy smell of blood in them. Virginia Chen stopped and faced Sylvie. 'Now, Sylvie, I wish you to do something.'

Sylvie nodded very slowly.

'I want you to pretend you are the blind man in the story. Do you remember? We once had a story with a blind man?'

Sylvie nodded very slowly.

'Now, close your eyes tight.'

Sylvie closed her eyes tight. Virginia took her by the hand. As she led Sylvie down the corridor, through the ward, Sylvie kept her eyes closed tight. They had to skirt round things that were in the way, and at one point Sylvie's sandal squelched in something, which made her feel sick. Then at last she could sense the hot-oven air outside, which did not smell of Dettol and death.

'Keep them closed!' Virginia dragged her on. Finally, she turned a corner, out of sight of the hospital. 'Now!' said Virginia.

Around them was the urgent press of people with nowhere to go except purgatory. But here no one was dead or dying.

Once more Virginia half-squatted to look Sylvie in the eye. 'I want you to go right to the end of this road and see if you can get a rickshaw back to number nineteen, and tell Simon and my grandmother what's happened. Tell them I am safe and have stayed to help. I must stay to help. Can I trust you to do this? You are a clever girl. Tell them that the Japanese are at the hospital but I am safe. They will have heard what is happening and will wonder about me and about you.'

'Will they worry?'

Virginia shrugged. 'Nothing would be served by that. Now go!' She put her face close to Sylvie's. 'Promise me not to stop. Go straight there.'

Then she was gone. Sylvie put her nose round the corner and watched her departing figure, slender and determined, in its blood-stained overall. Then she moved back round the corner of the building to see what was going on. She crouched down to make herself very small. The space in front of the hospital was just about deserted except for a platoon of short men in peculiar sea-green uniforms. They had big canvas boots and some of them had blood on their uniforms. They were standing to attention before a more smartly dressed officer with a sword, which was so big it dragged on the ground. She was disappointed in him. He would not even come up to her father's shoulder. He was no taller than Cookie. He was barking away at the men. One man spoke up and he slapped him hard across the face. Sylvie wondered if they were getting into trouble for killing all the people in the hospital, or for not killing enough of them. From her crouching position her glance moved down from the platoon of soldiers in the distance to the toe of her own shoe in front of her. It was covered in blood. She kicked out at a hovering fly. She crawled round the corner on her hands and knees for ten yards and then stood upright to run.

She woke what seemed to be a sleeping rickshaw man and asked him to take her to Beach Road. Eventually they jogged past knots of British soldiers sitting on the low wall that surrounded the *padang* in front of Government House. As they dodged among the soldiers, she held her ears tight between her palms to stop the crack and thump of the bombs breaking up her brain. She coughed in the black smoke from burning rubber in the *godowns*; looked up to see the flames shooting into the sky darkened already with the ash of a hundred fires.

The rickshaw man threaded his way through a narrow street and was stopped by the fire engine that was soaking the blackened front of a shophouse. Breathing hard, Sylvie watched as a little lady, very like Virginia's nana, came through the blackened door. She went from one blackened fire fighter to the next, offering each one of them a china cup of tea from a lacquered tray. The woman bowed her head and said something to one of the fire fighters. He held up the china cup in his sooty fingers, in some kind of salute to the old woman. A crystal moment of silence acknowledged this civilised act, then the world of falling bombs and crashing houses closed in again, and Sylvie hurried on.

Great zips and crackles way to her left made her turn her head swiftly to see a glorious display of whooshing, whizzing fireworks as another *godown* went up in smoke. The shooting stars and the rainbow waterfalls rose above the pall of blackened air before being engulfed again into the destroyed city.

Many doors were shut. In Orchard Road some of the washing poles already showed the red rising sun of the Japanese flag.

Number nineteen Beach Road was closed fast and, very unusually, locked. Sylvie banged and battered on it. 'Simon Chen! Nana! Let me in! Uncle Chu!' It was opened so violently she almost fell on top of Simon Chen, who had unlocked the door. He held on to her and peered up and down the deserted street. 'Where is Jin Kee?' he said. His voice was funny. Dry and hard, like when her father was forcing himself to say something nasty to her.

'She's at the hospital. She sent me . . .'

He stood her still inside the door and made her tell him what had happened. She did this, hiccoughing with tears. '. . . And I have blood on my sandals.' She started to wail and he slapped her face. She thought of the Japanese officer and stopped crying.

Simon Chen stroked her cheek. 'I am sorry about that. Now we must go and tell my grandmother. She will be pleased that Jin Kee does not yet meet her ancestors.'

'Why did you lock the door?'

'Looters are about.'

They walked, Sylvie in front of Simon Chen, up the narrow staircase.

'Let me tell the nana, Simon Chen. I know that she understands me. I could tell this morning.'

'It is not respectful. I will tell her.'

They were on the third landing. His voice came from behind.

'Why do you use this word "nana"?'

'Because she's like my mummy's mother at home. My grandmother. My nana. I like her too.'

143

They were at the door. The grandmother was in her usual place on the high seat. She wore a grander gown than usual and was fanning herself in the stifling air with a black silk fan with ribs of carved ivory.

Simon Chen was speaking almost before he got through the door, rattling out the information. Sylvie watched the grandmother's face carefully. It did not change.

'You're pleased, Nana?' she said urgently. 'That Jin Kee was not killed like those other nurses?'

The grandmother spoke to Simon Chen, who said, 'My grandmother says that Jin Kee was saved for other things. To take care of you, perhaps. The ancestors are not ready to receive her.' He paused. 'She says that obviously you are pleased, but you don't know about the ancestors.'

'What's this about ancestors?'

'That we do not worry about dying because in dying we meet our dead ancestors and this is what we lived our lives for.'

'And if Jin Kee had died would she have met with her mother and her French foreign devil father?'

The grandmother stopped fanning herself and said something.

'She says she is not entirely sure of the French foreign devil father, but certainly her mother, who was Hokkien, like any civilised person.'

Sylvie's lip went out and she trembled. 'I don't like being a foreign devil.'

The grandmother spoke quickly and Simon Chen led Sylvie to the carved bench. 'Sit here,' he said. 'And my grandmother says that when she dies she hopes to meet her own grandfather, who was a foreign devil. And her grandmother, who was *karayuki-san*. That is a Japanese lady who entertains many people here in this city. Even so,' he said, a serious frown on his face, 'the grandmother, who is the sister to my grandfather, is truly Chinese.'

Sylvie dangled her feet from the bench and thought about the Japanese officer with his long sword. She frowned. 'So was Nana's nana a *Japanese* lady?'

At last the old woman smiled. 'A courtesan,' she said slowly in English. 'My mother very beautiful courtesan.'

'Is that like a courtier?'

The old woman smiled even more broadly. 'Lived on Tregannau Street,' she said. 'Help men to enjoy themselves. A *karayuki-san*. She help my grandfather to enjoy himself.' She turned to Simon Chen. 'Tea!' she said in English. Then she brought up her fan and stirred the stagnant air before her face.

Three hours later, when Virginia returned to number nineteen, Sylvie rose very stiffly after sleeping again on the carved bench. Simon Chen had woken her once, thrust a bowl of rice in her hand and stood and watched her eat it. Then she'd slept again as though the eating of the rice was a dream.

In the low light of the room she could make out Uncle Chu and Uncle Wo, Simon and Virginia, demure but tired-eyed. She was talking to them in rapid Hokkien.

Sylvie shook her head to get it awake, and wriggled her feet to bring back the feeling. Virginia Chen came to sit beside her and put an arm around her. 'It is nearly over, Sylvie. We will have to consider what to do. They have killed many soldiers, taken the guns from the rest. They are hunting down the young Chinese. They have already killed many of these, so Simon Chen may not be safe. And then, there is you.'

Sylvie scowled. 'Do you want me to go on a sinking ship?'

Virginia shook her head. 'No more ships, Sylvie. The time for ships is over. They say some soldiers are setting off on little barques for the islands. But they also say the military will surrender any minute now. There will be no more ships.'

'We will get you some papers,' said Simon Chen. 'A man will take your photograph and we will make you some papers. Syl Vee Chen, another child of my aunt and the French foreign devil.'

The uncles smiled and nodded and chewed their pipes. Sylvie thought they, like the grandmother, probably understood English. She frowned, trying to force that thought into her head, which had had to accommodate so many new things in the last few days.

'We will have to be very careful in the next few days,' said Virginia. 'We do not want attention from those dogs. We will have to keep the shop closed until . . . until we know what's happening.'

'All the shops are closed. We will earn nothing,' said Simon Chen. 'We will become very thin.' He glared at fat Uncle Chu and translated his own words into Hokkien to reinforce his concern. 'How can we eat?'

'My mother's boxes!' said Sylvie. 'There are lots of things in there – some of her pearls, some fine clothes and shoes.

We can sell something and buy some food for you – for us all.'

The grandmother stopped fanning herself. 'No sell,' she said. 'We have much money. We very rich.'

Sylvie glanced at them, frowning. 'Oh. That's not polite, is it? I'm sorry.' She knew she'd stepped over some line but was not sure how.

Virginia stood up and pulled Sylvie to her feet. 'I think you should go to bed, Sylvie. There will be a good deal to do tomorrow if you are to be safe.'

'Jin Kee, I—'

'You must go, Sylvie. I have a good deal to talk about with Grandmother and Simon Chen. You will be bored.' She pushed her gently towards the door. 'Go.'

'The nana told me that her grandmother was a courtesan. What's that?'

'Did she not tell you?'

'Yes. Sort of.'

'Then that must suffice. Now, go!'

# Chapter Thirteen

## Identity

The next day Virginia left early to help at the hospital. 'Simon will take you to have your photograph taken,' she said briskly to Sylvie. 'Try your best to look at least half one of us.' She oiled and pinned Sylvie's hair back tightly, rubbed paste into her face and did something to her eyelids with black pencil. 'Be good, and do as Simon tells you.'

Simon nodded to Sylvie and led the way from Beach Road, through the warren of backstreets, then across the river and out on to a broader street, which Sylvie recognised. One or two of the shops here were opening for trade. The Japanese flag showed its face on two of the buildings. The air was filled with noise. The shriek of shells and the crump of bombs was almost continuous. If the bomb was near, people flattened themselves on the ground. Then they stood up, dusted themselves down and went on.

She bumped into Simon as he stopped outside one building. He took her by the shoulder and peered into her face.

Then he bent down and wiped his hand on the fire-blackened dust of the pavement and rubbed it down the edge of her cheek and into her jawbone. Her skin stung as he rubbed it. 'There,' he said, 'not so English. Inside, you do not speak. Remember, do not speak.'

The photographer was a slim Chinese man in a clean linen suit and a soft tie. He sat her on a chair and fussed with the lights, dragged the camera on its tripod this way and that. Then he stopped, looked Simon Chen straight in the eye and said something. Simon Chen barked something back. Sylvie could see he was angry. The photographer bowed to him, then said something more, very quietly.

Sylvie bit her lip, dying to ask what it was about. She stared wide-eyed at Simon Chen, willing a question in his direction. He stared at her, then stared at the photographer, then reached into his pocket and laid some notes on the small, ornate table that stood against a wall.

The photographer smiled faintly, and bowed. Then he made a slight adjustment to the tripod and proceeded to take his photographs.

Sylvie blinked as they came into the bright air. 'What was it? What was it all about? Why did you shout at him, Simon Chen?' She hurried to keep up alongside him, to get in front of him, to make him answer.

Simon sat down on the pavement with his back to the wall. She sat down before him.

'He was very greedy. Wanted lots of money.'

'Did you have a lot of money?'

'No.'

'But he still took the photographs. What did you say?'

'I said the Nippon were not yet in these streets and there were those among us who do not care for people who consort with these dogs. That there was still time.'

'Consort?'

'That shop, those cameras, they used to belong to a Japanese photographer who has worked here for many years, as his father did. Those photographs of Virginia and my aunt were taken by him. That man there was his assistant, his slave.'

'But where is he now? The old photographer?'

'The British transported him with the other Japanese to Australia.'

'Where is Australia?'

'Not far.'

She watched the slow bustle of people as they made their way along the street. Some were dirty soldiers, peering in the front of the open shops, sometimes going in. 'Look at them,' shouted Simon Chen over the crack of yet another bomb.

'The soldiers?' She peered more closely.

'A week ago, a month ago, they were marching off the ships to save us poor creatures from our enemies. Bright uniforms, blancoed belts. "How are the mighty fallen!" '

'What's that?'

'It's the Christian Bible. Book of Samuel. You wouldn't know about it, of course. You've never been to school. Virginia told me this.'

Sylvie scraped the earth a bit, wiggling her toe in her sandal. The blood on it had now gone black. 'Why are we waiting here?'

'We are waiting for your photograph. If we went away he would keep the money and not develop it.'

'He might still keep the money. How can you make him do it?'

He reached under his blouse and brought out something that glittered in a ray of sunlight that was managing to cut through the smoke-pall. Sylvie reached out a finger and touched the sharp blade. 'Would you kill him?'

'I would. And he knows it. I showed this to him.' Simon looked at his handsome watch. 'Five more minutes,' he said.

That was when Sylvie decided Simon Chen was her hero. She knew she must not show it. She'd seen enough of the still faces in that house to know that you shouldn't show what you feel. 'I would kill him too,' she said, careful to keep her voice flat. 'Me too.'

A small spurt of disbelief played about his finely cut lips. 'I do not think so, Syl Vee. But one day, perhaps, you may have to do this.'

'Will you show me how?'

Again, the half-expressed laugh. 'There may be too little time.' He leaped to his feet and told her to wait. He was back in two minutes clutching a small brown parcel. He was smiling slightly. 'The worm was so afraid he has made you look like a good little Chinese.'

'Can I see?' She reached out her hand and grabbed at the package, but Simon held on to it.

'No. I must go on and give this to the man who will make the documents for you. He is true Chinese. Not like that Nippon-lover.'

She stood up, ready to follow him. He shook his head. 'No. You must return to the house. I have much to do – not just this errand on your behalf. I have other business too.' He gave her a little push. 'Straight up past three roads and left. You will see where to go.' Then he turned and was gone, and she was left in the street full of strangers with wild eyes who, like her, did not know which way to turn.

She wandered in the direction he had shown her, but was confused by the narrowness of the alleys. In some places a house had been bombed down so she had to go sideways. She did this twice and then was entirely lost. Then she thought she saw her mother: a tall woman with a baby on her hip and a little girl in one hand and a bulging cotton bag in the other. Of course, it wasn't her mother. This woman had scraggy, unkempt hair under a plonked-on straw hat. Her dress was creased and stained under the arms and in a spear shape on her back. The children were dirty and wore soiled, creased clothes. Sylvie knew her mother would never have stood for that. The wash-*amah* would have been in very big trouble.

But still, the woman was English. You could tell from her skin and her frizzy fair hair; the occasional weary word she would throw at the little girl by her side. Sylvie could not think where to go so, keeping five feet between them, she followed the woman.

Before long, the roads opened up and Sylvie started to recognise where they were. When they came into Raffles

Square, she breathed out her relief. Now she was all right. Now she could trace her way back to number nineteen. She relaxed. She could wait now to see what the woman was up to.

The woman stood outside Robinson's Department Store, in a crowd of women like herself with children. Sylvie caught excitement in the air, laughter, even a bit of crying. There was a queue going slowly forward. She stopped quietly beside a couple of soldiers lounging against a broken wall.

In front of them, causing the 'Oohs' and 'Aahs' and the occasional spurt of laughter, emerged a trickle of women and children. The mothers were as grimy and unkempt as the woman Sylvie had followed, but the children were dressed in new clothes. The girls wore summer dresses with their hair in ribbons tied behind; the boys were in colourful shorts and neat shirts. They wore new sandals with white crepe soles. On their heads were shady straw or cloth hats. In their hands were neat brown paper parcels. One woman took one of these from her daughter and showed it to the woman in the queue. 'The same,' she said, tears in her eyes. 'Two outfits each, and no charge. Can you believe it? All the children can have them. Can you believe it? Two outfits.'

Sylvie wandered forward and vaguely attached herself to the queue. If there were free outfits going she might as well have some. Virginia – no, Jin Kee – would be pleased.

The woman in front of her glanced at her and shooed her away as though she were a dog, or a monkey on a lawn. 'Go away, little girl. Go away! English only. Only English children. Shoo! Shoo!'

Sylvie backed off and rejoined the soldiers with their backs to the wall. One of them laughed, a harsh, desperate sound. 'Not for Chinks. Whites only, flower. I wouldn't worry if I were you. Getting new clobber to go to prison, poor kids. Talk about Whitsun wakes.'

'Too early for Whitsun,' grunted the other.

'New clothes,' went on the first soldier. 'Me mam got us new clothes every Whitsun, right down to shoes. Then down to the chapel to say my piece on Whit Sunday.'

'Aw, shut it, will you, Geordie? This fuckin' business is no joke, I'm telling you.'

'Well, mate, yer gotta laugh or you'd be crying in a second.'

Sylvie shelved the thought of insisting on her turn in the queue and declaring herself a white girl, just for the sake of a few clothes. She had clothes tucked away at number nineteen. In any case, this blouse and these black trousers, with her mandarin jacket for best, these would do her for now.

She should get back. At least she knew the way. She put her head down under the shade of her hat, sidled past the two soldiers and started to run.

When she got back to number nineteen the uncles waved their pipes at her and talked to her, pointing behind her, and up to the skies, which now seemed to be humming with the permanent reverberations of shells.

'Simon Chen?' she said desperately. 'He went off. He left me.'

This seemed to make them angrier. They gestured even more angrily at the sky.

'He just went away. Simon Chen just went away,' she protested.

To her relief, at that minute, through the whirl of bomb dust and smoke, she saw him trudging down the street. He was leaning forward to balance a big carton, which he carried on his back by means of a kind of rope cradle, which connected round his shoulders.

'Simon!' she said. 'The uncles . . .' He pushed past her and into the dark recesses of the room behind. His uncles followed him, talking loudly, their tones very severe. Sylvie made to follow them. Simon was untying the carton from the ropes. He looked up at her and pulled something from inside his loose jacket.

'Here are your papers. Go up to the grandmother. She will want to see them, to make sure they are correct. She knows about these things.'

She took the packet but kept her eyes on the carton.

'Go!' he said. 'You are a troublesome girl.'

She raced upstairs. The grandmother was sitting in her chair reading a *Picturegoer* magazine, her fingers moving swiftly along the lines of text. She took off her glasses to peer at Sylvie. 'Simon?' she said, her voice crackling like old paper.

'He – is – downstairs.' Sylvie tried to keep her voice very clear. 'He has a big parcel.' She sketched the size of the parcel in the air.

The old woman's eyes glittered. The severe line of her mouth loosened a little. 'Ah,' she said. 'Loot.'

Sylvie drew close to her chair. 'Loot, Nana?'

'The town in disarray,' said the old woman. 'There is much belong nobody, so Simon take it. Loot.'

Sylvie gave her the packet. 'I had my photo taken, Nana. The man was very nasty.'

The grandmother took the crumpled, brownish papers from the packet. She put on her glasses and held it nearer the light so she could see it. 'Ah, like old paper, very good,' she said. 'Good. See this, little sister. Chen Syl Vee. You say Syl Vee Chen. Like Jin Kee Chen. So?'

Sylvie took the paper and peered at it. It looked as though it had been through a hundred hands. There were English words on it and Chinese characters. Name. Address. Father. Mother. And a picture of a little Chinese girl. She held it closer. The face was hers and yet it wasn't. She looked at the name. Chen Syl Vee.

The old woman laughed a laugh as reassuring as a crackling fire on a chilly night. 'Chen Syl Vee, little sister to Chen Jin Kee. Virginia.' She said the last carefully in the English way.

'Simon Chen – does he have a Chinese name, Nana?'

The old woman laughed. 'All Chinese go English school have English name. They like English name. But have Chinese name also. Also Simon Chen.' She took the paper and returned it to the packet. She hooked a wiry finger to draw Sylvie closer to her, then tucked the packet in the inner pocket of her white blouse. 'Keep it safe and it will keep you safe, little sister,' she whispered. 'Talk no English in street as there are very bad men.'

She patted the low stool beside her and proceeded to show Sylvie the pictures in her book, naming the film stars one by one. They lingered over her favourite, Douglas Fairbanks Jr. 'Brave man,' she said.

Half an hour later, clatter and noise below heralded the sudden entrance of Virginia. Her skin was clay-coloured and there were dark smudges under her eyes.

Sylvie leaped up, her hand going to the pocket with her papers. Virginia pushed past her and went to open the painted humming-bird shutters. She opened them and let in the dark of the night. 'Listen,' she said.

The old woman put a hand to her lips.

'I can hear nothing,' said Sylvie.

Virginia nodded. Then she started to talk away in Hokkien with her grandmother, the words streaming into the air, snipping and cutting sounds in ways that Sylvie could not understand.

Sylvie hung out of the window. There were people in the street fluttering and rustling like moths. 'No bombs,' she said. 'No shells. No noise. Such quiet.'

Virginia came and put her arm round her from behind. 'No war, Sylvie. The war is won.'

'We won the war?'

'No. We lost it. Our general has surrendered.'

'Is he a coward?'

'No, Sylvie. It was all too much. Too much altogether for our poor soldiers.'

Sylvie shuddered and hiccoughed, the breath inside her

uncontrolled. 'They'll kill us, like they killed the people in the hospital.' Sylvie could feel Virginia becoming very still behind and above her.

'No they won't,' said Virginia carefully. 'This is our home place, our island. They have defeated the foreigners.'

'The red-faced devils?'

'Yes.'

The grandmother's voice crackled from behind. 'The little sister has her papers now, Jin Kee,' she said in English. 'Very good papers. No foreigner.'

They stood there for a long time, looking out into the eerie silence of the night. Then Virginia pulled Sylvie back into the room and locked the shutters. 'Now, Sylvie, we must find some supper, then see about naughty Simon Chen.'

'He's been collecting loot.'

Virginia looked across at her grandmother. 'I saw it downstairs. Cigarettes. Uncle Wo is rubbing his hands.'

'Nana says there is stuff which belongs to nobody now. That's what they loot.'

Virginia shook her head. 'Now, Sylvie, it belongs to the conquerors. Already there are leaflets in the street saying looters will be shot.'

'Will they shoot Simon Chen?'

Virginia shook her head. 'We will hide his loot. It will be useful for us to trade. There are hard days coming. At this time, in these moments, he has done the right thing. Trade will be important in the days ahead.'

# Chapter Fourteen

## Looting

'Come and see this.' Simon pulled the hard bench away from the window and made room for them all. Even the grand-mother alighted from her tall chair to take a look over Sylvie's shoulder. Simon pushed the shutter wide open. The road below was full of people, but there was no hum of trade, no calls of business, no sirens, no crump of bombs.

Stretching her neck, Sylvie could see soldiers in the road. They were in four formation, marching along. She blinked. In these last days she'd overheard conversations that Jin Kee translated as talk of just what they must do now the Japanese were in charge. She'd peered down in the street, now empty of those other – 'our' – soldiers, to see groups of Japanese soldiers. She'd asked Simon where they'd gone. 'They gath-ered them on the *padang*. They have to go somewhere.'

'What for?'

Simon's eyes glittered. 'They will shoot them. Though how they can shoot so many—'

'Simon!' Jin Kee's voice was as sharp as a blade. 'They are gathering there so they can count them, Sylvie. They like to count people. Then the soldiers will be put under guard in one of the army camps. They say it will be Changi.'

'We were at Changi at the beach once. We had a picnic . . .' said Sylvie.

'There's an army camp there, and a jail,' said Simon. 'Here they are! They are walking to Changi,' he added 'Look!'

The first groups marched, head high, in neat formation, swinging along in time as though they were going off to war. After them came small brown soldiers, in clean, pressed uniforms and rakish hats, marching in step.

'The Gurkhas!' said Simon. 'Such dignity.'

After that the groups of soldiers were less organised, less immaculate. The endless line soon broke down into clumps of soldiers with heavy packs, pushing or pulling carts with belongings. Some soldiers were on crutches, helped along by their comrades.

'Why are there no guards?' said Jin Kee. 'No Japanese there at all?'

'They take themselves,' said Simon. 'Lambs to the slaughter. They are ordered so by their own officers. They are on their honour.'

'How hard for them,' said Sylvie, 'to march to prison on their honour.'

'There are thousands of them,' said Simon, his tone lowering. 'The flower of the Empire? Well, not quite so now. These they sent to protect us. The flower of the Empire.'

The grandmother spoke sharply to him. He turned

to Sylvie. 'I apologise, Syl Vee Chen, for insulting your ancestors.'

Now Sylvie had her head right over the wrought-iron guard on the windowsill. 'See, Jin Kee! See! At the end, pushing that other man in the rattan chair with wheels on. It's my father. My daddy!' Sylvie opened her mouth to shout, but Jin Kee clamped her hand over it and pulled her away from the light of the window.

Over Jin Kee's hand, Sylvie's eyes widened to take in as much as she could of the sight of her father's rusty head bent down over the chair, talking cheerfully into the ear of the man he was pushing. His Volunteer's uniform was crumpled and stained, and there was a dust mark on his cheek. He used to lean like that over her mother's shoulder when she sat in her long chair. He would talk and chatter to her; making her laugh even when she had decided to be miserable, which was quite often.

And he didn't know. He didn't know she was here. Her tears dripped over Jin Kee's knuckles. Finally she broke free. She ran across to the edge of the balcony but now there were only a few stragglers, soldiers in no formation at all, wandering along in a dazed fashion as though they didn't know where they were.

She turned on Jin Kee. 'Why did you do that? Why did you stop me shouting to him? He should know I was here.'

Jin Kee shook her head. 'The Japanese—'

'There were no Japanese soldiers there. You saw that.'

Jin Kee glanced at Simon. 'There were spies in the crowd. They will tell the Japanese. And they will come here and put us in prison. All of us. Including Simon and my grandmother.'

The grandmother eased herself into a chair and said something to the others. This was followed by a gale of talk from Simon and the uncles.

Sylvie pulled Jin Kee on to the hard bench beside her. 'What is she saying? Why doesn't she speak in English so I can understand? I know she can . . .'

'She speaks in her language, Sylvie. This is her country.'

Sylvie felt heavy inside, from her chest right down to her stomach. Tears welled in her eyes again. 'But I don't know what they're saying, Jin Kee,' she said. 'I don't understand.'

Jin Kee put an arm on her shoulder. 'They talk about Simon. The Japanese will gather all the young Chinese men together and take them away.'

'And what will they do? Will they kill them?'

'This they don't know. They killed many Chinese in Nanking. And in Hong Kong.'

'So that's worse than my daddy going to prison?'

'It might be. No one knows. Simon is the youngest in the family. He is clever. He is the hope. Without him the family has no future.'

'What about you?'

Jin Kee smiled. 'I am only half, am I not? Less than half. Not sufficiently white for your mother; not truly enough Chinese for my grandmother. Half and half.'

'A *stengah*!' said Sylvie.

Jin Kee shook her head. 'That is such a rude thing to say of a person, Sylvie.' Then she hugged her to stop the promised tears. 'But you and I are sisters now, Sylvie. The papers say this. Sisters until all this is over and you are back with your daddy and your mother and Feargal.' Jin Kee Chen had made up her mind about this – that Mrs Sambuck had survived – even though it was widely reported that so many of those boats had been blown out of the water. Better to believe her ship had got away.

That night Jin Kee organised a little truckle bed with a tented mosquito net in the corner of her capsule of a room, so that the two of them could sleep more coolly, each in her own space. She rooted in a cupboard and found a little doll with a cloth face and black, flat-cut hair and placed it in the bed beside her. 'Her name is Ayoshi. She slept with me till I was fifteen years. She was my mother's doll before that. And my grandmother's. She comes from Japan. Her name is the same as my grandmother's mother.'

'The courtesan?'

'The *karayuki-san*,' said Jin Kee.

'I have toys.' Sylvie was sleepy. 'I have my puppet.'

'We'll get that out tomorrow. Now lie still and try to sleep.'

The door clicked behind her and Sylvie could hear the murmur of voices next door: the mumble of the uncles, Jin Kee's clear-cut tones, Simon's youthful voice almost singing, undercut by the insistent croak of the old woman. She felt walled in with sounds she did not understand. So she put Ayoshi against her cheek. 'You understand English, Ayoshi. I know you do.'

Sylvie woke up next day and listened for several minutes to the silence before she told the doll called Ayoshi the story of how she was here and why. She told her the story of the little girl seeing her father in a line of tramping soldiers; of the little girl who hid in the top of a cupboard while, out on the landing, soldiers put their gun-knives through a man in pyjamas, and stamped on his face. And how that little girl was forced to live in a place where people opened their mouths and closed them and quacked and squawked with no meaning so the little girl thought she was deaf.

'Sylvie, are you awake?' Jin Kee's voice floated from behind the mosquito net, found its way through Sylvie's net and landed sweet as syrup in Sylvie's ear.

'Yes,' she said. 'I was thinking how quiet it is.'

'No bombs, no guns,' said Jin Kee.

'Just Japanese,' said Sylvie.

'Just Japanese,' said Jin Kee.

'What will happen today?' said Sylvie.

'I don't know. I suppose the Japanese will take charge.'

'How will they do that? Will they be the policemen and firemen? Will they be my daddy in his office?'

Jin Kee sat up, pulled aside her net and stretched her toes to the floor. 'I suppose the Japanese will tell the Europeans what to do.'

'They will not kill them? They will be on their honour?'

'Not if they need them to do something.'

'Will you go to the hospital?'

Jin Kee poked Sylvie with her toe, making her wriggle and giggle inside her net. 'No. Not if it is to help those dogs. And the Europeans took their sick with them to prison, so I don't think . . .'

'So what will we do?'

'We should lie low and see which way the wind blows.'

'What?'

'See what the dogs will do. Already, according to Uncle Chu, they are making lists of Chinese boys. The young men are to report for listing.'

'And then?'

'And then, heaven help Simon or any of his friends.'

Sylvie stood up, smoothed down her vest and pulled up her knickers. Jin Kee laughed. 'Clean knickers, Sylvie. Do you have some?'

'Yes. In my little case. One full change.'

'Then find those and I will show you how to wash the ones you've got on.'

'Wash them?'

Jin Kee shook her lightly by the shoulders. 'No wash-*amahs* here, Sylvie.'

Later, they made their way through streets which were bustling again with life, but in a minor tempo, with people glancing behind them as they went about their work. The wrecked houses were still being cleared by squads of Tamils, no longer in fear of bombs as they worked. Ambulances still hauled away the dead and the dying, some of them driven by Europeans. Obviously on their honour, thought Sylvie. But hanging from many washing poles were flags adorned with the symbol of the rising sun. And twice they saw men in pale green uniforms sitting upright and watchful as birds, one in a rickshaw, one in a Ford taxi.

They were making for the shop of Mr Wang, a friend of

Uncle Chu's. It seemed he had stocks of spare petrol and Jin Kee was going with money from the grandmother to secure these. On the far side of the road a young Englishman in white, with a clergyman's back-to-front collar, was careering along the narrow road on a bicycle, swerving to miss the rickshaws and the holes in the road. Sylvie craned her neck to watch him. She ended up walking backwards.

Then she felt a thump on her shoulder and was on her face in the dust. 'Sylvie.' Jin Kee kneeled at her side in the dust. Then she in turn was sent sprawling by a well-placed, highly polished boot.

Sylvie looked up into a harsh, folded face under a pale green cap. He was shouting at Jin Kee and pointing at Sylvie. Jin Kee hauled her to her feet and, keeping her head down, said something to the soldier, who looked, Sylvie thought, as though his face was made of fireworks. He passed his gun into his other hand and cracked Jin Kee across the face with his open palm. Once one way, once the other.

'Bow! Bow down low,' muttered Jin Kee through swelling lips. She tugged hard at Sylvie's elbow and Sylvie bent down so low her nose was touching her knees. More words were said and papers rustled as Jin Kee passed over their documents. There were more gruff shouts, another slap, which sent Jin Kee sprawling back into the dirt and then, through the corner of her eye, Sylvie saw the gleaming boots depart, stepping over Jin Kee's sprawling figure.

Sylvie kneeled beside her and, with the assistance of a hawker-woman who'd been watching beneath the shadowy brim of her hat, she helped Jin Kee across to the hawker-woman's stool. Jin Kee put a hand on her brow. 'Those dogs,' she said.

'Jin Kee, it's my fault. I bumped into him. I was watching the vicar-man on his bicycle.'

'It's not your fault,' said Jin Kee thickly. 'Those dogs are at fault.'

The hawker-woman gave Jin Kee a drink from a tin cup she had chained to her belt, muttering all the time as she did so. Now Sylvie was crying. 'What is she saying? What is she saying, Jin Kee?'

'She is saying the white foreign devils were one thing, but those dogs are the dirt beneath your feet.'

Sylvie stopped crying and looked at the mild-faced woman in surprise. The woman put a hand on her shoulder and nodded reassuringly, talking as she did so.

'She said that if it was up to her she'd fry his gizzards.'

'Good,' said Sylvie. 'Good.'

'Now you can help me go home.' Jin Kee hauled herself to her feet. 'Mr Wang will have to wait.'

Back at the shop the uncles clucked and cooed over Jin Kee. They sat her on a chair at the back of the shop and gave her something strong to drink from a crystal cup. The beating of the stick from the room above made her haul herself to her feet and climb the stairs to face her grandmother.

After the attack on Jin Kee she and Sylvie stayed in the house, watching events from the window. The pavements now filled with more Japanese soldiers and there was a great deal of bowing. Simon's face darkened with anger when he saw how

Jin Kee had been hurt. He went off to talk with his uncles and his uncles' friends about this, but they could do nothing. They went to powerful men in the old societies but they would do nothing. They said wait, only wait. The dogs would screw on their own axis. It would end. Just wait. Take no risks.

Messengers were sent to every district ordering young men to assemble at certain places to be registered. Simon set out to go to his designated place but was turned back by a man from one of the old Chinese clans. He told him stories of killings and hooded men. Simon took a rucksack of his things, including packs of cigarettes, and vanished.

'Where has he gone?' said Sylvie. 'Where did Simon go?'

'Up on to the peninsula,' said Jin Kee. 'There are groups in the jungle who fight the Japanese, harrying them like the dogs they are.'

'What's "harry"?'

'Cause them big, big trouble.'

'Can we go up on the peninsula and do this? I would really like to harry them.'

Jin Kee looked at Sylvie and thought how she herself would have done just this if she had not a little European girl to watch out for. 'They will not let women fight,' she lied. 'We have to stay here and wait, like the old ones say.'

After some days the two of them started to venture out again, watching warily for the soldiers, crossing the road hurriedly or moving up alleyways to avoid them. Sylvie wandered down to the docks where gangs of Europeans in ragged clothes, sweatbands round their heads, worked to repair the damage and sabotage they themselves had caused during the siege. She looked hard among them but couldn't see her father. It made her think of other times she'd been down in that place with her father. There had always been gangs of men working, but they'd been Tamils, or Malays with shady hats. Now there were men like her own father doing coolies' work.

She looked and looked at the dark, sweat-stained faces. Once she thought it was her father, but when the man stood up to stretch his back and wipe his sweating face with his hand she saw that it was a younger man; a man with lank red hair.

It was on one of her trips that she saw Japanese soldiers push three Chinese men into an alley and shoot them. She cowered behind a column and watched as one of the soldiers took his long gun-knife and hacked off the heads of the men. The first took so long that the officer took out his sword and sliced the other heads off in two swift blows. All the time there was screaming and wailing.

The screams and shouts, the hoarse mutters of satisfaction, the bark of an order, all these went into Sylvie's head and sealed themselves there, to come back into her brain when she wasn't looking. Now she watched as other Chinese were dragged forward to take up the severed heads and tie them, still dripping, to washing poles that stuck out into the street.

As the days passed by at the shophouse, Sylvie began to understand a little more of what was being said. The words for daily living were said again and again in the same tone, so they were not so difficult to grasp. She never ventured to speak the words herself. Although she knew what they meant she couldn't work out how to say them in the high tones that the nana and the old men used.

The uncles spoke no English at all, but patted her and nodded to her, pushed an occasional sweet or chocolate in her hand, sometimes straight into her mouth as though she were a baby. She could show them with her hands what she wanted and they understood. She felt comfortable with them, and always safe.

The grandmother watched her play on the hard bench with the doll called Ayoshi and the lionfish puppet. She spoke haltingly with her, then watched a play Sylvie made up that involved both the doll and the lionfish.

The old woman clapped her hands at the play. She made Sylvie a present of her second-best jade fan and showed her three more photographs of her grandmother's mother who had been the Japanese *karayuki-san*, a woman who entertained men. The woman in the picture was about as old as Jin Kee was now. She sat on a sofa, leaning to one side, her face cupped thoughtfully in her hand.

'She's beautiful,' said Sylvie. 'Like a film star.' She tapped the top copy of *Picturegoer* and nodded.

In time Jin Kee, Sylvie's beloved friend, became more distracted, more distant. Sylvie came to treasure the dark hours of the night when she would come to their tiny, shared space and they could talk in English about what was happening. That was how she learned how all the *mems* and their children had, like the soldiers, been herded into a camp.

'Will they kill them, like they killed all the Chinese boys?'

Jin Kee shook her head in the dark. 'I don't think so. They don't fear them as they fear the Chinese.'

They talked about Simon. 'What does he do in the jungle?'

'He shoots Japanese; blows up their cars. He trains hard to become a soldier for the last battle.'

'What's that?'

'When they come back to make us all free.'

'So it will be the same as before?'

'Simon says it will not. He says the Chinese will be in charge then.'

'Not the *angmoh kwai*?'

'No. Not them.'

She asked Jin Kee why she was always out, never just there, like the grandmother.

'I talk to people to get money, or goods to sell to help Simon and his comrades.'

'To harry the Japanese?'

'That's right.'

Sylvie lay there for two nights in the dark and thought of her father's fair head bowed over the man in the rattan chair with wheels. 'There is my father's treasure,' she announced one night. 'Under the hibiscus hedge. He will want to help in the last battle. He would want to help to harry the Japanese.'

Jin Kee sat up in bed. 'I had forgotten that. Do you know where it is?'

'Exactly.'

'We would have to do it at night.'

'You're always out at night.'

'Night is the only time anything can be done with those dogs around.'

'Will you take my father's treasure for the last battle?'

Jin Kee put her hand on Sylvie's arm. 'I will. I will. It will make so much difference, Sylvie.'

Somewhere in the middle of the next night Sylvie crept out of the house with Jin Kee and they met two Chinese men in the shadows of Malabar Street. It seemed a very long walk in the dark up to Leonie Hill Road. The men gave Sylvie a hitch up so she climbed the locked gate first. When she looked up to the house a thrill as harsh as lightning flicked through her. The lights were on and the hot draught of cooking food wafted down the lawns to the hibiscus hedge.

'Miss—'

Jin Kee clapped a hand over her mouth.

'They are not back,' she whispered close to Sylvie's ear. 'The Nippon have taken it. Officers live there.'

Moving through the shadow of the flame trees then, into the dark lee of the high hedge, Sylvie led them to the place where Wong Mee and her father had buried the tin boxes. Fortunately, the lawn rose in a high roll in front of them and the rough lalang grass had not been cut. They were invisible from the house. 'Watch!' said Jin Kee in Sylvie's ear. Then she and the men set to with *chungkols*, breaking the lalang, then digging into the soft earth below.

As Sylvie watched, two men came to the edge of the veranda, talking in gruff tones. They stood just at the spot where she'd laid out the game of dominoes in those last days.

One of the men laughed and the other clapped a hand on his shoulder. She had seen just such a gesture not so long ago between her father and his friend Mr Hoxton.

A hand came on to her shoulder and she jumped. 'We're done,' said Jin Kee in her ear. 'We have taken just one tin. There is too much for one trip. We have only two rucksacks.'

At the gate they parted from the men. The older man put a hand on Sylvie's shoulder and was gone. The trip back down to Beach Road was more carefree. Sylvie felt happy and wanted to talk. 'Have we been looting?'

Jin Kee laughed in the darkness. 'You cannot loot yourself, Sylvie. You can only loot what belongs to others.'

Back at the house Jin Kee produced two silver cups. 'I got these for you.' She held the cup towards the light of a lamp. 'See, your daddy's name is on them.'

Sylvie peered at her father's name engraved there. 'John Beaufort Raine Sambuck. That's my father's name.'

Jin Kee stared at her. 'Sylvie Beaufort Raine Sambuck. That is also your name.'

'But for now Syl Vee Chen,' said Sylvie.

She was enfolded in Jin Kee's arms. 'Just for now, Sylvie, just for now.'

Sylvie decided she'd keep only the smaller cup. The big one seemed too much to be responsible for. She signed to Uncle Chu if he could sell it for her, so she could give Madame Chen money for food. He nodded gravely and put it on the shelf among some wood and brass beakers. Sylvie was in the shop, sitting on a stool in the back, when he sold it. There was some haggling but it finally went. The buyer was the bicycling clergyman who'd drawn Sylvie's interest and caused the bother that led to Jin Kee being beaten. She looked the man right in the eye but his glance peeled over her as though she were one of the rolled carpets leaning on the wall beside her. That was when she realised that she fitted quite well into this household of old men and women.

She kept the small cup in her pocket and stroked it from time to time, tracing her father's name with her fingertips.

Virginia Chen: Her Book

All our young Chinese men have been called up to be counted and accounted for. They gathered them together in huge crowds. Men with hoods moved among those crowds of young men – sons, brothers, even fathers from our community. They pointed to those who were guilty of being anti-Japanese, friends of the British, people who worked for the British. The worst was that some of the men with hoods were from our own community. Some were Singapore Japanese who returned with the invaders. We were told about those betrayers who were our own men. 'True citizens of Syonan,' they say. This is what these creatures say we must call Singapore – Syonan. In the end so many young men were taken, not only the ones who were pointed at by the men in hoods. No one quite knows how many, but it was enough to quieten any sense of revolt in the city. They say tens of thousands. I heard one story that hundreds were driven into the sea to drown. Uncle Chu told me a story he had heard that thousands were taken out to sea in an old wrecked ship, which was sunk underneath them.

But at least Simon Chen got away before they came for him or he was caught. We had some arguments in those last days but now there is so much he said with which I agree. I feel now he is right in his attitude to the British *tuans* and the way in which they have let us down. He is right when he says things will never be the same if – when – we win back our city from these creatures.

I am so very relieved now that Simon Chen has gone up on the mainland. While he was here he took such risks. He dealt in the black market and sometimes got too near the Japanese soldiers. Sometimes they would sell to the soldiers goods that have come into their hands through the European exodus. Let us not say the word 'looting'. (The penalty for looting is instant execution.) The soldiers get things very cheaply, of course, so they have nothing about which they can complain. But sometimes they lose their tempers and seize the goods anyway. (They might even shoot or knife the seller.) The uncles, traders ever, urged Simon on. But they stayed in the shadows themselves.

Simon talked about groups in the jungle, armed and led by the British, who sabotage the Japanese. 'They have guns, weapons,' he said, his eyes gleaming. 'They can kill these snakes.' So now he has gone. I think he might be safer out there than he was here, roaming the streets of Singapore with his bulging rucksack. Simon is lucky still to be alive.

I think it is more important than ever before to keep this book but it occurs to me now that I should keep it hidden. I have a good place. One doesn't know what will happen day by day and there is sufficient to hang me in these pages. I must be very careful now because of Sylvie. She is settling down quite well, quite relishes calling me Jin Kee, and is a great companion for Grandmother. We have had to register the family with the authorities, so her new papers were essential. So she is now officially my sister. Some nights she cries and moans in her sleep (not surprising!) but there is little I can do about that. Nightmares are perhaps the price of survival.

# Chapter Fifteen

## The Time Between

As a year, then another, passed at the shophouse, life settled down to some kind of routine. Jin Kee became involved in the shop with Uncle Chu and Uncle Wo, trading not just in curios but in everything they could get their hands on, new or not new at all. She also busied herself selling the contents of Sylvie's boxes and everything she herself could spare. The money went to the society dedicated to supporting the jungle men. The societies themselves were hard-pressed, as the Japanese authorities were demanding vast sums of money from the Chinese in reparation for daring formerly to be enemies of the Nippon Empire.

The rationing based on the family registration bit very hard as the Western allies blockaded the supply routes. Uncle Chu knew about this as, after curfew some nights, he visited his friend Mr Wang who had a wireless. The increasing shortage of food in the markets was, said Uncle Chu, a warning. Things would get worse. *Very much worse!* They should stockpile everything they could put their hands on for the days to come.

Jin Kee insisted that Sylvie did lessons every day, working with her through Simon Chen's early schoolbooks in maths and science, and reading the old-fashioned English story-books on the grandmother's shelves. They came upon a small book with a single poem in it. *The Song of Hiawatha* by Longfellow. Sylvie took two weeks to learn this off by heart and would chant it for Uncle Wo, who clapped his hands, chuckling wildly at her efforts.

She got Sylvie to read out loud to the grandmother from the old *Picturegoer* annuals. This made the old woman laugh and ask for a repetition of details about her favourite stars.

Through this time Sylvie also learned off by heart all the songs that blared out from the grandmother's gramophone. Her favourite was about a blue moon which saw you standing alone without a dream and without a love. They had to play the gramophone quietly these days, as songs in English were banned.

Joining in the fun, the grandmother got it into her head that Sylvie should learn Hokkien. Jin Kee murmured that perhaps Mandarin, being higher class and more generally spoken, would be more useful. Both she and Simon had been made to learn Mandarin at school as well as English. The old woman waved her hand at this and started a painstaking process. She would make Sylvie collect a tray of objects from her room and they would spend the day pointing and repeat-ing, pointing and repeating. Sylvie tried, but none of the words seemed to lodge properly in her head, even though day-today phrases about food and the playing of the gramophone welded themselves into easy poetry in her mouth.

During these first two years an uneasy quiet settled on the city. People, as far as they could, went about their business. Barbed wire often stopped them going where they would in their own city. Trading still proceeded, much of it barter now as the new Japanese currency held very flimsy value. The real price of everything climbed steadily. With the destruction of the docks the secure hum of trade inwards and outwards, to and from this ancient trading city, had come to a clanging stop. Rice, quite plentiful at first, became poorer and poorer in quality. The farm produce, always so abundant, became scarce as the conquerors regulated movement across the Straits into the peninsula and creamed off the best for their own purposes.

Just once Jin Kee and Uncle Chu managed to get out to Uncle Chu's first father-in-law's farm and return unscathed with a load of pineapples and coconuts. Virginia explained that Uncle Chu had married twice. Each wife died within a year. After that he decided that remaining wifeless was safest for all concerned. They tried to get to the farm another time and came back beaten black and blue, their loaded cart confiscated by prying, greedy guards.

Virginia Chen: Her Book
As time goes on we, like many others in our city, have to manage on less and less food. Even that which is available is of very poor quality. You see more beggars in the street; more people with the stigmata of disease. Sicknesses that were under control are now rife. Those

who aren't in favour with the conquerors, have access to very little indeed. It is only Uncle Chu with his friend Mr Wang, with their shady contacts, who help us to manage to raise ourselves above starvation level. Rumours are rife in this city, but the wise discount any optimism. This war is a very long haul.

More than once, in the night, Sylvie was woken by Jin Kee stepping over her pallet and going into the middle room and talking to someone. The first time she sat up and eased the door open a crack, she saw Jin Kee and Simon Chen knee to knee, talking in loud whispers. As she talked, Jin Kee was decanting bottles of tablets into cardboard boxes and stuffing them in a rucksack.

Simon looked darker. His broad face had narrowed. His smooth hands were rough and calloused. His hair was longer, kept in place by a dark green sweatband wound round and round his head. Sylvie longed to burst through the door and greet him, pleased that he was safe, that his head was not up on a pole. But she did not. The old Sylvie, who had lived in Leonie Hill Road, would have done this. But the Sylvie who had lived for so long now in this house of restraint desisted. Jin Kee would tell her in good time.

The next night as she settled down under her net, she asked about him. 'How is he, Simon Chen?'

'I think he is well. He is well away from this strangled city.'

'He was here last night.'

In the dark, she could hear the rustling as Jin Kee tucked in her mosquito net. 'He was visiting.'

'Won't the Japanese catch him?'

'He is too wily. Like the jungle tiger. They do not see him in the bright light.'

'Why was he here?'

'He was here for supplies.'

'I saw you giving him the tablets. Was that all he wanted?'

'He wanted other things.'

'Did he get them?'

'You would have to ask Uncle Chu about that. He was downstairs making parcels.'

The day after Simon's third visit Uncle Chu vanished. For two days Jin Kee went around with a grim face and Uncle Wo sat in the corner of the shop wrapped up in his own thoughts. He did not look up when Sylvie came in. Sylvie sat beside him and thought of Uncle Chu feeding her with chocolate as though she were a little bird. The grandmother played British military music on her gramophone. It was very loud. Jin Kee had to persuade her, very politely, to turn it down.

And two nights after the removal of Uncle Chu, Jin Kee was playing mah-jong with her grandmother. Sylvie was playing on the floor with Ayoshi. There was a clattering of feet on the stairs and the door burst open. The room was filled with growling voices and green uniforms. There were only two men but they seemed like more.

Jin Kee frowned, began to protest. The younger soldier used the hand not holding the bayonet to pull her to her feet by her hair. He made her bow. The grandmother stood up in front of her chair. Jin Kee whispered through the side of her mouth, 'Bow, Sylvie, bow, for goodness' sake. Make Nana bow.'

Sylvie, Ayoshi still in her hand, bowed, her nose nearly on her stomach, as she had been shown. The grandmother looked at the older soldier then, very stiffly, bowed very deeply. Then the older soldier growled and sang in his language, spitting words at their bent backs. The younger soldier poked Sylvie's doll with his bayonet, speared it, and started talking excitedly to his superior.

Through the corner of her eye Sylvie was horrified to see the grandmother haul herself upright. She waited for the one with the bayonet to strike. Then the grandmother spoke, her gargles and singing tones matching those of the older soldier. Sylvie caught her breath as she heard the words *karayuki-san*. There was a short burst of laughter and the doll was dropped again near Sylvie's hands.

The older man spoke to the grandmother, then said something more to Jin Kee. He looked at the family registration papers. Through the corner of her eye Sylvie saw him bow his head slightly in the direction of the grandmother. The door clashed and they were alone.

Sylvie sat on the floor and clutched at the doll, whose soft woollen insides were pouring from her wound. Jin Kee helped her grandmother to her chair and they murmured together. Jin Kee turned to Sylvie. 'My grandmother says that her cousin Chu has been sent to his ancestors by the *Kempai Tai* at their torture rooms at the YMCA. They went for Mr Wang but he got away. They accused them of spying with the wireless set and of sending guns to the men in the hills. It seems that in the end Uncle Chu was too weak to be useful to them. His ancestors spared him the pain. So they came for me.'

'But they didn't take you.'

Jin Kee put a hand on her grandmother's shoulder. 'He recognised Ayoshi. She is a doll by a famous maker. And my grandmother talked to the officer in her mother's language, which was also his. He tells her his name is Captain Kageoki. She talks of the *karayuki-san*, the Japanese women who came to Singapore from Japan. Her mother was one of these. Do you remember the photograph she showed you? She was a countrywoman of the captain. Grandmother tells him I am an ignorant slut who has the misfortune of a European father and am much hated by the zealots who claim Singapore for China. And you, as my little sister, are likewise polluted. You have the misfortune to have me as *onesan*, older sister.'

Sylvie frowned, trying to understand.

'Do you see, Sylvie? Grandmother gave him a choice: me at the YMCA, being made to tell the *Kempai Tai* about Simon, or me beneath both their contempts as a half-breed.'

'So you are all right?'

Jin Kee laughed and shook her head. 'It is the lesser of evils, dear Sylvie.'

Sylvie shook her head.

'The officer, Mr Kageoki, has said you and I are to be ready tomorrow, as they will come to intern us, to put us behind bars.'

'To prison? Can't we run away, like Simon?'

Jin Kee shook her head. 'Not you and I, Sylvie. That way lies certain death. And I promised I'd take care of you, remember?'

\* \* \*

Later that night, they had a visit from Mr Wang. First of all he bowed to Jin Kee and thanked her for the help that she had given the comrades in the country. Then he told them they must pack as much as they could, as the camp where they would be taken, in Sime Road now, not Changi, was bereft of any comfort. He reached into his pocket and handed Jin Kee twelve gold coins, telling her to stitch them under their clothes. Also a roll of Dutch guilders. 'They use these in the camp.'

'He says we must pack in rings, Sylvie,' Jin Kee translated. 'The most essential things we must tie very close to us, then less essential things and less and so on, but to take as much as we can, as it will help us inside the prison. He hears of many things. He says the Dutch women have even taken in their sideboards and their sewing machines. Many things.'

Sylvie looked round the exotic, cluttered room. 'We don't have a sewing machine.'

'No, but we can take needles and thread and buttons and cloth. And lots of clothes. And books, because now you will really have time for study,' Jin Kee said gaily. 'And shoes. We will pack them in one of Grandmother's boxes.' She pulled out a carved box that stood underneath the window bench.

Sylvie looked down at her stained white tunic and black trousers.

Jin Kee shook her head. 'No Chinese maiden now. Another disguise. You will truly be my sister, a fully fledged *stengah*. Now no one must know otherwise or they will take you away from me and I will not be able to look after you.'

They packed 'in rings', as Mr Wang had prescribed, the

last ring being parcels of cloth which might or might not get through. The inner circles were more essential and they tied them next to their skin. They packed the rest of the things into the carved box. Jin Kee made Sylvie put on three vests and three dresses. She washed the oil from her hair and combed it down in its fringe, but she could do nothing about her skin, which was more golden now than it had ever been.

But the next day the officers did not come back. The dresses became patchy with sweat and Sylvie had to remove two of them.

The day of Uncle Chu's elaborate funeral came and went and still the soldiers did not come.

'Is it a joke?' said Sylvie to Jin Kee that night at bedtime. 'Are they playing a joke?'

Then the next morning the grandmother and Jin Kee were at the window. Sylvie was playing on the floor with Ayoshi, now neatly mended by Jin Kee. At eight o'clock a small truck drew up and parked tightly on the pavement before the shop. The grey-haired soldier, Captain Kageoki, jumped out. The driver was a different man from last time.

'It's time.' Jin Kee turned to Sylvie. 'They are here, Sylvie. We have to go now. We must go.'

They peered down at the officer. He looked up, bowed slightly to the grandmother, who bowed back.

'We must go,' repeated Jin Kee. She took her daybook from its place among the books and climbed on to a stool beside the door. She removed a papered panel in the wall above the door and slipped the daybook inside.

Sylvie walked slowly across to the old woman and put her

arms round her and pushed her face into her shoulder. At first, the old woman stiffened. Sylvie could feel her softening, the light touch of the grandmother's hand on her shoulder. Then she pulled the two extra dresses, crumpled as they were, over her head.

'We must go.' Jin Kee pulled Sylvie away. 'Come on.'

Uncle Wo was loading up the carved box, unhindered by the officer, who was looking up at the window, at the old woman. Finally, his gaze came down to Jin Kee and Sylvie, who were standing by the car.

He stepped towards them and Sylvie flinched. 'So!' he said. 'Very lucky not at YMCA.'

Jin Kee bowed very low, pulling Sylvie into a bow beside her.

'Honourable grandmother speak truth. Records say. Stupid foreigners. Safer in camp.'

Jin Kee bowed even lower.

'Now into truck!' He stepped in to the passenger seat.

The driver watched as Jin Kee took Sylvie under her arms and jumped her into the truck. Uncle Wo hurried out with a box ladder so that Jin Kee herself could climb into the truck without too much loss of dignity.

The door of the truck slammed, the engine roared and people in the street who were averting their gaze allowed themselves to watch as, in a swirl of dust, the Japanese removed more people from their midst. The whisper now was that all the Eurasians were being taken. Their usefulness to the new administration was at an end. Their loyalty had always been questionable.

It was only as Sylvie was settling in a corner of the truck that she made out the bundled figure of a woman with a narrow white face who sat in the opposite corner of the truck. Words came out of the face. 'Well then, how did you two manage to stay out so long? It must be two years.' A hand, encased in lace gloves, was thrust forward for them to shake. 'Snowdrop Raven. You may call me Snowie, Miss Snowie, that's what I prefer.' The voice was tightly elocuted and thin as a flute. The grip on Sylvie's hand was like a tiny vice. 'How do you do?'

Sylvie rescued her hand, sat back and took a closer look at Miss Snowie Raven's face, which was a network of creases and wrinkles, the hair hanging in straggly orange clumps beneath the upturned brim of a childish straw hat. She started to laugh.

'Sylvie!' warned Jin Kee, and started to laugh herself. She gasped out her own name, grasped the lace-gloved hand firmly and then introduced Sylvie.

Miss Snowie Raven chuckled. This made them all laugh and, as the swaying truck threw them on to each other's knees, and into each other's parcels, it seemed as though they laughed all the way out of the city, past all the checkpoints to the edge of the jungle and to Sime Road Camp.

In front of the truck Captain Kageoki stared straight ahead, ignoring the growls of disgust emanating from his driver at the antics of their passengers. They'd heard many things in this truck, including the moans of the dying, but they'd never heard laughter that seemed to sustain itself on its own strength.

# Chapter Sixteen

## The Charge of Angels

A tall man in a tight turban lounged by the wire at the prison gate. For a moment Sylvie thought it was the *jaga* from her father's office. What was he doing with that gun? But the man turned round and it wasn't the *jaga*. His face was altogether fatter, his mouth altogether thinner.

Virginia Chen's voice whispered in her ear. 'Remember now, you are Sylvie and I am Virginia. As English as you like.'

She looked up and saw, squashed into a circle of waving trees, row upon row of huts surrounded by a high fence. Clustered about these, in the open square towards the centre, bowing over *chungkols* in some kind of gardens were what seemed like hundreds and hundreds of women and children. Sylvie drew closer to Virginia, who was struggling with the carved box. Captain Kageoki barked an order and the driver, sulky-mouthed, jumped out of the truck and took it from her.

The Sikh guard was head and shoulders taller than Captain Kageoki. He bowed low and checked the paper handed to him by the captain. Then he led them through the gates and made his way to the third hut in the line. As he passed, the women and children about the camp bowed like flowers cast low before the wind. Then, rising from their bows, they raised curious eyes to the strangers making their way from the gate.

Most of them were thin and wiry. They wore very little: mostly shorts and improvised suntops. Their headgear – worn against the blazing sun – was a fine assortment: conventional straws, coolie cones, battered *sola topees*, cloths tied peasant-wise, strange things constructed from shredded attap leaves. Many were barefoot, but some wore clumsy mules made of some kind of thick rubber.

Some of them started to walk towards the newcomers. Others rushed to help with the box.

The Sikh went into the hut and came out with a tall woman, thin as a crow. Her hair was very severely cut. Her face was pale compared with the women who were drawing ever closer. She bowed deeply to Captain Kageoki, who nodded his acknowledgement. 'Miss Chen and her sister, Dr Renhardt. And also Miss Snowdrop. Perhaps you have a corner for them?'

She bowed again.

The captain turned to Virginia. 'And here you see, Miss Chen, the generosity of the Nippon finding safe haven for the deserted women of the cowardly servants of the British Empire.'

'But my daddy—' started Sylvie.

Virginia forced Sylvie's head down in a bow. 'Thank you, Mr Kageoki.' She bowed herself, and stayed bowing until the captain had returned to his truck and driven away.

The Sikh, no longer respectful, held his gun flat before them. 'Now you go inside with this woman. Quickly!' He took a step towards her.

'Quickly!' repeated the doctor. 'Come on. We'll give you a hand.' Suddenly there were women taking their things and their precious box. Virginia started to protest but bit her lip. Surely these women would not steal their things. They were not looters. The doctor was not so sure. 'Mrs Corbridge, be careful with that. Straight to Hut Five.' The woman so called shot a poisoned look at the doctor, but followed meekly enough. As they walked down the hut lines small children came to stare and women stopped their work on battered rows of vegetables to check out the strangers.

When they got inside, the blast of heat reflected from the iron roof met them like a ship's furnace. The smell of dust and sweat unrelieved by the fragrance of oils made it a different, more deadening place than the grandmother's room above the shophouse. Sylvie thought it was worse than the coolie hut across the yard from the house at Hibiscus Lodge. Much worse.

They found themselves inside a long hut with wooden walls, which, like the roof, had gaps through which you could see the outside world and through which the hot sun could easily find a way. There was a central aisle, on either side of which was a raised platform, with small mats and markers to show possession. The hut was now filling with its women.

Each woman went to sit in her place, and stared boldly at the newcomers.

There was one unfilled space by the wall.

'Ah yes,' said the doctor. 'Poor Mrs Simpson and Miss Mills. We lost them yesterday. The place is clear. We divided their goods today. Thank goodness they both left wills. That saved a lot of bother.'

Sylvie looked at the narrow space and shuddered. Goods divided. What did that mean?

'This will be very nice,' said Virginia.

'There should be room enough for three if you squeeze a bit.' She paused. 'We have a . . . woman, Mrs Lamont in Hut Two. Perhaps she is more your . . . well, perhaps we should see if there is room there.'

'Do you mean Eurasian, Doctor?' said Miss Snowie Raven sharply, taking her hat off and shaking her head to cool it. 'No. We three came together and we will stay together.'

'Well, I thought perhaps . . . Miss Chen would be more comfortable. It would be easier.'

Virginia exchanged glances with Miss Snowie. 'You will excuse me if I say that I do not get on with, or necessarily gravitate towards Eurasians, Dr Renhardt, any more than I get on with Chinese like my grandmother, or French people like my father, or English people like my teachers' friends and employers. It all depends on who they are and how they are with me.'

The doctor rose to her full six feet of height. The fact that she was all skin and bone made her seem even taller, like a great heron. 'It was merely a thought, Miss Chen. Now, ladies, if you will stow Miss Chen's numerous parcels, and Miss Chen, if you could release that child from two layers of clothing before she asphyxiates . . .' She turned to go.

'Doctor?' said Virginia, starting to unfasten some of the small parcels she had stowed about herself.

'Yes?'

'I brought some medicines, some vitamin pills, some other things.'

The doctor's demeanour changed. 'Medicines?' she said. 'What did you bring?'

'To be honest I don't quite know. My cousin Simon Chen – he's Chinese, not Eurasian you'll be pleased to hear – obtained a parcel of medicines from Maynards during the upheaval. There are some M & Bs there, a bit of quinine, I think.'

The doctor sniffed. 'I was told there was looting.'

'Do you want this looted medicine or not?' said Miss Snowie, watching the proceedings beady-eyed.

'Of course I do. The M & Bs are like gold dust. We need something to fight these infections.' The doctor had to stand while Virginia raked among her things.

'There!' It was a box inside a canvas bag. She gave it to the doctor. 'It might be some help.'

The doctor poked among the contents. 'No doubt about that, Miss Chen,' she said gruffly. 'They'll be pleased about this at the hospital. Sorry about blethering on about Mrs Lamont. The woman's an infernal nuisance and I thought you might get her off our backs a little. Mistake, of course. Damned illiberal of me.' She paused in the doorway, a spidery figure outlined in the white light of the midday sun. 'The parcel showed some forethought. I thank you for that. The child –' she went on – 'we have a school here. Some very good people teach the children. Devil makes use of idle hands, you know. No better place to see his work than in here.'

After she had gone, the women in the hut relaxed. A woman who said she was Mrs Grassington introduced them to the others. Mrs Warren, Mrs Morris, Miss Lomax, Mrs Lou Granger – these were the names Sylvie could hang on to.

There were eager questions about Singapore and any news from the outside. Mrs Josie Warren commented on how they'd managed to stay out so long. 'Two years!' she said. 'You've missed the worst of it. This place is paradise compared with Changi. Two years in that hole before we got to this green and pleasant land.'

'Paradise!' said Miss Lomax. 'Now there's a joke.' Sylvie intercepted some sidelong glances at the heap of cases and parcels, but no one asked what else they had brought besides the precious medicines.

Mrs Morris heard Sylvie call Virginia Jin Kee. She said, 'Jin Kee? That is unusual.'

'It is a pet name,' said Sylvie. 'Her real name is Virginia, Virginia Chen. You can call her Miss Chen.'

The women turned their gaze on Sylvie as surprised as though a monkey or a marmoset had spoken.

'There!' said Miss Snowie Raven cheerfully. 'The child has it in a nutshell. Now can we unpack?'

* * *

Virginia decided not to unpack the box before all the staring eyes. That would be too unkind. Instead, she pushed it hard against the slatted wall so it took as little space as possible. From her own parcels she unpacked a rug on which she and Sylvie could both lie, and a rolled extra rug for Sylvie. And their mosquito nets.

'New mosquito nets!' groaned Miss Lomax. 'What I would give for a mosquito net!' Sylvie unpacked her own little case and put Ayoshi and the lion puppet side by side on her rolled blanket. Her white silk coat gleamed in the bottom of her bag and her mother's pearls rattled in the side pocket.

Beside her, Miss Snowie Raven was unpacking her modest pack. On top of her bedroll was a thick book with a curling leather cover, its pages somewhat mildewed. On top of this she placed her straw hat.

The hut began to empty. The women wandered off to their various jobs and rendezvous. The three newcomers were soon left on their own. Virginia got up to follow the women. 'I will just look around this place, Sylvie; see what we have to do here, how things happen. I don't know what things mean here, and will need to find out.'

Miss Snowie Raven sat down cross-legged in her place and leaned over and touched the lion puppet. 'This is a strange object. What might this be, Miss Sylvie?'

'It's my Singa Pura. My lionfish.' Sylvie held it up and spread it out so that it made a black shadow in the air. 'Look, here's where Amah mended the holes with bits from my gloves.'

'It's a very old, very fine lion.'

'Virginia and I got it from the puppet man in the Great World. He'd made new ones so he gave me this one. It was to bring me great luck.'

'Well, dear, it kept you out of Changi, I suppose. Although this place is somewhat grim, I must say. So what will you do with this?'

'Well, I make up this play with him and Ayoshi – that is my doll here. They meet in a place by the sea, have many adventures and live happily ever after.'

'And you can do all that without even a stage? Or lights?'

'The puppet man had a stage and a strong light. The lion in his play could fly. I just pretend.'

Miss Raven nodded. 'It is an old, old art.' She suddenly kneeled up on her mat, folded her hands together and bowed her head. Sylvie held her breath; for a second it seemed that the whole of the camp, the whole of Singapore, held its breath while this little woman bowed her head.

Then she raised her head and the world breathed again. She brushed one hand against the other as though she were disposing of great care.

'What were you doing?'

'Don't you know?'

'It looked funny. The world became still.'

'I was praying. Haven't you seen praying before? Have you never been to church?'

'Yes. But they are noisy places. You made the place quiet.' She pulled Ayoshi on to her knee, and straightened her dress. 'What did you do when you prayed?'

'I said part of a psalm. "For he shall give his angels charge over thee: to keep thee in all thy ways." And I asked God to take care of you in your innocence and all of us in our pain.'

'I feel no pain.' Sylvie frowned.

'Did you see the thin faces? The hungry eyes? The veils of care?'

Sylvie shook her head. The people in here were no thinner, no more hungry-looking than many people on the streets of the city. Perhaps they were a little dustier. Perhaps their eyes were veiled. She had not had time to notice.

Miss Raven patted the wooden slats of the bed space. 'Here, and there where you're sitting, two women lay. And they died of the sickness that is taking so many, here and in the city, and upcountry where I was before.'

'Did the Japanese find you there? Upcountry?'

'So they did, in the end. The people whom I was caring for quite sensibly ran back to their *kampongs*. I stayed there a very long time until the soldiers finally came. I think they were so surprised they just put me in a truck and brought me to the city.'

Sylvie looked into Ayoshi's black, button eyes. 'I saw a dead lady on the quayside, bleeding blood. And I saw the soldiers cut off three heads.'

Miss Raven closed her eyes for a moment. 'Oh dear. How awful for you.' There was a stillness in the place again.

'And I saw the soldiers hurt my friend Virginia, and I heard them kill a man at the hospital.' It took her a second to realise she had said something wrong.

'Your friend?'

'My sister, Virginia,' said Sylvie hurriedly. 'Virginia.'

'Well,' said Miss Raven, 'I can pray for all of these people if you want me to.'

'You said about angels having charge of us. How can an angel have charge of me here?'

'Well, dear, in truth I don't really know. Perhaps He has sent you an angel in your . . . sister, Virginia, who most definitely has charge of you. And perhaps too in some way He has put you in my charge.'

'And you, Miss Snowie? Are you in my charge?'

'I am not sure, but I think it may be something like that.'

Sylvie nodded slowly, quite pleased about this.

Then the hut filled with a dark energy as Virginia came through the door, bringing dust and hard bars of pure sun in with her. Her face was grave. 'We have come to a terrible place, Sylvie. These poor women . . .' She looked at her parcels, frowning.

'Go slowly, my dear,' said Miss Snowie Raven. 'Do nothing in a hurry. Your first duty is to yourself and this child. Your . . . sister, is it?'

Virginia's glance dropped to the Bible. 'That is rather an odd thing for a Christian to say, Miss Snowie. What about St Francis? Or the parable of the loaves and the fishes?'

Miss Snowie Raven frowned. 'You admonish me with justification, my dear. But a month in the wilderness out there on my own rather refined my notions of survival. Think of it. Before you came, they had nothing and were getting on with it. Now . . . well.'

'Miss Snowie was on her own for years upcountry before the soldiers came,' volunteered Sylvie.

Virginia looked hard at the other woman, then nodded. 'Perhaps you are right, Miss Snowie. There will be plenty of time to think about what to do with all this.'

But later, in the long queue for their midday meal of thin soup and a thimbleful of grey rice, the decision was taken from Virginia's hands. Dr Renhardt invited her to Hut Three, which was the dispensary attached to the larger hospital hut, for what she called 'induction'. Sylvie went too. There were three other women who were introduced as 'the committee', who in effect managed the camp for the Japanese. The fourth woman was Mrs Grassington, their acquaintance from Hut Five.

Dr Renhardt talked about the importance of 'things in common'. And that there were some very selfish people who held all their goods to them and used them for trade, which was frowned on. So, of course they were delighted with the parcel of medicines, which would indeed save lives, at least in the short term. Now, if Miss Chen had any other goods that would contribute to the common weal, and felt she could hand them over, it would be highly appreciated. Then they would be distributed as and when needed by the management committee.

'Well,' said Virginia, 'I thought from the first I should do something with the stuff. I brought as much as I could so that Sylvie and I would cope with whatever—'

'What have you got?' said one woman, almost too quickly.

'There are some clothes, extra shoes, combs, needles, threads, scissors, some cloth, though we had to leave the biggest bale behind.'

'Needles!' said the other woman. 'We have to pay one dollar for a single needle.'

'There are some notebooks and schoolbooks for Sylvie. Some lipstick. An extra blanket. Ribbons. Some towels. There is some Marmite, because Sylvie likes it on bread.' She stopped. Would there be bread here? And she was not going to tell about the gold coins Mr Wang had made them sew into their clothes. 'And there are some cigarettes. Oh, and some soap.'

'Do you smoke?' asked someone.

Virginia shook her head.

'Right!' Dr Renhardt looked up from the list she was making. 'Any spare clothes? Needles? Threads? Keep the basic necessities for yourself. Of course, you must only give this willingly. Only remember that there are those here much worse off than you – women and children who came down the peninsula with only the clothes on their backs. You have already declared the medicines. The rest is your choice.'

'The Dutch women rather tend to cling mightily to their possessions. They pay others to work for them. That is not seen here as playing the game,' put in the woman who'd asked about the cigarettes. 'We like to do things better here.'

Sylvie leaned into Virginia so that she could feel the weight of her body. She wanted Virginia to know she was there and she didn't have to do what these women said unless she wanted to.

'I will think about this,' said Virginia. 'I have just arrived and Sylvie and I need to find our feet, to see how we will cope in this place.'

Dr Renhardt sniffed. 'That is up to you, Miss Chen. But we must remember that we are a community here. We care for each other.'

Virginia and Sylvie walked back from the meeting just ahead of Mrs Grassington. 'What will you do?' asked Sylvie. 'Give them all our stuff?'

'We will sleep on it,' said Virginia.

Mrs Grassington scurried to catch up with them. 'I hope you won't think Dr Renhardt too severe,' she gasped. 'She's a bit of an old stick but she means very well.'

A work detail of women, hauling a kind of sledge loaded with sawn wood, looked curiously at them as they came into the worn, sandy *padang*. They were mostly young and dressed in shorts or brief sarongs with suntops. They were wiry and brown, and two of them had dry, cracked lips. One had sores on her face. At the gate they dropped their burden and bowed deeply to the two Sikh guards, who laughed and waved them on.

'Do you always have to bow? Even to those Indians?' said Virginia.

'Always, always,' said Mrs Grassington. 'A few of us with bigger ideas got a good slapping for it in the early days. It was murder at Changi. They are very keen on the bowing. We bow to the Sikhs and Koreans as well as the Japanese. The Sikhs and Koreans bow to the Japanese, or *they* get a good slapping. Then they make us bow to them or we get a good slapping. We had a meeting about it and decided we would always bow but, while bowing, think very disrespectful thoughts.'

Virginia laughed. 'A very British compromise.'

Mrs Grassington looked her up and down. 'I suppose it is,' she said. 'Perhaps it's different—'

'No, it's not,' said Sylvie, picking up her very clear meaning. 'We're British. Just as British as you.'

'Yes, yes, of course you are,' said Mrs Grassington smoothly. They were back in the hut, which was empty except for Miss Snowie Raven, who was sitting cross-legged on her mat, reading her dog-eared Bible.

Mrs Grassington walked with Virginia to her place. 'Now, my dear, perhaps I should enlighten you as to the market value of these goods of yours. Charity is a fine thing but charity, they say, begins at home, don't you know? Trading is one of the most important things that goes on here . . .'

Virginia Chen: Letter to Albert Taft

I am resorting now to one of Sylvie's exercise books for this. Albert asked me for letters so I intend to write him letters and post them to his village when I get out. He made a great appeal to me, although I do not know whether it was the love-at-first-sight affair that he mentioned.

Dear Albert,

I wonder where you are now. Safe, I hope, with no troubles. That evening with you was, I think, the last carefree evening of my life, and often in the two years since, I have thought of it and can still remember your face so I think you must be safe. And when you mentioned love-at-first-sight I was a little shocked. But every day since your face has been with me and I think if we had had a little time we could have been much more to each other. It is this war, always this war. You asked me to write to you so here goes. It might be a very long time until I post it, but still . . .

Sylvie (my little sister!) and I find ourselves in this dusty place far from the city on the edge of the jungle. It is the women's internment camp. There is a men's internment camp not far away. We are to be here for the duration. The bed spaces here with their pitiful heaps of worldly goods tell their own story. The prisoners have endured time in Changi, a very fearsome place, I think. Then they were brought here. Some of these are women from upcountry, and had been wandering round destitute in those last days before the defeat. Some had been picked up at sea, survivors from bombed boats 'rescued' by the Japanese with everything they owned on their backs.

It is a strange atmosphere here. Warm and yet desperately threatening at the same time. When I think of what these women have gone through I am very sad.

Dear Albert, writing to you cheers me up and makes me think of better times.

Your friend Virginia Chen

# Chapter Seventeen

## The Women

The newcomers' first few days in camp were very busy. The day after their arrival there was a hut meeting, run very efficiently by Mrs Grassington. She introduced the three of them again and made some suggestions as to ways in which they might make a contribution to the community of the camp. 'Miss Chen, being fit and strong, it's pretty certain you'll be incorporated in the wood and water rota. We are currently short of one strong pair of hands on the wood. Now, what else can you do?'

Virginia looked at her blankly. 'What d'you mean?'

'Do you sing, do you dance, do you paint? What d'you do on the outside?'

'Well, nothing since the occupation. Unless perhaps you count staying alive. But before that I was a teacher. I taught children at home. I helped in the hospital . . .'

Mrs Grassington frowned. 'Full complement of teachers at the moment. Nurses too, until one of them gets sick.'

'Well, I don't sing, I don't dance.'

'Pity. We have a little concert coming up – a skit on British monarchs.'

'I know a good rhyme about King Alfred,' offered Miss Snowie. 'I used to think it quite comical.'

'Good, good, that's the ticket. And you, Miss Chen, we'll just assume perhaps you'll sign up for the wood and the water for the time being.' It seemed there was no option not to volunteer.

Mrs Grassington went on to pass an important message to the women from the management committee about clearing up the main areas of the camp, and the inside of the huts. 'Our dear commandant, His Imperial Majesty, has said we are a shame to our race, insisting on living like pigs as we do.'

The women groaned. Miss Lomax, sitting cross-legged in her bed space, clapped her hands together very slowly, three times. 'Fat choice. Good old Cloth Ears. Tell him to get us brooms and soap, boxes for our stuff. That would be a start.' The others shrugged. Virginia thought they must have heard this argument many, many times.

'Well, ladies, it's Hobson's choice. Seems Cloth Ears has a bigwig coming to see what a wonderful time we have in this holiday camp. So we have to do it, soap or not. Otherwise someone'll get a slap. Or they'll cut the food by half.'

Miss Lomax let out a wild laugh. The other women muttered and moaned but there was no real dissent.

Mrs Grassington turned to Sylvie. 'Now, young lady, what about you? We have our little school here. You'll soon fit in.'

'You will like it there, dear,' said Mrs Granger. 'Children of your own age.'

Mrs Morris called across that Mrs Grassington was on the school committee and was very keen on that kind of thing.

Sylvie stared at her. She'd managed very well so far without children of her own age, thank you. 'No, thank you,' she said. 'I don't go to school. Me and Virginia will do our lessons like always.'

Virginia, who was re-sorting all the stuff in the wooden box, looked up at the sound of her name.

'You should go to school,' said Mrs Grassington. 'All children go to school. One of our great aims is we try for this normality for our children.'

'It's not normal for me. I have never been to school.'

Suddenly there was real tension in the room. 'Oh God, another bloody spoiled brat,' said Miss Lomax, lying back on her bed and closing her eyes. 'Lord save me from spoiled brats.'

Sylvie looked from one to the other. 'I don't go to school. I've never been to school,' she said. 'Never in all my life. I'm sorry.'

If the child had been properly defiant, Mrs Grassington could have handled it. She'd have given her a slap for her pains and the child would have learned the error of her ways. But this even, matter-of-fact tone was baffling. 'You must, Sylvie. It's a rule. All the children go to school. Even the Eurasians. Two hours a day.'

'*Even* the Eurasians?' Now Virginia spoke up. 'I'll continue her lessons, if you don't mind, Mrs Grassington. She will have her education in here as she had it outside.'

Mrs Grassington looked sharply at Virginia, then at the

carved box, which was now draped with two towels. 'You don't understand, Miss Chen. It's a matter of camp discipline. We cannot have the children growing into hobbledehoys.'

'I would not grow into a hobble-de— whatever you said,' said Sylvie, her eyes now filling with tears. She'd not cried – not in all this time. She blinked to stop herself.

Now Miss Snowie rose to her feet and adjusted her hat. 'Perhaps Sylvie and I can go and look at the school, Mrs Grassington? I could offer myself as teacher and Sylvie can offer herself as a pupil.' Her tone, mild as it was, brooked no refusal. She looked Sylvie deeply in the eye and marched to the door of the hut.

Sylvie looked at Virginia, who shrugged her shoulders and smiled. 'Go, Sylvie, go with Miss Snowie. She'll take care of you.'

Sylvie ran with a hop, skip and a jump to catch up with Miss Snowie. 'I don't want to go to school,' she said. 'Like I said to that woman, I don't go to school.'

'You should go,' said Miss Snowie calmly. 'You will probably learn no more than you would with your sister, perhaps less. But you should keep the peace in this instance. You need to keep your powder dry in a place like this. Save your fight for when it really matters.'

*Keep your powder dry.* Sylvie would remember that.

The school was an end section of a hut that was open on three sides to catch the breeze. There were rough joiner-made forms at which children kneeled or sat to write. When they raised their eyes, the children could see past the clumps of lalang and the sword grass, and through waving trees and the perimeter fence to the distant shimmer of water. Sometimes they caught sight of the sleek-tailed squirrels and the opulent yellow butterflies that hovered in the shrubs beyond the fence. In the canopy above an unseen army of birds and insects whirred away like a giant saw.

Gathered in the classroom there seemed to be a great crowd of children, some not much older than Feargal, and some much older than Sylvie. They all looked up with interest as Sylvie and Miss Snowie moved into the schoolroom space. Miss Snowie introduced herself and Sylvie to the teacher, a willowy woman with large eyes, who smiled eagerly at their approach.

'Ah, new blood!' she said, shaking both Miss Snowie and Sylvie very vigorously by the hand. 'I'm Mrs Wallace, today's teacher. Sylvie Chen?' she said. 'Is that . . . ? Are you . . . ?'

'Yes,' said Sylvie, staring at her defiantly.

'You would hardly know,' said the teacher with professional kindness. 'How old are you?'

'Eleven.'

'How lovely! Well, dear, you can go and sit beside Beryl Bridges in the corner. She's eleven and she's sick of being the only eleven-year-old in the class, is that not so, Beryl?'

Beryl stared at Sylvie with bright blue eyes through a fringe of greasy fair hair. She moved along the bench. The class started to buzz as Mrs Wallace and Miss Snowie conferred at the front.

Beryl looked greedily at the pristine notebook and pair of pencils that Sylvie had in her hand. 'Where d'ya get that?'

'I brought it in with me.'

'Brought it in? You're not from another camp? Like the Dutch?'

'No. I was in the city. They just came for us.'

Beryl whistled and tossed her head so that her long plait swished behind her. Sylvie noticed that the bottom of one of her front teeth was missing. 'Were you a spy?' said Beryl.

'No!' said Sylvie. 'They didn't come to get us at first – the Japanese. My family is Chinese, you see.'

'Eurasian, though, aren't you? It's different for them. They let three of your lot out of here yesterday. To go back to the city. My mum says you can never trust them anyway. One minute they're all over you, the next they're snuggling up to the Nips. Half of them are Nips' girlfriends.'

'It's not true. They're not.'

'It is. One got us put on half-rations 'cause she betrayed us to her Nip boyfriend.'

'It's not true.'

'It is. How would you know? You're just a—'

'What?' Sylvie turned and grabbed Beryl by the throat with such force that they both crashed to the floor. Then Beryl was on top of Sylvie, fingers digging into her throat. Sylvie brought up her knee in front of her and flexed, pushing the weight of the other girl off. Then it was her turn to be on top of Beryl, her knees on Beryl's upper arms. She pounded away at her face for all she was worth. When she got tired of pounding she pulled Beryl's long plait as though she were playing tug of war.

She closed her eyes. She was back in the hospital cupboard, hearing the thump as the soldiers kicked the man at the top of the stairs. Then she was aware of the other children around them shouting and Beryl screaming. The screaming of the people on the quayside. Her mother going up the gangway, dragging Feargal by the hand. Then hands were pulling her away and she could smell the musty lavender of Miss Snowie's black alpaca frock.

'Now then, Sylvie, what's this?' murmured Miss Snowie.

The willowy woman was kneeling beside Beryl, lifting her head and shoulders. She looked up. 'This won't do at all, Sylvie Chen. Miss Snowie, you should take that wildcat away and teach her some manners. There is no room for wildcats in here, miss. Education's a privilege. I suppose we can't expect any more from these families. Volatile temperaments.' Her eyes, cold now, met Miss Snowie's, expecting some kind of agreement. Mrs Wallace, the sister of a Methodist missionary from Penang, had heard of Miss Snowie Raven and her work on various parts of the peninsula. She'd been looking forward to getting to know her. A new face was such a treat in this stifling atmosphere of tense women. But now her confiding glance was met with a scowl.

Miss Snowie put an arm round the shaking Sylvie and shepherded her away, saying over her shoulder, 'I would advocate a bit of Christian tolerance, Mrs Wallace. This child has seen some terrible sights in these late times. Enough to make anyone wild.'

Sylvie's blood was coursing through her so hard that she thought it would bruise her skin from the inside. Sitting there astride the girl, punching away at her face, she'd felt really elated, happy even. As she was slapping that face she felt inside her the man who had slapped Virginia, and the soldiers bustling the poor Chinese in the corner before setting about them with their bayonets. She was breathing hard, feeling a stone melting inside her. She was not sorry she had hit Beryl Bridges. Not sorry at all.

'Expelled?' said Virginia. 'So soon?'

Miss Snowie sat down on her bed space, folded her legs underneath her and pulled her hat more closely on to her head. 'I'm afraid Sylvie set about another girl with a somewhat vengeful demeanour.'

'She called us names, our family,' said Sylvie. 'She said you could never trust us, that we were spies.'

'Us?' said Virginia.

'Us people with Chinese families.'

'But . . .' Virginia's glance met that of Miss Snowie. 'That was very unfair of her, very uncivilised. But still, you shouldn't hit people,' said Virginia.

'People hit you,' said Sylvie. 'They shot those men. They stamped on the face of that man in the hospital.'

A shadow of distaste passed across Virginia's face. She put her hands on Sylvie's shoulders and brought her own face close. Her touch was as hard as a slap. 'Don't *ever*, *ever* talk about what those dogs did as justification for what you may do.'

Sylvie held herself stiff, resisting for a moment, then pulled away and turned her back on Virginia.

Miss Snowie stirred on her lowly perch. 'Be careful, Sylvie. You too, Virginia. They infect us with their terrible spirits,' she said. 'If you two became bad friends then those bad ones have won. Turning the other cheek is the most powerful thing you can do. This puts you above, *outside* all these terrible things. It is different for them. It will stain them to the heart. For ever and amen.'

Virginia put a soft hand now on Sylvie's shoulder. 'Come on, Sylvie.'

Sylvie nodded slowly, then sat down in her own bed space and crossed her legs like Miss Snowie.

Miss Snowie beamed. 'That's better. Now then, we will make our own school for you. Two hours a day, Miss Chen? Mrs Wallace says this is what the children do. We can split it between us. I will take mathematics, science and geography and you can take English, French and biology. We will have to show the sanctimonious Mrs Wallace that we can manage without her. And those people on that blessed school committee rota of theirs.'

'I might manage the French. I can make up the exercises for that. But biology! I forgot all that straight after I did the exam.'

Miss Snowie nodded at the carved box against which Virginia was leaning. 'It seems the key to everything here is exchange. There must be people here with that knowledge in their heads. I'm sure someone will be agreeable to tutor Sylvie for, say, some soap, or some needles.'

'I'll find somebody,' said Virginia. 'So when will we start?'

'We'll start tomorrow,' said Miss Snowie firmly. 'Mathematics, then science, then you can do English and French. We'll rotate the subjects throughout the week.' She patted her mildewed Bible with one finger. 'They'll be begging her to join their school, soon. You believe me.'

'Stop!' said Sylvie. 'This is me you're talking about.'

'Yes,' said Virginia.

'I can't do all that work, every day.'

'You will surprise yourself, dear girl,' said Miss Snowie firmly.

Sylvie dropped back on the blanket and brought Ayoshi close to her face. 'It would have been easier, Ayoshi,' she said, 'to stay on that bench beside that rotten Beryl Bridges.'

Virginia returned to her list-making. Miss Snowie returned to her Bible. The air was hot and still. Somewhere a frog croaked and if you listened hard you could hear the flies buzz as they hovered in their hundreds, busy and engorged, over the latrines. The whack of a ball and the fizz of laughter filtered through the hut lines from the other side of the camp where some kind of bat-and-ball game was going on.

The buzzing calm was broken by the rumble of male voices and the shrill pipe of whistles. Mrs Grassington put her head round the door. 'Come on now. The Nips want to count us. Come on!' She shepherded them out of the door into the harsh light of midday. The women stood in even lines, standing one body space apart. The square was very full. As she passed along her line, Virginia noticed three women who were pregnant. They must be late arrivals like themselves, she thought. She looked at the soldiers with their loud voices and shuddered at the alternative.

The Sikh guards looked on as two Japanese soldiers walked along the line and pushed and pulled in vain to make these messy women conform to some military idea of order. Then both soldiers started to count.

Mrs Grassington whispered through the side of her mouth to Miss Snowie, 'Those Nips? Four Eyes and the Snake. Takes them ages. They can't keep numbers in their head, do you see?'

Miss Snowie, who as a young woman had taught in Japan, did not think this was so. But it did take the soldiers a long time, and the sun on the backs of the women started to burn. Two women started to sway. One woman fell down. No one moved to help her.

At last there seemed to be some agreement between the grumbling soldiers and one of them stood in front of the lines of women, his legs spread wide, his rifle upright before him. The other tramped back to the big building by the gate and in minutes was scuttling back behind two officers, one short, one tall. Sylvie recognised the tall officer as the one who had taken them from the grandmother's house: Captain Kageoki. The soldier Mrs Grassington had called the Snake barked something and all the women bowed. At another shouted word there was a mutual sigh of relief as they all stood up, easing their aching backs. One woman helped the collapsed woman to her feet.

A murmur rumbled through the assembled women as through the gate, a soldier on either side, walked a woman, head down. The shorter officer started to speak and the Snake barked out some kind of translation. Listening hard, Sylvie could make out something about the kindness of the Japanese and the overwhelming excellence of the Emperor and the hundred years of order they would bring to the poor bereft people of this island, exploited and robbed by their European masters. How the worthless women would all die as old women there behind the wire.

Then the woman was pushed forward. She had a purple bruise on her cheek and red marks on her legs. The shorter officer took a belt, which Four Eyes was holding, and it snaked up into the air and back again. The front row of women shrank inwards together like wheat in the wind. Then Sylvie could hear some words again. How this disgraceful, dishonourable woman had put letters in her belt and carried them to the men outside. Did they not know it was forbidden? There was kindness: the kind Nippon permitted messages. They had even allowed meetings between men and women. But these were secret messages, not between husband and wife but between strangers. This was forbidden. So this woman had been punished for this dishonourable act. Four Eyes pulled her forward and turned her to face the women, then he whispered hard in her ear and forced her head up. He barked in her ear again.

Captain Kageoki looked on, his face blank.

The woman dragged in a breath. 'I-carried-messages-when-I-was-in-the-wood-detail-and-this-is-a-dishonourable-disgraceful-thing,' she said in a monotone. 'It-shows-ingratitude-to-the-kindness-of-the-Emperor-expressed-through-his-glorious-Nippon-army. I-ask-his-forgiveness.' She lifted her head a little and her voice became clearer. 'And-I-ask-you-to-forgive-me-this-dishonour.'

A mutter of appreciation flowed through the women like a breeze.

Then the Snake poked her with his bayonet and she sank to her knees in the dust. The women muttered.

'And now,' the officer's voice stilled the women in a second, 'you will stand still for inspection.' The two officers walked along the lines of women slowly, looking at each woman from the top of her sun-bleached head to her dirty feet. They reached Virginia and stopped. The officer leaned back to say something to Captain Kageoki, and they both nodded and grunted.

'Come,' said the first officer, putting a hand on Virginia's shoulder.

'She can't come!' said Sylvie, grabbing Virginia's arm. 'Please, she can't come. She's my sister and she has to stay with me.' The woman either side of them froze into terrified stillness.

Then Captain Kageoki put a hand on Sylvie's head and said, 'Where your doll today, girl?'

She twisted under his hand to look up at him. 'Ayoshi? She's in my hut. Do you want her for your little girl? You can have her if you'll leave my Virginia, my sister. I need her here with me.'

Captain Kageoki laughed a growling laugh and the tension went out of the air. 'No doll and no sister. Leave them.'

'Not today, then,' said the first officer, laughing as though a great joke had been made. 'Not today. Come back another day.'

And the two men turned and strolled away as though they were two schoolmasters turning their backs on naughty schoolgirls.

The women relaxed and the lines broke up. The doctor and three other women went to help the kneeling woman to her feet and half-carry her to the hut where the doctor had her clinic.

'That was a close shave,' said Mrs Grassington, as they walked back to their hut. 'They do that, sometimes. Come and collect girls as though they are taking goods from the shelves of shops without paying. You were lucky, Miss Chen.'

'That's looting,' said Sylvie.

Mrs Grassington laughed. 'That's a new name for it, I suppose.' She stood beside Sylvie's bed space and stared down at Ayoshi. 'I noticed that before. A Jap doll, isn't it?' She glanced up at Virginia. 'Queer thing to give a child in these days. A Jap doll.'

'It was a present from my . . . our grandmother for Sylvie. It is a very old treasure from her own mother who was,' she paused, 'Japanese herself. That was a long time ago. Not the present times.'

'Japanese, though!' Mrs Grassington clicked her teeth and shook her head sorrowfully. 'Always a mistake, this mixing. Japs or no Japs.'

Virginia flushed and folded her lips very tight.

'That's an unfortunate viewpoint,' Miss Snowie's voice cut in. She was back in her bed space. 'The doll Ayoshi, it seems, saved Virginia once before in Singapore. And now again. She is doing good service.'

'And Ayoshi stopped them taking my Virginia this time as well,' said Sylvie. 'I offered it to the captain so he wouldn't loot Virginia. He wouldn't take it but he didn't take Virginia either.'

'So our Japanese ancestor reaches down through time and rescues us, Mrs Grassington,' said Virginia. 'To be perfectly honest, I would have thought that was a good argument for what you call "*mixing*".'

The other woman sniffed. 'Well, perhaps you're right. I'd not thought of it in that way, *to be perfectly honest*.' She changed tack. 'Miss Chen. Those cigarettes! You said you didn't smoke?'

'Yes. I do not smoke.'

'Had you considered sharing them? Or perhaps you intend to sell them?'

Virginia reached into the carved box and pulled out the sealed tin. She threw it at Mrs Grassington, who caught it awkwardly. 'There are only forty,' said Virginia. 'Perhaps you will share them round the hut?'

Mrs Grassington looked at the tin blankly. 'I honestly don't know why you don't keep them for barter. Everything is up for trade these days.'

Virginia stared at her. 'You are to share them round the hut, Mrs Grassington. Share them. You must not use them for barter.'

Mrs Grassington held her gaze. 'Mustn't I?'

There was depression at that night's hut meeting at Mrs Grassington's announcement that the food ration would be cut for three days because of Miss Rainton's indiscretion with the notes in her belt. But then the depression lifted when Mrs Grassington referred to Virginia's gift to the women in the hut. Everyone, smokers and non-smokers, took their allotted two cigarettes. Many of them were traded on for pieces of banana or slices of pineapple, so Virginia's ban on trading was not perfect. But with her act of generosity she'd earned her place in Hut Five and in the days that followed, when others in the camp regretted the inconvenient presence of these Eurasians, they protested that they were not all the same. There were exceptions.

From Virginia Chen
20 July 1944
Dearest Albert,

I hope you are well. It does me good to think of someone outside this place. I thought I'd tell you about what happens here and about the people in this hut. It is not so bad during the day but after curfew the hut is so crowded with all these women. (That is, unless there is special permission for a concert or something.) I hear tales of many concerts and pantomimes. Mrs Granger, the doctor's wife, told me of a Christmas concert performed by the men for the women, and a proper party afterwards. With food. She also told me that messages *were* allowed from time to time between husbands and wives and parents and children. Flirtations and speculations are strictly forbidden, though, she said, they do occur. It was very trusting of her to tell me this as some of these women are suspicious of me. Even so, the tin of cigarettes seemed to soften the atmosphere somewhat. Cigarettes here are prized above gold.

During the day most of the women make their way stiffly out of the stuffy confines of the hut and go into the open areas of the camp. Everyone who is fit has chores and duties, depending on the rota. There are work details for the cooking, the wood-gathering, latrine-cleaning and . . . oh dear . . . emptying of same; cleaning the commandant's office (an honour!); a sewing and laundry detail, which takes care of the needs of the Nippon soldiers who so kindly guard us from ourselves. There is a gardening detail, which seems the least unpleasant, although scratching meagre rows of underwatered spinach, could, I think, be a little depressing. A young Chinese woman is scratching away there today. I have no desire to find out anything about her. It is a difficult enough task to keep Sylvie occupied (Miss Snowie is a blessing there) and to become accustomed to the people we have to share our lives with in our hut.

These are the individuals I have sorted out so far. The queen of the hut is, of course, Mrs Grassington. She is tall; extremely thin now, of course, and has her hair plaited in a kind of rat's-tail plait down her back. Each night she takes that plait out and each morning she combs it for five minutes with a comb with only half its teeth. Then she replaits it. She has a funny harsh accent (not like Mrs Sambuck's genteel tones nor that of many women here). I watch the others looking down on her and muttering about her even while they do as she says. She has small gleaming lizard eyes and thinks a great deal of herself. However, perhaps there is a need here for someone who is a bit bossy to combat the lethargy. The undertone of discontent makes the air prickle sometimes, and there is a great weariness. This is not at all surprising after two and a half years in these terrible conditions. They must all be angels in some kind of way.

Then there is Mrs Josie Warren, who is much younger, perhaps not much more than thirty. She told me she'd been married to a planter up by Kuala Lumpur. She makes jokes about coming East on the 'fishing fleet' and having the pick of the desperate European men when she arrived. The others roll their eyes when she talks about this. They must have heard it many times over. She is short and wiry and has cut her hair short like a brush; her big eyes and small mouth bring a small, quite friendly animal to mind.

Mrs Warren is absolutely best friends with Mrs Ann Morris, wife to some kind of law officer on the colony. She is older than Mrs Warren, perhaps nearer forty. The skin on her neck and her upper arms is in folds and creases, parched for the missing fat. I imagine she was a very pretty woman when she had her weight.

She and Mrs Warren are bosom friends. They call each other by first names (not usual here), refer and defer to each other and go everywhere together. They take walks, arm in arm, round the perimeter of the camp. Even inside the hut they usually have their heads together, giggling. They are prone to whispering. The other women do not really like this.

It is easy to see that this is a source of irritation to the others, especially to Miss Lomax, a very explosive character. She is in her late thirties, clearly a spinster: some kind of administrator in the medical service. (Miss Snowie is a spinster too, but it sits better on her.) She (Miss Lomax) has very spindly legs in her ragged shorts. (Her legs are even more spindly than others whose legs are more *thin* than spindly.) Her eyes are bright as stars and gleam and glitter in her head. Her hands move jerkily for much of the time. She is very jumpy and suspicious.

Mrs Granger (the doctor's wife, who has been the least unfriendly to me so far) told me that Miss Lomax is in this hut 'on trial'. She has been voted out of four huts already. It seems she gets very angry and shouts at people for little reason. When she gets to the stage of pulling hair and throwing punches they vote her out. There is something about Miss Lomax that I like. There is a logic to being angry at this situation. And she works hard. I have seen her working on the water detail and she seems to move twice as fast as the others.

Then there is Miss Snowie, a real angel, and exceptional person, who moves about little but seems to bring light with her. And this is not because she is a God-woman. She is deeper and more consequential than that.

Morning duties done, there is still quite a lot of movement about the camp. The women go to visit their various friends and have activities to keep them busy – music, Scottish(!) dancing, quilt-making, language classes, art, painting and so on.

Apart from being put on the wood detail (where I am

working with a Mrs Smith-Court and Mrs Lamont) I am sort of left alone so far. Except that yesterday I was asked by an American woman called Freddy to go and have tea with her and her friend. The friend is not American. She is from Scotland, I think. Two thirty sharp. I fit it in before my two-hour afternoon shift on the wood. I am prompt and turn up with a small tinned fruitcake from the box. This is received graciously and put on a high shelf. I am served very weak tea and skeletal rice biscuits at a makeshift table with a very decent cloth on it and a fish tin filled with flower heads. Freddy winces a little as she sits down and I see she has sore, ulcerated feet.

The two women ask me about affairs outside in the city and shake their heads at the bad state of things for the people who have little food if they have no money for the black market. I tell them what I know about the Allied victories and they look pleased. The friend says, 'It is only a matter of time.' When she learns I am part French (did I tell you this? I think I did) Freddy tells me about a jolly time she once had in Paris and I talk to them about my studies at the Sorbonne. (They both raised an eyebrow at my mention of that august place of learning but say nothing. Surely they know that to be Chinese, or even part-Chinese, is not synonymous with being poor?) Anyway, Freddy says that perhaps I can retell one of the great Maupassant stories for the camp newspaper of which she is the editor. She mentions '*La Parure*', the one about the necklace, which I know well.

They ask a few questions about Sylvie but I guard our secret. I must talk to Sylvie also about this. I distracted them by asking about the camp. Freddy rolled her eyes and said don't sign up, don't get involved with *anything*. 'There's so much infighting, honey, it ain't worth the biscuit.' She has a lovely American drawl. Like the films.

When I make my way back to our hut the skies open and there is a heavy afternoon deluge. I am grateful on behalf of the dry spinach in the garden. But I am soaked to the skin. Our little group agrees to wait till the shower is over before going out for the wood. As I dry myself Miss Lomax bawls at me that it must indeed be a luxury to dry yourself with a whole towel. There is much hurt in that woman.

Sylvie is nowhere to be seen. I hope she has found herself some shelter in this heavy storm. I think she is settling down a bit now.

Take care of yourself. Thinking of you and remembering our perfect, civilised evening keeps me going in this place.

Your loving friend,
Virginia Chen

# Chapter Eighteen

## Beryl's Dog

Sylvie stood in the warm rain and let it flow down her like a river. Her shoulders, like two cliffs, made waterfalls that splashed on to her bare feet, swilling away the dust and much of the dirt. Women were standing outside every hut, offering their faces, their bodies to the cleansing, welcome rain. Many were wearing just their brassiere and knickers. Some had taken off their brassiere.

Sylvie stood there for ten minutes until the rain thinned, then suddenly stopped. She waited for a few moments, drying in the hot air as the sky retrieved its blue mantle and the sun was restored to its brassy, insistent glare.

Then she made her way, soggy toilet paper in hand, to the latrines, which were called *Heaven* according to the notice tacked on to the wall. Heaven was not hard to find: something to do with the stench and the flies. Sylvie squatted and tried, as Virginia had carefully taught her, to think of other things than this rank place. Today she thought of her mother's table with its lit candles and its gleaming silver. Later she swore at the limitations of precious toilet paper gone soggy in the rain.

On her way back down the steps her way was barred. At the bottom was the squat figure of Beryl Bridges. Sylvie moved one way and Beryl barred her way. She moved the other way and Beryl moved to stop her. Then Sylvie sighed, climbed back up two steps and sat down at the top. 'What's the matter with you? Let me by.'

'Nothing. It's nothing to do with you why I'm here. You're only a filthy *stengah*. My ma says so.'

'So what if I am?'

'Who do you think you are?' Beryl sniffed.

Sylvie started to prickle. Perhaps the girl had seen through her and she would tell her ma and they would take Virginia away from her. 'I'm me, that's who I am. That's all.' She stared Beryl Bridges in the eye until the other girl's gaze dropped.

Beryl clambered up the steps. 'Hitch up. I wanna sit down,' she said. Sylvie moved and Beryl sat beside her. 'They say you have a big box in your hut, with towels and soap and everything. A carved box.'

'How do you know?'

'Everyone knows everything in this place. You might as well put an adver*tise*ment in the American woman's paper. This American woman has this newspaper here. They put in about the Hallowe'en concert, and when people have birthdays, things like that.'

'Anyway, so what? Don't you have towels? Didn't you bring them?'

'We brought nothing,' said Beryl. 'We even had to borrow sailors' shirts and boots to get here. My ma works and trades and we have a few things now.'

'You were in the water?'

'The Japs bombed our boat with all our things. We got to the island and they came for us and brought us here.'

'And you don't have a towel?'

'Well, I have a quarter of a towel. The Committee for the Destitute gave Ma a whole towel and she cut it in quarters and hemmed them. To make them last out, see? We're on our fourth quarter.'

'I can get you a towel,' said Sylvie.

'I wasn't saying it because of that,' Beryl sniffed.

'I know you weren't.' Sylvie knew, though, that that was exactly what Beryl Bridges was on about. 'It's all right.'

Their particular peace was broken by the doctor, who shouted up at them to *get down from the steps of that filthy place unless the Chen girl wanted to contract cholera in her first month*.

They jumped down. 'We can go for a walk,' said Beryl.

Sylvie looked along at the huts and the long fence. 'Where?'

'Lots of places.' Beryl led the way through the trees to the perimeter, weaving round the isolated clumps of sword grass. They were watched by women lolling outside their huts and the big Chinese girl who had come to scratch in the mud round the spinach. The guards on the gate also watched them with disinterest, and continued smoking.

'See her?' said Beryl, nodding towards the girl.

'That girl?'

'She's only one year older than us. They'll have us digging before long.' Then she stopped and peered through the fence at the hillside opposite. A space had been cut in the dense cover of trees to make some kind of a smallholding. There was a hut with a deep, overhanging roof made of attap. Outside ducks, pigs and children ran about and played outside. Two women, one old and one young, returned the girls' gaze, their eyes shaded under wide hats. In the cleared space beside the hut a man, also in the deep shade of his hat, was digging with a *chungkol*.

'See them?' said Beryl. 'They're free. And we are in prison. And they have pigs and ducks and we have filthy rice and thinned stew. A duck would taste nice. Chewy, I think.'

Sylvie stared hard at the tiny, doll-like figures in the distance. 'Why do we have to be prisoners?'

'Because we lost the war.'

'So when will we get free?'

'My ma says it doesn't bear thinking about, but Mrs Smith-Court in our hut says our air force will come, and our soldiers, and they'll rescue us. But my ma says they're a long time a-coming.'

'Will the air force harry them? My cousin Simon Chen is harrying them in the jungle. Killing them too. With a gun.'

'See those trees?' Beryl pointed to the canopy in the distance. 'What can you hear?'

Sylvie closed her eyes and listened to the dense hum, which was part of their landscape, day and night. 'Insects. A bird,' she said airily.

'Hundreds and hundreds of birds. Thousands. There's one called a bulbul. And there are owls. But no one sees them 'cause the trees are so high.'

'How do you know there are hundreds of birds up there, if you never see them?'

'I have this book. A woman in our hut who died – she left it me in her will. I have to keep it in a biscuit tin because of the ants. It'd have made a fine old dinner for them.' She skipped over a lump of sharp grass, ran on and looked back at Sylvie. 'The birds, see? Up there in the canopy. We can't see them and they're there. It's like the RAF boys. We can't see them but they're there. They'll come for us one day, never fear.'

Sylvie ran to catch up with her.

'It's a good thing those birds are up there too high,' said Beryl, 'or the cooks'd've had them for the pot, no fear.'

'They'd be a change from slimy rice with chips of old fish.'

'So, why don't you come to school?' said Beryl. 'You've never been to the school. Not properly.'

'I got expelled for beating you.'

'That's what they said, but I said it was not fair. Why should you get off school for beating me? It should be me. So you get to do nothing. Like I say, it's not fair.'

'I don't "do nothing". I have my lessons with Miss Snowie, who was a teacher, and with my sister, Virginia, who teaches me French. Miss Snowie in the morning. But I can't have Virginia till the afternoon as the doctor came and told her she had to go and help to bring the wood.'

'What does that Miss Snowie do with you then?'

'She does geography, which is countries. It's mostly Africa and China because she has been there missioning. She tells me and I have to write things in my book. Same with science. Newton and Galileo and all that. She has it all in her head. She must be very clever.'

Beryl whistled. 'Sounds worse than the school to me.'

'Probably is.'

They walked along in silence. Ahead of them, beyond the high fence, they could see a narrow winding road through the jungle. 'If you go down that road far enough you come to Changi Beach. When we were in Changi, the other place, the Nips let us go for a swim sometimes. The sun and the water. It was lovely. But then they stopped it. There's no predicting those Nips, my ma says. That's the worst of them.'

Sylvie imagined the push of salty waves against her sticky, overheated body and sighed. That would sluice down the dust all right. Better than the rain. 'Why did they stop it?'

'Somebody did something wrong. Disobeyed one of the rules. Or they thought someone had done something wrong. My ma calls it "pyromania".'

'Pyromania? What's that?'

'It's when you think everyone's doing you down but really they're not. My ma says.'

A brown, rough-haired dog appeared and jumped up at Beryl, barking high, sharp barks. 'Get down, Caesar.' She ruffled his head and his neck, then turned to Sylvie. 'This is Caesar. I got him for Christmas. Mr Lieman brought him over from the men's camp at Christmas. Then Susie Lieman died, so now I share him with the Liemans. He likes me best. Here, give him a stroke.'

Sylvie touched the dog's rough coat. The small head turned up under her palm and Caesar looked up at her with glistening brown eyes. Her own eyes prickled with tears.

Beryl nudged her to move on and the dog followed them. 'You said Mr Lieman brought him over from the men's camp?'

'Yes. At Christmas. The men made Christmas presents for the children here. And they let them bring them over. And some of them visited us. Mr Lieman was there. They only let him stay five minutes. Mrs Lieman was so mad about that, she smacked Susie real hard for crying.' Beryl stopped. 'Look!'

Two men were walking through the grass beyond the corner perimeter, with *chungkols* over their shoulders. They were burned brown and very thin. One wore a rag on his head to protect him from the sun. They were clearly European.

Beryl started whistling and shouting but the men didn't look up, just kept trudging along, their chins low on their chests. Sylvie clung hard to the wire, peering to see whether the dirty head cloth hid some vestige of her father, but there was nothing in the face that she recognised.

Beryl started to shout. 'Do you know Mr Lieman? He's my friend. Do you know him?' she bellowed.

Sylvie joined in. 'Do you know my dad? His name's Bo Sambuck. Do you know him?' she yelled till she thought her lungs would burst. Still the men did not look up.

'Postnatal depression,' announced Beryl.

'What?'

'That's why some of them are so miserable. They get postnatal depression with having to bow to the Nips all the time. My ma says. It affects your head.'

They turned the corner and picked their way through more gardens. The ground was pockmarked with sad clusters of plants struggling to live in the heat. The air stank with the slurry that was being tipped on to it by two women who, working very slowly, had carried the buckets from the latrines on a home-made pole like milkmaids in one of Sylvie's nursery books.

'Pooh!' said Beryl. 'I'm not gonna eat anything that grows on there.' She suddenly stopped and grabbed Sylvie's arm. 'Hey, it can't be your dad,' she said. 'In there with the men, in the men's camp.'

'It is!' said Sylvie fiercely. 'I saw him marching with the others on their way. He was pushing another man in a wheelchair.'

'The name you shouted was Bo Sambuck.'

'So it is.'

'But you're Sylvie Chen. A . . . well, you've got a Chinese name.'

Sylvie thought very quickly. 'Of course I have. Chen was my mother's name,' she said airily. 'Virginia and I thought that would be safer while we were still out in the city, among the Chinese.' She ignored Beryl's wide curious eyes and kneeled down to take Caesar's face in her hands. 'How old do you say he was?'

'Ten months. He was born in the men's compound. He was only a puppy when he came.'

They lingered in the doorway of Sylvie's hut. 'Well,' said Beryl, 'I'd better get back. I promised Ma I'd put her hair in rags for her. She can't reach the back, y'know.' She turned to go.

'Wait!' Sylvie raced into the hut and raked in the carved box for the green towel, which she knew was lying in the bottom layer. She pulled it out, replaced all the other items and ran to the door. She thrust it at Beryl. 'Here. You can have this.'

Beryl's round eyes grew rounder. 'A whole towel? You're sure?'

'Take it.'

Beryl took it. 'D'you wanna go for a walk tomorrow?'

Sylvie nodded.

'Right. After school.' Beryl whirled round, whistled for Caesar, then raced down the line to her own hut to show off her booty.

Miss Snowie was sitting stitching Ayoshi's obi. She caught Sylvie's look. 'Virginia asked me to mend the obi, dear. It was coming loose.' She tied off the cotton. 'Was that young Beryl?'

'Yes.'

'So you're friends now?'

'Seems like it.' Sylvie flung herself on to her bed space. Empty and disappointed now, uneasy at what she'd just done.

Miss Snowie added to her uneasiness. 'It might be a mistake, my dear, to think that one can buy friends.'

Sylvie, dismissing that thought, looked down at her watch with its yellow strap. 'When will Virginia be back?'

'Yesterday, it wasn't until five o'clock. Did you see those blisters on her hands, poor dear?'

'She might have been better if she'd been looted.'

Miss Snowie frowned. 'Oh, no. I don't think so, my dear.'

Sylvie sat down, pulled out Ayoshi and held her close to her face. She was comfortingly heavy and solid. Sylvie closed her eyes. She felt very sad, very low down. Her cheeks and her chest felt very heavy. She scrunched her eyes tight to stop the tears squeezing through. She thought perhaps she might be suffering from *postnatal depression*. Or *pyromania*. That was always a possibility.

# Chapter Nineteen

## This Camp

### A Compostion by Syl Vee Chen

There are a lot of women and children in this camp and a big fense in case we escape and get back to the city. A baby was born yestarday so the numbers are growing. There are boys as well as girls but when the boys grow up they go to the men's camp. A boy called Tim Lott had to go to the men's camp just before we came here. Beryl Bridges says Tim Lott came back to visit two weeks later and he was fater. She says this was because the men are beter traders than we are and grow more food. The men are fater than the women. Last night I dreamt of a boy I think I knew once, a boy with white hair. He was a good jugler. He jugled with me.

Jin Kee has got quite thin. There is almost no food but she has some guilders so she manages to buy some extra things from traders which helps a bit. Everything costs a big lot of money and the guilders are going fast. She keeps warning me about being discreet. <u>Discreet</u> is one of her favourite words.

The women here are all very thin. Some are so thin that their body goes in where it should come out. You feel they will cut you when you touch them. Then there are some with very fat legs who have to go to the clinic because they are ill. Some people die in the clinic and are beried on the hill. The woman whose bed space I have is on the hill. I never met her. I have seen her little grave.

One day I saw a funeral, a big one. The men and the women gathered at the gate sang abide with me and the Nip they call Cloth Eers who runs this camp stood at the gate and saluted. They only let a few women go to the funeral, including the American woman called Freddy. Jin Kee, who is quite friends with the American woman, says the man was with the tauturers at the same time as the American woman was and came back very very sick and now has died. Freddy had poorly legs when we first met her but they are better now.

The children are not quite so thin as the women, as they are fed first and sometimes the Nip soldiers send in speshal food for the children. It was like Captain Kageoki saving Jin Kee because of Ayoshi and me. Miss Snowie calls it the appeel of a child. She says the Nips can be very sentamental when they want to be. But the problem is you don't know when, which makes it all worse. Beryl's ma calls it unpredictabelity.

Beryl's ma is not so thin now. She must be a good trader.

She has curly hair because of the rags and wears lipstick. She uses long words and makes me laugh. She calls you names but you know she doesn't mean it. She has been looted a couple of times, but she came back. Beryl told me she came back with presents and tins of corned beef from our own Red Cross parcels that the Nips haven't given us. Mrs Warren in our hut says Beryl's mum is a common tart. Mrs Granger says she was the wife of some low level creeper upcountry who was taken with her looks.

Ayoshi was getting very fat and I investigated the reason and found out why. I think it is something to do with Miss Snowie and Jin Kee, a kind of surprise. But I won't tell them I know. I think secrets can be nice.

The doctor goes on at us about sickness and the <u>dredded anophele fly</u>. (I made the doctor write that down for me on a piece of paper. I thought that was quite a nice name for a fly.) She says we must keep clean, clean clean. But this is not very easy as there is not so much water. Almost none some days. The strong women go to get it from a muddy stream. But they have to get water for the Nips before they get ours.

At least me and Jin Kee still have a very little bit of soap. Jin Kee has given some soap away and people think she is very strange because she won't trade. She just gives it and it makes them uncomfortable.

Jin Kee gets things for her and me and Miss Snowie because of the guilders. Some Dutch women still have things or seems they can get them.

What I like best about the camp is going for walks and playing games with Beryl Bridges. She is very quick and funny and uses long words. She knows about birds. She swares. I've never had a friend before, if you don't count Jin Kee. And Beryl Bridges is my friend, even though she is bossy.

We go all about with each other and have some fun. I thought Cristmas would be fun as she told me other times in here Cristmas had been fun. But it seemed a dusty Cristmas to me. Except for Miss Snowie, who read the story of the baby from her bibel and made up a song for everyone in the hut to sing about hope and heart and things. I thought of my mother with Feargal when he was a baby curled up against her. I kind of see it but cant remember my mother's face. Miss Snowie gave me her straw hat as a Cristmas present and I wear it every day. She wears a cloth tied round her head backwards. It's all right cause she doesn't go out very much except for the counting. She just sits there in the shade and reads her bibel and writes songs and poems and things for people. A lot of people come to see her and talk to her.

Jin Kee is tired when she gets in from the wood detale. The other ladies on the detale got sick and she has some new helpers now. Her hands are as hard as lether. She has to have a rest before she can give me my lessons. The other day we didn't have lessons at all as she had to go to tea with the American newspaper woman. She writes little stories for the newspaper. She says if this compostion is good enough it will go in the newspaper.

The lessons are OK. English is easy. We are now into sub-ordinate clauses. And I can write this compostion for as long as I like and it still counts as a lesson.

My least favourite person here is Mrs Grassington, who is very nice to us to our faces because of the carved box, but is as dry as old paper when you talk to her, as though there is no smiles or frendliness in her. She got Miss Lomax voted out of the hut for shouting, but I liked Miss Lomax and I was sorry. I think shouting is very sensible as it's really horrible in the hut. I don't think Miss Lomax likes Jin Kee and me, though, cause she shouts at us and calls us names.

My biggest worry every day is that the Nip officers will come back and loot Jin Kee and I will be on my own. I have to be very discreet about this. (My other worry is what dinner will be and when there will be sugar again.)

My greatest hope is that the AIR FORCE will rescue us and me and Jin Kee will go back up to Hibiscus Lodge and find my Daddy and Mummy in their long chairs on the veranda. And Ah So and Feargal are there playing pat ball on the lawn.

Sylvie Chen Sambuck
Aged eleven
Hut Five
Sime Road Camp
Nr Singapore
Nr China
The World

Afterwards.

Miss Snowie said this compostion is very good indeed a few spelings but not to worry about that but says it is too privit for the paper. That I should not show Beryl. Beryl would not read it anyway. She thinks it's really bad luck that I don't go to the scool as the lessons are much easier there. Miss Snowie says that I should keep it somewhere secret and that I should not say anything. So I will fold it under Ayoshi's obi and show it to my Daddy afterwards.

# Chapter Twenty

## The Anniversary

One afternoon after a very dry spell at the beginning of February there was heavy rain that lasted two whole hours. It rattled like marbles on the tin roofs of the huts and rendered the sandy walkways into temporary swamps. The rough drain overflowed on to the road, spreading another level of rank air across the camp.

At first it was good. Everyone washed their bodies and clothes in this welcome glut of water. They brought out pans and dishes to collect every precious drop. Even the old women came and stood with their faces up to the unseen skies. Only Snowie Raven stayed inside.

Then all the women got down to washing. They scoured themselves and every washable thing with the precious liquid. They drank. The doctor nagged and nagged about boiling it before using it. The hospital was full enough with the sick and the very sick, she said. And bad water was the cause of that. Next to bad food, that was. Or no food at all.

There was muttering behind the doctor's back about how she thought it was possible to boil every drop with this continual shortage of wood.

Beryl and Sylvie danced in the downpour, naked except for their knickers. They rolled in the silty mud, rubbing it on their face and arms, then standing in the rain and letting the rain sluice them down. Then the rain stopped and the world started to steam before their eyes.

Mrs Grassington called them into the hut to hear her announce that there would be festivities on the thirteenth of the month, to celebrate the liberation of 'Syonan' from the British imperialists.

There were shouts and catcalls at this. Beryl put her fingers to her mouth and managed a great piercing whistle.

Mrs Grassington shook her head. 'Can't look a gift horse in the mouth, ladies. Cloth Ears has informed our committee that we will be furnished with parcels of milk powder, tins of jam and a barrel of pickled pork to assist us to join their celebration.'

'Our own Red Cross stuff,' said Mrs Morris. 'Don't we know it.'

'Been here for months,' said Mrs Warren. 'In their storage places.'

Mrs Grassington said there was to be a count, a *tenko*, to check on their gratitude. The commandant would speak to them of the glories of the liberation. And they would have to bow to the Japanese flag.

At one o'clock they endured the usual fumbling, inefficient count. Even the walking ill from the hospital had to be there in the midday heat. Then a flurry of senior officers walked from the gate across the dusty quadrangle. They clustered around the commandant like dark pigeons.

Today he did not deign to speak in English. His translator, an even smaller man with a worried, sweaty face and a briefcase, conveyed the speech to them. They listened to familiar phrases about the liberation of Syonan from under the imperial heel of the British and the eternal Empire of the East that was now growing in strength with each and every day.

Sylvie stopped listening and searched the crowd of officers with the side of her eye. She found one man. Captain Kageoki. She stared hard at him and he looked at her.

Then the commandant, followed by the officers, made their customary parade up and down the lines of women.

'Here we go!' Sylvie heard Mrs Bridges spit out behind her. 'Whipsnade Zoo.'

One of the officers, built like an Oxo cube with a turnip for a head came to a stop before Sylvie and Virginia. Sylvie flinched as the man's hand came out to touch Virginia on her shoulder, just above her breast. He growled something to the man behind him, who laughed. Then from behind him came Captain Kageoki's voice. They walked on. Captain Kageoki stood in front of Virginia and looked first at her then down at Sylvie.

'I send for you,' he said. 'Or that officer send for you. Better that it is me.'

Later, after the people in Hut Five had shared in the feast of tinned milk and corned beef, two guards bustled into the hut.

The women stood up and bowed low then waited in prickling silence.

The taller guard strolled down the hut and pointed at Virginia. 'Come,' he said. 'You come. Bring bag.'

The women watched in horrified silence as Virginia thrust a few things in her rucksack. More than one of them felt guilty relief that it was Virginia Chen who had been chosen.

Sylvie grasped Virginia's arms. 'Don't go. Don't go, Virginia.'

Virginia kept her eyes on the soldier and shook off Sylvie's hands. 'Go and stand by Miss Snowie, Sylvie. She will take care of you,' she said carefully. She glanced at Miss Snowie, who took Sylvie's hand tightly in her own. Her other hand she put on her left breast and nodded to Virginia. It was a promise of the heart. 'I will go and I will come back, dear Sylvie.' Virginia's voice was steady but there were unshed tears in her eyes. 'Remember always to be discreet. Look after Ayoshi. I will come back, I promise.'

Miss Snowie pulled Sylvie very close to her. Sylvie could feel the fragile birdlike bones of her arms and her breast.

'Woman come!' The soldier took another step towards Virginia.

She nodded vigorously. 'I come,' she said. 'I come.'

The women clustered to the doorway of the hut to witness Virginia's steady walk with the soldiers trudging behind her. In other parts of the camp, women stopped whatever they were doing and stood up and watched as the three made their way to the perimeter gate. One woman whistled the funeral march and was hushed by the woman beside her.

'And who,' said Mrs Warren, glumly, 'will take her place on the wood detail? She was the strongest of the lot. Did you ever see those muscles? Like whipcord.'

Miss Snowie pulled Sylvie back into the darkness of the hut and sat down with her on the bed space. 'Don't worry, my dear. Miss Chen will be all right. She's a very resourceful young woman. Very clever.'

'She's been looted,' said Sylvie, pressing her lips together. 'She really has been looted this time, hasn't she?'

'Looted!' Josie Warren looked down at the old woman with the child in her arms. 'The girl has no idea, does she?' she said shrilly.

Miss Snowie rocked Sylvie to and fro in her arms. 'It's hard enough for the child, losing her sister.'

Sylvie pulled away from Miss Snowie and stood up. She scowled at Josie Warren. 'What will they do with her? What will they do with my Virginia?'

Josie stared at Sylvie, her own panic leaking away at the sight of the child's wide eyes. 'Well, dear, they will make her . . . work for them,' she said slowly.

'Will they hurt her? I have seen them hurt people. I saw them kill some men in the city.'

Josie Warren flushed. 'I don't know about that, dear. Let us hope not. You should know—'

'That's enough, Mrs Warren.' Mrs Grassington's voice came from the end of the hut. 'The child has had enough to take.'

Josie Warren went and plonked herself on her bed space and Sylvie subsided back beside Miss Snowie. She looked at her friend. 'Will you do a prayer for her? One of your prayers?'

'I most certainly will. You could do a prayer for her yourself, dear.'

'I can't do that.'

'Why not?'

''Cause I can't.'

'Well, will you do something for me?'

'What's that?'

Miss Snowie put a hand on Sylvie's forehead. 'Close your eyes.'

Sylvie closed her eyes. Miss Snowie's voice came from beside her. 'Now think of your Virginia. Think of her in the best place you and she have been together.'

Sylvie thought of Virginia, fatter then, walking in a pale dress down the sunny lawns of Hibiscus Lodge, smiling and holding her hand out to take hers.

'Can you see her?'

'I see her.'

'Keep that picture in your head. Every time you miss her and think about her keep that picture in your head. Can you do that?'

'I think I can.'

'Good. You do that and I'll say my prayers and between us we will keep her safe.'


From Virginia Chen

My dear and best friend Albert,

   It is a comfort to write to you just now in this difficult

time. I imagine you there in some house with a tile roof, perhaps eating an English dinner, then smoking your pipe. Or on the deck of your ship scanning the far horizon.

I have to tell you that in the end, our hosts(!) came to the camp to get me. I managed to bundle my exercise book into my bag. I always keep it wrapped in a dress so it wasn't too difficult. They are half blind anyway. I was not sure what would happen but they just bundled me into a truck and to my great surprise they brought me here to Beach Road. Beach Road! The house of my grandmother! I could not believe it. The streets of the city were ribboned with Nipponese flags and I could hear fireworks. The celebration of the anniversary of the Nippon liberation of 'Syonan' was well advanced.

Uncle Wo was in the shop, which is half closed now. There are few curios left. He nodded and smiled when he saw me and asked me where was the child. He shook his head when I told him, but told me I was most welcome and that business was not too bad when he could get hold of the goods. These days he sells anything he can get his hands on. The societies do not interfere. They have other fish to fry. The war is turning round and they know the time will come for us to take back our own city.

My grandmother was sitting playing with cards, the gramophone roaring out some Gilbert and Sullivan chorus. When she saw me she put down her cards and leaned over stiffly to lift the needle off the gramophone. 'Granddaughter,' she said.

I went across and kneeled before her. She put her hand on my head. She looked behind me as far as the door. 'The child, where is she?' I explained the circumstances and emphasised how good and kind was Miss Snowie Raven. My grandmother nodded and left it at that. Of course *I* cannot leave it like that. Sylvie and I have been more than sisters, more than mother and daughter for two years. I have to trust in Miss Snowie, and in the other women to take care of her. But in this uncertain world there is no certainty that she is, or I am, safe! In the simplest terms I miss her! How I miss the sight of her face, her bright searching eyes, every minute of the day. My mission now is to survive to get back to her. I will do it.

I explained to my grandmother about Captain Kageoki and she shrugged. 'You will deal with him,' she said. 'He is only a man.' I wish I were so sure! But then she is a descendant of Karayuki San.

After tea with my grandmother I wash and change into a decent dress that still hangs in my room. I am swimming in it like a fish. I have to tie my belt closer and pleat the skirt to make it look decent. When I join my grandmother she has a tray on the small table with clean white rice and plump fish and pomegranates. I look at this feast and wish I could parcel the whole lot up for Sylvie and Miss Snowie. 'Eat!' commands my grandmother. I have to say I devoured the food in a trice, thinking all the time I should save some for Sylvie.

Sylvie will be safe, I know, under Miss Snowie's protection. She is a quiet woman but the other women are, I think, a bit frightened of her. That is helpful. Otherwise they might try to get Sylvie out of the hut, and send her down with the other Eurasian children. That must not happen. They can be very selfish, but I suppose that is how, in the end, they have managed to survive that awful place. Paradoxically they are often very unselfish in the way they support and care for each other. There are some very fine women there and I have to trust Sylvie with them.

Sylvie has grown so much taller (and thinner) in there! I wonder if Grandmother would even recognise her now. How I miss her, even after a day!

I will just take this time as a rest and get back to her as soon as I can. There will be a knock on the door soon, I know. But there may be ways in which I may persuade the captain that I must go back to Sylvie, or she can come to me. I will make any – any – sacrifice for that. You will have to understand, dear Albert. I will explain to you one day. Sometimes, whole families do get out of the camp. Chinese, Eurasian prisoners – money passes hands – they bring the whole family. Not this time. I have to be careful not to draw scrutiny on the sisterhood that Sylvie and I claim. I just have to wait for a knock on the door. I will see what I can do. I must do something for Sylvie.

But I will build my strength for the future and look

forward to the time when things are better and perhaps we will all meet again in sunnier times. I was wondering what it was like there down in the West of England. I looked on my grandmother's map of Great Britain. I know you are there on the high seas somewhere but I try to think of you at home in your little village. Perhaps one day I will see.

With loving best wishes from your friend Virginia Chen.

# Chapter Twenty-One

## Stories

On the night after the looting of Virginia, there was a birthday party for Mrs Grassington in Hut Five. This celebration of birthdays, even wedding anniversaries, was common in the camp. So once in a while the women could celebrate their individuality, the network of their friendships. All afternoon, women called with bunches of flowers picked at the peripheries of the site and formed into bouquets any London florist would be proud of. There were presents of left-over ribbon, small pieces of soap and a barely worn pair of pink camiknickers. There was a small packet of tea and a tin of Irish stew without the label. They knew it was Irish stew because 'Irish Stew' was scratched on the lid.

Mrs Grassington caught a certain look on Miss Snowie's face. 'You're surprised at this largesse, Miss Snowie?'

'Well, under the circumstances, I think it is, well, unexpected.'

'You above all must know the miracle of the loaves and the

fishes, Miss Snowie? Well, here we have it. And we bring it into play to show these heathens that we are civilised, that they can't grind us down.' She smiled a wintry smile. 'And it's said to keep up our peckers as well!'

Later that day, Miss Snowie copied a Bible text on to the blank end sheet of a book and decorated it with a border of English robins. On Miss Snowie's urging, Sylvie raked out a short length of cream shantung, a needle and some thread from the carved box. 'Why should I give her a present?' Sylvie asked from the raised lid of the box. 'I don't like her. She doesn't like me.'

'She's hut captain,' said Miss Snowie placidly. 'It is to keep everybody's spirit up, Sylvie. And it helps to keep our powder dry.'

Sylvie didn't really see why, but she did as she was told. She smoothed out a piece of old wrapping paper from Robinson's. When she gave her present, it was the wrapping paper (hers was the only *wrapped* present) that made Mrs Grassington cry. 'It even *smells* of Robinson's,' she said, gulping back tears. She patted Sylvie's head. 'Thank you, my dear. Miss Chen will be so missed at my do. Perhaps she would have danced for us. That would have been fun.'

'She doesn't dance,' said Sylvie, frowning. There was something in what Mrs Grassington said that worried her. She thought of Virginia going off to the pictures and then on to dance with Albert Taft. She wore her best blue silk cheong sam, and, Sylvie thought, was probably a beautiful dancer. Probably Albert Taft fell in love with her there and then. You could tell, the way he looked at her. 'Well, not on her own.'

'But they all dance . . . well.' Mrs Grassington caught Miss Snowie's glare. 'Let us not worry ourselves about that, shall we? It's my birthday, after all.' She moved to the next present, a quarter of a pineapple carefully wrapped in a shred of palm leaf.

The party was set to start at five, and women strolled in from various parts of the camp just before then. They all carried some small thing. It might be a single flower, a conical hat made of leaves, an old and scratched fountain pen, a coconut (unused), a battered tin of beans (unopened). When everyone was assembled, Mrs Grassington's friend Dora stood up and read out a eulogy. It had some rhythm and rhymed here and there. It told of Mrs Grassington coming from Richmond on a fishing boat (there was laughter at this mention of a fishing boat), of a planter she met, of the parties they had in their house, and her prowess at tennis and golf, and her travails with a series of cooks whom she never managed to train.

At each familiar reference there was a gale of laughter and clapping.

Other people got up and did their pieces – a song, a poem, home-made or stolen from the dwindling pile of books that constituted the camp library.

Then there was a lull. Mrs Grassington's eye alighted on Sylvie, sitting on the carved box. 'What about you, Sylvie Chen? Don't you have a piece? Stand up on that blessed box of yours and sing me a song.'

The murmur went round and Sylvie climbed up on the box. 'I can't sing,' she said.

'Tell a story, then,' Miss Snowie said quietly. Beryl, sitting at the end of Sylvie's bed space, said, 'Yes, tell us a story!' Her mother, sitting resplendent beside her, in ringlets and purple lipstick, joined in. 'Yes, tell us a story.'

Sylvie thought hard and something popped into her mind. 'Well, this is about four dragons. One time there were no rivers and lakes on the whole earth, but only the Eastern Sea, where there were four dragons: the Long Dragon, the Yellow Dragon, the Black Dragon and the Pearl Dragon. These dragons were flying around and saw many people putting out fruits and cakes, and all sorts of things for gods. They were praying for rain because their crops would fail and then they would have nothing to eat and drink.'

The women murmured, glanced at each other.

Sylvie hurried her story along. 'Well, these dragons went and saw the emperor of everything. He told them to think of the answer themselves but they couldn't. The people had to eat bark and grass roots like we do and the dragons were really sorry for them so they decided to solve the problem themselves. So they scooped up the sea water in their mouths and spilled it on the land, making four big rivers, which saved the crops and the people. The people were not hungry any more. These four rivers are the great rivers of China. The emperor was so mad that he turned the four dragons into mountains, but they had saved the people so they didn't worry.' Sylvie had run out of breath. 'The end,' she gasped.

There was a pause before the applause this time. Then the applause was mixed with murmured words and stricken looks.

'Well done, Sylvie,' said Miss Snowie. 'What a lot to remember.'

'That's what we need, a few dragons from the sky,' said Mrs Warren.

'Dragons called the RAF,' said Mrs Morris.

'A lovely story,' said Miss Snowie. 'Where did you hear that, dear?'

Sylvie frowned, pulling it out of her memory. 'My daddy told me it when I was very small,' she said. 'I was frightened in the night and he told me it.'

Miss Snowie nodded. 'The Chinese have such wonderful tales,' she said. 'Such wonderful metaphors for the beginning of the world.'

'But Sylvie's dad's not—' said Beryl.

'Shut up, Beryl!' said Sylvie. She herself wanted to shout that her daddy was not Chinese, that his name was Bo Sambuck and he had learned the story from his *amah*. But she looked around at the eager, devouring faces and she couldn't do it. Virginia said *be discreet*.

The doctor came to help Sylvie down from the box. 'That was very nice, my dear. Remarkably allegorical, given our present situation. Perhaps your age . . . you didn't realise the import. Such a clear voice. I was shocked just now to learn from Mrs Bridges that you still don't attend our school.'

'I have school here, with Miss Snowie and Virginia. Well, before with Virginia. I'm always doing lessons. Too much.'

Beryl squealed with laughter. 'So she says. It's not so hard as school.'

The doctor nodded. 'Well, poor Mrs Wallace has come down with the dreaded anophele fly and is in the clinic. So we need Miss Snowie to go on to the teaching rota, and Miss Chen, alas, is no longer with us.'

'She'll be back. She said she would come back,' said Sylvie. 'I know she will come back.'

The doctor nodded. 'We hope so. We very much hope so. But in the meanwhile, I think you should go to our school. The days are too long for you to be here in the hut on your own.'

Miss Snowie was nodding at Sylvie and she knew she'd have to give in. Beryl would be there, of course. And Miss Snowie. It might be worse.

It was the next day, when both Sylvie and Miss Snowie were away in the school hut, that Virginia's box was taken. The whole of her bed space had been tidied. At its head was a small pile of clothes and a rolled blanket. The carved box had vanished.

Sylvie ran the length and breadth of the hut, looking under people's blankets, sending the pitiful piles of goods flying. 'Where is it? Where is it? Who has stolen Virginia's box?' The women tried to stop her but she bit and scratched them. She ran outside and made her way from hut to hut, shouting at people, asking for the box.

She ran into the clinic, shouting and yelling for the doctor. She hesitated a little as the stench of human waste and sweat met her, then peered in the gloom of the pulled mosquito nets for the doctor. Patients lifted their heads, some raised themselves to their elbows to see this small tornado who had disturbed their Stygian peace.

The doctor finished talking to her patient, the teacher Mrs Wallace, who was at last allowing the raging infection to inhabit her body. The doctor tucked the grubby net in beside her, walked swiftly to Sylvie; she took the girl's upper arm in a punishing grip and dragged her out into the glittering day. 'Get out of my clinic, you stupid, selfish child.' She started to shake her. 'What do you think you are doing?'

Miss Snowie had caught up to them, Mrs Grassington close behind, with the dog Caesar snapping at her heels. 'Someone has stolen her sister's box while she was in the schoolroom. Do stop shaking her. The child is distraught.' The old woman's tone was reproving.

Many years ago, in a small girls' school in Somerset, Jemima Renhardt, later to be Dr Emma Renhardt, had had a teacher who used to speak to her in just that tone. Her hand dropped from Sylvie and the child stood still, rubbing her upper arm. 'Are you accusing me of taking the box?' the doctor said frostily.

'Of course not,' said Miss Snowie evenly. 'But the child – and I – imagine you are in charge here and feel that you may be able to do something about it.'

Sylvie took a deep breath. 'Someone here has looted Virginia's box, Doctor. It has Virginia's and my things in it. Just a few things left. It's not fair. You have to find them and give it back. It must be here when Virginia gets back. It must be.' She stumbled towards Miss Snowie, who put an arm round her shoulders.

Miss Snowie looked the doctor in the eye. 'This will not do, Doctor. What are these women about? Stealing from a child? We are no better than those savages we pretend we do not despise.' Holding Sylvie by the shoulder she turned and marched away. She did not lead her to the hut, but to the edge of the camp where, through the wire, they could see the reflection of ice-pink clouds in the haze above the trees.

As they stood there, Miss Snowie told Sylvie the story of Li Chi, the youngest of six daughters, who fought and defeated a great serpent whose habit was to loot young girls. She defeated it with the aid of rice balls sweetened with malt sugar, a sharp sword, and a snake-hunting dog.

Sylvie squatted down in the dust and fondled Caesar's ears. 'Like Caesar?' she said.

Miss Snowie nodded. 'I wouldn't be at all surprised if he were quite like Caesar. It is my view, dear, that help comes to us from the most surprising places.'

# Chapter Twenty-Two

## Retrieval

That evening, the doctor called a meeting of the hut captains to discuss the issue of Virginia Chen's box. Someone mentioned that Miss Lomax was a bit giddy but another woman said that the poor woman was mad, not bad. Surely she wouldn't do such a thing.

The outrage of the doctor and Miss Snowie was not universal. There was some discussion of Miss Chen's removal to God-knew-what fate; of the fact that while it must be said she was generous with the contents of her box, she didn't do the decent thing and give them outright to the Committee for the Destitute so they could be shared, fair and square. Now she wasn't there, the logic was . . .

'But the box is not there for us to share!' said the doctor. 'We must respect property. If we do not do this we are all looking into the abyss. Anyway, this is all academic. Some very greedy and very stupid person has stolen this box. What's more, they have stolen it from a child. It was all she had left of her sister. We are in desperate straits here, but are we really in such straits that we would steal from a child? Are we such barbarians?' She looked round, meeting the gaze of each woman in turn. 'This is unforgivable. I want you to tell the people in your huts that if the box is not found, then I shall put the case in the hands of the authorities.'

'The Nips?'Mrs Bridges whistled. 'You couldn't do that? Last time—'

'Well, perhaps we should have learned from the last time.'

There had been another time when a woman's case had been stolen. As no one admitted taking it, the Japanese were told and all the women in the camp were punished by being made to stand outside in the heat for three hours. Eleven women fainted. Still the culprit was not found.

'You can't do this,' said Mrs Bridges. 'Not again, for God's sake.'

'Perhaps it will not be necessary,' said the doctor. 'Perhaps the culprit will feel properly guilty and will return the box. If you do your jobs as hut captains, then I am sure that will be the outcome and there will be no need to inform the Japanese.' She turned and stretched her head and shoulders to relieve the tension there. 'Now, ladies, if you will be so kind . . . I have two new patients and they need close attention if they may get through this bout safely. And we have this great batch of new internees coming. Jewish people, I'm told. And others. Where we will put them heaven knows. There could be sickness among them. There is typhoid in the city, I hear.'

The hut emptied and for a second the doctor was on her own. She put her head in her hands and thought again of the clever, stern little girl in Somerset who had a teacher just like Miss Snowdrop Raven. She looked up and there, in the dappled sunlight of the door, was the object of her thoughts. Miss Snowie held out her hand. In it was a very small pot of jam. 'I kept this from my time upcountry. I want you to have it.'

The doctor took it and turned it round in her fingers. Strawberry.

'You are doing very well here, my dear,' said Miss Snowie. 'You have an impossible job.' Then she was gone and there were only the bars of white light that had crept in under the thatch.

The doctor tucked the jam into the small cotton sack in which she kept all her treasures. It is the case, she thought, that we were all a child to someone.

Mrs Bridges had offered Sylvie a bed space in her hut beside Beryl (there had been another death in that hut), but Sylvie said she would keep to the space with Miss Snowie. When Virginia came back she would want to find her own space still there. She'd collected all of Virginia's things that had, fortunately, not been in the box, and made a neat pile of them by her bedroll. She put Virginia's sleeping rug under her own, and hung the two mosquito nets together on the rail. Three separate women came to ask her to sell them Virginia's net or her bed blanket but she shook her head. But for the eagle-eyed presence of Snowdrop Raven beside her, she might have suffered more pressure in these matters.

Despite herself, Sylvie started to enjoy her school hours. There were jokes and company, tricks and laughter. She and Beryl were usually together inside and outside the school hut, with Caesar at their heels. There were school things to do on some afternoons as well: some games and songs to be learned, and short forays into the bits of jungly woodland that reached into the camp, to learn the names of plants, familiar to her since she was a toddler, whose names she had never really known.

The jungle walk was led by an occasional teacher, the tall American woman called Freddy Bloom. She was thin and wiry, like the rest, but she still hobbled a bit along on her sore feet, a reminder of her time with the brutal *Kempai Tai*. Her direct, dispassionate gaze stilled the more riotous children, and her interest in the thing at hand, whether it was a piece of poetry or a strange jungle plant, focused everyone's attention and made them understand. At her heels was a small, frisky dog called Judy, which followed her everywhere.

Caesar came to school with Beryl and Sylvie, and was good friends with Judy. They barked at each other a good deal, and leaped about, their heads poking up from time to time through the tall grass. 'Mrs Bloom,' said Beryl one day, 'do the dogs know they are in prison?'

The tall woman laughed at this. 'Look at them. What do you think?'

Sylvie nodded. 'Nobody can tell them that. They don't realise. Not like us.'

'Hah! You can't talk. You've only been here less than a year,' said Beryl scornfully. 'We've been in a proper prison, with grey walls, an't we, Mrs Bloom? Over at Changi was nothing like this. Grey walls and dark places. Treading over people on the staircase. Much better here, innit, Mrs Bloom?'

The women had been relieved to get to Sime Road, out of the stench and stew of the prison with its high walls and its crowded landings. Here at least you could see trees and the dusty green all around. Here the sky seemed wider, less enclosed. But the huts leaked and rats thrived, as did the dreaded anophele fly. And the water was short and had to be hauled a long, painful way. The women soon learned that here too life was painful and often unjustly short, and that their guards were just as free to indulge in occasional casual violence.

The American woman picked up her little dog and hugged her. 'A bit better, Beryl. More trees. More space. You forget. But we won't be even here long. You watch, honey. The word is, we're winning this old war.'

Sylvie looked at the hands that held the dog. They were brown and very sinewy, but the nails were perfectly mani-cured: like her mother's when she had spent half the afternoon trimming and filing them. She could suddenly remember the hands even though she could not bring the face to mind. 'My mother had hands like yours,' she blurted out. 'Smooth nails.'

Mrs Bloom splayed the fingers of one hand out and looked at them with a small smile. 'I can't tell you what it takes to keep them like this, honey,' she said. 'But it's worth it.'

Sylvie closed her eyes and tried really to bring up a picture of her mother's face, but she could not. She could see the hands with the long, tapering nails, but the face was shadowy, indistinct. 'Oh! Oh!' she said, rubbing her eyes, and ran back through the huts until she got to Hut Five.

Miss Snowie looked up from her self-appointed task of pulling the bugs off Sylvie's net and putting them in a special tin box that she kept specially for this task. (When the tin was full, she would walk to the edge of the jungle and set the monsters free. Sylvie had an image of them marching in formation, like Japanese soldiers, right back to the hut from which they had been displaced.)

'Miss Snowie, Miss Snowie,' Sylvie hiccoughed. 'I can't see her face. I can't see my mother's face. I close my eyes and I can't see her.'

'Ssh. Ssh,' said Miss Snowie. 'Look, Sylvie, look!' She pointed. Sitting there at the head of Sylvie's bed was Virginia's carved box. 'I went to Heaven and it was here when I got back. Unfortunately I've been to Heaven five times this afternoon.'

The tears dried behind Sylvie's eyes. She kneeled beside the box and opened it. Then, one by one, she took out the boxes and packages, the cloths and braids.

'Is everything there?' said Miss Snowie.

Sylvie touched the items one by one. 'I don't know. There were five soaps and here are four. And there were four packs of needles and now there are three. The cloths are still there. There was some purple braid. That's gone. And my mother's pearl necklace. But the rest's here, I think.'

'So that is good, isn't it? The doctor must have appealed to the better side of whoever this poor woman is, the one who took your box. Three years in the wilderness can drive even the nicest woman to desperation. Remember this, Sylvie.'

Content now, Sylvie started to ram the things back in the box. Miss Snowie put a hand on hers. 'Why not take something for the doctor? To show how pleased you are that she helped you?'

Sylvie scowled at her. 'I have to keep this safe for Virginia. For when she comes back.' She clicked the box shut and added the illusion of security by sliding the broken lock. 'I can't give them away.' She threw herself on to her bed and picked up Ayoshi, holding her in the air and making her turn somersaults. Ayoshi's nose and the stitched knuckles of her fingers were blackened with so much loving.

'And you had a satisfactory afternoon, I hope?' said Miss Snowie, picking up the bug-infested net and peering at it closely through the thick lens of her glasses.

'It was all right. We were on a nature walk with Mrs Bloom. Caesar came with us.'

'Mrs Bloom? Now there you have a very brave woman.'

'She's American. She calls you "honey". She says, "The wu*rr*d is, we're winnin' this ole war." ' Sylvie was proud of her imitation, derived more from the films she had seen at the Cathay Cinema than Mrs Bloom's actual voice. 'And she has a little dog called Judy. Why is she brave?'

Miss Snowie met the child's beady eye. She was a great believer in telling the truth to children, but she held her tongue. It was hard to tell a child whose mother had gone heaven knew where, and whose sister was in the hands of the Japanese, about this woman who had survived the worst experience up in town with torturers, and come back after six months, very thin, with septic feet to show for her ordeal. 'She is very brave,' repeated Miss Snowie. 'Things you don't want to know about.'

Miss Snowie had learned from Mrs Grassington about the day in October 1943 when the Japanese secret police, the *Kempai Tai*, descended on the civilian internment camp, convinced they would find an organised spy ring transmitting messages and organising sabotage on the island. This had led to the imprisonment, torture and sometimes the death of a number of prisoners, including two women. The American woman actually survived six months of dreadful treatment and returned to the camp. She did not talk of her experiences but was regarded by all the women with the respect due to a heroine.

'I like her, she makes jokes,' said Sylvie, 'and has this big laugh. Ha. Ha. Ha.' She closed her eyes again and saw Mrs Bloom's long fingers. Then she lay back and placed Ayoshi over her eyes and conjured up the image of Virginia's face. That was better. She could see Virginia and she knew she was all right. 'Your box is back, Virginia,' she whispered. 'So everything is all right, isn't it?'

There was a rustle, beside her. She opened her eyes to the unusual sight of Miss Snowie actually hurrying, with a skip and a hop, to the door. 'The toilet,' she gasped. 'Sixth time today. Tummy's playing up.'

Sylvie watched the door swinging for a minute. She opened the carved box again. She put everything out in a line on the bed, then returned to the box one packet of everything: soap, ribbons, needles, threads, one towel. The rest she wrapped up in the remaining towel and staggered across with it to the hospital hut. She knew the doctor would be there.

Beryl, still dawdling along behind Mrs Bloom, ran to catch up with her, Caesar snapping at her heels. 'Whaddya doing?'

'The box came back. I'm taking this stuff to the doctor. I don't want it.'

'Why?'

'You heard Mrs Bloom. "The *wurrd* is we're winnin' this ole war." '

'My ma says we beat the Italians, and the Germans are nearly beat.'

'So I don't need any of this stuff.'

Beryl grabbed her shoulder and squeezed it hard. 'Give it to me. My ma would really like all that stuff.'

Sylvie pulled away. 'No. I wanna give it to the doctor.'

'Give it here!' Beryl grabbed for the parcel.

Sylvie clung on tight and kicked Beryl hard on the shin. Beryl fell down, howling. Two women bending down over their gardens looked up from their labours. When they saw it was Beryl Bridges, they returned to their careful watering. That Bridges child was always kicking up a racket for one reason or another. And the other was the Eurasian child. So volatile, those children. The camp children were spoiled brats, you couldn't deny it.

Sylvie pushed through the hospital door and spilled her booty on the table that served as the doctor's desk. The doctor peered at the jumble of packets that covered her precious notes. 'What's this?' she said.

'Someone brought the box back. Here's the stuff from inside it. I kept one or two things. And the box. For Virginia. She'll be back soon.'

The doctor poked at the packets. 'Well, I am glad, truly glad the box came back, Sylvie. But I am not sure that Miss Chen would wish—'

'I wanted to put my own stuff in the box,' said Sylvie. 'And Virginia isn't here, is she?'

'As you said, she might come back.'

'Yes, I know that. In any case, Mrs Bloom says the war's nearly over, so I'll be able to go and look for Virginia.'

The doctor pushed one package towards her with one finger. 'Still, I don't think I should take all these.'

Sylvie sighed. 'Virginia kept the stuff 'cause she thought you would like her better with them. Miss Snowie told her that you can't buy another person's regard. She told me that.'

'Why would Miss Chen think that?'

'Because she is . . . *we* are what they call *stengahs*. I heard Mrs Bridges call the Richards family "black-and-tans". That's the same, isn't it? Virginia thought you would like her more if she gave this stuff away bit by bit.'

'Well, I don't think that is the case, Sylvie. Surely you don't think that?'

'It doesn't matter now. I've given it to you. Now no one, not one woman, will come and loot Virginia's box when there's nothing in it.'

The doctor stood up and came round the table. Her hand on Sylvie's shoulder felt like a claw. 'You are quite a sensible girl, Sylvie. I see this now. If you want anything, anything at all, you come to me, do you hear me?' Then she put Sylvie away from her. 'Now, my dear, perhaps you would go and play? I am rather busy here.'

The doctor sat down and watched the child trail out from the dark interior of the clinic to the blinding light outside. Strange child. Strange indeed. She stared at the open door for several minutes. Then she piled the packages on the floor and got back to her notes, which were charting a worrying increase in the incidence of dysentery. The old ones were dropping off like flies. It was so irritating to have kept them going so long, just to lose them at this point in the endgame. For endgame it was. For three years, first in Changi, now in Sime Road, the rumours had been rife. But now the messages from the men's camp were firm. They had a wireless. Italy down, Germany tottering. For sure Japan would not be far behind. They must hang on, blast them, they must hang on.

# Chapter Twenty-Three

## What a *Susah*!

At the end of that week Miss Snowie collapsed in the doorway of the hut and was carried to the hospital by Mrs Grassington, with Sylvie holding on to her ankles and trying to keep her sandals on her feet. 'How terrible this is,' gasped Miss Snowie. 'How terrible.'

The doctor sent Sylvie away while they made a space for Miss Snowie in the crowded ward. The nurses hovered, ready to clean her up. Sylvie ran to the hut, jammed Miss Snowie's straw hat on her head, grabbed Miss Snowie's mildewed Bible and ran back to sit on the ground outside the hospital.

Beryl came and threw herself down beside her. 'I'm not your friend, you know,' she said. 'You kick people.'

'I know that,' said Sylvie. 'I don't care.'

'Whaddya got that Bible for? Found Jesus, have you?'

'It's for Miss Snowie. She had it all that time on the peninsula when she was saving all the natives for Jesus. Then they ran away to their *kampongs* and left her. Then the

Japanese took her to the cathedral. Then she came here. She's in the hospital. Got the runs.'

Beryl whistled. 'Whaddya do if the old biddy dies? Then you really will be an orphan. They'll not keep you in that hut. My ma says those biddies in Hut Five have no time for you. Never wanted a kid, and especially—'

'If she's a black-and-tan.'

'Well, my ma said they should have put you down at the end with all the rest of them. The Richards and the Tongs and the rest. Mebbe they'll send you down there now. If Miss Snowie kicks the bucket.'

'Well, they can't.'

'Sure they can. The old biddies on the Committee – their rule is law, my ma says. She says they're too big for their boots. And she's one of them, being our hut captain.'

Sylvie wanted to shout at Beryl, to shake her and tell her that anyway, she wasn't a black-and-tan, that Virginia was her friend, not her sister, and that she was as white as . . . well, as white as anybody. She looked at Beryl's burned brown face. As white as Beryl, anyway. She started to giggle.

'Whaddya laughing at?' said Beryl, scowling.

'I was thinking you looked like a bit of a black-and-tan yourself.'

No. Virginia *was* her sister. The old woman *was* her grandmother. They *had* lived together. They had told their stories. They belonged together in a family, didn't they? That was all there was to that. 'Virginia's coming back,' she announced. 'I know that for certain.'

'How d'ya know that?'

'The doctor said she had a message.' There. That would keep all the biddies quiet. Lots of stories went round the camp, many untrue. This could be one of them. Beryl's ma would see to that. Sylvie picked up a stick from the dusty ground and threw it for Caesar. He went running for it and brought it back, wagging his tail. Then it was Beryl's turn to throw. Mrs Bloom's dog, Judy, loped up and joined in. The dogs barked and jumped and the racket brought an irate Dutchwoman on to the scene. Her hair was pulled tightly back from her head and she had a very long nose. She had a large stick, with which she laid about both dogs. The dogs then ganged up on her. She had to be rescued by two very cross women from her own hut.

By this time, Mrs Bloom had come running down to retrieve Judy, and the Dutchwoman had a shouting match with her before peace was restored. Caesar came to lie on the dusty ground at Sylvie's feet and put his head up for a stroke.

'Whaddya think?' said Beryl. 'What a *susah*! Have you ever seen such biddies?'

'Not in my life,' said Sylvie, tickling Caesar behind his ears in the spot he particularly liked. 'Not ever in my life.'

'Some of those biddies got the other dogs shot when we were in Changi,' said Beryl.

'But not Judy and Caesar.'

'Nah. Mrs Bloom and my ma got a petition up and all the children signed it. The Nips shot the others but Caesar and Judy were saved. Here!' Beryl hunted in the pocket of her overlong shorts and pulled out a stick. 'Here. Sugar cane. Just chew it. Lovely!'

Sylvie sat back, content now that, for the moment, Beryl (and Caesar) were her friends again.

# Chapter Twenty-Four

## Two Visits

There was another kind of *susah* that night when some bigwig general made a visit to the camp. There was a big *tenko* of all the women, including the 'walking sick', to hear the general's words interpreted by the small man with a briefcase. The women listened to gruff sentences about how very kind the Japanese were to their captives and that they must say if there was anything, anything at all, with which they were discontented.

As they dispersed to stand to attention in their huts, Sylvie enjoyed a *sotto voce* comment from Mrs Bridges that the Nips were lying bastards whatever their rank. After that the general came to visit each hut where he commented on the great efforts the women had made to render these places cheerful. He complimented the artists on their paintings, the teachers on their classroom and the gardeners on their gardening. This latter was so important, he said, when supplies were so short. He lectured them on how the people of

Singapore city and the brave Imperial soldiers had to endure the shortages and it was well that the prisoners, lowly as they were, made this effort.

In Hut Five, he spied Ayoshi on top of the carved box. Sylvie had to explain who she was and how she came to be there. The general grunted as his interpreter spoke in his ear.

The interpreter, a neat man with glasses and highly polished boots, said, 'The name of your – ah – sister – what is this?'

'Her name is Jin Kee Chen. And she lived on Beach Road. Jin Kee Chen,' she said more loudly. 'I wish her to be back here to take care of me, sir. I am alone.' Then she bowed as low as she could so that her nose almost touched her knees.

There was a strangled gasp from the general that was the sixth cousin to a snort of laughter. Then he and his fidgety, fluttering attendant left the hut and all the women relaxed. Mrs Grassington came across and put her hands on Sylvie's shoulders. 'That was very brave of you, dearie. Very brave indeed.'

Sylvie put her head on one side and looked up at her. 'Who was he?'

'That was the big cheese. The biggest cheese in Singapore.'

Mrs Josie Warren, in the corner, piped up, 'For the time being, my dears. Just for the time being. We have our own big cheeses in waiting. Did you hear those bombers last night?'

There was laughter all round at this and everyone relaxed. Sylvie picked up Miss Snowie's Bible in one hand and Ayoshi in the other and made her way through the muttering, murmuring women towards the clinic. The general and his entourage were still hovering at the gate and some women were hanging around the doors, talking and chattering. Relief spun in the air like dragonflies.

When Sylvie asked about Miss Snowie, the doctor shook her head. 'Quite poorly, dear. Sleeping now. But we do what we can do.' She nodded towards the two Australian nurses, moving from bed space to bed space.

'Can I see her? I'd like to see Miss Snowie,' said Sylvie.

The doctor was about to hold forth on the uselessness of this gesture when she saw the Bible. 'You will read to her? What a nice thought, my dear.'

As she watched the child weave her way down the dismal, crowded hospital hut, the doctor thought that perhaps the reading would at least do the child some good. Not much good for the old girl, of course. Out for the count, poor old duck.

As she made her way carefully through the prone bodies, breathing in that sticky death smell, Sylvie thought of that first time, with Virginia leading her through the bodies of dead men in the hospital at Singapore. And the blood on her sandal.

Hurtled now into *reading* the Bible instead of just giving it to Miss Snowie, Sylvie sat on the end of the bed wondering what to do. Then she stood the Bible up on her knee and let it flop open. She read: ' "*For he shall give his angels charge over thee: to keep thee in all thy ways. They shall bear thee in their hands: that thou hurt not thy foot against a stone.*" ' She flopped it open again and read: ' "*Heaviness may endure for a night but joy cometh in the morning.*" '

'That's it, then!' said the Australian nurse trying in vain to feed the woman beside Miss Snowie. 'Would ya believe? Old Hitler's gotta be on his uppers. Sure as shot. We've got angels lookin' after us and we just need to wait for the joy to cometh.'

It took five days, despite Sylvie's increasingly desperate readings from the Bible, for Miss Snowie to come back from the misty world she'd been visiting to the sticky heat of the hospital hut and the desperate murmur of people coping with no resources.

On the fifth day, Sylvie stood at the end of the clinic and looked at the clutch of old women at the far end of the hut, hunched under their mosquito nets. She remembered one time when she walked down Sago Street in Chinatown with Virginia to buy paper boats and houses from the paper man. There were the dying houses there: old ones were brought there to die in narrow spaces with shrines and kneeling, patient people at the entrances. The paper things were for them to take with them to their ancestors.

Here in the hut, that quiet attendance of the doctor and her nurses, moving calmly in the stifling gloom, made her think of all that patient, respectful waiting. She shuddered and strode down the hut and whipped away Miss Snowie's mosquito net. Then she laughed as she saw Miss Snowie was awake.

'You seem cheerful today.' Miss Snowie looked up at her from her makeshift pillow. 'I wonder why that is?'

'Because you're not waiting.'

'Waiting for what?'

'To die.'

'You can be sure of that,' said the old woman, hauling herself up into a sitting position, swaying slightly. 'Now then. Is that my Bible there? Would you be so good as to pass it to me?'

For the next half-hour Miss Snowie and Sylvie sat reading, Miss Snowie turning the pages of her Bible and Sylvie engrossed in a battered camp library copy of *The Secret Garden*. After ten minutes she looked up to let her eyes follow a procession of a nurse and a tall man with a beard, led by the doctor. When they reached the prone body of the old woman in the bed beside Miss Snowie the man bent over and said words under his breath. Sylvie had witnessed, in the last two days, a growing drama around this old woman, wife to a vicar. She was very poorly, about to be transferred to the big Myako hospital for treatment, more probably to die.

As the tall man with the beard raised his voice and started to chant something in a high, almost whining voice, Sylvie blinked in surprise.

'Ah!' said Miss Snowie. 'The good reverend.'

Sylvie could tell that the tall man had heard, but he kept chanting. Then, assisted by the doctor, he gently lifted the unconscious woman and they moved with difficulty through the door of the hut. Sylvie knew there would be a car or truck at the gate, ready to take the woman to the hospital. It had happened before.

She turned back to Miss Snowie. 'So you're really better, Miss Snowie?' she said.

Miss Snowie gave what would have been a cheery grin if she'd had her bottom set in. As it was, it had all the appearance of a leer. 'Good as gold, Sylvie. How lucky I've been to have such a guardian angel. Many days I could not see you, but I could hear you reading so well.' Miss Snowie patted the bed. 'Sit here, Sylvie, and tell me what has happened in this microcosm while I've been away.'

'Microcosm? What's that?'

Half an hour later the bearded man was back, standing by the bed. 'Miss Raven! How good to meet you at last! The bishop has told me of your sterling work. The doctor says you are on the mend.' He put down the rucksack he was carrying and grasped her frail hands in his. Sylvie noted the fine fuzz of thick blond hair on the back of his knuckles. Miss Snowie introduced her to the man. Her own hands were grasped by firm, slender fingers.

Sylvie looked up into his face and thought for a split second that it must be her father, Bo Sambuck. He too was tall and fair. He too might have a beard now. It wasn't him, of course. This man was far too young to be her father. Still, Sylvie stared up at him, wishing that he would change. The man absorbed her stare for a moment, then turned back to Miss Snowie and asked her about her last months up on the peninsula when she was left without help.

Then he bent down and took some things from his ruck-sack: a kind of cup; a bottle of water; a soiled piece of cloth tied round some small squares of bread. He looked around, pulled a crude table across.

The man placed the bottle and the bread on the table. 'Now.' He beamed from one to the other. 'We are set.'

Miss Snowie hitched herself up a bit further until she was sitting up very straight. 'Kneel down,' she croaked across at Sylvie. Sylvie knelt by the table. 'Put your hands together and close your eyes. Like they tell you at school.'

Sylvie did this, just as she did at school. She'd never been troubled about this folding of hands and closing of eyes. It meant nothing to her. She did relish, though, that world behind her eyes.

The man's voice murmured on about forgiving sins and the Father, Son and Holy Ghost. 'The body of Christ.' Sylvie had seen the picture in plenty of books. The body of Christ could be no worse than that. She lifted her lids slightly so she could see through her long lashes. It was just those bits of bread. No body. What a poor thing.

'And the blood of Christ.' She opened her eyes wider. The cherub-faced man was holding the cup with both hands and offering it to Miss Snowie. It was very plain, on a stem. It gleamed in the half-light of the hut. She leaned forward to see more clearly. The man kept on muttering away. Then he put the cup back on the table. She leaned over and peered at it. 'Presented to Bo Sambuck, 1937 Champion' with a design of crossed tennis rackets above it. The hairs on the back of her neck stood out like pokers. Her whole body prickled with pain and pleasure. She knew this cup. It was the one she'd sold in the city. She had a small version of this cup, marked '1936 Champion', in the carved box. (The thief had returned it. Another part of her mind wondered about the thief. Who she was and why she'd done that thing? It probably was Miss Lomax. She was very angry about the box.)

At this moment she wanted to shout out, 'That's my daddy, that is my daddy,' but she bit her lip and stopped the words coming. That would blow it all open. Be discreet. She would never get Virginia back, if they knew about Bo Sambuck.

Miss Snowie was breathing more easily now, eyes open, smiling faintly. 'That is a fine communion cup, Reverend.'

The man smiled, a boyish pleased smile. 'At first, communion was only offered in Changi with a tin cup. I was still outside then, with the bishop at the cathedral. We went into Changi to offer communion. So I bought this at a shop in the chaos and when I came in here full time I brought it in with me.' He drank the rest of the water and cleaned the cup carefully with the white rag. 'It has done great service, this cup. In Changi. Down here at Sime Road. Better than on some planter's mantelpiece.' He tucked the things back into his rucksack. 'I have to go, Miss Raven. I only have a chit for three hours out. And there was Mrs Black to send off to the hospital.'

Miss Snowie smiled faintly. 'Poor Mrs Black's misfortune is my good fortune.'

The man stood before Sylvie and put a hand on her head. 'May the Lord bless you and keep you, my child.'

Then Sylvie remembered something: the time in the street when this man sent her flying, causing all that bother for Virginia. She thought about Virginia and her bruises. Perhaps that's what they were doing to her now that they had looted her. What was this man doing? Why was he there, interfering with them, coming like some kind of saviour to Miss Snowie? This man. He made her think about those men who had hurt

Virginia. She ducked to loosen her head from his hand, but he didn't seem to notice. This man. She did not want his blessing.

He bent down to Miss Snowie. 'Hold on, Miss Raven,' he said quietly. 'It won't be long now. Just hang on.'

Sylvie looked at him again. Perhaps he was a good man. Not really like those soldiers at all.

'I thought they were all rumours,' murmured Miss Snowie. 'There are always rumours.'

'We have it that Italy has surrendered and Germany is on the point of capitulation. And our planes are clearly seen in these skies. We have it on good authority.'

'Thank you, Reverend.' Miss Snowie had heard about the wirelesses in the men's camp, replaced at last after that first frightening October '43 Japanese purge. She shuddered slightly. She remembered again what Mrs Grassington had told her. How the American woman and this young man's bishop were among the seventy souls to be taken by those butchers, the *Kempai Tai*.

Sylvie watched the priest as he walked to the door, having a word here, a word there, with women he obviously knew. The women watched this young man with motherly affection, with lover-like relish. They thought of the sons, husbands and fiancés that the war had snatched from them.

When he was safely through the door Sylvie turned to Miss Snowie, who was lying back on her makeshift pillow, looking exhausted. She burst out, 'He could be wrong, you know.'

Miss Snowie frowned slightly. 'Wrong? He is a very good man. Young and earnest. But very good.'

'He could be wrong. It might *not* be a planter's cup. It could be a doctor's cup, or a shopkeeper's cup, or a cup from a man who takes care of an office in a *godown*.'

'I don't know what you are talking about, child. That cup is a blessed cup now, whoever it belonged to before. A hundred times a week. It's blessed a hundred times a week. It purports to hold the blood of Christ. What matter if it was a planter or a doctor – or a tinker or a tailor, for that matter? It is a holy cup.'

Sylvie stayed silent. She wanted to say that it matters if that cup belongs to your daddy and was stuck on *his* sideboard once upon a time in Leonie Hill Road.

'Well, child, why so glum?' Miss Snowie adjusted the net. 'Why don't you come right inside my net and read your book to me? The part where she first finds the garden and she's walking down the paths and the roses are still blooming. Don't you think that would cheer us up now?'

Beryl was quite pleased to hear that Miss Snowie was getting better. 'So she'll be back in the hut soon?'

'The doctor says so.'

'Ma says the Committee were talking about having you out of the hut and down the bottom of the camp with the others.'

'The others?' Sylvie was sick of hearing about this.

'You know who.'

'Anyway, who says?'

'My ma argued with them and said it was a crying shame.'

Sylvie didn't know whether that meant Mrs Bridges

thought she should go or she shouldn't, so she changed the subject. 'I was wondering if they knew who'd taken my Virginia's box. The doctor said they'd find out even though I got it back.'

They were walking the perimeter with Caesar in tow. Beryl picked up a chip of wood, and threw it for him to chase. 'They do, but they ain't doing anything about it. Ma says.'

'Why not?'

''Cause it's Miss Lomax. They found her wearing your ma's pearls because she's potty. But she said she was going to commit suicide if they made her come and say sorry to you.'

'What's suicide?'

'When somebody kills themselves. My ma says it's surprising there's not more suicides in here.'

'Oh.' Caesar had dropped the wood at Sylvie's feet. She threw it high in the air and it stuck in a tree. They went to the tree and started to kick it and shake it to try to free the bit of wood. It was very tenacious.

Beryl soon got sick of kicking. 'Leave it. It'll come down when it rains.'

'It's not going to rain.' The water was very low. Everyone was looking very grimy. That was why more people were sick.

Beryl shrugged. 'I know,' she said, 'let's go and see Mrs Bloom. She said she'd show me how to play mah-jong.'

'I know how to play that,' said Sylvie. 'My grandmother showed me. So I don't have to learn.' That was a lie, of course. But it didn't matter because she'd never volunteer to play a game and Beryl would never find out. So that was all right.

# Chapter Twenty-Five

## Booze and a Smocked Dress

'The old biddy's on her pins again, is she?'

Sylvie nodded. It was a relief to have Miss Snowie back. It stopped the other women looking longingly at Miss Snowie's space, and talking when Sylvie was there about the child being better off among her own, down in Hut Two.

It was evening. They were sitting on a piece of high ground up behind the hospital hut, one of the few spots free of the ferocious gardening that was going on around every hut. The women used their gardens and the more common central patch of garden to supplement the bleak rations, which had been cut by half again, according to Cloth Ears. The Imperial soldiers were on restricted diet because little food was getting through the blockades. So, of course, unworthy prisoners must eat less.

For Sylvie, hunger was as perpetual as the flies that buzzed and attacked you day and night. It was there, and it bothered her, but she didn't waste time thinking of it. Beryl, though, did like the idea of food. She was obsessed with it. It was an old custom in the camp to talk about food, or the lack of it, or to savour with talk some recent treat that had been wangled, bought, or conceded by the unpredictable captors. One frequent pastime was to communicate in detail the whole menu of the dinner they would give when they got out. Another was to reflect in graphic detail the meals in restaurants they had had with their husbands and lovers.

'Ma and some others are sewing stars on Nip uniforms to get some more food,' said Beryl, after they had just discussed how very hungry they were, despite the fact that the Nips had let the camp have two Red Cross parcels two days ago and they had had their microscopic share. 'You should hear the biddies on about her doing that. "Giving comfort to the enemy" and all that. They do get on their high horses.'

'They're not making bombs, are they? Or guns?'

'Exactly.' Beryl reached into the cloth bag she always carried round her neck and produced a tin bottle. She unscrewed the top and offered it to Sylvie. 'Here. Try this.'

'I'm not thirsty.'

'It's not water. It's hooch.'

'What's hooch?' said Sylvie.

'Booze? You know booze? Like gin. Gin *pahits*. Like cocktails.'

Sylvie lay back and looked at the night-dark sky, trying to find an image of her mother drinking gin *pahits* in the dancing room at Raffles. 'We're at Sime Road, Beryl, not Raffles.'

'It is! My ma bought it from a Dutchwoman who made it.'

'How'd she make it?'

'From rice slops and some bits of raisins and yeast.'

'Yeogh!'

'Try it. G'wan! Otherwise it'd not be worth me stealing it from her. She'll go crazy and beat me, anyway.' Beryl nudged Sylvie's arm with the tin bottle. 'Go on!'

Sylvie sat up and took the bottle. Really, Beryl got on your nerves. She took a swig and choked.

'Go on!' urged Beryl. 'It always hurts at first.'

Sylvie took another painful swig and thrust it back at Beryl. 'Take it,' she gasped. 'You have some.'

Beryl took a swig and only coughed a little.

Sylvie opened her mouth and breathed in slowly, so that even the hot evening air cooled her burned mouth and throat. 'It tastes like poison,' she managed finally.

Beryl licked her lips. 'Doesn't it?'

Sylvie opened her eyes very wide and then a retch started at her heels and travelled up her body.

'Keep it in!' warned Beryl.

Sylvie swallowed hard, took a shallow breath through her mouth and the boiling mixture stayed down.

Beryl screwed on the top of her bottle and put it back in her cotton bag. 'There! How do you feel?'

'Swimmy.'

'Good!' said Beryl. 'That's how you're supposed to feel.'

Sylvie blinked. Before her the row of huts detached itself from the dark foliage of the gardens and hovered just a foot in the air. Above them, low in a dark hibiscus sky, the sun was round as a cartwheel. Its daytime fire had simmered down to a custard yellow as it shot warm arrows of orange into the last dying lights of day.

Beryl pushed at her shoulder, so that she turned right round. 'Look!'

In another part of the sky, like a pale reflection of its sister, the moon was rising, a thin disc of insubstantial silver. The sky around it was dense. Darkness unrelieved was on the ascendant.

Sylvie closed her eyes. 'Magic,' she said.

'No, hooch,' said Beryl. 'D'you like it?'

'No,' said Sylvie. She wanted to be sick again.

Beryl lay back in the lalang grass. 'Do you ever think of before?' she asked. 'When we were real?'

Sylvie thought of the veranda and her mother and father in the long chairs. She thought of the silver cups with the crossed racquets.

'No,' she said. 'I never think of that.'

'My ma,' said Beryl, 'says there are more Red Cross parcels. So there'll be treats.'

'They're always saying that.'

'She says it's true this time. The Nips have promised.'

'Treats,' said Sylvie. 'I'm hungry as a hog.' She thought of marshmallow and liquorice, chocolate and tinned cheese. Eggs piled on top of each other in a kind of egg mountain.

It turned out that there certainly were parcels. The women who worked for the Nips had seen them. They were not given out. This made the sloppy rice with scraps of blackened seafood taste like grit in Sylvie's mouth.

The next rumour was about money. The message was brought by Mrs Bracegirdle, now hut leader, as Mrs Grassington was in the hospital with beriberi, having blown up like a balloon and split open her clothes. The Nips said the prisoners were to make a list of all the jewellery they had, and give up any money they had more than one hundred dollars. Sylvie wondered if Miss Lomax would declare her mother's pearls. That would be quite funny.

'My pink dress needs mending,' she announced loudly to Miss Snowie. 'I'm bursting out all over. I'll have to shorten it and put the bits in the side.'

Miss Snowie looked at her over her glasses. 'How clever of you, dear. I'm afraid I am a bit of a duffer when it comes to sewing.'

'I was until –' Sylvie paused – 'until Jin Kee and I went to live with our grandma. Uncle Chu showed me how to cut cloth and make small stitches.'

'You are a lucky girl.'

'I'll go by the fence to do it. Watch for the aeroplanes.'

'Will the sun not be too bright there for you?'

'I'll wear your hat and sit under the flame tree. There's shade near the edge where the jungle is.'

Miss Snowie sighed. 'The hut seems so much a darker place when you are not here, Sylvie.'

'You come with me,' said Sylvie. 'I'll carry your rug; hold your hand.'

The women in the other huts watched the Chen child lead the old woman through the hut and down to the boundary. That was something. The old dear never came out of the hut, except for *tenko*, and that time in the hospital for her bout of dysentery.

The tree had had all of its ground-level branches lopped for fuel but the high canopy still cast a narrow band of deep shade. They tucked themselves inside this, and Sylvie laid out her pink dress with its elaborate waist smocking. Beside this, she placed Ayoshi, face down. She lifted up Ayoshi's elaborate obi, removed a piece of paper and put it underneath the pink cloth and proceeded to use the sharp points of the scissors to pick out the stitching. Then she pulled out most of the wiry stuffing.

'Goodness me, child, what are you doing?' said Miss Snowie.

'Watch,' said Sylvie. She turned the dress inside out and started to unpick the lining on the back of the smocking. She poked her fingers inside and pulled out the coins, laying them, in rows of five, in the sandy soil. 'Five, ten, fifteen . . . forty,' she counted. Then she proceeded to put the coins into Ayoshi, packing them round with bits of stuffing. 'They can go with the ones which you sewed in.'

'You knew that?'

'She seemed so heavy so I took a look.'

'Of course we are told to surrender our money,' said Miss Snowie. For her, the order was academic, as she had no money.

'But why should we do what the Japanese say?'

' "*Render therefore unto Caesar the things which are Caesar's.*" '

'Caesar?' Sylvie frowned, thinking of Beryl's little dog.

'He was a great Roman Emperor. The great authority in the time of Jesus. Some might say the aggressor.'

'Like the Nips?'

Miss Snowie was flustered. 'Well, not quite. Perhaps there were similarities. The point was, when the argument rose about paying the taxes to the Romans, Jesus said, "Render therefore unto Caesar the things which are his." They were trying to trap him, you see,' she floundered.

'So I should give this to the Nips as a kind of tax?' Sylvie bit off a length of thread and started to stitch up the hole.

'Well, no. To be honest, my dear, I am not certain.'

'I promised the grandmother I would keep the gold coins safe. I promised.'

'Well, then, that's all right. "Honour thy father and thy mother." That might just cancel it out.' She watched Sylvie close the hole up with small stitches. 'So it was a story, then, that you were going to alter the pink dress?'

Sylvie shook her head. 'No. It *is* too small. And I said that so the people in the hut would hear. If they saw me stitching the coins into Ayoshi . . .'

'They would understand.'

Sylvie shook her head. 'Someone took my box, Miss Snowie. I think I know who it was but she's mad.' She shook out the dress in front of her. 'Look!' she said. 'Do you think I need to cut off the bottom? All I have to do is undo the smocking.' She picked out the bits of cotton, shook out the dress again and held it in front of her. 'A bit like a pink tent,' she said.

'I must admit, my dear, I like you in your little shorts and blouse. You look – how shall I say it – carefree?'

'I'm not the kind of girl who would wear a little pink frock?'

'I don't think so.'

'Perhaps I will sell it. Or give it to the doctor for the Destitute.'

'The latter, I think, my dear girl. After all, you always have Ayoshi. You are a very lucky girl.'

# Chapter Twenty-Six

## Transgression

The next day it seemed some parcels had indeed been liberated. Miss Snowie and Sylvie shared a teaspoon of sugar on their rice at breakfast and found extra tinned beef swimming around in their lunchtime soup. They were promised bread and tinned cheese for tea, and – a miracle – tinned fruit after that. The day pulsated with treats.

In school, Sylvie's little group of four practised quadratic equations, rehearsed again the whole of *The Song of Hiawatha* and continued their invention of an epic story of Wallace the bear, who discovered the Americas. This latter was only actually written down by Sylvie, as it was her turn for the notebook.

After tea, Sylvie and Beryl went to the doctor's clinic for their monthly appointment to be measured and weighed. The doctor was meticulous about this and each child, every month, was shown her own personal graph. The clinic, like the rest of the camp, seemed these days to buzz with the invasive prickle of almost unwilling optimism. The doctor now had two new boxes of quinine pills, and a box of vitamins in her cupboard, and two jars of Marmite, a crucial source of vitamin B, in her drawer. She almost smiled. The nurses tackled the nursing of the nearly dead with the thought that these, at least, might be the last.

Near the door, Beryl's mother, May Gallaher Bridges, sat very still while a persistent suppurating sore was tended by a young South African. Mrs Bridges' hair was coiled in fizzy springs and her lipstick was in place.

'Well done, Beryl,' grunted the doctor. 'You've grown inches since we first found ourselves in Changi. Unfortunately, your weight is rather less than when you came.'

'She's a bloody beanpole,' Beryl's mother called from the other side of the hut. 'Ouch! Go easy, will you?' she said to the back of the head of the nurse who was tending her wound. 'It's the only left leg I've got.'

'If we don't keep them clear,' the nurse said, 'you'll have no left leg at all.'

The doctor's hand clutched Beryl's bony shoulder. 'This one could do with a few egg-and-bacon breakfasts, I suppose.'

Beryl twisted out of her grasp and moved to stand by the door. Now it was Sylvie's turn. 'Only nine measurements for you, Sylvie,' said the doctor. She stood Sylvie against her home-made measuring stick. 'Only an inch taller, but you're not quite as skinny as your friend.' Carefully, she lifted the weights to balance the scales. 'A little down again. You were well covered when you came in to us.' She glanced across at her nurse. 'Please God, it's not much longer before you'll be able to put it on again.'

Beryl took Sylvie's arm and dragged her out of the hut into the sunlight. 'The old bag,' she said. 'You'd think we were prize pigs and she was sending us to market.'

Sylvie grinned. Beryl had this wonderful way of putting things. They went to their usual high place behind the huts.

'What's wrong with your ma's leg?' said Sylvie.

'She banged it one day when she was out doing the wood,' said Beryl. 'It won't close up. She's really mad. Keeps on about her legs always being her best feature and here she is scarred for life. She says it's a good thing my dad skedaddled, or he'd vomit at the sight of her.'

'Skedaddled?'

'He went off with this floozie from the Great World. Went to Hong Kong with her and vanished into thin air.'

'What's a floozie?'

'A bad woman who sells herself to the highest bidder, my ma says, and women who go with Japanese. There are some here in the camp. This floozie made my dad take all our money and skedaddle.'

'So what did you do, left on your own?'

'My ma got a job selling lipstick in Maynards and we had to live with her friend, Beattie, who had two sets of false teeth. One for weekdays and one for Sundays. So there was always a pair of teeth grinning at you in the bathroom.'

'So what happened to Beattie?'

'Drowned when the ship went down, like all our stuff. Except for the lipsticks.'

'Lipsticks?'

'Ma had fourteen tucked in her brassiere. She had to dry them out, but she says those lipsticks have kept her going.'

Sylvie lay back in the sharp grass and thought of the rows of lipsticks on her mother's dressing table. She screwed her eyes tighter, and among the bright points of light she could see a face: a perfect oval with arched brows and full, lipsticked lips. Then all she could see were the lips.

Beryl shook her arm. 'Hey, Sylvie! Open your eyes. You look like a monkey. Or a Nip.'

Sylvie shook off her arm, but the vision had gone. She opened her eyes. 'I could see my mother, just for a second,' she said. 'I'd forgotten her face.'

Beryl stood up. 'I have a new game,' she said.

Sylvie leaped to her feet. 'I'm in,' she said.

Beryl explained that the game was that they had to walk backwards right along the perimeter and count the steps. 'Backwards, mind you.'

'Me in front?' It didn't seem such a bad thing to do. Sylvie had done this walking backwards once before, walking all the way down to the town with Virginia, from Hibiscus Lodge. The world which crept into being from behind her was a different world from that seen forwards. She liked it.

'OK. You in front. We have to keep one hand on the wire at all times. That's the rule.'

Freddy Bloom and her friend, exhausted by the heat and the obligation to dig out a whole row of sweet potatoes, stood up to stretch their backs and watch the two little girls loitering by the fence. Beryl Bridges tripped Sylvie Chen and they both collapsed into giggles.

'Oh, the joys of youth,' said Freddy.

The two women quickly bent their backs again as they spied Four Eyes and the guard they called Cyclops, gaunt and unusually unkempt, detaching themselves from the gatehouse and coming into the camp. Cyclops hesitated at the end of their garden, so the women stood up again and bowed deeply. Cyclops laughed, showing his broken teeth, and said something to Four Eyes, and they walked on. Freddy Bloom put her tongue out at the receding backs and bent down again to her work.

Sylvie and Beryl had done three-quarters of the wire when they heard a shout. 'Hey, kids, what are your names?'

Three men, *chungkols* over their shoulders, were trudging back towards the men's compound. The one who had shouted was tall and bony, and wore glasses tied with string. 'Go on, kids, we might know your dads,' said a smaller, stringy man, whose red hair was shaded by a rag and the vestiges of an army hat.

The girls pressed their noses on the wire. 'My name's Beryl Bridges,' shouted Beryl, 'and my dad skedaddled off to Hong Kong. And she has a Chinese name because she is a Child of Love.'

The men laughed at this. Their smiles faded suddenly, and they put their heads down and hurriedly trudged on.

Sylvie stayed at the wire. 'Bo Sambuck!' she bawled. 'Do you know Bo Sambuck?'

A hand pulled her away from the wire. 'Beryl!' She turned

angrily to stare into the beetle-browed face of Cyclops. 'Get off me!' she bawled. 'Get off me!' She could see only the back and bottom of Beryl, who was bowing low beside her, her neck held firmly down by Four Eyes.

Cyclops held Sylvie by the shoulder and slapped her face one way, then the other. 'No talk to men,' he grunted. 'No talk to men!' Then he hit her again.

Her head was ringing with the blows; her sight went fuzzy. Across in the garden, Freddy Bloom and her friend were crouching over their sweet potatoes. Other women in doorways stared at a safe distance. Mrs Bridges was in the doorway of the clinic, shading her eyes.

'Come!' The men pushed the girls before them with their sticks. They were moving in the direction of the guardroom by the gate. Mrs Bridges came towards them in a limping hurry. 'What is it, Beryl?' she said. 'What the hell have you done?'

A blow from Cyclops' stick sent her sprawling. The soldiers marched on, harrying the girls in front of them like malevolent sheepdogs.

In the guard hut Four Eyes grunted something to the sergeant at the desk and he nodded to a corner beside a tall cupboard. Cyclops hurtled the girls into the corner, saying, 'Now kneel, now children kneel.' He forced them down so they were kneeling, half facing each other, half the wall.

The sergeant seemed angry about something. He growled at the soldiers and then gestured towards the little girls. He grunted something else and Four Eyes went off.

Being in the hut, with its grinding fan, was cooler than being out in the sun. But their corner was dusty and smelled of sweat and sweet tobacco. Beryl was pale under her tan, and breathing hard. She'd known women come to the guardhouse for punishment, never to be seen again.

Sylvie winked at her and mouthed, 'It's all right.' She didn't really know whether it was all right. She just knew she should say it to Beryl, to lessen her terrible pale stare.

The wooden floor was hurting her knees and she tried to bring her leg up to ease it. Cyclops poked her in the shoulder with his stick and she stayed very still. If she tried very hard, she thought, she could convince herself that the ridges in the floorboards were not daggers in her knees. They were soft cushions like those Virginia's grandma had on the carved bench. Soft cushions. Really soft.

After a very long time the door opened and in limped Mrs Bridges and the doctor in her washed-out hospital smock. The two women bowed low to the sergeant. The sergeant nodded at Four Eyes, who shouted, 'Children by fence. Talk men. Is forbidden. Bad training for children.'

Mrs Bridges started to say something but the doctor grasped her arm. The doctor ignored Four Eyes and spoke directly to the sergeant. 'The children are very naughty, but they are children.' She spoke very slowly, gesturing towards the girls in the corner. 'Very naughty *children*.' She held her hand out flat three feet from the floor. 'Small.'

'They pass messages to the men prisoners,' said Four Eyes.

The doctor shook her head, staring steadily at the sergeant. 'These are fatherless children,' she said. 'No fathers. It makes them curious about the men. They miss their fathers.'

'Their fathers in camp?' said the sergeant.

The doctor glanced at Mrs Bridges and shook her head. 'No fathers. This is the mother of Beryl.' She pointed first to Mrs Bridges, then to Beryl. 'But the little one . . .' she pointed to Sylvie and shook her head, 'has no one in the camp.'

'My sister, Virginia Chen,' burst in Sylvie, undeterred by a poke on the shoulder from Cyclops. 'She left the camp and has not come back. Virginia Chen.'

The sergeant made a note in his book. In the long minutes which followed the silence was broken only by the buzzing of a large, lazy fly, which was finally swatted on the desk by the sergeant himself.

The doctor tried again. 'Perhaps if the sergeant could find it in his heart to allow these naughty girls to go, we could punish them ourselves, so they never do anything again.'

The sergeant stared at her. Then he took a cigarette from a tin in the pocket of his immaculate tunic, lit up and stared first at her and then at Mrs Bridges through the veils of smoke.

Mrs Bridges suddenly bowed very low. Sylvie watched her corkscrew curls bounce as she stood up. 'I will punish my daughter, Sergeant, I promise you. I will punish her very, very hard.'

Then the sergeant started to laugh and waved his cigarette at the girls. 'Take girls and punish,' he said. He took a long bamboo cane from behind his desk, and handed it to the doctor. 'Corporal make sure punish.' He waved towards Four Eyes.

Sylvie and Beryl stood up. 'Come on, you naughty girls,' said the doctor grimly. 'Take your punishment.'

They were marched through clusters of women to Hut Five. Four Eyes wanted to follow them in, but the doctor barred his way. 'We punish, you listen.' She pointed to her ears. 'I show you after.' She got them into the hut and firmly clashed the door behind them.

She turned. 'Now! Lipstick,' she said. Mrs Bridges scrabbled in her waist pouch and produced one.

'Now!' said the doctor grimly. 'Howl, girls! Howl like you have never howled before.' She started to slap a bedroll with the stick. 'First Beryl, then Sylvie Chen. Mrs Bridges, you use your lipstick to give the child marks so I can show the voracious Four Eyes.'

Miss Snowie stood by her bed, one hand to her mouth.

Then Beryl howled while Sylvie was painted with rubbed-in lipstick weals on her bottom and her legs. After that Sylvie shrieked while Beryl was anointed with her bruises.

'Now!' said Mrs Bridges grimly. 'Keep crying and scream-ing.' She dragged them, whimpering, to the door and opened it. Four Eyes had been joined by Cyclops and they were leaning on the side of the hut smoking cigarettes.

She placed the girls before them and pulled up their dresses. Four Eyes nodded and exchanged a giggle with Cyclops. 'Good punishment,' he said. 'Now no dinner for anyone in this hut. No dinner ration.'

They strolled off. 'The cheek of it!' said Mrs Warren, who had been watching the pantomime in the doorway. 'Why should all of our hut suffer? What about your hut, Mrs Bridges?' She glared at Beryl's mother. 'It's not fair.'

'Who knows,' said the doctor, 'how their little minds work? Don't worry, Warren, we'll have a share-out. And there's still something left from the Red Cross parcels. Nobody'll starve. Well – not quite. Now!' She looked from Beryl to Sylvie. 'No more shouting through the fence, you girls!'

Beryl burst out sobbing at this, and Mrs Bridges put an arm round her. 'Come home, sweetheart. You need a wash down and a rest after all that.' She glanced at Sylvie, who was standing frozen-faced by the doctor. 'I keep telling you, Beryl, you should be careful who you play with.'

'That's enough!' Snowie Raven chimed in. 'Come here, Sylvie dear. These are children, Mrs Bridges. This is an insane situation.' She touched Sylvie's arm. 'Come on, my dear. I think you'll need my help to get those nasty marks off your back. I think we have a bit of soap in the box, don't we?'

Sylvie looked Mrs Bridges in the eye. 'Do you have soap?'

'No, we don't,' snivelled Beryl. 'I'll never get these marks off my back.'

Sylvie ran to the box and brought back a carefully cut quarter of a bar of soap. She put it into Beryl's hand. 'Here.'

The ire went out of Beryl's mother like air out of a balloon. 'Thanks, love. No hard feelings, eh? Just worried about my Beryl.' She ushered her daughter away towards their own hut.

Snowie Raven tugged at Sylvie's sleeve. 'Come on, dear. Come with me. We will have to beg some precious water from the doctor.'

Only later, having had her back and bottom cleaned by a very considerate Snowie Raven, and having eaten her very sparse tea, Sylvie lay on her bed and allowed her misery to overtake her. In her mind, she saw repeated dozens and dozens of times Mrs Bridges' action in pulling Beryl close to her, hugging her to her side as though she'd never let her go. Sylvie tried in vain to think of a time, even once, when her mother had hugged her like that.

But still she wouldn't cry. She hadn't cried all day and she would not cry now. She wouldn't. It became a real labour to stop herself crying but then she slept through the night and dreamed of a garden in a dark, grey land. In this garden the white-haired boy juggles balls, then somehow juggles her whole body before returning her to her high perch.

'Sylvie! Sylvie!' It was Beryl shaking her arm. 'Come on, it's morning. Come and see!' She dragged her out of the hut towards the far end of the fence. Sylvie pulled back. 'Don't go by the fence.'

'We don't need to. Look!'

They stood fifteen feet from the fence but could see none the less on the sandy rising on the opposite side that some stones had been laid out in a pattern. 'Look!' said Beryl. 'It spells the name that you said. B. O. S. A. M. B. U. C. K. H. Bo Sambuck. Then H. Isn't that the name that got us into all this trouble?'

'No H.' Sylvie stared. So. He was there. Somewhere beyond the long fence.

'Who is he? This Bo Sambuck?'

Sylvie stared at her. 'It's . . . it's the man who was my mother's husband. I told you we had to use her name so we could stay in Chinatown.'

'Well. He's there. That says so.'

At intervals throughout the day the girls went back to the place and stared at the stones and wondered about the extra H. They were still staring at the stones as the sun grew pale in an ice-pink sky, then fell almost with a plop over the horizon. The next morning Sylvie ran back to the place to see the stones again, but the name was gone. Stones were scattered and kicked around in the lalang grass.

Still, Sylvie hugged to herself the idea of her father and kept smiling when, as the food was cut back yet again, she had no reason to smile at all.

# Chapter Twenty-Seven

## A Puppet Play

The next afternoon after school Sylvie and Beryl were on the mound that Beryl had christened Primrose Hill, playing chess with a home-made set from Beryl's hut, when they noticed a flurry of activity by the gatehouse. A camouflaged car had pulled up at the gate and an officer jumped out. He was tall. Sylvie frowned, trying to get him properly into focus. There was something about him. Something. Then a tall, slender woman with a case got out of her side of the car. Sylvie started to run. Beryl raced after her; the chess pieces tumbled about her feet.

'Sylvie! Sylvie, what in Hades is it?' Not as fit as Sylvie, she struggled to keep up.

The soldier went into the guards' hut with the woman. The woman came out, on this side of the fence, with Moonface. She looked just the same. She had on her best blue cheong sam. Slimmer, perhaps, than when she first wore it, but rounder than when she left the camp. She looked a little worn about the eyes. She was carrying a small suitcase and a bag with two handles.

'Jin Kee!' Sylvie threw herself at her so hard she dropped the bags. Virginia hugged her. 'Sylvie! Are you all right?'

'I've kept your bed space, Virginia,' Sylvie babbled. 'I told them you'd come back. I told them. I kept your bed space. They stole your box. A mad woman did that. But she brought it back. Come and see!' She picked up the smaller bag and led the way through the women who, as always for any stir, any new activity, were gathering. 'I counted the days. Fifty-six days. Eight weeks. I knew you'd come back. I knew it.'

Inside the hut, Snowie Raven put down her Bible and stood up. 'Ah!' she said, shaking Virginia heartily by the hand. 'Now Sylvie will be all right. We've had a bit of a trying time, I'm afraid, my dear.'

Virginia sat down on the carved box. 'I heard about this,' she said. 'There was a report. It was this that encouraged Captain Kageoki to allow me to return. Something about the general. It seems that he met Sylvie. Sylvie demanded my return.'

'He was the Big Cheese. Beryl said so,' said Sylvie.

Much later, away from the crowded hut, Sylvie and Virginia sat on top of Primrose Hill scraping out the remains of a tin of condensed milk Virginia had brought back with her from the town. (They'd shared it out in the hut: one small spoonful for each woman.) Sylvie looked over her sticky fingers at Virginia. 'Did you see the nana?'

Virginia smiled. 'I did see her. She asked about you, as did Uncle Wo. I said you were very good. The best of sisters.'

'Are they all right?'

'Well, the shop is rather lacking in curios. They sell anything these days. But they eat, because people pay huge sums for things on the black market.'

Sylvie licked her thumb, her stomach still luxuriating with the sweetness of the milk. 'Did you see Simon Chen?'

Virginia shook her head. 'Uncle Wo says the jungle fighters are doing good things with the British upcountry, providing intelligence for the Allies. Uncle Wo says things are drawing to an end. He says things will be very different afterwards.'

'It all means . . . it means . . .'

'That means the war will soon be over, Sylvie. We will be out of this place, you and I.'

Sylvie scraped the very last smear from the tin with her fingers, peering into its silver depths. She frowned. 'Why did they loot you, Virginia?'

'Well, it was Captain Kageoki. He looted me to save me from another nastier man.'

'Did he hurt you? Beryl says they hurt you hard when they loot you. Her ma says so. And I thought of those soldiers who hurt you in the street.'

Virginia shook her head. 'The captain was not like that, Sylvie. In a funny way it was harder. At first I thought he would do some awful things. But he just visited me in Beach Road. I had to dress up. Give him tea. He talked to me. He talked to Grandmother. He talked of his family in Nagasaki. I had to work with some of the other women at the Officers' Club – you know they took Raffles for that? – but . . .' Virginia looked closely at Sylvie. 'I remained always under the captain's protection.'

'So that means you are a floozie.'

'Who told you that word?'

'Beryl. Her mother told her. She says women who go to the highest bidder and women who go with Japanese are floozies. Her father ran away to Hong Kong with a floozie.'

'Beryl's mother speaks nonsense, Sylvie. Nonsense! You shouldn't be using words like that. Beryl has a low way of speaking sometimes.'

'She's my friend,' said Sylvie.

'I know,' sighed Virginia. 'I know she was a friend when you needed her. That is very important, especially in these times.'

Sylvie licked the very last sweetness from her finger. 'Was Nana all right?' she said.

'She became ill, and the captain got her medicines. He brought food. There is so very little food in the city.' She blushed slightly. 'He asked for nothing in return, I promise you. I was much luckier than some of the women who had to work at the club, I must assure you.'

'And is the nana still ill?'

'She is so much better.'

'What does Simon think of Captain Kageoki?'

Virginia laughed. 'Simon would be horrified. But Grandmother is more practical. She does not see Simon but sometimes there are parcels of gratitude at our door. Not from him, but from comrades who applaud his fight.'

'He would kill Captain Kageoki if he knew he was coming to Beach Road.'

Virginia hugged Sylvie to her. Sylvie nestled into Virginia's thin form, and thought of the way Beryl's mother had hugged her. 'So how d'you end up back here, if it was all right there at Beach Road?'

'I chose to come.'

'What?' Sylvie sat up straight and looked at her.

'Captain Kageoki had a message from the general about you. Then he was informed of some further trouble regarding you and we discussed whether you should come out and stay with me in Beach Road.'

A ripple of disappointment washed through Sylvie. 'Why didn't you?' she said. 'Why didn't you let me come back? I could see the nana.'

Virginia shook her head. 'The times are changing, Sylvie. Germany's finished. The captain would not say it in so many words, but the Allies are gaining ground. The comrades say that in a very short time they will invade Singapore and chuck the Japanese out. So it is much safer for you and me to be in here for this short time. In the changeover there will be questions regarding the girls who worked in the club or had a Japanese – protector – like me.'

Sylvie frowned, thinking about the months in the hut on her own, except for Snowie Raven. 'But I was on my own, Virginia. You should have let me come before.'

'Before this time the captain would not allow it. Like most men I think he wanted me on my own. He is essentially a selfish man. But now things are drawing to an end. This trouble with you allows me to be brought back to the camp for a reason, as a kind of punishment of me for your misbehaviour. It is convenient. And that is right. Because at the liberation, this is the place to be. Good credentials.'

'You are making my head ache,' said Sylvie. 'All this stuff.'

Virginia laughed. 'Now, your turn,' she said. 'Why are you a bad girl?'

Sylvie told her about the walking backwards and the shouting to the men and the beatings from Four Eyes. Then, she told her about the stones spelling her father's name.

Virginia sat very still. 'Did you tell them you were shouting for your *father*? Sylvie, I—'

'Nah. I was discreet, like you said. That would upset the applecart, wouldn't it? We'd all be in trouble. It did spill out with Beryl but I said we were called Chen because that was our mother's name and we were safer in town with that name. She didn't tell. She promised not to tell. But it does mean my daddy's there, doesn't it?'

'Yes. I think so. Don't worry. We'll soon find out. Change is in the air. Why else would the captain bring me back?'

That night, Snowie Raven succumbed to a second attack of dysentery and was taken to the hospital hut. Virginia stayed by her bed, nursing and washing her, rather to the annoyance of the South African nurse, Miss Chorton, who objected to 'just anyone' being allowed to do this specialised work. The doctor soothed her, and pointed to the other six women who needed bed care, not counting the dozen or so day patients they would have with cuts and sores to deal with. 'Miss Chen can cope with Miss Snowie perfectly well. You know it and I know it.'

Sylvie overheard this emphatic statement and decided that these days the doctor was her heroine. 'You know it and I know it,' she muttered on her way back to Hut Five. She infused more authority into her voice. '*You know it and I know it.*' She bumped into someone.

'First sign of madness, my ma says, talking to yourself,' said Beryl.

'Miss Snowie's in hospital again,' said Sylvie. 'And do you know, the doctor told that Miss Chorton off. She said, "Miss Chen can cope with Miss Snowie perfectly well. You know it and I know it." I think that doctor's like the queen.'

Beryl threw herself on to the ground beneath a tree. 'Mrs Wallace says instead of school this morning, everyone has to make an entertainment for their hut. Ma says the old biddy's sick to death of the sight of us. What point a camp school when soon we'll be in bricks and mortar? Worse luck.'

'I know, I know all that,' said Sylvie crossly.

Beryl held up what looked like a bundle of sticks. 'I thought we'd get the puppet working,' she said.

'Where d'you get that?'

'I got it from your hut. Virginia let me have it. We'll do it up on Primrose Hill. Bring Ayoshi and we'll make a play and we can show Miss Snowie when she gets better.'

This time, with the help of a new supply of tablets gratefully received by the doctor, Snowie Raven was well enough to come back to the hut in two days. She helped with the rehearsals, telling them tales of times when she'd made puppets in her school in China, to tell the story of the Good Samaritan to people who had never heard of Jesus. By then the play – about a princess who was first captured, then released by a lionfish – was ready. Sylvie got Virginia to help her fix up a screen made of bamboo. Across this they draped a scrap of cream silk out of the carved box.

'It'll only work when it's dark, Miss Snowie,' said Sylvie. She looked at the other women in the hut, who were lounging around entertained by all this industry. 'I want all the lamps off after dark,' she announced. 'I want to show Miss Snowie my puppet play.'

Mrs Grassington put down the skirt she was mending. 'So are we all invited? What an honour!' These days there was a new feeling in the camp. The Nips were releasing more supplies and had almost stopped slapping and pushing people. The women were being kinder, more tolerant of each other. The long wait, the sheer pressure of the place, the quarrels and the paranoia, all these in the end had split the women up into tight groups who only trusted each other. Now, with the end clearly in sight, was the time to open up, broaden out, pretend to oneself that one was normal. There had been times when Mrs Grassington would have insisted on a meeting to ban this kids-play in the hut, to declare that the black-and-tan kid was causing a disruption. But this was not the time.

As it happened, that night the lights – and the water – were off right through the camps, so the girls' puppet play would have to be executed in complete darkness, except for the spirit torch that illuminated the white silk screen.

Mrs Grassington said the Japs were practising for the invasion and that's why the lights were off. Water as well.

'We can still do our play, though,' said Sylvie, 'can't we?'

That night, the hut was crowded with all the women from

Mrs Bridges' hut, the doctor and two of her nurses, the teacher and as many children from the school as could cram in. Even the American woman and her friend came. Miss Lomax slipped in and stood fidgeting at the back.

The play started with a soliloquy from Ayoshi, held up before the screen, illuminated by a single lamp held by Miss Snowie.

> By the shores of Singapura
> Lived a maid called sweet Ayoshi . . .

So, to the rhythms of *The Song of Hiawatha*, Sylvie and Beryl told the tale of the young girl who was threatened with horrible deaths by fire and drowning by enemies with names like Moonface and Four Eyes, Cyclops and Fatso. Then the lights in front of the screen went out and went on behind, and the rearing figure of the lionfish pranced before them in shadow. Then Ayoshi, our heroine, came before the screen to recount how the swooshing, rearing lionfish killed Moonface, Four Eyes, Cyclops and Fatso and a monster called Cloth Ears, and brought the maiden Ayoshi safe to her homeland by the shores of Singapura.

There was a second's silence as the poem came to an awkward end, with the spotlight back on Ayoshi. Then there was clapping and tentative laughter, then cheers not quite in proportion with the virtues of the performance. Then, one of the women started to sing 'There'll Always be an England', and the other women joined in. They sang other things from 'Danny Boy' to 'September Song'.

Then the door clashed open and there were Four Eyes and Fatso with big flashlights. Beryl clicked off the lamp behind the screen.

'Out! Out!' screamed Four Eyes. 'Own huts! Own huts!' They pushed and kicked the women as they passed them, even the doctor.

In the dark Sylvie felt something pushed into her hands. The Hut Five women stood by their beds and the two soldiers made their way down the centre space. Fatso spied the screen.

'What this?' he said.

Sylvie could smell the sharp, sweet smell of alcohol. He swayed backwards and forwards beside her. She clutched the present (beads as far as she could tell) behind her.

Snowie Raven looked Four Eyes in one of his eyes. 'The children have had a concert,' she said steadily. 'With puppets.' She held up the bundle of sticks which was the lionfish.

He grabbed the puppet from her and stamped on it, breaking the sticks in several places. Then he tore down the screen and stamped on the white silk so it became a dark rug beneath the dust on his rubber boot. 'No concert!' he shouted. 'No concert. No lights. All signals.' He picked up the small lamp and threw it to the waiting Fatso. Then he stumbled back to the door and went off with Fatso, clashing the door behind him.

The women scrambled on to the beds in the unrelieved blackness.

In the darkness Sylvie held the beads to her face but could not see them. 'I hate them,' she shouted into the darkness. 'I hate all of them.'

'Attagirl!' Mrs Grassington's voice rang in the darkness. 'Attagirl! Just you hang on, my dear. It won't be long now.'

Sylvie fingered the beads, put them by her face, and then a thought came to her and she knew what they were. They were her mother's pearls. The mad woman Miss Lomax had given them back.

So that was all right, then.

From Virginia Chen
11 June 1945
My own dear Albert,

It seems something of a paradox to say I am happy to be back here at Sime Road, but I am. My place, in these days, is with Sylvie or she will be in jeopardy. She had been watched over by Miss Snowie but this lady is not so well. She has just survived a second bout of dysentery and may get more. There is no way in this place that rules of cleanliness may be observed. (I have just realised what a gross understatement that is!)

The camp is buzzing with rumours that we will not be here much longer. The guards are alternately subdued and very bad-tempered. This week more of the parcels, which are ours, are being given to us and there is more food to be shared out. This makes people generally more cheerful and friendly.

Sylvie coped very well when I was away. A disturbed woman stole her mother's pearls but she got them back. The said disturbed woman seems remarkably sane at present. Perhaps the trajectory of her illness reflects the madness of our incarceration here. It seems we are indeed at the end of it all.

I have not heard from the captain but then did not expect to hear. He seemed to me to be a very lonely man, missing his family in Nagasaki.

While I was away Sylvie discovered that B. S. – you remember him? That night when we talked on the veranda – is somewhere here and I am in a quandary about this. He can't be here in the civilian camp. As a Volunteer he must be at Changi with the military. There are family visits here now on Sundays. This is hard for her. I have forbidden her, however, to mention B. S. to anyone. I have explained that this will put our position here, even at this time, in jeopardy. If our deceit is uncovered our friends at the gate will arrest me with heaven knows what consequences. I impress her always with the need to be discreet. I have explained to her that it will not be long and soon everything will be as it was. She will have him back.

Soon, very soon I will be able to post a letter to you in reality. I wonder if I will post this long book letter to you, or will I write a polite letter just to remind you of me? I have been pondering this. You may have found some other friend on some far distant shore. I have begun to wonder whether I have conjured you up to save my sanity in this place.

Still, I believe I am, even now,

Your loving friend, Virginia C

# Chapter Twenty-Eight

## Endgame

The end, when it came, came almost too quietly. There had been weeks of extra roll calls, official paranoia about lights, the reduction even further in rations for all because of an incident to do with the theft of tapioca. Now, in a new and vindictive move, everyone was only to be permitted one suitcase, one bed, one stool.

Virginia borrowed a blunt saw from the wood detail, sawed the carved chest in half down the middle to make a stool each for herself and Sylvie. They stuffed their belongings into Virginia's new case and Sylvie's old one. Any surplus had to be shared out or given up to the Japanese. There were sufficient needy people in the camp that nothing had to be given up.

In these last days, there was less and less to eat, and in the hospital hut some of the very old and the very ill gave up, some of them hung on. Virginia spent most of her time at the hospital now, doing what she could. Even she, who had come

316

back into the camp relatively well covered, was growing thin again now. The discussions were increasingly repetitive. 'What scraps of rubbish will we have to endure for our next meal, which might be our last?' 'Exactly when do you think the end will come?' The now-frequent messages from the men's camp were adamant that the game was afoot. Some big thing had happened. In Japan itself.

School was just about abandoned, and Sylvie and Beryl, with Ayoshi, spent much of their time on Primrose Hill, scanning the skies for friendly planes. The planes that did come over dropped parcels of precious quinine and vitamins, and the Nips did not prevent them picking them up and delivering them to the hospital.

One day they were shielding their eyes to make out a formation of seven planes that were surely American. Sylvie leaped up to shout and scream at them.

Beryl pulled at her. 'No, Sylvie, the Nips, they . . .' Her eyes travelled to the guardhouse at the gate. 'Look, Sylvie! There's no one there! They've all gone. Look!' There were no men in uniforms. No jungle-painted car.

The Japanese were not all gone. Moonface and some others came back with a truck of Red Cross parcels, some much labelled and quite old. They brought sacks of mail which had been standing for months, even years. Beryl and her mother had letters from Mrs Bridges' sister in England, dated 2 April and 4 June 1943.

As Sylvie had no letters of her own (How could she? Who knew she was there, after all?) Beryl read hers out to her. They were very ordinary letters, about British rationing and bombs and babies being born and old people dying, and queues, queues, queues. They were from people Beryl had never met and would not have recognised, but she knew all about them from the stories her mother told, and for her these letters were matters of delight.

Alone again under the tree on Primrose Hill, Sylvie closed her eyes and imagined a letter in her mother's flowing hand. The letter would have a South African stamp on it. It would be addressed 'Miss Sylvie Sambuck, Sime Road Camp, Singapore'. Inside, it would say 'Dear Sylvie'. Not 'Darling Sylvie', not 'Dearest Sylvie'. Just 'Dear Sylvie'. And it wouldn't talk of rationing and the bombs. It would talk of lipstick and dancing and fine food and wine, flowers and sunshine. And it would probably complain about the servants. But still, Sylvie would like to have such a thing, a letter of her own.

'Aren't you sorry you don't have letters?' she said to Virginia one day.

Virginia shook her head. 'There is only my grandmother and Uncle Wo. And Simon, wherever he is. He would not risk a letter. I think of them and they think of me. That is sufficient.'

'Beryl says many of the biddies have love letters from soldiers. You should have a letter from a soldier. What about Albert Taft?'

'Albert?' Virginia flushed.

'The sailor who went to the Great World with us.'

'What a long memory you have, Sylvie.'

'You liked him and he liked you. You in the blue cheong

sam, like Cinderella at the ball. And Albert was Prince Charming.'

Virginia laughed. 'That is a very nice way to put it.'

'He gave you his address. Will you write to him?'

Virginia thought of the pile of battered notebooks that were first her own daybook, then, in a desperate act of optimism, letters to Albert. 'I think I probably will after the war, Sylvie. It's not after the war. Not just yet.'

The next day, Sylvie and Beryl, from their spy-place on Primrose Hill, saw the American woman and her friend, fully lipsticked and dressed up to the nines. They were tippy-toeing to the fence. Their dresses hung in soft folds around their thin figures, but there was something about them that made you see them like they must have been before the war. They had a man with them, one of those from the men's camp, who'd been over this way every day since the Nips lowered their profile. He held up the barbed wire and the two women scrambled underneath. Then he scrambled through himself.

'Where are you going?' shouted Sylvie.

'We're gonna catch us a taxi up to Changi, honey,' said the American. 'To see our menfolk. Wanna come?'

'Ain't got no one there,' said Beryl. Her voice echoed the easy American style. 'Not at Changi.'

'Can you ask about Bo Sambuck, please?' called Sylvie. 'He was . . . he is a man I know and . . . he was very nice to me. I need to know about him.'

'OK, honey. Will do.' The women turned then, linked arms with the man and tottered off in search of their taxi.

'Last we'll see of those two,' said Beryl. 'Wanna game of five-stones?'

But it wasn't the last they saw of the two women. They returned four hours later, brought right to the gate in their taxi. They were laughing and cuddling each other and flaunted themselves past the lone soldier at the gate, secure in coming 'home' to Sime Road. Sylvie sidled into their hut as they were removing their shoes and, amongst much laughter, bewailing their sore feet.

'Did you see him, Mrs Bloom? Did you see Bo Sambuck?'

The women exchanged glances. 'No, honey,' said Freddy Bloom. 'There was no man of that name there.'

The days drifted on. Men from the other camp started to come into the camp to talk to the Committee and to take the helm in the affairs of the camp. There was the official announcement of the ending of the war. At the very end of August there was a storm to end all storms. The roads in the camp were awash with water, the camps drummed and dripped with falling rain. The women, as usual, stripped off and stood in the healing rain.

Miss Snowie nodded, and said to no one in particular, 'Tears to wash so much grief away.'

'There are men around,' said Mrs Grassington. 'They shouldn't strip off like that. It's not decent.'

Later that day, the earth steaming, Sylvie and Beryl were up on Primrose Hill when they saw, marching along the perimeter, a small squad of tanned, powerfully built men wearing army berets. They were fatter, stronger than any men they had seen for years. Their faces shone like those of gods. Their uniforms were immaculate, their red berets placed just so on their brows. They were marching steadily, purposefully towards the gate.

Sylvie and Beryl raced to the fence. 'Who are you? Who are you?' shouted Sylvie, shaking the fence. 'Who the hell are you?'

The tall man at the front said, 'Eyes right!' Simultaneously, the line of soldiers turned to them and saluted, faces grinning, teeth gleaming.

'Who are you?' repeated Sylvie, her nose right up to the barbed wire.

A short fair man, last in the line, called softly to her. 'We're the cavalry, love. That's who we are.'

By the time Sylvie and Beryl got to the open gate, there was a large crowd of women and a sprinkling of men who had come over to Sime Road. Right and left, hands were shaken. 'About time. About time.' The words flew into the air like so many soap bubbles. 'Where have you been?'

Beryl pushed through the crowd so she could be at the front. Sylvie walked slowly back to Hut Five, where Snowie Raven was sitting, and Virginia was standing in the doorway.

'They're English,' said Sylvie. 'The man said he was the cavalry. They're saying Japan really has surrendered. The Yanks dropped these huge bombs on Japan.'

'Thank God for that,' said Snowie Raven. 'It was a long time coming properly.' She was sitting on one of the carved-box stools.

Sylvie crouched down beside her. 'What will happen now, Miss Snowie?'

'Well, my dear, I think the camp will be invaded by men of one kind or another.'

'They think they're the cavalry.'

'They've got to think that, dear.'

There was a spurt of laughter from Virginia. 'Miss Snowie, you are a cynic.'

Miss Snowie fingered her mildewed Bible. 'No, my dear. I am a Christian woman who knows the frailty of man.' But she smiled as though Virginia had paid her a compliment.

'Where will you go when we get back to town?' said Sylvie.

'Well, dear, the doctor has told me that I must go to the hospital to be checked. From there I will write to the Mission Secretary in London. There will be work to do somewhere, I feel quite certain.'

'Miss Snowie,' protested Virginia, 'you need to go home. Have a good rest. Retire.'

Miss Snowie shook her head. 'I am fifty-nine, Virginia. I have been hereabouts since I was twenty-six. Where is my home? China, if one were to tell the truth.'

There was a feast of food that night and much laughter in the huts. Some women wept uncontrollably. Virginia helped in the hospital hut, which now boasted a rather bossy male doctor as well as their own doctor, who looked very frail beside him. Virginia stood by in the still of the night while two old ladies, thin and not responding to the new injections, just seemed to fade away into the sticky, humid air. The doctor threw up her hands and said that it wasn't fair. She went to her own private space, now a curtained-off corner of the ward, and drew the curtain. There she cried.

Sylvie did not sleep at all that night. Thoughts buzzed in her head. She thought, now is the time. Now is the time. Now is the time. I can tell them who I am and who I am not. I am Sylvie Sambuck. I can tell them to tell my father about me. Surely he's had a letter now, from my mother, saying I am left behind. I'll ask them if he's there. I'll write a letter and give it to him.

It was very dark when Virginia came in from the hospital, but Sylvie sat up straight. 'We have to look for my father,' she whispered. 'He must be there. In Changi.'

'Ssh,' said Virginia. 'Soon it will be time.'

From Virginia Chen
8 September
Dearest Albert,

What a month it has been! In the most recent days we have discovered that things have been happening about which we did not know. It seems that our side dropped two enormous bombs on Japan, one of them on Nagasaki. (I thought about the family of Captain Kageoki. He must be desolate.) New inventions – very powerful. It was worse than London, worse than Coventry. You must know all this, of course.

That happened back in the first week in August although we didn't know. Things did change though. Our guards became downcast, conciliatory. Some cried. They are poor things really. There was a circular outlining the Emperor's surrender speech. It made good reading. He forbade suicides, raping, killing and looting so that was felt to be a relief, although Mrs Grassington said she had no problem at all with Four Eyes and Fatso indulging in a little hara-kiri. Still we hear there is starvation and hunger in the city, and much disease. I worry about my grandmother. But I will not insist on going there until my time comes as that might draw attention to me and Sylvie, and they may take her from me.

The new authorities – our own men from the other camps, not yet our own invading military – began to make themselves busy making lists, of who we are and where we want to go. (I have again urged Sylvie to be discreet. She talks about her father. We will get away from here and deal with our own problems.) The business of rescue and repatriation will be an enormous job. The soldiers say there are more than sixty camps of one kind or another, and six thousand souls to deal with. What a job.

After that first flurry, things slowed rather too much. Oh, we can listen openly to the BBC now, which was balm to our ears, and there are medical and food supplies to meet all our needs. Still, there are ripples of discontent at how slow everything is. Everyone wants to go home. People go out but there is still a curfew. They come back here. Some of them see Sime Road as their home, which is very ironic. I tell Sylvie to be patient. We do not want to draw attention to ourselves.

I don't really know why I think this. The habit of caution is ground into our bones.

Dearest, dearest Albert, I imagine you celebrating, there in England, the victory of right over might. I imagine there will be dancing in the streets. I will risk now a little letter to you. You and I will start again on the basis of that first fragile evening. And if ever we do become really close again, I will give you these letters to show how I have been thinking of you and how you have kept up my spirits in these hard times.

Your very good and loving friend,

Virginia XXX

# Chapter Twenty-Nine

## The Grandmother's House

After what seemed like weeks being herded around by soldiers in a rather more benevolent manner than that which they were used to, Virginia Chen and Sylvie Sambuck found themselves free in the streets of Singapore. They'd had to leave Snowie Raven in the Alexandra Hospital. When they left her in the ward Sylvie returned the straw hat to Miss Snowie. 'I liked wearing it but I want you to have it,' she said. 'It really is yours.'

According to an immaculate Canadian doctor, Miss Snowie was suffering from serious malnutrition and a degree of dehydration. She needed more vitamins and the dressings on her legs needed changing every four hours. But she was very well, considering. They would hang on to her for twenty-four hours. 'Tomorrow, the ambulance will take her to Raffles,' said a plump, smooth administrator. 'We're using that as a dispersal point for the repatriation. You will find her there. Leave it till four o'clock. Then you will find her.'

At the camp, they'd had to sit at a desk with a brisk sergeant, who wanted to make a note of who they were, where they'd been, and where they were going. He looked closely at their Chinese papers and the photograph of Sylvie in her silk coat on the lawn at Hibiscus Lodge. He looked her over from head to foot and for a second, she thought this was the time to ask about Bo Sambuck, her father. But he pushed the papers back towards them, the moment passed and they were in the truck to the hospital, holding on to Snowie Raven to save her from the bumps. 'Can we still be sisters, Jin Kee?' said Sylvie. 'Just for now?'

At the hospital too, they'd had to say goodbye to Beryl, who was stuck there with her mother. Mrs Bridges, resplendent in her lipstick and springing curls, and rather excited by the presence of whole, handsome men, was propped on a bed, having her leg treated.

'Where are you going?' said Beryl.

'We're going back to the shophouse,' said Sylvie, glancing at Virginia. 'Where we live. Our grandmother is there. And our cousin Simon Chen. He'll probably be back from up-country where he was harrying the Japs.'

Beryl nodded. 'We're gonna be repatriated. We're going back to London where my grandma is. Home. On a great big ship.'

'Oh,' said Sylvie. 'That's good. I guess I won't ever see you again.' She looked around, behind Beryl in the busy corridor. 'Where's Caesar?'

Beryl shrugged. 'A soldier took him. Said he had one like him at home and he'd take care of him.'

'So, we won't see him again?'

'Guess not,' said Beryl.

They eyed each other for a second, then Sylvie turned away.

The streets were dirty and cluttered and less colourful than before. The Japanese flags had been replaced by Union Jacks, which were everywhere, like a rash of red, white and blue. The city was scored by bomb-holes and still littered with barbed wire, but the shops were open; trading, the lifeblood of the city, was gathering strength again. There were still many beggars in the street, and the faces of many of the citizens were thin and emaciated, not unlike those of the internees with whom Virginia Chen and Sylvie had spent the last year or so. But gone from the streets was the atmosphere of fear and rigid watchfulness, replaced now by a subdued buzz. The city was like a clock, stopped for a long time, being wound up again.

The shophouse was bolted and deserted. There were no ginger jars and mahogany cupboards, no delicate, jaunty Uncle Wo, no Grandmother. With a stony face, Sylvie looked up at the building. This was it then. The Nips must have got them. The grandmother was dead and everything was finished. She felt worse, much worse than she'd felt any time in the last year. This was worse than being slapped by Four Eyes; worse than imagining her father floating dead in the dock.

Virginia Chen grasped her shoulder. 'It's all right, Sylvie. Leave your *barang* here.'

Sylvie looked at the locked-up shop and then down at her luggage. There was very little in the case: Ayoshi; the wrapped-up scraps that had been the lionfish. (These had only just escaped the eagle eye of the British Army sergeant who was collecting bug-ridden camp stuff to burn before they could get on the hospital lorry with Snowie.) The white silk Chinese coat. A new issue vest, knickers and socks. Her school books. *The King of the Golden River*. A Max Factor lipstick, which was a present from Beryl Bridges, courtesy of Mrs Bridges. Beside the case was her carved chest stool. Virginia carried the other half.

She looked each way along the road that was teeming with people. 'I am not leaving my things here,' she said. 'They'll steal it all.'

'Bring them with you then,' said Virginia. She led the way next door, into the dark interior of the jewellery shop owned by Mr Lam. When he saw Virginia, Mr Lam bowed very low. He was thinner, and seemed to have shrunk in height, but his close-necked gown was just as neat, his eyes plain and watchful as ever through his round glasses. 'Miss Chen,' he said, 'I see you are well.'

'I wish to know of my grandmother,' she said steadily.

'There was no stock in the end, Miss Chen. No money. Simon Chen was to come to help her but failed to come. The Society arranged for Madame Chen to go into the country on a farm with her kinsman Mr Wo – those farms which those dog-Japanese set up there to get us out of the city, now in the hands of Chinese patriots.' He coughed slightly and rubbed his hand down his silk sleeve. 'The British are not so happy about this! Our comrades still out there with their guns . . .'

Sylvie clapped her hands. 'The nana is all right then,' she said.

Virginia smiled. 'So Grandmother is not with her ancestors?'

Mr Lam shook his head. 'She is in the country eating good rice every day. She is getting fat again. I believe this.' He sighed. 'There was a messenger.'

'Your health, Mr Lam?' said Virginia politely. 'Are you well?' She looked round at the shop, which was bare and dull, with no glitter of jewellery to lighten the gloom.

'Alas, my last bright things were sold a year ago. The finest items for just a few dollars. Bread and rice have reached the price of diamonds. Those dogs killed my brother, my sons and my nephew and then bought my gems for cents.' His voice was mild. 'But now, I will start again. This is the time to start again.'

'I cannot enter my grandmother's house,' said Virginia. 'It is all bolted and screwed down.'

Mr Lam bowed. 'I will find someone and give him tools and he will take down the bolts. But now, I will show you a particular doorway to Madame Chen's house. Simon Chen has used it many times.' He led the way to the first landing and pushed an empty display case to one side to reveal a plain wall. Then he took a long metal pole from under the case and placed it in a hole low down in the wall. He used this as a kind of lever, and the wall cracked open. 'So,' he said. 'Now take up your place in your grandmother's house, Miss Chen.'

They were on the first landing leading up to the grand-mother's sitting room. Sylvie raced up the stairs into the dark room, across to the window and unbolted the shutters. The bright afternoon light flooded the crowded, intricate space. 'There!' she said to Virginia. 'Now we're home. The nana will come back and we'll all be together again.'

Virginia came to stand with her by the window. Below them, the street hummed with movement. Sylvie leaned out. 'Look!' Walking steadily along the street was a troupe of six Japanese soldiers, two abreast, shepherded by a British soldier with a rifle. An island of whispering silence followed them as the crowd made way and watched quietly as they passed.

'Look!' said Sylvie. 'It's Four Eyes. Hey, Four Eyes!'

The man raised his head to look up at the girl and woman in the window. Sylvie stuck her tongue out and her fingers in her ears and waggled them. Four Eyes' head went down again and the British soldier's eyes rested a moment on the monstrous face at the window before they passed on.

'That showed him,' said Sylvie. 'I wish Beryl were here. She was very good at gargoyle faces.'

'Sylvie!' Virginia commanded. 'That was dreadful. Very rude. You must never do this again. It is very rude.'

Sylvie flung herself on to the carved bench. 'He deserved it,' she said. 'He's a horrible monster. I hate him. He deserved it.' She scowled, overcome with misery and cast down by Virginia's disapproval.

Virginia peered again out of the window. 'Look!' she said. 'Mr Lam's friend is here. He's unscrewing the bars and opening the shop. Now we can prepare for my grandmother's return.'

\* \* \*

Virginia Chen: Her Book

Now I have ventured to post a real letter to Albert Taft I have to return to my daybook proper.

Sylvie is asleep beside me and now I can relish being back at the shophouse and the chance to write this unguarded and without worry regarding its disclosure. Sylvie breathes slowly and deeply but now and then she cries out. She has been very good, near to tears now and then, but while awake quite stoical.

While settling Miss Snowie in at the Alexandra I talked to a doctor at the hospital, an Indian fellow, medical assistant whom I knew before the war. It seems in some ways Sylvie and I have been lucky. Foul as the conditions were at Sime Road, apparently the conditions of some of the camps on the islands were unbelievable and those few who survive are in a poor state. He also spoke of the horrifying state of some of the men who had worked for the Japanese upcountry and (not many of them) survived. What things are come to! We have looked into the depths. (They took all the fit men upcountry to build a railway. I have fears for Mr Sambuck. The next task is to deal with that for Sylvie. I must go gently.) But even so, we two have survived. It will be wonderful to sleep at last within the sounds of the city and the perfumes of my grandmother's house. There are still, however, many things to do. The first of these is to look for Bo Sambuck.

# Chapter Thirty

## Raffles

The next day, before they went along to Raffles to visit Snowie Raven, Virginia and Sylvie set about cleaning and polishing the grandmother's parlour. Every item was dusted and polished and replaced in its usual spot. They worked to the sound of jazz played on the grandmother's gramophone.

Sylvie kept giving the grandmother's throne-like chair a wide berth. It was just too empty. 'Will she come back?' she said. 'Will she come back from the country?'

Virginia smiled. 'She'll be on her way now. This is her city, Sylvie. Simon is out at the farm with her. He will make sure she comes home.'

Hundreds of people with sacks and bags were being dropped off at Raffles. Its lofty halls echoed to the shouts of soldiers and the click of army boots. Ex-internees, in new issue boots and a motley of clothes harvested from the newly opened Red Cross parcels, clattered shyly into the concourse. Jackets hung from thin shoulders, dresses were belted round very narrow waists. A cautious eagerness lit faces set now in lines of wary relief. But there was little laughter, no shouting. Many of these people had been queuing, bowing for life essentials and doing as they were brutally told, for three and a half years, and the habit bit deep.

Virginia took one look at the confusion and pulled Sylvie into the shortest queue of women. 'We'll have to wait and ask this soldier.'

At an inlaid mahogany table at the bottom of the stairs sat a young white-haired soldier with a big logbook before him. He had pale blue eyes and almost white lashes. Sylvie could see this because he raised his head to look into the eyes of each woman to whom he spoke. Then he wrote their names down in the book and gave them a room, a place, where they would be billeted until their repatriation to Britain. One woman asked him, 'When? When? When will it happen?'

'There are troop ships specially assigned, madam. But it'll take time to organise it. We have thousands of people to process.'

'Process!' groaned the woman. 'Ye gods! *Process!*'

Sylvie looked hard at the white-headed soldier, who glanced across at her. She saw again into his bright eyes. Something stirred in her, a gripping pain at the base of her stomach. They moved nearer to the table. She recognised the next two women who were being dealt with: Mrs Morris from Hut Five, and Mrs Lamont, the Eurasian woman from that group in Hut Two.

'Right, ladies,' the soldier said, after checking their papers, taking down their names and their ultimate destination in his ledger. 'That will be room seventy-nine. It is quite small, but there is ample room for two. Up the stairs and along the balcony there.' He was enjoying himself. It was nice to be *doing good*. He'd heard in the mess of the dreadful conditions at the camps: the crowded huts and the low state of many women there. It was good to be doing this for them. Raffles, too!

Mrs Morris took in a very deep breath. 'I can't do that. Absolutely impossible,' she said. 'I can't do that. I can't share with *her*.'

The young man looked from one to the other, frowning. Then his frown deepened. Mrs Lamont's dark looks suddenly made the issue clear. 'The hotel is crowded to bursting point with internees, Mrs Morris. There are men sleeping on the floor of the billiard hall, in the residents' drawing rooms. It's a case of beggars can't be choosers, I'm afraid.' Now he was *not* enjoying himself. 'That is your billet.' He looked down again at his ledger.

The two women picked up their bags and walked stiffly to the stairs, two clear feet of space between them.

'Yes!' The soldier looked up again. Sylvie's heart jolted.

'That was not very tactful,' said Virginia severely.

His light blue eyes took in Virginia in her grey silk cheong sam and the girl in the gingham dress beside her. No dusty internees, these. 'I'm sorry?'

'Calling those women "beggars". Talking about "process-ing" them. After the last three and a half years of the Japanese "processing" them, of those Nippon creatures calling women names of all kinds . . .'

He held up his hands as though fending off blows. 'Sorry, sorry, miss. It was careless of me. I was a bit struck, though, that snobberies like that still survive. Survive all this . . .' His voice was soft and well-modulated. It reminded Sylvie of Mr Attwood, their doctor in the old days.

Virginia took a deep breath. 'If you think being in a camp makes people into cyphers, without their original passions and prejudices, you are as bad as the Japanese.'

The man's cheeks reddened. 'I say . . .' he said. Then, with great effort, he looked down at his ledger. 'Perhaps you would give me your name?' he said. He could see the women behind her moving restlessly. 'I need to check your papers.'

Virginia showed him their papers, then, while he was writing it down, said, 'But we do not need a bed for the night. I wish to find Miss Snowdrop Raven. She was discharged from the Alexandra hospital this afternoon. We wish to visit her to see how she is.'

He buried his head in his ledger again. 'Room thirty-three, second floor,' he said. His eye passed on to Sylvie, then away.

'Do you still juggle?' she said.

His gaze swung back to her. 'What on earth . . . ?'

'Captain!' A sharp, female Australian voice came from behind them. 'I've been waiting here for an hour and my legs are killing me.'

Sylvie followed Virginia towards the stairs. 'What was that about, Sylvie?' said Virginia.

'I thought I recognised him. From home.'

'Home?'

'Priorton, where my nana lives. I saw that boy. I dreamed about him, Jin Kee. I dreamed about him at Sime Road.'

Virginia was counting the room numbers. She stopped on the corridor and looked down at Sylvie. 'You really should call me Virginia again now, Sylvie. Not Jin Kee. We are friends now, not sisters. And you are Sylvie Sambuck. The time for Sylvie Chen is over, don't you think? We'll start by looking properly in all this mess for your father. He must be here somewhere.'

'Or he's dead,' said Sylvie. She'd thought very carefully about this when she'd seen the men – fathers and husbands, thin, fit, hobbling or running – coming from the men's to the women's camp at Sime Road. Those men made their way through the crowds of excited women and children, taking possession of their own. She'd been sure, that day, that her father would come and get her. Surely he would. She'd thought he *must* come and find her, and sweep her up in his arms and take her back to Hibiscus Lodge. And Ah So would be there. And Wong Mee and Cookie. But that had not happened. So he must be dead. 'He must be dead by now,' she said as they made their way along the cluttered dusty corridor.

'You don't know that he's dead, Sylvie,' said Virginia. 'You don't know at all. Ah! Number thirty-three. Did that soldier say thirty-three?'

It turned out that Miss Snowie had been billeted with Mrs Grassington, resplendent now in a new red linen dress and white sandals. Already her skin looked less leathery and her

337

hair softer. In a few weeks she would return altogether to the Mrs Grassington, respected teacher and woman golfer, that she'd been before the war. Relieved at her own survival, she would take months to digest properly the now painfully fresh news that her husband, Jock, had been killed on the railway in Thailand. In the meantime, Miss Snowie, with her battered straw hat and her Bible, was a calm and quiet presence. Not uncongenial company. More importantly, it turned out that Miss Snowie was to be Mrs Grassington's early ticket home.

Miss Snowie was placidly pleased to see Sylvie and Virginia. She told them of a visit from a superintendent of the Mission Society who'd told her that, after six months' rest in their retreat in Eastbourne, Sussex, they thought they *might* find her a place in their China Mission. 'Dr Pleasance has told me they might find a berth home for me very soon. Any day now. They want me better. With the defeat of the Japanese, there is even more work in China for people who knew the Chinese. And isn't it nice? Mrs Grassington is coming with me. She will take care of me.' She opened her eyes wide and Sylvie knew she didn't mean that at all.

After the first flood of comment and conversation, there seemed very little to say, except to express their mutual pleasure that they were all free. 'Perhaps you would give me an address, dear,' Miss Snowie said to Virginia, 'so I can send you a card from Eastbourne. And I can visit you if ever I come East again. Now, perhaps, you have better things to do than chatter to an old woman.' She held out a hand and

Virginia shook it energetically. Then she turned to Sylvie and opened her arms and Sylvie was held against the sparrowlike breast a second. 'You were wonderful companions on a very difficult part of the journey. I will always pray for you.' She tipped Sylvie's face towards her. 'Now perhaps, dear, you'll find your own family, whoever they are. Virginia has been a wonderful sister to you, I think.' Then she put Sylvie away from her. 'Maybe you'd better get on.'

She was in charge. There seemed nothing to do but go. They had so much in common, after the last year. But those very things meant that all there was to do was to part, and get on with their own lives.

Mrs Grassington showed them to the door. She shook hands with both Virginia and Sylvie. 'Be sure that I will take care of her. Dr Pleasance said he was very pleased. I can take care of Miss Snowie on the voyage. There is nothing, after all, to keep me here.' She frowned a little. 'Nothing at all.' She shut the door very soundly in their faces.

Virginia and Sylvie stared at the closed door. 'Well,' said Virginia heartily, 'isn't it good to know that Miss Snowie is in such good hands?' She took Sylvie by the hand. 'Now, I think we really need to make you Sylvie Sambuck again. The charade is just about over. Miss Snowie realised it all without our telling her.'

'What is it, Jin Kee?' said Sylvia. 'Are you mad at me?'

'Not you, little sister. Not at you. Just the world out here that means we lose our friend Miss Snowie. Not at you. But remember you must call me Virginia now.'

\* \* \*

At the bottom of the sweeping staircase they were met by the white-haired soldier, who'd now relinquished his ledger to an older, heavier-looking soldier, a sergeant with rusty hair.

'Miss Chen!' He came forward. 'I was waiting for you. Do you have a moment?' He led the way through the crowd to a quieter corridor and a small table by a long window.

'What is it?' said Virginia, keen to get away, to dissolve the upset over Miss Snowie in the sanctity of the shophouse. Sylvie stood behind her, watching the white-haired soldier very closely.

'I wanted to talk to your . . . sister, is it? What did you say her name was?'

'I can talk,' said Sylvie. 'My name is Sylvie Sambuck.' She stood up very straight. 'What's yours?'

He pulled out a little notebook. 'Your papers said Sil Vee Chen,' he said. 'I copied it. You are sister to Miss Chen. Born 1932.'

She watched him steadily. 'I am Sylvie Sambuck,' she said. 'Me and Jin Kee – Virginia – pretended to be sisters so the Japs wouldn't take me from her. She takes care of me.'

He frowned, staring at her. 'How did you know about the juggling?' he said. 'What made you say that thing about the juggling?'

'What's *your* name?' said Sylvie. She raised her voice. 'I asked what was your name.' Virginia Chen put a hand on her shoulder.

'My name is Jamie Chase.'

'I saw you juggling once, in the market when I was a very little girl, but I don't know whether that was a dream. But I did see you in a castle in a garden in England. At the Spitfire party.' She frowned. 'I don't think that's a dream.'

'I do juggle,' he said.

'I saw you juggling,' said Sylvie. 'All the balls in the air, then me, going round and round.' She started to shiver, then collapsed to the ground like a leaf falling.

Virginia shook her, but could not wake her. She looked up crossly at the soldier. 'There!' she said. 'See what you have done? She's gone all through this, steady as a rock. Three and a half years like a little soldier, and you make her sick. You are a dolt! That is what you are! A stupid, stupid idiot.'

# Chapter Thirty-One

## Jamie Chase

In the end Captain Chase took the two of them back in an army vehicle that he called a Jeep. Virginia sat in the passenger seat with Sylvie tucked in beside her. In recent days the city had been tangled with military vehicles of various kinds, but still this open vehicle, with its blond-haired driver and its striking pair of passengers, drew some speculative glances. They passed a working party of Japanese prisoners of war clearing some debris with *chungkols*. They were guarded by a couple of gum-chewing army privates. Sylvie and Virginia afforded them but a single glance.

Sylvie was still subdued after her outburst and collapse in Raffles. The other two talked in a desultory fashion as though they'd just been introduced at a party. The subject of their conversation was the city and its particular delights.

'Have you been to the Great World, Captain Chase?' asked Virginia.

'I've strolled through it with my friends. A strange world.

Very colourful, I must say. Popular with other ranks.' He glanced down at Sylvie, who was staring at a trishaw, whose driver was wobbling along with a load of tethered pigs in his vehicle. 'I saw a jolly good juggler there one day. Juggled with pineapples and this curled-up creature. It was alive, whatever it was.'

'Sylvie used to love it, before the war,' offered Virginia.

Sylvie was staring at a street hawker who was selling sweet cakes from a tray. She sniffed the sweet toffee smell.

The captain manoeuvred the Jeep around a stationary bullock. 'How long were you in that camp?' he asked.

'We'd been there just more than a year. Many of those poor women had been there two and a half years already, there and at Changi, which was even worse. Some were in the camp for less time than us – the Jewish families. But some of those were in such a bad state when they arrived, their conditions in the city were so bad. Sylvie and I were lucky.'

'Lucky?' Jamie Chase could not conceive of any person here in this place since February '42 feeling the least bit lucky.

'Well, as I say, some of the people had been behind the wire for the whole three and a half years. Many died. And bad as Sime Road was, I was told at the hospital that the camps on the islands were worse. I also heard about those soldiers working on the railway.' She glanced down at Sylvie, who was still watching the road with rapt attention. 'Too terrible.' Jamie caught her eye and she shook her head, closing that subject. 'There were some very brave women.' She told him about Freddy Bloom and Mrs Nixon.

'But *you* were not mistreated?' Jamie kept his tone even. The tales he'd heard in his mess had made his hair stand on end.

Virginia laughed thinly. 'Well, there was always bullying. And a good deal of drunken harassment. Some women suffered much more than others. But the worst for all those women was persistent starvation, food bad before it was given, the careless neglect of the needs of the sick ones. Malaria, beriberi – they were rife when the Nippon had the M & Bs and the quinine that could have saved them, from our own Red Cross parcels. The Japanese could not be bothered to open some of them, much less let us have them. They might have been warehousing pigs. How many times the prisoners were told that they were the coolies now, not the British masters.'

'You say "they" and "them",' said Jamie Chase. 'Did you not feel part of "them"?'

'You're very sharp, Captain Chase. In many ways we were not part of them. We had not shared their more terrible experience in Changi. And in any case, they saw Sylvie and myself as not *of them*. Not properly British. Even in that dirt and dust they liked to place you in your little pigeonhole.' She paused. 'We went in there fatter than them, carrying resources. So we came out not so thin or wasted. Even though our friend, Miss Raven, who went in at the same time, came down with dysentery more than once. She was an amazing woman, of great spirit.' She paused. 'She was the one we were visiting at Raffles.'

'But Jin Kee,' Sylvie's sepulchral tones emerged from the soles of her new sandals, 'Jin Kee, you were looted. It wasn't easy for you.' She kept looking out of the window.

'Looted? What—'

'Here we are, Captain. This red door,' said Virginia crisply. 'Thank you.'

He jumped from the Jeep to help them both down. He lifted Sylvie down wholesale, as though she were a doll. Virginia took his hand and tripped down daintily from the truck. 'Thank you, Captain.'

He held on to her hand and looked past her at Sylvie. 'I say, could I come in and talk, perhaps? We should talk about Sylvie here. I'm afraid I will have to report about her – that she's not one of you . . . I'm sorry but . . .'

Virginia relinquished his hand and led the way through the shop and upstairs into the grandmother's sitting room. She sat the captain on the carved bench by the window and perched herself on her grandmother's great chair. Sylvie stood beside her, leaning slightly on her shoulder.

He looked at them. They were so alike, these not-sisters. He sat quietly then as, between them, they began to tell an abbreviated version of their story, from the time in the milling crowds on the quayside when Sylvie missed the boat, to the day they walked out of Sime Road camp.

'The *Felix Roussel* got away,' he said. 'It got to South Africa. I saw the report.'

Virginia glanced down at Sylvie. 'We did not know this. There were no letters. There wouldn't be, would there? Sylvie's mother wouldn't know that her daughter was now Sylvie Chen.'

'And what about Sylvie's father?'

'*My father*,' said Sylvie. 'His name is Bo Sambuck. And he was in the Volunteers. A soldier for Singapore.'

'So he would have been in Changi. That's where the military were at the end.'

'When I was in Sime Road the men were working outside. They made a message for me in stones outside the wire: "BO SAMBUCK H".' She spelled it out. 'They got a bashing for it. I don't know what the H was. But that was my daddy's name.'

'Your father?' He glanced at Virginia. 'Who is Bo Sambuck to you, Miss Chen?'

She shook her head. 'My employer. Sylvie was my pupil. She is the daughter of Mr Sambuck. And Mrs Sambuck who went off on the *Felix Roussel*. Sylvie was left, so I took care of her.' She stared unblinkingly at Jamie Chase. 'So she is English, English as you are.'

'But I saw her papers. Syl Vee Chen. Born 1932. And look at her. You look alike.'

'Papers are easy in this half-world. We are sisters under the skin. It was the only way I could keep her safe.'

Jamie had heard talk of this in the officers' mess. Of how people were trying anything just to get to England, out of this chaos. It could be a ploy. They were trying all sorts of ploys. They were wily, these people. But perhaps these two were different. Perhaps the girl really was English, dark as she was. He turned his attention to the girl. 'So how did you know that I juggled? Where did you see me do that?'

Sylvie frowned. 'I can't properly remember. But it must have been Priorton. Like I said, there is a market. It's where my nana lives. My nana is my mother's mother,' she explained.

'There is a castle place somewhere near.'

'Tell me about Priorton.'

She felt waves of pain buzzing through her as she made herself remember these images from before. They buzzed through her brain like blood pulsing into a wound. 'Well, there is a market on Thursdays and Saturdays. On Thursdays they sell the cows and the sheep. There are big wheels that drag the coal up from the ground. And there is a priory with a big gate and a clock. And a town hall with a tower. They run things from there, like the Japs in the gatehouse.'

He was still staring hard at her as though he could peel off her skin and peer inside. 'So your mother . . . ?' He glanced at Virginia.

'Her mother, she comes from this place called Priorton. She is very English.' She smiled slightly. She knew his problem. 'Sylvie's father always used to tease her, say she was a bit of a throwback.'

He nodded. He took out a notebook from his tunic pocket. 'Sambuck, you say? Will you spell it again for me?'

Sylvie did so. 'And there was an H after that in the stones. They made an H.'

He stood up. 'There should be something I can do.' He shook Sylvie's hands with both of his. 'My own people are from Priorton,' he said. 'As you speak I've a vague recollection of a little girl in a tree.' That had been before Sandhurst, before France, before Belgium. His own mind was buzzing. What a coincidence. 'Right at the beginning of the war.'

'You were juggling,' she said. 'With white balls.'

'So I was,' he said. He went to the door. 'Give me a few days, will you?' He put on his cap, saluted them and turned smartly and left the room, closing the door firmly behind him.

As he put the Jeep into gear and worked his way through the streets back to Raffles, Jamie Chase reflected on the fact that in truth he had had a very good war. Commissioned just in time to join the push in Normandy. Action as far as Germany. The overwhelming sense of growing victory. Home leave, wondering whether to resign, and then being shipped to Singapore to give the Japs their proper due, and help to get the POWs on their way. And now tomorrow Mountbatten to take the formal surrender! Chance to see the man who was a legend in the flesh. He'd take a dekko at that.

And now here was this little half-Chinese who wasn't really that, who'd seen him juggle when he was a sprig of sixteen, a world ago. Jamie wasn't very given to strange thoughts but he wondered for a second if all that had happened to him in the last four years had led him to this point where, if there was any justice in the world, he'd really dig up this girl's pa and present him to her on a plate.

When he got back to Raffles he took over the desk from his sergeant.

'Nice-looking Chinee, sir,' said the sergeant, with the shade of a wink. 'The one you took off there with the little girl.'

'What? Oh. Yes. Topping.' But it wasn't the beautiful, over-thin woman in the cheong sam who was in his thoughts. It was the little girl with stick-like legs and eyes like those of a veal calf.

# Chapter Thirty-Two

## Kota Tinggi

Two days later Sylvie had pulled back the shutters and was peering down into Beach Road when an old Ford with no windscreen drew up in the dust outside the shophouse. Simon Chen – a taller, barely recognisable, older, more wiry Simon Chen – was driving. As he unfolded himself from the car and looked up, his eyes were blank as pools as they passed over her. Beside him, squashing down the slight figure of Uncle Wo, was a raggle-taggle mountain of parcels. On top of this was a closed basket, which squawked angrily and sprouted the occasional feather. In the centre of the back seat, sitting bolt upright, one hand clasped over the other on the jade handle of a parasol, sat Virginia's grandmother.

Sylvie clattered downstairs on the old *trompahs* she'd kept from Sime Road. She shouted, 'Nana! Nana!' and held open the car door as the grandmother climbed out with a kind of stiff glamour. Sylvie smiled so broadly that she thought her jaw might break. She knew better than to throw herself at the old woman, even though that was what she really wanted to do. 'Nana! You've come home.'

The old woman nodded and touched her forearm, then she put her arm through Sylvie's and allowed the girl to help her into the shop then up the two staircases. Either the grand-mother had shrunk or Sylvie had grown but now Sylvie was half a head taller than she. Uncle Wo, Virginia and Simon Chen struggled up behind them with the parcels. Sylvie could smell dust and animals, incense and old spices. She gloried in the tight claw-grip of the old woman's hand. She was brim-ming with pleasure. She took in the struggle and the clatter of talk behind her but she did not care. The grandmother was home.

Inside the room she led the old woman to her own chair. She sat down and looked round. 'Very clean,' she said in English.

'Me and Virginia cleaned all up when we got back here from Sime Road,' said Sylvie.

'Very clean.' The old woman nodded, then pointed with a hooked finger. 'Music now,' she said.

Carefully Sylvie wound up the gramophone, then lowered the needle on to the American record of piano jazz. The room filled with larruping, crick-crack sounds. Sylvie clapped her hands in time and the grandmother let her parasol drop to the floor and joined in. Simon and Virginia Chen struggled with the parcels into a room that was full of music and clapping.

'Just like old times,' said Virginia.

Simon Chen did not respond to the mood. 'It is not like old

times,' he said firmly. 'It will never be like old times again.' Then he turned and stamped out.

Sylvie scowled at Virginia. 'Is that Simon Chen? He doesn't look like him. He doesn't sound like Simon Chen.' She wrinkled her nose. 'He doesn't smell like Simon Chen.'

Virginia smiled slightly. 'Do not worry, Sylvie. He has seen many bad things. Perhaps he has done some bad things. He needs now to see some normal things.'

Sylvie felt dull, like an unsharpened knife. She was worried but she didn't know why. Despite Virginia's reassurance she did not understand Simon Chen's sullen looks. How could he look like that now they were all back together again?

The grandmother picked up the parasol and struck the wooden floor with it. 'More music, Syl Vee,' she said. 'Soldier music only the best.'

Sylvie chose the record with the military band, set the needle on it and removed the baffle from the big horn so the sound came out full blast. 'That's better,' shouted the grandmother. 'Now, Virginia. Tea!'

The next day Simon Chen went on his way in the city. Sylvie felt glum about this and, using signs, asked Uncle Wo where he might be. The old man shrugged his emaciated shoulders. 'Go see man,' he said. 'Big Chinee. Simon Chen with big Chen men. Go hall see ancestors.'

She knew the wider Chen family had a special place, a hall where they met. But she was prevented from pursuing her enquiries any further by the grinding of gears as an army truck pulled up outside the shophouse. It was driven by a thickset soldier with wild red hair. Captain Jamie Chase jumped down from the passenger seat. 'Just the girl!' he said.

Sylvie examined him closely. 'You've found him,' she said. 'You've found Bo Sambuck.'

'Sorry, old thing.' He shrugged his shoulders. 'I do have a few feelers out. There was a problem, but I think things are clearing now.'

'So you will find him?'

'I have great hopes of finding him, believe me, but in the meantime I wondered if you and Miss Chen might like to go for a swim. Get the dust off your feet. Mac, that's my sergeant here, tells me of a wonderful place with waterfalls up on the mainland. A proper place to get the sand out of your toes. Place called Kota Tinggi.'

'We're not allowed on to the mainland, Captain Chase.' Virginia Chen's quiet voice came from behind Sylvie. 'Not without special permission from the military.' Simon had told her. The crossing was guarded by the British. They examined the papers of everyone who crossed. In the new peace they were cautious about the communist guerrillas who had been their allies in the war against Japan. For the British the liberation did not mean self-determination for the people of the island. It meant a return to the ways of the old colony.

Jamie Chase grinned. 'We *are* the military, Miss Chen. And will you call me Jamie? This is all so formal.'

She did not tell him to call her Virginia.

'Can we go swimming?' said Sylvie suddenly. 'I'd like to go swimming, Virginia. It's so long since I went swimming. Didn't I go swimming with my daddy, Virginia, at the Tanglin Club?'

'So you did,' said Virginia. 'But you have no costume . . .'

'We can go to Robinson's,' said Sylvie in a flat voice which she hoped did not show how much she was willing Virginia to say yes. 'Use Ayoshi's money. She has gold.'

Virginia looked at Jamie. 'We will need to buy a costume. Sylvie has grown so tall.'

'We'll take you there, miss,' called the tousle-headed sergeant in the driver's seat. 'We'll wait.'

Within the hour they were stirring the dust in the Bukit Timah road, heading for the Johore Straits. Clutching her Robinson's bag with her new costume, Sylvie sat in the back beside Virginia. Behind them was their alibi – military-looking boxes and cartons. Their feet rested on a basket of food and another basket clanking with bottles of Tiger beer.

They had gone six miles when 'Oh-oh!' said Mac. 'Check-point! Dive-dive-dive!'

'Cover yourselves with that tarpaulin,' said Jamie. 'Do it! Quick!'

So they found themselves clutching each other under a tarpaulin smelling of rubber and gunpowder. Sylvie's heart was beating. She thought of that time at the camp when she and Beryl had had to kneel in the corner in the Nip guardroom. She wet herself.

Above them they heard the gruff exchange of male voices, the rustle of papers. Then they set on their way again.

Sylvie whispered in Virginia's ear, 'I've weed myself.'

'Don't worry,' whispered Virginia. 'Lift your dress up. It will have gone through the floor. I will think of something.'

'Up-up-up!'

Virginia pushed away the tarpaulin and they raised their heads to find the men whistling and calling like truanting schoolboys. 'Here we go!' shouted Mac.

Sylvie looked round her at the road and the invading green of the jungle. They passed Tamils driving overladen bullocks and Chinese and Malays trudging and cycling in both directions. She pulled at her dress to make sure that she did not sit on it.

The men started to sing,

> 'Bless 'em all, bless 'em all,
> The long and the short and the tall.
> You'll get no promotion
> This side of the ocean,
> So cheer up my lads
> Bless 'em all.'

Virginia smiled quietly at them, a smile which Sylvie remembered from even before Sime Road, from the first time at Beach Road. She used to smile like that at Hibiscus Lodge when Sylvie had one of her giddy fits. Sylvie thought again of Hibiscus Lodge, her head began to fill with the sounds of that house: the gentle clash as Tang Peng presented his dishes, Ah So calling for Feargal, the swish of her mother's dress as she swept into the room, the clink of ice as it landed in a long glass. She sniffed hard to keep the tears back.

Virginia put an arm round her. 'Are you all right, Sylvie?'

Sylvie shook her off. 'Yes. I'm fine.'

When they got to the long bridge they had to dive under

the tarpaulin again at yet another checkpoint. In five minutes they were in the air again. They seemed to drive for hours through dense vegetation, wrecked rubber lines and some burned houses.

'Was this where Simon Chen fought the Japs?' Sylvie whispered.

Virginia shrugged, her eyes on the two soldiers. 'I'm not sure about that, Sylvie.'

They could hear the water before they saw it. Then the jungle seemed to open out and they had to crick their necks to take in some rearing rocks. Then they saw the water gushing down over the rocks, through the trees in two great succeeding spirals, splashing and steaming in the air.

Sergeant Mac whooped like the Red Indians did on the pictures, and found a place to park. They scrambled upwards to the second waterfall, aiming for a place where there was a flatter reach of land where they could sit. Here the gush of water brimmed into a vast saucer of stone before it careered further down the slope. Mac, clutching the beer basket, led the way, followed by Jamie, who had the food.

They waited by the pool for the girls to reach them. Mac was mopping his brow with a khaki handkerchief. 'How you pair keep cool,' he said, 'I don't flipping know.'

'We play two hours of tennis a day,' said Sylvie without hesitation.

The men raised their eyebrows.

Virginia shook her head. 'We are acclimatised,' she said. 'It takes time to acclimatise yourself to Singapore. Sylvie was born here. So was I.'

Jamie squatted down to fashion nooses for the bottles so they could hang them in the water and keep them cool. 'I suppose it makes a difference, being born here,' he said. He dangled the bottles, making sure his noose was securely tied to a young sea-apple tree. He stood up. 'Now for swimming,' he said. 'Last in is a corncrake.'

Sylvie had no idea what a corncrake was but ran behind a shrub just the same. Virginia followed in a more leisurely fashion. Carefully Sylvie peeled off her wet knickers. She looked at Virginia.

Virginia told her to leave them there and leave her clothes beside them. 'I'll take care of them,' she said.

They changed into their costumes and Virginia tied a sarong round hers. 'Aren't you swimming?' demanded Sylvie. She thought suddenly how Beryl would have liked this. What a lark it would have been to have her here. How most probably they would have jumped into the water fully clothed. Then she thought of swimming lengths in the Tanglin pool with her father and how keen he was that she should be a good swimmer. 'Could save your life, this, one day, old girl.' She could hear his voice now, behind the rush of the water.

Virginia had not been allowed to swim at the Tanglin, of course.

'Can't you swim?' she said slowly now to Virginia.

'Well, I was too busy studying to waste my time learning to swim,' she said. 'But I can dangle my feet very nicely.' She scooped up the pile of clothes and followed Sylvie to the water's edge.

'Virginia can't swim,' Sylvie announced. 'But I can. At least I think I can. I hope I remember.' Then she walked into the water up to her waist, turned over and swam a very efficient back crawl to the other side of the pool.

The two young men looked uncertainly at Virginia.

'You go.' She waved her hand. 'Give that little madam a swim for her money. I'll wash through her dress and things. She has caught a great streak of oil in that not-too-clean truck of yours.'

She knelt down and sloshed the dress and the knickers in the sparkling water and laid them on a rock to dry. Then she sat on the edge, dangling her feet in the cool water, watching the child-like antics on the other side of the pool.

After a while the sergeant swam back towards her and stood up in the water. 'Reckon it's the bounden duty of me and the young captain here to teach you how to swim. Never know when it might come in useful.' His tone brooked no opposition.

For the next half-hour the two men held her up, showed her the strokes and hauled her out of her depth, but she didn't trust the water and kept sinking like a stone. Then they abandoned her under her grandmother's parasol on the bank and went back to chasing Sylvie round the pool.

Mac gave in first, got himself a cool bottle of beer and joined Virginia. 'Oh, for the energy of the young,' he said, throwing himself down beside Virginia.

Jamie Chase was splashing around with Sylvie by the waterfall. He called to her. 'Your sister . . . your teacher might walk like an angel on the ground but, by golly, she sinks like a lead carrot in the water.'

Sylvie splashed him with a great armful of water and set out for the far bank. He pursued her and ducked her until she begged for mercy. When he released her she clambered on to his back and held him under to get her revenge. Then she raced to the side, jumped out of the water and sat down beside the other two, who were having a conversation about the invasion of Normandy. Virginia had on her sarong and her wet hair was tied back under a bandeau. She was taking bird-like sips from the neck of the bottle of beer.

Mac went for the food basket. 'What about *chow*?' he said.

They ate bread, cold fried chicken, guava, mango and peaches. Sylvie ate hers very quickly, then burped.

'Sylvie!' said Virginia. 'Really!'

'Jin Kee,' grinned Sylvie, 'you just reminded me then of my mother. The very same voice.'

'Don't say that, Sylvie.' Virginia dabbed her hands on the snowy cloth that had wrapped the bread.

'Do you know what I was thinking, Jin Kee?'

'What?'

'How all the food in that basket would have fed six huts at Sime Road. For two days. Three days with some rice.'

Mac, who was just finishing off the last of the chicken, choked. 'Must have hit a bone,' he said. 'I told Cookie, "No bones!" '

Jamie gathered the cloths and the detritus of their meal to put in the basket. 'Why'd she call you Jin Kee like that?' he said.

'It's a pet name!' shouted Sylvie, too loud.

'It is a family name, a familiar name. It was appropriate for her to call me this while she was my little sister. Now,' she frowned theatrically in Sylvie's direction, 'she must call me Virginia or else.'

'I used to call her Miss Chen in the old days. But that would have given the game away at Sime Road, wouldn't it, Virginia? If I'd called you Miss Chen like I did at Leonie Hill Drive?'

'So your name's Virginia?' said Mac, who'd been trying in vain to get closer to this woman all afternoon.

Virginia smiled slightly. 'It is even more complicated than that. My real name is Virginie, so called by my father who was more or less, in his Eastern way, French. Virginia is my English name, my school name. I went to an English school.' She looked at the red-faced sergeant. 'You may call me that if you wish.'

Jamie shook his head. 'All so mixed up.'

'That's just about right, Jamie. It *is* all mixed up.' Virginia looked at her watch. 'We should be setting off again, Captain Jamie, if we want to reach the island in daylight. The soldiers will be suspicious.'

It was not so. They were challenged at none of the checkpoints. It was dark by the time they drew up at the shophouse. They all jumped down from the truck and stood on the pavement. Virginia shook hands with both men. 'Thank you so very much. How wonderful it was to be carefree once more. Sylvie! Say "Thank you"!'

Sylvie curtsied first to Mac, then to Jamie Chase. 'Thank

you for a nice day, Sergeant Mac. Thank you for nearly drowning me, Jamie Chase.'

He grinned. 'It was a pleasure.' He reached inside the truck. 'Here,' he said, handing her a neat brown paper bag. 'That should make up for the drowning.'

'Well!' said Virginia, peering at the truck as it roared off.

'Well, what?' said Sylvie, suddenly tired and a little bit angry. She tore at the bag in her hand and out dropped three balls, not quite as big as tennis balls. 'Juggling balls!'

Virginia bent down to pick up a paper that had fluttered from the bag. 'Your first note from a young man.'

Sylvie scowled at her.

'What does it say?'

Sylvie peered at it in the residual light from the shop. ' "Next time the battle of giants." What does that mean?'

'It means you'd better get on and practise your juggling. Pretty damn double quick.'

# Chapter Thirty-Three

## Juggling

Over the next few days Sylvie tried very hard. At first she could do it with two balls only, using two hands. Then, encouraged by Uncle Wo, she managed to do it with two balls, using only one hand. But she couldn't cross over and bring the third ball into the game. She couldn't quite get the idea that the second ball in one hand had to be the first ball in the other.

She'd been obliged to practise down in the shop because the constant throwing of balls distracted the grandmother from her music. Uncle Wo became her trainer, her very appreciative audience. He picked up dropped balls and it was he who clapped when she – very temporarily – managed to get three balls in the air.

One day, Simon Chen came in, carrying boxes. His face was unsmiling and when she asked him if he could juggle he said any circus brat could do that. She stood in his path and pushed the balls into his hands. 'You show me then.' He tried three times, each time dropping the balls. When he retrieved them the third time he thrust them into her chest and said, 'All children's stuff.' He stalked off.

Uncle Wo caught Sylvie's eye. 'Simon Chen fry big fish,' he said.

'Was he very brave in the war, Uncle?'

'Brave warrior,' he said. 'An honour to the Chen family.'

Virginia Chen: Her Book

What an amazing thing it was to see Sylvie at Kota Tinggi, cavorting in the water like a little porpoise, playing childish games with Jamie Chase. The last strands of childhood revisited. (Why do men find it so much easier than women to revert to the child inside themselves?) When I watched Sylvie and Beryl Bridges play at Sime Road it was a much more wearying experience, like watching a pair of small English witches brewing potions of survival in a dark world. But here, splashing in the water, she and Jamie Chase might be two children at play, having all of their childhood in the present. There seems little difference between them. Sylvie is thirteen now. The boy is, after all, just out of school. And the English of that class are, I have found, so very late in growing up.

I must press him for more news of her father. He knows something, I can tell, but if there is no proper news we must start to think of how we may get Sylvie back to whatever there is for her in England. This will be painful for me but it is not my needs which must be paramount. Dealing with his playmate, the Scottish sergeant, is not so easy. He is eight or nine years older than Jamie Chase and casts himself in the role of guard-dog as well as playmate. He is both brave and senti-mental. He came through the Normandy landings with Jamie and it seems the two of them chased the Germans single-handed, back over the Rhine. He has two small children back home, whom he has barely seen, and a wife whom he badly misses. He showed me their photographs, battered and creased from their campaign experience. But still he seeks female company. He was frank about this. 'When there is no war, Virginia,' he told me, 'the companionship of the mess is quite hollow.' He rolls his Rs when he says *warr*, which is quite attractive. He is not 'after anything', he insists, merely interested in some gentle company, rehearsing for when he gets home. In this he is not unlike Captain Kageoki. He too had photographs of his family.

The Scotsman made me think of Albert Taft and that well-remembered evening at the Cathay, watching Vivien Leigh in *Gone with the Wind*. And the dancing under the stars and the Coconut Grove. I have written a letter to him at the address he gave me. I wonder if he is still there. The letters I wrote at Sime Road will keep for later. If there is a later.

It seems to me that Sylvie and I are waking from a long sleep, like the princess in the fairy tale. We have the unspoken pact not to dwell on our shared nightmare. Nor on Captain Kageoki, nor on Beryl Bridges; not even on the angelic Miss Snowie Raven. That is all behind us now. We do not speak of it. We can only look to the future. And the future for Sylvie is in England with her father, if possible. Her mother too. The English say blood is thicker than water and sadly with all Sylvie and I share we do not share blood.

Simon Chen turned up last night. He had had his hair cut, European style, and was wearing a very well-cut lounge suit. He looked very handsome and much younger again. He is full of the importance of hanging on to, even fighting again for, the gains we Chinese have made through the war. They have orders from their own leaders not to hand back the weapons with which they have fought for the Allies. Of course, the powers that be are getting very windy about this. He says that the British should not be handed back all the advantages on a plate. Things should not be as they were.

But, for the time being the British authorities are very pleased with him and his work against the Nippon. So he brought the news that his Raffles Institute scholarship, gained before the war, will afford him a place at Cambridge. He is to do his degree. This is somewhat amazing.

But there is common sense in it from the British point of view. If there is to be some kind of insurgence, it is better that people like Simon Chen should be out of the way. When he comes back, though, he will be very useful to the comrades in their struggle. The British are, perhaps, mistaken in thinking that his loyalty may be bought by their self-serving generosity.

Perhaps I am becoming too suspicious, too cynical. In the end, in the camp it seemed to me there was one informing ethic: that of dignified survival. Simon Chen is keen to go to Cambridge. It is the dignified thing and I think it will make him no less radical. So the British investment in goodwill may very well backfire.

Sylvie and I are to be taken by the Scotsman and young Jamie to fly kites on the esplanade. More shades of the times before!

I wonder where Mrs Sambuck is now? On the high seas coming back here? Or on her way to England? Or is she there already? We are certain now that the *Felix Roussel* got to South Africa. So Mrs Sambuck should be safe. It is a strange thing but in all her yearning for her father Sylvie has never once mentioned her mother or Feargal. I can't remember whether I missed my parents when they died. But no, I was with my grandmother always, so excess of grief would not have been appropriate.

(Much later.)

Simon Chen has just been to say that the military have fixed him up with a passage. That was quick. They must be keen to get rid of him. He is to travel to Britain on the *Felix Roussel* on Tuesday! He tells me that this ship is the only one of the prewar vessels taking part in the repatriation exercise.

Well, well!

Tomorrow the kite-flying! Sylvie should like that.

# Chapter Thirty-Four

## The Get-out

The barbed wire put up to secure certain parts of the town by the Japanese was being torn down on the instructions of the military. The people of the city could walk their streets without fear of intimidation or grotesque casual violence. Trishaws – rickshaws balancing on bicycles – had more or less replaced the prewar footman rickshaws that the Nippon authorities had said were the symbol of British colonialist oppression. The *padang* outside Government House was being properly cleared and resown to restore the great greensward that had been there for more than a hundred years. Cricket would be played again.

Sylvie and Virginia – out with Jamie Chase and Sergeant Mac – led the two soldiers to the kite seller who had sold them the mandarin kite before the war. This kite was fine silky paper and shone like water when you held it to the light. This time the kite seller sent his cousin's son to sky the kite for them. He explained to Virginia that the Japanese had taken both his sons and had not returned them.

They made their way along to the esplanade. Mac and Jamie tipped the cousin's son to leave them to it. The captain and the sergeant raced to an open space to try it themselves. Mac held the winder and Jamie ran with the silvery kite, then released it so that it rose higher than the highest tree and hovered there like a dewdrop.

Sylvie kept a worried eye out for dogs but they had other visitors to annoy and ignored the silver kite. She took the string holder from Jamie and moved it this way and that, making the kite swoop and dance in the sky. Mac had a go and, in his attempt to follow the kite, ended up galloping into a palm tree.

Only Virginia was not tired when they finally hauled the kite in, wrapped it into itself and walked back to the Jeep. Sylvie found herself telling Jamie about the shadow puppeteer, and her own puppet, and the show she'd given with Beryl in Sime Road.

'Aha,' said Jamie. 'You'll have to let me see that play.'

'No good,' said Sylvie. 'They stamped on it and spoiled it.'

'Who . . . ?' said Jamie.

'Bloody Nips!' said Mac.

They went to Robinson's for high tea. Having demolished four scones and three pieces of fruitcake, Jamie Chase looked straight at Sylvie. 'How's the juggling?' he said.

'I can do three but not four,' said Sylvie cautiously. She glanced round. She hoped that he'd not make her show him here. Just like him to have some balls with him.

'She practises all the time,' said Virginia. 'She's very

assiduous. My uncle supervises her and says her skills increase.'

'You'll have to show me when we get back to the shop-house,' Jamie said. 'There's a little trick I can show you which will help you with four.'

Sylvie nodded and spooned some cream on to her chopped fruit.

Jamie glanced at Mac, then at Virginia, then back at Sylvie. He coughed. 'There's a bit of news about your father, Sylvie. I thought I'd keep it till now.'

Her head jerked up. She stared at him, then looked round the room. 'He's here!' The room was busy. There were crowds of off-duty RAF boys. Waitresses hovered by the door like an elegant cluster of magpies.

'No,' said Jamie. 'He's not here.'

Sylvie's head went down. 'Dead,' she said. Only she heard the word.

'He's not here in Singapore, Sylvie. He was flown out with the very sick to a hospital in Ceylon, not long after we landed. We'd have discovered this sooner but I'm afraid the first dolt we made the enquiry with got it down as Samson. Seemed Bo Samson didn't exist. I got back to them, corrected the name and, hey presto, we found the record.'

Virginia put a hand on Sylvie's arm. 'So Mr Sambuck is in Ceylon?'

'Well, they checked again for me. Now it seems he's been shipped out of there as well. Ship this time. To an English hospital. Somewhere on the seven seas just now.'

At that point Sylvie leaned sideways and managed to miss

the table as she vomited her English high tea in its entirety, complete with two teaspoonfuls of fruit and cream, on to the carpet.

In an instant a blank-faced waitress was in attendance with soft paper and a cloth.

Virginia led Sylvie to the ladies' powder room and held her head over the basin. 'Nothing left?' She sat her down in a silver gilt chair. 'You stay here and I'll get a warm cloth to wash your face.'

While she was gone Sylvie's eyes wandered to the mirror and surveyed the shining anxious eyes of the person who looked back at her. Her face was different. Her hair was not what it should be. She was so much browner. Her father wouldn't have recognised her anyway. He would have walked by her in the street. And he would have left her, like he did before. Perhaps she would have missed him. She had been trying recently but could not conjure up his face, only his laugh and his clean-sweat smell. If a person couldn't recognise their father, or even their mother, then she really was alone. She sniffed.

Virginia came with a bowl and hot towels and a lavender water spray. Sylvie allowed herself to be anointed like a china doll. 'There,' said Virginia. 'We'd better go up now and thank Captain Jamie for all his detective work.'

'It's no use!' said Sylvie. She shouted the words so they pinged off the elegant tiled walls. 'I'm left behind, Virginia, and that's it! I can't even remember their faces. I can't remember his face. It's finished. Ayoshi and me saved the gold for him and it's no use. Now we're left behind.'

'Come on, Sylvie! No theatricals,' said Virginia briskly. 'They will be waiting for us. It's rude to leave them for so long.'

Jamie and Mac were sitting at a different table, their backs firmly turned against the people still clearing the floor and the table behind them.

Jamie smiled a very sweet smile when he saw her. 'How are you? I—'

'She's fine,' said Virginia briskly. 'A bit of a tummy upset. Our tummies have been somewhat volcanic since Sime Road. This food is very rich for us.'

Sylvie sat in the chair and looked at her scrubbed hands.

'You didn't wait for me to finish, Sylvie. There is a stack of letters out of store for Mr Sambuck. Some from South Africa, some from England. You'll have to collect them.'

Sylvie closed her eyes to a vision of her mother's flourishing, over-inked handwriting. 'My mother . . .' she said.

'And there is something else.'

'Bloody magician, this boy. Excuse my French, ladies.' Mac sat back, beaming all round.

'I have this distant cousin, who's not too far placed from Mountbatten. Well, not to put too fine a point on it, I've sold him your sob-story and you have a berth for England in three days. So you'll see your pa soon enough, Sylvie. Don't worry.'

'I can't do that. I can't go to that place.' For the first time, dratted tears. 'I will stay here with Jin Kee. Jin Kee! She's my sister and it'll not be safe if I leave her. Everyone will be gone. It's no good. No good.'

'Sssh!' Jamie Chase put a finger to his lips. 'All top notch here, Sylvie. Miss Virginia Chen is to accompany you as your chaperon. She will be charged to hand over your good self to your esteemed father or mother *in person*. My cousin's cousin says that they know at headquarters what men like your father went through, those blokes on the railway. Small things like this salve his conscience.'

'That's like the kite seller,' sobbed Sylvie. 'Your cousin's cousin.'

'What ship is it?' said Virginia suddenly.

Jamie Chase took a sheaf of letters from his pocket and leafed through them. 'The *Felix Roussel*,' he read. 'French ship, so I'm told. Bit of a workhorse but it floats.'

'That's the one I missed,' said Sylvie. 'My mother and little brother caught it, though. I let them go.'

'Well then,' said Mac, 'now it's your turn to catch it. I tell you what, I'd give my eyeteeth to come with you and see my old lady and the kids.'

'You *are* coming with me, aren't you?' said Sylvie, suddenly very wary of Virginia's absolute stillness. 'You *will* come?'

Virginia let out an enormous sigh. 'Oh yes, Sylvie, I will come with you. I cannot stay there, but I will come. I'll take you to your father.'

Mac was staring at Virginia in open admiration. 'I suppose it's been a bit of a long job for you, Virginia.'

'What does he mean, "long job"?' demanded Sylvie.

Jamie Chase put his hands flat on the table. 'Enough of this chatter,' he said. 'We have but a short time to improve

371

your juggling, young Sylvie.' He pulled out her chair as she stood up and followed her out of the crowded restaurant.

Virginia caught Mac's eye. The sergeant shrugged. 'Seems he's took a fancy to the kid. I think he'd adopt her if he could.'

Virginia Chen: Her Book

I am very sad to leave my grandmother and Uncle Wo. But with their family sense they understand my duty to this child who is my adopted sister. Simon Chen is torn. He is pleased that I am to travel to England on the same ship, that I too am to go to England, at least for a time. On the other hand he sees I am continuing my feudal duties towards my colonial employers, my country's oppressors. More than ever before I understand his feeling in this. But Sylvie is a child and I feel great affection for her: the affection of an equal. I take the joy of friendship in completing this task.

But when I return I will never again take up a role where I am barely distinguished (at least in the eyes of people such as Lesley Sambuck) from a simple *amah*. When I return I will join Simon Chen and his comrades, do what I can for a Singapore where I can be properly visible.

It is interesting to watch young Captain Jamie with Sylvie. He is so anxious about her in a way of which she is not aware. He watches her as you would a small bird with claws. He is anxious to please her. In some ways it is more than a man would feel for a child. But then he is not quite a man and she is not altogether a child.

I have written another letter to Albert Taft and will try to see him when I am in England.

# Chapter Thirty-Five

## A Day at School

Virginia Chen: Her Book

It was a very necessary thing to do but it was with great sadness that I finally left Sylvie with her grandmother in Priorton. The sea journey took weeks but one part of me was not happy for it to end. Sylvie and I spent a good deal of time with Simon, whose jungle crust started to wear away, allowing the old Simon to emerge now and then, which pleased Sylvie. In our conversations and in listening to the talk of the ex-internees who filled that vessel, it occurred to me that Simon was lucky. He could go into the jungle and fight those beastly people with their own ruthless weapons. He lost comrades and he risked his own life many times, but he was active. One part of me wished I could have gone with him. But for Sylvie I might have done that.

Both he and I are benefiting from my grandmother's care and generosity. She gave each of us a parcel with gold and banker's orders before we embarked. She was concerned that we would not go to England – her husband's country, after all – as paupers.

But there were many poor men aboard – Europeans – who had been denied the right to fight by the ineptitude of their leaders, on the island and in their home countries. They had to suffer humiliation and pain, see their comrades die without dignity, know their women were unprotected. Even rescued, even 'going home', they were still full of deep bitterness. The Nippon, when they realised they were not winning, used to tell us many times that the war would last a hundred years. On that ship I wondered if for some of these poor men the war would indeed last a hundred years because of the shame they had been forced to endure with no fault in themselves.

It took nearly two days on trains and rickety buses to get to the far North of England to the home of Sylvie's 'nana' in a dark town called Priorton. England to me is green and cold; the people have a kind of blankness that I find hard to fathom. They are polite enough but shout at me in a very loud voice as though they are afraid I might not understand them. I have to admit that I felt some curiosity in going to the childhood home of Mrs Lesley Sambuck. I imagined it to be a castle or a large country house such as you encounter in the stories of Elizabeth Bowen.

It was not that at all. It is a small house – only four bedrooms, the end house of a row of stone houses near the centre of that old English town. It is comfortable in an overcurtained and overstuffed kind of way. Although it was mid-afternoon when we finally arrived the sky was overcast and the nana had three lamps on and a roaring coal fire. I had expected an older version of Mrs Sambuck, haughty and distant. It was not so. She is stout and florid-faced, dressed in a tailored wool dress with a lace collar. Her black hair is pulled back from her face into a chignon at the back. Her face lights up when she sees Sylvie and she clasps her to that bosom to the point where I feel Sylvie will be suffocated. She wriggles away but I can see that she is comfortable with this woman. Though the two grandmothers – hers and mine – are worlds apart, this child responds to both of them with the same trust.

Sylvie looks round the room, her eyes wide. The grandmother shakes her head. 'They're not here, pet. I've had the wire that your daddy will come here from hospital soon, perhaps in a week. And your mam is on the ship and will be here in a week or so.' Her voice is strange. It is warm but it is low, almost gruff. And her accent does not have the cut-glass edge of her daughter, Mrs Sambuck. This is interesting.

Over the three days of my stay she waits for Sylvie to go to bed, then she makes another cup of her eternal tea and settles down to ask me, in detail, Sylvie's story. I admire her delicacy in not interrogating Sylvie herself. She is worried that bad things have happened to the child. She, like others, has read the newspapers, which are full of the most atrocious details about people's experiences in the camps. I try to be as honest as I can but I omit to tell her of the time I was taken from the camp and Sylvie was alone. I am haunted by this myself, and fear I would make it sound worse than it really was. It was bad, of course. One must admit this.

After three days I have to go, first to see Simon settled in at Cambridge, then down to Plymouth to visit Albert Taft, who is on demob leave. He sent me a wire on the ship. He had used some navy intelligence to discover me there. Then there was a letter when I landed, full of interest and cheer. I wonder if I will know him? Like him? This is a very strange journey.

Up in Priorton there are tears and stubborn looks from Sylvie, and I try to explain that we must get on with our lives, that our own particular interlude is over. I have to promise solemnly to write to her every week, every single week, before she lets me get into the taxi. Her grandmother looks at me over Sylvie's head and thanks me very sincerely for taking care of her grand-daughter.

In the days since, I have been looking over my shoulder for Sylvie. It is like walking without your own shadow.

'Did they torture you, then?'
'Did they pull out your fingernails?'
'Did they hang you up by your toes?'

Sylvie pulled her school satchel to her chest and held it tightly there. She was sweating underneath the thing her nana called a 'liberty bodice', which made her feel anything but free; on top of this a vest, a petticoat, a blouse, a cardigan and a blazer.

She looked round the bodies – similarly loaded with clothes – and the broad pasty faces that encircled her. She recognised them from the class where she had been taken yesterday afternoon by the headmistress and her nana. 'One C,' the teacher had announced to the highly attentive girls, 'this is Sylvie Sambuck. She will be joining you tomorrow. I know it is mid-term but this is a special situation. Here in Britain we have had the Blitz and the Battle of Britain and rationing. But Sylvie here has been in sunnier climes, enduring hardships which we just cannot imagine. Only now is she back with her grandmother after many years. I want you to be particularly kind to her.'

As they walked back along the cream-glossed corridor the headmistress said to Nana, talking over Sylvie's head, 'One C is, I think, most suitable. We don't know Sylvie's standard and in her state we would not wish to tax her, would we?'

'Nothing like that,' Sylvie said now to the hovering circle of girls. 'They never touched me.'

'Sing-sing, sing-sing, talks like a Chinkee,' said the small girl on the end.

'But did you see them?' the tall girl at the centre persisted. 'Did you see them do anything? You must have seen them.'

'You must have seen them,' said the shorter girl, who stood at her elbow. She pushed Sylvie on her unprotected shoulder. 'It says in the papers. You must have seen.'

Sylvie closed her eyes. She could see the hut with Miss Snowie sitting cross-legged reading her Bible, and Mrs Grassington with her head bent low over a scrap of sewing. Of its own volition her stomach wrenched with hunger despite the fact that she'd just eaten a fried egg and a slice of bacon and two slices of fried bread. Her nana had said to Virginia almost as soon as they came through the door that they would have to build the child up.

Virginia had brought her to the empty house. No father. No mother. No Feargal. Just her nana folding her uncomfortably in her broad arms.

Now the girl to her far right said, 'They make lampshades out of human skin. My dad read it out of the paper.' The other girls nodded and murmured in agreement to this patent truth.

Sylvie looked around. There were seven girls standing shoulder to shoulder. There was no break in the circle. She remembered the Japs bullying the Chinese men in the street. 'I saw them chopping off the heads of three Chinamen,' she offered. 'They put them up on long poles in the street. As *a warning.*'

Aah. The tension in the circle relaxed but the girls' focus on Sylvie became, if anything, sharper. 'Sing-sing,' said the smallest girl. 'Hear that? Talks like Fu Manchu.'

The tall girl took up the interrogation. 'But the women,' she said. 'What did they do to the women?'

'They slapped them.'

A disbelieving mutter went round the circle. 'Show me. Show me how they slapped the women,' the tall girl said.

Carefully Sylvie placed the schoolbag on the ground. Then she stepped up to the tall girl, drew back her whole arm and swung it towards her with all her strength. The girl caught her forearm before it landed and hung on to it, gripping it painfully tight. She was very close to Sylvie now. She said right into her ear. 'What else did they do? What else?'

'They . . . they looted them.'

'Looted? *Looted?* What's that mean?' said the short girl.

'They took them,' said Sylvie, gasping now with the pain in her arm. 'They stole them away and sometimes they hurt them. Then they came back. Later. Sometimes days, sometimes weeks.'

A snigger went round the circle. 'Oh you mean *raped*!' said a red-haired girl.

'What's that?' said Sylvie.

'Oh, that's when they make you lie down and put their—'

'Girls! Girls! What's this, Jane Hetherington?' A small fat tornado with a helmet of blonde hair broke into the circle.

The tall girl released Sylvie, who rubbed her arm and bent down to pick up her satchel. 'It's Sylvie Sambuck, Miss Levitas,' she said. 'The girl who was in the newspaper. From Singapore.'

'Ah!' Miss Levitas surveyed Sylvie kindly through round lenses. 'Well, my dear, you can be sure you will only meet kindness at The Mount. We have a special brief to take care of you. Your mother was an old girl here, I believe?'

'Yes,' said Sylvie.

'Yes, Miss Levitas,' instructed Miss Levitas.

'Yes, Miss Levitas.'

The girls in the circle, having now dropped back a step, sniggered.

'Where were you at school before, Sylvie?'

'I was never at school . . .'

'Miss Levitas,' prompted Miss Levitas.

'I was never at school, Miss Levitas. Except in the camp.'

'And what kind of school was that?'

'I can't really say, Miss Levitas. I was banned after the first day.'

'And why would they ban you from a – er – camp school?'

'For fighting, Miss Levitas.'

There was more laughter around her.

'Well, well, I never.' Miss Levitas put a whistle to her lips and blew three ear-piercing blasts. 'Now, girls, line up. We can't be chit-chatting all morning.' She bustled off to supervise the five long lines that comprised the whole school. One by one the queues numbered themselves off.

Sylvie, who was second in the queue to Jane Hetherington, shouted TWO! when her turn came, then afterwards whispered to herself, '*Tenko!*' As the lines peeled off to go into school and girls passed Sylvie three girls whispered 'Jap!', two whispered 'Nip' and one whispered 'Chink'.

Sylvie found the morning's work in mathematics and English grammar very easy. She finished long before the others and the teacher, a long-faced mild-tempered woman called Miss Sinclair, supplied her with two extra pages of work in each subject. She worked with her head down, wondering what she would do about playtime. The bell clanked through the school and the girls put their work inside their desks, sat up straight and then, dismissed, erupted from the classroom in a raging horde. Sylvie stayed at her desk.

Miss Sinclair glanced up at her from her pedestal desk. 'What is it, Sylvia?'

'I don't feel very well, Miss Sinclair.'

Miss Sinclair bit back her usual retort for malingering. This was a special case, after all. 'I suppose this is rather overwhelming to you,' she said, 'being brought back to civilisation in this fashion. Perhaps if you just quietly read a book . . .'

'Yes, Miss Sinclair.'

'Your standard of work is very good, Sylvia, and yet I hear . . .' she'd heard the amazing story that this child had been expelled from a camp school, 'you've had little schooling.'

'I never went to school, really. But I was taught by Miss Snowie, who was a missionary. And Miss Chen, who was my tutor.'

'Miss Chen? She would be . . .' (Miss Sinclair reflected on the firm directive from her headmistress that something must be done about the child's dreadful accent.)

'She was my friend. Like my sister. She was very clever. She had two degrees.'

Miss Sinclair nodded sagely. 'One can see that has engendered great benefit. Now,' she gathered up her capacious handbag, big enough to carry a small child, 'will you need to attend the offices?'

Panic ripped through Sylvie, targeting the pit of her stomach. 'What's that?'

'What's that, Miss Sinclair?' said Miss Sinclair patiently.

'What's-that-Miss-Sinclair?'

'It is the lavatory, Sylvia.'

Sylvie thought of Heaven at Sime Road. 'No thank you . . . Miss Sinclair.'

'Well done, Sylvia. Now there is a book called *Little Women* on the shelf behind you. You may read that.' She fastened her long cardigan, picked up her bag and swept out of the room.

Sylvie waited for the door to click behind her and started to laugh. She laughed so much that tears came to her eyes.

At dinnertime Miss Sinclair is not so complaisant. Sylvia simply *must*, for the sake of her health, get some nice fresh air. It is a cold day, to be sure, and it is threatening rain, but it is bracing.

Jane Hetherington and the others are waiting for her. She moves away from them but they follow her until they corner her in a space created by a deep bay in the old house that has been transformed into this small girls' school. Here the daughters of traders in this market town get sufficient education to launch them on the world. Some of them, in years to come, will find they are cleverer than their school recognised and will get a real education elsewhere.

She turns to face them, no schoolbag to protect her now. 'What is it? What do you want?' She thinks of Beryl Bridges and the hooch, which brings a smile to her face. Beryl would have been good to have at her shoulder now. She has sent

Beryl her nana's address but there has been no letter. The red-headed girl pushes her hard. 'What're you laughing at, lass?'

'She's laughing 'cause she's here,' says Jane Hetherington. 'Here instead of in that stinking hole with the Japs.'

A girl with glasses at the edge of the crowd says, 'I say, girls, I think she's a Jap. Look at her, yellow as old custard.'

'Here!' Jane Hetherington pushes up her cardigan sleeve. 'Do this.' She grabs Sylvie's arm, pushes up her sleeve and places it alongside her arm. The girls crowd round to view the two arms side by side. Sylvie looks with interest herself. It's true. Jane's arm is lily-white, and her own arm, with its faded tan, is a sallow muddy yellow.

'It's true,' says the red-headed girl.

'Right,' says Sylvie. 'If you say *it's true* . . .' Then she brings back her arm and delivers Jane Hetherington a slap that would have done Four Eyes proud. The tall girl crumples to the floor. Sylvie turns then to mete the same treatment out to the red-headed one, then the one with glasses. Some girls scream and run away. Jane and the redhead get up and turn on Sylvie. For a minute she gives as good as she gets. Then the redhead pushes her over and Jane is sitting astride her and delivering effective punches, first her left cheek, then her right.

'Girls! Girls!' Miss Levitas is pushing her way through the crowd. 'Really!' she gasps.

'Whew,' says Jane, looking very relieved. 'Thank heavens you're here, miss. Sylvia Sambuck just went berserk. The little ones were terrified. She was flailing about like a windmill.' There was a murmur of scared agreement in the crowd.

'Get up, for goodness' sake,' says Miss Levitas. 'You too, Sylvia Sambuck. Come with me.'

She takes hold of Sylvie by the upper arm and leads the way to the headmistress's study, Jane Hetherington and the redhead in tow. Once in that sombre and cluttered sanctum the evidence seems irrefutable. Jane has obviously been frightened by the strange reactions of the newcomer and one can understand her wanting to protect the little ones. The situation is not helped at all by the fact that Sylvie Sambuck offers not one word of explanation for her behaviour. She just keeps her eye on the toe of her right sandal. The headmistress sighs a deep sigh. 'We understand, Sylvia, that adjustments have to be made, but this is intolerable. In this school we expect good order and good manners.'

Sylvie lifts her head and looks the woman in the eye. 'There's no order in this bloody school, I can tell you.'

'Sylvia!' says Miss Levitas, her pale cheeks ruddy now.

Jane Hetherington swallows a snigger and then the room is silent for a full minute.

'Miss Levitas!' says the headmistress finally. 'Perhaps you will escort Sylvia to her grandmother's house and explain to her the problem we have here. Unacceptable behaviour makes unacceptable people. I am afraid that Sylvia is not welcome in this school.'

Miss Levitas stands over Sylvie while she collects her bag and Burberry. No word passes between them. It's raining outside and the teacher makes a great business of putting up a black umbrella. As they walk the quarter of a mile to the grandmother's house she doesn't invite Sylvie to share it with her.

Trudging along beside the black mushroom apparition of Miss Levitas, the rain beating down on her like cold chips of ice, Sylvie thinks longingly of the sluicing tropical rain, which steams off in minutes after it has fallen.

Nana opens the door to Sylvie, who is standing there, Burberry drenched, black hair sticking to her bruised face. Then she looks up into the round face of Miss Levitas, dry and powdered under her umbrella. 'What's this then?' she says. 'What on earth have you been doing to her?'

# Chapter Thirty-Six

## Pictures

Sylvie listened to the rise and fall of angry women's voices from down below. She stripped to the skin, then dressed again, this time in a kilt and green jumper her grandmother had bought for her from Doggarts. Sylvie held up the liberty bodice then threw it on to the pile of damp, discarded uniform.

She made her way to sit on a step halfway down the stairs. She heard her grandmother's voice say, 'Well, Miss Levitas, I know you'll convey to Miss Corrigan my extreme displeasure. Tell her how very disappointed I am that she – and you – could not act with charity to a child, who, if I may say so, has been injured by history.'

'Mrs Conrad, I—'

'Goodbye, Miss Levitas.'

Sylvie heard the front door clash and walked slowly down the rest of the stairs.

Nana held out her hand. 'How about some cocoa, dear?'

In the kitchen, which, as well as its modern electric cooker, still had a cosy black range, Nana set about making the cocoa. 'That was a lot of fuss about nothing,' she said. 'Teachers nowadays! That Miss Levitas was a pupil of your grandpa, you know. He always said she had the initiative of a slug.'

Sylvie laughed.

'That's better.' Nana poured the milk and stirred in the cocoa. 'A smile will wipe it all away.'

'They called me "Jap", Nana. And "Chink". They said I talked funny.'

Nana laughed. 'You do talk with a bit of a lilt, pet, but who's to be surprised? And that's what they do at that school, iron out accents. They ironed out your mam's accent in a month. Gave her no end of airs and graces. Your grandpa was very pleased. The way I talked always made him click his tongue. He liked my Sunderland looks but didn't like my Sunderland twang. But I wouldn't lose the way I talked, not even for him.' She put a mug of cocoa in front of Sylvie and took hers to the other side of the table. 'What did you do? Give them a bashing?'

'Yes. Sort of.'

'Good for you. I can see you've learned to stick up for yourself. No bad thing.'

'And they bashed me as well.'

'So I see. Don't worry, pet. You won't be going back there in a hurry.' Nana leaned backwards to the dresser behind her and drew a box on to the table. 'I thought we might take a look at these, love. Just to put you back in the picture.' She chuckled. 'Aren't I clever. Back in the *picture*!' She tipped the box up and out came dozens of photographs and cards.

She turned them face up and spread them so each one had its own space. 'Look, there's your mam when she was your age. A beautiful child, though I say it myself. The apple of her daddy's eye. I didn't get a look-in. There she is again in her school uniform. Loved that school, she did. Not a fighter like you. Knuckled down. And there they are on their wedding day. Handsome couple, everyone said.'

Sylvie took the picture and held it close to her eyes. Her mother looked really young, younger than Virginia now. She was wearing a draped silk dress. Then there was Daddy, big and bluff, grinning at the camera like a Cheshire cat.

'I always liked your dad,' said Nana. 'Hard-working. Generous to a fault. He's another one we'll have to feed up when he gets here.' She sighed and stared into the fire for a second.

He was in a hospital somewhere. They had taken him there straight from the boat. Sylvie had read the letter he'd written to her nana. The writing was very shaky. Sylvie held on to the card too long. Her nana peeled it out of her fingers. 'Look at this one, pet. Your grandpa.' Sylvie stared at the tall figure with its vigorous head of what might be fair or might be grey hair. Good bones. Handsome. Rimless glasses. A very severe look.

'You can tell where our Lesley gets her looks from,' said Nana. 'Talking of your mam, she'll be here in two weeks. She can be a madam, our Lesley, but it'll be good to see her.' Lesley knew about Sylvie now. Nana had wired the ship to tell her. 'She'll be that excited, love. She thought you were gone, you know, consumed in those first days. She wrote to me about it. I couldn't believe you could be lost like that. But seems they were those kinds of times, in that place.'

'What's this?' Sylvie picked up another card with a younger version of Grandpa: an explosion of blond hair and an actor's looks. Beside him was a tall beautiful girl with smooth black hair piled on her head. She was holding white lilies and was wearing the same draped silk dress that Lesley wore in her wedding picture. Sylvie put a finger on the face. 'She's really beautiful. Who is she?'

Nana gave a gurgling chuckle. 'What a nice girl you are! Why, that's me, pet. On my wedding day to your grandpa. He was the youngest headmaster in the region and was visiting Sunderland one day to talk at the training college there. I was learning to be a teacher. He took one look at me and was lost.' She chuckled again.

Sylvie frowned. 'You were a teacher, Nana?'

Nana shook her head. 'Not in those days, love. One sniff of a wedding ring and you got the sack. I gave up. Not cut out to be a teacher, anyway. Cut from too coarse a cloth.' She shrugged. 'There was plenty to do, with Grandpa being headmaster and all that. Then Lesley came along so it was all fine.' She paused, then reached for another photograph. 'Now look at this. Here is a photo of me when I was your age! Twelve years old.' The girl in the picture was wearing a long-waisted dress with a wide sash. Sylvie picked it up and looked at it closely.

'Who does this girl look like?' said Nana.

'Me! Nana. It looks like me!'

Nana laughed again. 'I thought you'd spot that.'

Sylvie picked up another photograph of a small child in a knee-length dress. 'What's that? That thing she's holding.'

'It's a he. Your grandpa. The boys wore dresses till they were three.'

'What's he holding?'

'That? Oh, that's this doll he had. He told me once – in a moment of weakness – he really loved that doll . . . Sylvie, where are you going? Sylvie?'

Mrs Conrad sat back, listening to the scrabbling and clashing overhead. At least the child's mind was off that disastrous episode at school. She should have known. It was too soon, far too soon. How stupid to think that school would make things more normal. She thought of the wide stubborn eyes of the child brought to her by the Eurasian woman. How powerless and guilty it made her feel. She was determined to make up for it, whatever that took. But it would do no good going on at the child. No good at all.

Sylvie clattered back down the stairs. She came into the circle of light and placed Ayoshi carefully on top of the pictures in front of her nana. 'There! See! I have one too. And Grandpa had one.'

Nana touched the battered doll with her forefinger and tried not to wrinkle her nose at the strange smells that emanated from her. 'What is she called?'

'Ayoshi, and she has been with me right through. And see, under her obi? Some gold coins I saved for Daddy for him to start again.'

'Well, child,' said her nana, blinking, 'what a nice thought. Where d'you get her?'

'Well, Virginia gave her to me. But she got her from her grandmother. She is a very, very old lady. I like her. She really, really loves music.'

'Well,' said Nana. 'Well, I never.'

'Where did Grandpa get his Ayoshi?'

'Well, pet, I think he was given her by another very old lady.' She paused, pulling Ayoshi's gown down so she was very neat. 'But that's a tale for another day, love. Let's clear these photos and you can help me set for the tea. Then it'll be time for *Children's Hour* on the wireless. You're getting to like that, aren't you?'

# Chapter Thirty-Seven

## Homecoming

Mr Borridge, the school board man, came to check why Sylvie was not at school but he quickly retreated when he realised the grandmother was the widow of the famous headmaster Conrad. He had to believe it when Mrs Conrad said that for the time being the girl was being educated at home. Did she not need time to recover from her recent ordeal? The child's world had been shattered. Her father – who had been forced to work for the Japs in the war – was due home any minute and how was the child to face that? How would Mr Borridge – who unfortunately had not made it himself to the war to do his bit – face that?

Sylvie, who had been listening at her sentinel place on the stairs, watched him go and came down to say, 'Does that mean I have to do lessons? With you?'

Her grandmother shook her head. 'Time enough for that, Sylvie.' She wondered if Sylvie had heard all that had been said. 'But I thought you might do some nature study with

Frank; help you get to know your *own* country.'

Frank was a friend of Mrs Conrad, a former colleague of her husband, now retired. He came to tea twice a week and brought Mrs Conrad vegetables from his allotment. He'd never been married and was intensely shy. Sylvie already liked him because he didn't ask her direct questions and only commented on the weather and the quality of the scones. Her grandmother said it was quite all right to call him Frank because that's what he liked.

Now Sylvie's head went down. 'My own country's Singapore, Nana. I was born there.'

Mrs Conrad frowned at her. 'Let's say you're a lucky girl. You have two countries. And you need to learn about this one so you know it as well as the other one.'

Frank came the next afternoon and they caught the bus to Killock woods. He wore field glasses round his neck and carried a long umbrella, which he used as a walking stick. He occasionally used it to point out different species of trees and the few fugitive squirrels. In the main, though, he and Sylvie walked companionably through the narrow pathways. They stopped by a spreading oak tree and the umbrella pointed to an exactly circular path that led round the tree. 'The children call those fairy rings,' he said.

She looked round. 'Fairies?' she said.

He gave a short snorting laugh. 'I fear not. I'm told it is the roe deer. Perhaps the grass just there at the edge of the tree canopy is very juicy. Or perhaps they pursue each other round and round when they do their courting.'

'Courting? What's that?'

'When a girl and a boy become close to each other before they are married.'

She walked on, her mind charged again for a second over the reaction of the girls about 'looting'. Then for no reason at all Jamie Chase came into her mind. He would be out there in the hot sun. He might even be flying a kite on the esplanade.

They clambered higher, where the forest opened up, and there, down below them, sprawled the wall and the keep of a castle. 'I didn't know there was a castle here,' said Sylvie.

'We're just by Killock Castle,' Frank said. 'Lord Chase lives here, when he's in the North, not in his big house in London. He owns many of the mines round here just for the present. Not for long.'

'Has he sold them?'

'Not exactly. The government'll take them from him and they will run the mines on behalf of the people. It will be a very good thing.'

Sylvie was frowning, shading her eyes so she could see it better.

'Would you like a closer look?' He handed her his binoculars and showed her how to adjust them.

The binoculars drew the castle in very close. She could see the large gateway where the Spitfire stood on that day; the central court where flags were sold on behalf of the war. She scanned to one side with the binoculars. Yes, there was the garden with the long surrounding wall, and the tree in which she lay and watched the boy juggling. She looked for a long time, then handed the binoculars back to Frank.

'You seem very interested in the castle,' he said.

'I think I was there when I was very little. There was a boy there, Jamie Chase, who was juggling. Then he was in Singapore and he was a man soldier. He taught me how to juggle there. And he helped me and Virginia, my sister, to get back here.'

Frank settled the binoculars over his head and on his chest. 'Ah, a very timely coincidence,' he said. 'And do you still juggle?'

'Yes, but sometimes if it's four balls I drop one. But sometimes I am quite good.'

'You must show me. I think I would like to see you juggle.'

Frank had to get back to feed his cats so he said he would leave her at the back gate of her grandmother's house. As she fiddled with the sneck he spoke to her stiffly, his mouth almost closed. 'Your grandfather was a very great man, Sylvie. Perhaps it will help you to know this.' He gulped, as though he had swallowed something very hard, and strode off.

In the kitchen Sylvie wrinkled her nose at a half-forgotten, yet familiar smell. There was something in the air. Something. Miss Snowie flashed across her mind, sitting cross-legged in the bed space. A murmur of voices trickled through from the front room.

'Sylvie!' her nana's voice sang out. 'Come in here, won't you?'

As she pushed open the door the first thing she saw was the blazing fire. This was unusual. Nana kept a blazing fire in the kitchen, but the sitting-room fire was kept cold, graced by an embroidered screen. Beside the fire, in the best chair, sat an old man in a loose fitting suit.

'Sylvie?' The man spoke. His voice, anxious now, but with laughter waiting at the edges, was very familiar.

She looked again. The hair was thinner, the face was so much narrower. But of course it was him. Bo Sambuck. Her feet took her forward. 'Daddy!'

'Come here, sweetheart. I won't break.' He hauled himself to his feet and opened his arms. She ran into his embrace, feeling the bones of his chest under her cheek. 'What a big girl you are, what a big girl you are.' He kept saying this. Then: 'What a long time it's been. How long, Sylvie?' Then he swayed and dropped back into the chair and she fell with him.

Sylvie disentangled herself, feeling awkward. Bo closed his eyes for a second.

'Now then,' said Mrs Conrad briskly, 'your daddy's not too good on his pins just yet. He needs a bit of building-up, like you did.' She pulled up a chair close to the best chair in which Bo was sitting. 'You sit there, love, and talk to your daddy and I'll get the tea on. I've got a nice bit of steak from under the butcher's counter and new potatoes from Frank's allotment. You just get yourselves up to date now.' She closed the sitting-room door behind her with a click.

Sylvie looked at the flickering fire, then back at her father, who was now emerging from the old man's husk. She could see him properly now. She could see his bright eyes and how his lips curled up in that old way at the edges. She could see his large hands with their long tapering fingers. She looked closer at his fingernails, thinking of what Jane Hetherington had said about the torture. They were all there.

'I looked for you, then I thought you were dead.' The words burst out of her like an accusation. 'For a long time I thought you must be dead or you'd have come for me.'

He took a breath. 'There were times, sweetheart, when I thought I was dead too. But, as you see, I'm not. A bit older, a bit wiser. But I *am* alive.' The last words were said through gritted teeth. 'And now at last I've come for you.'

'I shouted at them, the men, Daddy. Through the wire. And they spelled your name for me in stones. With an H afterwards.'

'I was in the military hospital. Those were brave men, Sylvie. They would get a beating for their pains.'

'H for hospital?' she said.

'That would be it. When I came through that dose of sickness, I asked them to check on the women's camp. They had their means. I couldn't believe it. I hadn't heard from your mother but I knew the *Felix Roussel* had got away. There was one Red Cross letter, two years old, from your mother, asking if you were with me. I could not believe it. Then they said someone shouted my name in the women's camp. So I got them to check. There were channels.'

'Some of the fathers came on Sundays towards the end.' She was staring hard at the fire as she said this.

'I would have come. I would have come, sweetheart. I would have crawled there. How I would have loved to come. But there was no one called Sambuck listed in the women's camp. Even the Nips checked.'

She brought her gaze back to him. 'I was Syl Vee Chen in Sime Road. Virginia Chen took care of me.' She was unsmiling. She would not let him off the hook. 'In the camp I was her sister. Not Sylvie Sambuck.'

'Thank God for Virginia Chen.' Bo Sambuck looked at his daughter, now very nearly a woman. He was consumed by the hollow waste of years. That was the crime. For nearly four years he'd avoided such despair, counting steps, marking days, marking birthdays: the common ones and those of the King. Counting shows and performances, Christmases with excess in proportion. Counting grains of rice to make the sharing more equitable, counting strikes of the *chungkol*, blows of the blunt axe at work. Counting the living, only the living. Counting shows, counting meals, counting guards, counting poles slung with wire. And even afterwards, safe in the English hospital, counting injections, counting showers, counting meals, still counting grains of rice. Then counting telegraph poles on his journey to the North of England. It was the counting that kept him in the present as he focused on the survival of each particular day.

Now this daughter of his, staring so intently, was making him consider the past, look to the future. The very sight of her convinced him finally that survival was in his grasp. She'd been dead to him. Lesley had written, in the required twenty-five words. 'Trust Sylvie is with you. Not on ship. Feargal, self safely in Durban. Lodging with the Cranstons. Always thinking of you. Much love, your Lesley.'

He had the words off by heart. And in his heart from the

early days he felt Sylvie was dead: dead as the baby's mother struck on the quayside by shrapnel. Dead as the comrades on the railway, who dropped around him like savagely wounded sparrows. But he was alive and he kept counting. And his daughter (it was carved on the inside of his skull), who was funny, defiant, a great turner of cartwheels: she was suspended in death at the age of nine.

But she was not. She was here in front of him staring with those cool dark eyes. She was longer-limbed now, and had a longer face, a bigger nose. Her eyes, though, had that same self-regarding glint, that distinctive challenge. 'Do you still turn cartwheels?' he said.

She frowned. 'I don't know. But I can juggle.'

His grin lit up his wasted face. He leaned forward and took her hand in his. 'Tell me everything, Sylvie. Every little thing. Right from the quayside.'

So Sylvie did this. She continued her story when Mrs Conrad called them into the kitchen to eat their steak and potatoes. She went on with it as they were eating, as they were drinking the tea that Mrs Conrad poured out for them. Mrs Conrad sat silently as Bo prompted Sylvie for more and more details. Sylvie would wake up for weeks remembering some other small thing and save it like a treasure for Bo when they were alone.

But for this day she drained her memory as far as she could. In this way, as far as was in her power, she gave her own missing years back to her father. 'I have your tennis cup,' she said finally. 'In my luggage. The vicar used the big one, like I said, for the Blood of Christ.'

'Seems to me that your friend Beryl Bridges is quite a number,' he said.

'She knew how to go on. She was funny. I liked that,' said Sylvie.

'Very handy, to have a friend like that.'

Mrs Conrad stirred finally in her seat. 'Seems to me we have a lot to thank that Miss Chen for, Bo.'

'I'll say.' He looked at Sylvie. 'So where is Virginia Chen now? Did she go straight back?'

Sylvie frowned. 'Well, she's either at Cambridge with Simon or at Plymouth with Albert.'

Bo laughed. 'Two men?'

'I told you,' said Sylvie, 'Simon Chen was her cousin but he was proper Chinese. He's at Cambridge to study. He was a hero. He fought the Japanese in the jungle,' she added.

Bo pursed his lips. 'Would that we could all have done that. Fight the . . . fight those evil men.'

'Simon says things will be different in the new Singapore. No more European bosses. That's what he says.'

'He does, does he? Clever chap!'

'And Virginia says there is good sense in what he says.'

'She says that, does she? Well, perhaps his years at Cambridge will quieten him down.'

'He says he knows they think that. That's why they let him go. He explained that to me on the ship.'

'What about Plymouth?' cut in Mrs Conrad.

'Well, that's Albert Taft, who's Virginia's sweetheart. It was love at first sight. Like Cinderella, you know? He wrote to her. She wrote to him. He's a demob now, from the navy.'

'Is he now?' said Bo.

'You remember him, Daddy. He was really, really hand-some.' She frowned, pulling back the memory. 'He took Virginia Chen to the Coconut Grove and my mother was so cross, wasn't she? I heard her shouting.'

'Is that so?' Bo exchanged glances with his mother-in-law. 'Well, that's water under the bridge now, sweetheart. As your friend Simon says, those days are over.'

'Now it's your turn,' said Sylvie. 'You tell me about you.'

His face closed up. 'Not now, sweetheart. Not just yet. Another time maybe.'

'That's right,' said Mrs Conrad, starting the routine bustle of table clearing. 'We need to get your daddy fit, love. Feed him with some good Durham food. Get him out in our fresh air.'

'He could come for nature study walks with me and Frank.' She turned to her father. 'Frank is Nana's friend. He has these lovely binoculars. They make the far away close up.'

Her father smiled thinly. 'That sounds just the ticket, sweetheart. If you ask me, a bit of nature study is just what I need.'

# Chapter Thirty-Eight

## Recuperation

In the next two weeks Bo consumed Mrs Conrad's wholesome meals washed down by pints of milk obtained off ration from the Co-op Dairy. The only thing he turned down was her rice baked in the oven with nutmeg. He ate with the dogged determination of an athlete in training. Every other day he and Sylvie went for a walk with Frank in Killock woods. There was no talk of war, although Frank had served on the Western Front in the Great War and had his own tales to tell. They passed the binoculars from hand to hand and talked only of abstractions: the new Labour government and hopes for the future in a more just society. Sylvie, listening carefully, thought that Frank, dry old stick that he was, reminded her of Simon Chen.

Their walks were short at first, with Bo using his late father-in-law's old stick to help to haul himself along. After a week the stick was put back in the stand in the hall and the trio got to explore the length and breadth of Killock woods, and the network of paths by the River Gaunt in the Priors Park. Here the talk was of the sighting of a golden plover and the yearly return of kingfishers to the River Gaunt. Bo told the scandalous tale of a friend of his, a naval officer, who once ate a golden oriole that his 'man' had trapped in the jungle of Singapore. Sylvie admired the easy way the men spoke together and wondered how she might get her father to talk about the thing that most concerned her.

In the evening they listened to the wireless, following the adventures of *Dick Barton, Special Agent* with avidity and learning of the goings-on in London from *In Town Tonight*. One Saturday night, when the play had just finished and Mrs Conrad was clearing away the supper dishes, Sylvie, slouching back in her chair, asked Bo, 'Were you ever struck down by the Dreaded Anophele Fly?'

Bo's face closed down. 'Well, yes, I was, as a matter of fact. Seven times in all. Struck down's the word.'

'How did you get better?'

'Well, first of all I had buddies, friends, who took care of me. And second I counted. I counted the days, the meals, the storms, till I got better.'

'Counted to show that you counted?'

A smile breezed across his face. 'If you put it like that, yes.'

'My friend Miss Snowie was attacked by the Dreaded Anophele Fly three times. But she got better. It was a Close Thing.'

'Good for her. I like the sound of your Miss Snowie.'

Mrs Conrad was standing in the doorway between the

kitchen and the scullery. She wondered whether Bo could take all this innocent questioning. Perhaps she should intervene. Bo glanced at her and, ever so slightly, shook his head.

'Captain Jamie Chase – you remember I told you about him? The juggler – he said you were on the railway.'

'So I was.'

'Was it bad?'

'It was very, very bad.'

'Do you remember that American woman? The one I told you about? The one with the dog called Judy?'

'Yes, I do.'

'She was a great heroine. She had it very, very bad with the *Kempai Tai*, so I know about all that. Six months. I thought you would like to know that.'

'That's very kind of you, Sylvie.' He blinked hard. 'It is nice to know this.'

'Now then!' Mrs Conrad swept into the room, filling it with her assured common-sense self. 'What a girl we have here, Bo! We should be proud of her. But now we need some good-night cocoa.'

Bo and Sylvie looked at Mrs Conrad and then at each other and laughed. Sylvie thought how much her father had changed in the last three weeks. He became younger every day. His flesh was growing on his bones. His face was filling out. His very hair was springing from his head in a celebratory fashion.

'Cocoa!' he said. 'What I would not have given for that in Camburi. Now there was a hell of a place.'

\* \* \*

A week later Sylvie and Bo came back from watching a film called *Good Old Soak* at the Priorton Odeon and caught up with the Post Office boy. He would not hand over the yellow envelope as it was addressed to Mrs Conrad. She tore it open and beamed at them. 'Lesley and Feargal. They're at Southampton,' she said. 'Just getting on the London train. They'll stay overnight in London and there is uncertainty of the times of trains up here. So many delays. You would think there was a war on. They should arrive tomorrow afternoon. Early evening.'

Sylvie looked at her father. She knew she should feel happy but she did not, quite. She saw the same look in his eyes.

'Lesley,' he said slowly. 'Your mother, Sylvie, she's coming. Won't it be wonderful to see her?'

'Yes,' she said. But she walked past them both to the door. Behind her she could hear the rush of her grandmother's voice and murmuring from Frank, who had come for tea, not the voice of her father. She walked steadily upstairs to her room. Out of her pocket she took a letter that had come from Virginia Chen this morning. She read it again.

My dearest Sylvie,

I have missed you each day although it is indeed a very big adventure, being in England, a country that I think I know in my heart from my studies and my grandmother's talk of my grandfather. But it is all very different. Not so dark, although much colder if one finds oneself in a room without a fire. I bought some woolly underclothes in Cambridge! There is a shock in hearing always and every time English spoken. But such strange 'Englishes'! I tell myself it is only like the many 'Chineses' spoken in Singapore.

I am pleased to say Cambridge English predominates at Cambridge. Simon Chen is now every inch the Cambridge student. His college is called Fitzwilliam. He has a thick tweed jacket and even smokes a briar pipe! He admires his teachers and has, I think, made an impression. He introduced me to one of his tutors, who sang his praises. He lives in a house with four other students. One is from Glasgow (ex-army). The others are Malayan of one kind or another. They are members of a Malayan forum and talk politics a great deal and plot their revolution.

It was a very slow train ride from Cambridge to Plymouth. So many changes. I thought the journey would never end. There is a great deal of war damage here, whole streets and squares in ruins and children playing on heaps of rubble. Albert Taft, much older and tougher now, was very pleased to see me and remembers every detail of our meetings before the war. But still so good-looking. I gave him some letters I had written to him while I was in Sime Road and, tough as he is, there were tears in his eyes. You always said he was my sweetheart, Sylvie, and I think he is. He is very 'smitten' as they say in the American films. He took me for a meal at his parents' house. The meal was English roast beef, carrots and cabbage (very wet). And beer. Very English, I imagine.

His mother and father and two brothers (still in the army) were very polite, very respectful. They talked of the war and the bombing of neighbours who had died. They talked around me as though I were a stray bird who had wandered on to their patch. Still, they are fine people.

Albert remembers you well and sends his loving regards. I have not told him all of our story as some of it does not bear telling. I had to tell him, though, of the sad fate of Singa Pura, your puppet.

I miss you every day and will never forget my little comrade.

Your Jin Kee

PS You can find me at this address for ten days. After that I return to Cambridge. Then I go to Paris to visit old haunts and talk to some people.

Sylvie sat down at her dressing table and wrote straight back to Virginia.

Dearest friend Jin Kee,

It was nice to hear your news and about Albert Taft. I think he must be your sweetheart now. You could tell before the war that he had fallen for you 'hook, line and sinker'. (Beryl told me once that that was how you say it.)

Isn't it funny the things you remember? The other day I told my daddy (he is back here now) everything that happened to us. (He wanted to know every single thing.) He won't tell me so much about what happened to him. He was on the railway line, like Jamie Chase said, but he won't say too much about it. He looked very old when he arrived but looks like himself these days. I have not yet given him Ayoshi's gold coins. I am saving that for a surprise for him.

I saw the place where Jamie Chase lives the other day. The garden and everything was there, so that juggling was never just a dream. I really, really like Jamie Chase. I have been practising juggling. I showed my nana's friend Frank and he is very impressed. I think Frank is quite keen on Nana but I don't know if you can have sweethearts when you are old.

My nana showed me a picture of herself when she was little and you know who she looked like? Me! Only very pretty. Also – very funny – my grandfather had an Ayoshi like mine but she wouldn't tell me too much about it.

My mother is coming home tomorrow and I am very worried about this as I can't remember what she looks like. Or Feargal. Do you think this will matter? I can't say this to Nana or Daddy as they might be cross.

Are you going home after Paris? You didn't say whether Albert was going with you. I bet he is. I wish I was coming with you. It's very cold here and there's no blue sky, only in a bit of the day. I think we'll have to wait to come home until my daddy is better. He is quite good now and can walk for miles without his stick. I will come and see you straight away when I arrive home.

And Uncle Wo and the old nana. I promise.

   Love from your sister,

   Syl Vee

PS I have decided that Jamie Chase will be my sweetheart but I'll probably not tell him until I'm old like you.


In the middle of that night Sylvie woke up and realised that she'd wet the bed. She lay in the warm space for a while, then went to her nana's room and told her. Mrs Conrad shook herself awake and padded along the corridor to strip and remake Sylvie's bed. She pulled Sylvie's wet nightie up over her head and replaced it with one of hers. 'There now. It's like a tent on you,' she said.

Sylvie lay in the newly made bed. 'I'm sorry, Nana.'

'No worries, deary. None of this is your fault. None of it.'

As she padded down the yard towards the washhouse with the bundle of wet sheets, Mrs Conrad wondered how any of them would ever recover from the guilt of letting a child go through what Sylvie had gone through. They'd really, really made a mess of things between them. Not for the first time she wondered how on earth her daughter had lost Sylvie on the quayside. If the child had been hers she'd have had her tethered to her with a rope. Wise after the event, of course. We were always wise after the event. Her husband the headmaster had preached that. It was only after a war that we discovered how we should have fought it.

\*   \*   \*

Lesley Sambuck swept into Priorton in the very largest taxi that could be obtained at Darlington station. The taxi driver leaped to open the door for her and lifted out several cases. Then he came to the house and asked for help with the trunk. Against Mrs Conrad's protests Bo went to do the honours. So it was when Bo Sambuck really got a look at his wife for the first time in nearly four years he was gasping over a heavy snakeskin trunk that he could have lifted single-handed before the war. He looked across at her and smiled sweetly despite the pain. 'Gathered a bit of moss in Durban, did you, Les?'

She frowned very slightly, her cheeks pink. 'You are always so sarcastic, Bo.'

The luggage stacked in the narrow hall, she paid the taxi driver from a full wallet and turned to face them all. In her close-fitting green coat and a matching hat decorated with felt flowers she cut an elegant figure. Feargal stood behind her in a tweed coat and cap. 'Bo, darling!' She went towards him and kissed him delicately on both cheeks. 'You look so much better than I thought, darling. The stories ... I thought ...' She shuddered. 'And Ma!' She shook hands with her mother. 'In the pink, I see. Frank! The faithful Frank!' She shook hands with him without actually looking at him.

Sylvie took a gulping breath. She could smell her mother's dense sweet smell.

'And Sylvia! What a naughty girl you were to run away like that. And look at you! You are so big! So tall.' She made no effort to touch Sylvie.

'I didn't run away,' said Sylvie. 'You all kind of left me behind.'

Lesley rolled her eyes at Bo. 'That accent! What company *has* she been keeping?'

Sylvie felt the comfort of her father's arm around her as he pulled her to his side. 'She's been keeping company with those who kept her out of harm's way and kept her alive and safe, haven't you, old girl?' he said quietly. 'They did the job we should have done. And we are very grateful, aren't we, Lesley?' He glared at his wife.

She flushed more at this, then shrugged. 'Whatever. Now, Sylvie, say hello to your little brother.'

Feargal stared at Sylvie from a face she could not recognise. She had barely thought of him in all the years. When she had thought of him he had been small, wriggling like an eel on his *amah*'s arm. But here was a tall boy with a fierce, serious face. He turned to look at Lesley. 'Mum,' he said in a clear, piercing voice, 'I'm hungry.'

'Course, darling,' said Lesley. 'Your Nana Conrad will get you something to eat, won't you, Ma?'

Mrs Conrad was staring steadily at her daughter. 'It's very good to see you so safe and well, Lesley.'

'Well,' said Lesley, irritated as always by her mother, 'we've all come through hard times, but here we are.'

'Was it hard in South Africa?' said Mrs Conrad. 'From where I'm standing, Lesley, you've put on weight, a stone at least. And from your letters it all sounded like paradise there. A veritable paradise.'

'Well!' Lesley looked at them, from one to the other. 'I *was* the lucky one, wasn't I?'

# Chapter Thirty-Nine

## Panorama

Under instructions from Mrs Conrad, Frank now started to take Sylvie out on her own each day. The house, up till now a sleepy haven of rest and self-discovery, had become a palace to tension, strained looks, whispered words and forced laughter. Most days Lesley sat in the front room in front of a blazing fire, dressed up as though for an afternoon party. Feargal, watchful and confused among all these strangers, especially his strange father who shouted in the night, stayed close to her. After one abortive nature walk with Frank and Sylvie, when he declared himself 'infernally bored', Feargal was not invited again.

Bo Sambuck shrank back into himself a little and took to using his father-in-law's stick again. He stayed longer in the little boxroom where, after two nights, he now slept. (His shouts in the night had disturbed Lesley.) And to Mrs Conrad's consternation, he began to eat less.

For Sylvie, who had not spoken directly to her mother

since she arrived, it was a relief to get out of the house with Frank. One day they caught the Favourite Bus in the market-place and took the long road to Durham City. Here Frank took Sylvie to the great cathedral and hauled himself after her up the hundreds of steps of the great tower. As they climbed, Sylvie told Frank that they had their own cathedral in Singapore. 'It's a big white place. Do you know, it shines in the sun. That man from the cathedral came to the camp once. The Reverend. He gave the Blood of Christ to my friend Miss Snowie. In a silver tennis cup that had been my father's.'

'Is that so?' Frank puffed.

At the top Sylvie pulled her scarf more tightly around her, to muffle the cutting wind. Then she blinked and opened her eyes very wide. Before them lay the whole city with its rearing castle, its coiling river, its steep narrow streets, its necklaces of trees. From the edge of the city green hills rolled into the distance where, tucked into the elbow-like gaps, the high tracery of colliery wheels dotted the landscape like punctuation marks.

It was comforting afterwards to go back down again into the cosier dark of the nave and hear the patter of boys' feet as they crossed the stone floor for choir practice. Frank led Sylvie to a side-chapel hung with ragged flags. There was a great book there in a case. 'This is the book where is written the names of the soldiers who died,' he said.

'Do you know the name of anyone in that book, Frank?'

'Oh yes. Many friends of mine. Boys who went to my school. Men who fought beside me in the Great War.'

'Is there a book with my father's friends in it? The ones off the railway?'

'I imagine there will be, Sylvie. Before long.' Frank rubbed his hands together. 'Now then. I think that afternoon tea might be the order of things. We need warming up.'

They found a café where the owner, a frowsty woman who was mistress of the art of Coping Under Rationing, produced a very passable high tea. At first Sylvie and Frank ate in companionable silence. Then Sylvie finished her second scone and looked at Frank. 'You know when we were up there, in the tower?'

'Yes. What an amazing panorama that is.'

'Well, our house in Singapore, Hibiscus Lodge, that's on a big hill too. You can see all round the city from there. You can see the harbour with the big ships and the sampans. You can see the docks with the big cranes. You can see the *padang* and Beach Road. That was where my friend Virginia lived. You can even, if you stretch, see Chinatown and the people's washing out on poles.' She was not sure how much of this she was making up. She was not sure of the exact perspective but she knew the facts to be true.

'It must be a wonderful city,' said Frank, neatly folding his napkin. 'Singapore.'

'Oh yes,' said Sylvie. 'Do you know that Singa Pura was a wonderful lionfish that started the city off altogether? And do you know there are moonflowers in our garden, which smell of heaven? And butterflies as big as your two hands?' She put both of her hands up before his eyes.

Frank linked his bony hands together and fluttered them in the air. Two women at the next table glared at him. Sylvie laughed. 'And do you know that in Singapore the sun shines every single day – well nearly – and no one, absolutely no one wears liberty bodices?'

It was Frank's turn to smile. 'I think you love your city, Sylvie. Perhaps you're homesick.'

'Homesick.' Sylvie rolled the word round in her mind. 'It's my home town, Frank. I'm Singaporean.' That was a word she'd learned from Simon Chen on the boat. Now she'd said it out loud.

'So you don't like our poor old North East of England?'

She looked around the crowded café, with its steamed-up windows. 'Not very much,' she said. 'I like you and my nana. And my nana's kitchen. But not the rest.'

Frank smiled slightly. 'Honest as ever, Sylvie. Honest as ever.'

Later they were bumping along in the afternoon dark of the Favourite Bus when Sylvie asked him if she could ask him a question.

'Certainly, Sylvie.'

'Will you answer it?'

'I'll try my best.'

'Are you my nana's sweetheart?'

The bus stopped and started again, and they watched as the conductor punched tickets for the new passengers.

'Are you?' said Sylvie.

'Well, I have to say I'm her very good friend, Sylvie. I like her company and I would do anything in the world for her.'

'Oh,' said Sylvie. 'Is it because you're old that you can't be her sweetheart?'

The bus stopped again. More passengers. More tickets.

'Once, long ago,' said Frank, 'when we were all very young, your nana, grandpa and I, I did want your nana to be my sweetheart. But she chose the better man.'

'My grandpa?'

'He was a great man.'

'But *you* loved her?'

'I love her still, Sylvie.' He moved his arm and pulled her hand through so it sat in the crook of his elbow.

'Frank?'

'Yes, Sylvie.'

'Do you think my mother loves my daddy?'

He shook his head. 'These things are private, Sylvie. We can't know anything of them.'

It had been a very difficult week for them all. First problem was the sleeping arrangements. Bo had disturbed Lesley in the night because of his shouts and screams. So he moved to the boxroom, which meant Feargal had to share with Sylvie. This worried her because of her bed wetting, so Nana very smoothly insisted that Sylvie sleep with her in her bed, saying privately to Sylvie not to worry about the wetting. They would deal with it together.

Then there was the problem of the photos: endless photos of Lesley's life in South Africa. She made them look at shots of swimming pools and safaris, cocktail parties and galas. They had to listen to her gospel of the great life to be had out there for anybody with sense and a bit of capital.

As well as this there were Lesley's ill-tempered tirades, endured by a stony-faced Mrs Conrad, about the miserable state of the dark North East with its stigmata of poverty and lack of any sense of appropriate service. This was usually linked to the fact that Mrs Conrad, since her husband's death, had refused to have help in the house.

Then there was the elucidation of Sylvie's faults. Her posture was slouching, her accent sing-song, her looks were too dark (this with a resentful glance at Bo). The air, in this formerly welcoming house, became pickled in a resentment so distilled that it might have bruised your skin.

One night Sylvie was turning over the photographs that Lesley had left on the sideboard. 'Who's this?' she said. 'The man with that hair all brushed back? He's on eleven of these pictures.'

Lesley glanced across at Bo. 'That will be Robbie Sleights-Bix. Colonel Sleights-Bix. I told you about him, Bo. Connected with De Beers. Rolling in it.'

Mrs Conrad looked up from her knitting. 'Lesley,' she said, 'sometimes you sound so . . . commonplace.'

Lesley turned then on Sylvie. 'What're you gawping at, girl? Go and find something to do, will you? Running wild for years has done you no good. No good at all. You creep around, you listen all the time.'

Sylvie trudged to the door and made her way across the hall. As she walked up the stairs, her mother's voice rang through the house. 'When we *do* go to South Africa, Bo, that child should stay here, go to boarding school, get all those dreadful rough edges smoothed off, get rid of that dreadful accent . . .'

Later, lying on her grandmother's bed she could still hear

the row raging below. Most particularly she listened to the strident tones of her father. The words were squeezed from him in a bitter stream. He almost sobbed with anger.

'Sylvie! Sylvie! Wake up.' Frank was shaking her. The bus was settling on its springs, easing to a halt. 'We're here. Home now. Fasten your scarf tight, it's blowing a gale out there.'

When they got back, at her grandmother's gate there was a small black car. Sylvie dashed into the house and there, sitting at her nana's table, under her nana's print of *Stag at Bay*, was Virginia Chen. 'Jin Kee!' Sylvie said, throwing herself into the slender arms of her friend. She gulped. 'Jin Kee.'

'And here is Miss Chen's friend,' said Mrs Conrad.

Standing behind her near the door, in a very ill-fitting demob suit, was a very *un*military but still handsome Albert Taft. He held out a hand. 'A long time since the shadow puppets, Sylvie.' He pumped her hand up and down with painful enthusiasm. Unlike her father Albert seemed much younger than before. His hair was fairer, his face ruddier. It must be the lack of uniform.

'Don't tell me how much I've grown!' said Sylvie. 'Please.'

Then they all laughed and the air was very warm. She looked round the room and at the ceiling, at Frank then at her nana.

'Your parents are out,' said Mrs Conrad. 'They went to Darlington to see an old friend of theirs. And I believe they had some business to do.' She turned to her old friend, who was hovering by the door. 'Frank!' she said. 'Come into the sitting room. I've been sorting Maurice's books. I thought you might like to take your pick. We could parcel up the rest for the bookshop.'

The door clicked behind them and Virginia, Albert and Sylvie sat down round the table. Sylvie sat forward in her chair, her elbows on the table, staring hard at Virginia Chen. 'Why d'you come here? Are you going home yet? Can I come with you?'

'Slow down, slow down, Syl Vee. Yes. We are going to Singapore in three weeks' time.'

Sylvie looked at Albert Taft, who was smiling like a cat. 'What about him?'

'He will come too.'

'What will the grandmother say?'

'She will be pleased. Grandmother has a weakness for foreigners.'

'I know that,' said Sylvie. 'Don't I know that?' She looked at them. Albert now had his arm round Virginia's waist and was smiling down at her, looking very pleased. 'What about Simon Chen? He'll not be pleased. Another foreigner in the house.'

'As you say. But he is here at Cambridge for another couple of years so he will not interfere.' Virginia paused. 'How are you? Your parents are both here?'

'My father was like a skeleton but my nana is feeding him up. And he shouts in the night. My mother is very fat. Nana says she has been feeding off the fat of the land in Africa while Dad and me starved in the camps and *she* had to have The Rationing.'

'Your nana said that?'

'Well, no, but I bet she thought it. My mother had a whale of a time in Africa and my nana says she has got very *commonplace* these days.'

'Is that so?'

'And,' said Sylvie, heaving a sigh from the soles of her sandals, 'she wants to go back to South Africa. She says any fool can make money there. She wants her and Daddy and Feargal to go. She wants to put me in a boarding school here. Beryl Bridges used to say that boarding schools were prisons for children. Like Sime Road only worse. No trading.'

Virginia smiled slightly at Albert. 'She's never even been to an ordinary school. Boarding school!'

Sylvie nodded at him. 'I'll probably sock somebody and get expelled. Again.'

'Something of a habit with her.' Virginia turned back to Sylvie. 'Syl Vee! I came to see that life was treating you well. But Albert knows how much I miss you. You and I were together too long not to miss each other. So we have agreed that, if you wish it, ever, you will always, always have a home with us in Singapore.'

'Yes. Yes.' Her mouth and cheeks were sore with smiling. She tried to stay calm, to stem the tide of her relief. 'I'd like that. That would be just fine. I will come with you.'

Virginia Chen frowned. 'Be careful, Sylvie. Your mother . . . your father. You waited so long to find him. Such a long time.'

Sylvie shrugged. 'They're going to Africa. They don't need me.'

Virginia Chen stood up. 'You would have to get their permission, Sylvie. No running away. But, given that, we'll get you a berth with us. Let me know. We're going to see Simon in Cambridge to upset him with our news before we go. No doubt he will have something to say.'

Virginia and Albert said their goodbyes to Mrs Conrad and Frank, then Sylvie and Virginia stood in the doorway as Albert went to crank up the car. Sylvie said, 'Will you marry Albert Taft, Virginia?'

Virginia shrugged. 'I don't know.' Then she laughed. 'I will try him out and see if he fits. I will consult my grandmother. Then, perhaps.'

Then she was gone, leaving only the scent of magnolia in the air. Sylvie wandered back into the sitting room where Nana and Frank had their heads down over a pile of books. 'Virginia wants me to go home with her and Albert. Back home with them,' she said.

The other two exchanged glances. 'Well, you'll need to talk to your parents,' said Nana. 'Don't know that they'd want you to do that.'

Two hours later, when Bo and Lesley swept back into the house laden with parcels, there seemed little opportunity to talk of such things. Bo helped Lesley stack her parcels in the sitting room and went off to change out of his lounge suit. Sylvie's mother kept her outdoor coat on and, parcels stowed, went off again with Feargal in the taxi, which was still waiting at the door.

As the air settled after the flurried exit Sylvie looked at her nana. 'I thought at first she really didn't like me. But I don't think that's quite right. She doesn't see me. I am invisible, like a ghost.'

Mrs Conrad sighed. 'Ah, Sylvie,' she said. 'That imagination of yours.'

Sylvie waited eight minutes, then climbed the stairs to her father's boxroom. He was sitting at a tiny table by the window, staring into the gathering dark. His glance as it moved towards Sylvie was unseeing. Then he coughed. 'Sylvie. What can I do for you?'

'How are you, Daddy?'

'Better by the day, sweetheart.' He took out a packet of Players Full Strength and lit one, pulling the air between his clenched teeth. 'And how are you? D'you have a good trip with old Frank?'

'Yes. Frank is really nice. We had tea. We went to the top of the cathedral.'

'Splendid.' He drew hard again on his cigarette. 'The thing is, sweetheart, your mother and I have been fixing things up today . . .'

'You're going to South Africa and putting me back in prison . . . sorry, boarding school.'

'Who told you that?'

'I heard you saying. I only find out anything by listening. Like a spy.'

'Well, sweetheart, it might sound bad but really it's somewhat worse. Your mother and Feargal, they are going to South Africa.'

'Not you? Not you?' *Somersaults. Cartwheels. Five-ball juggling.*

He shook his head. 'I can only tell you the truth, sweetheart. Somehow things are not right with us – your mother and I. She went away in very difficult times and came back a different person. And me? I'm like a bear with a sore head to live with. I have to try to go back to find the person I was before, before I can go forward.' He frowned. 'I have to make a safe place for the bad memories. Something like that. Your mother and I now, are snakes and bears. Different creatures.'

'So you can't be together?'

'The solicitor we saw today will sort something out.'

'So what will you do?'

'Go back to Singapore to take up the reins. Do what I can do with what's left. Build again. See if I can stake your mother on her new adventure. Sylvie—'

But she'd gone from the room. He could hear the clatter of footsteps on the corridor, the scrabbling in the far bedroom. Then she came back with Ayoshi and a pair of scissors. She lifted the obi, snipped Ayoshi's wound and extracted the gold coins. These she heaped in two neat piles on the table before him. 'I saved these for you all through the camp. We couldn't use them for trade because Jin Kee said it was too risky. So I said I'd save them for you after the war. That way you could use this to start up and I'll come and help you.'

'Sylvie, I don't think, just yet—'

'I'm coming anyway. Virginia was here to visit today and she said I can go home with her and Albert Taft. I said I will.'

He looked at her quietly. 'I've thought I couldn't live with anyone, that I have nothing left that I could share, that another person couldn't tolerate—'

'I wouldn't mind you shouting in the night,' said Sylvie. 'Not at all. I know about being behind the wire. And the shouting. There was this woman in our hut called Miss Lomax who was truly mad. And other things happened. I told you. I know about it. I'm thirteen now. Not a baby.'

He lit a new cigarette from the old one. 'You'd have to go to school.'

'I'll go to school, I promise. I'll go to school if I can go to the school where Virginia Chen went.'

'You can't go there. That's for—'

'It's for people like me,' she scowled. 'Simon Chen says things will be different in these new days. In this new world people like me *can* go to Virginia's school.'

That night, when Lesley came back from her visit, the house was quiet. She was more civil with them than at any time during her stay. Bo cornered her in the sitting room and told her Sylvie was coming home with him. 'With *you*? But you're not fit to have a child with you. Be honest, Bo. With your . . . difficulties. I thought a boarding school . . . We should be able to scrape together some money. Ma'll help.'

He shook his head and spoke very slowly so she would listen and she would hear. 'That child spent nearly two years in an embattled city, more than a year behind barbed wire. Putting her in school would be sending her back to all that. I won't have that.' He glanced at the closed sitting-room door where, he felt sure, Sylvie was listening. 'What is it about the child, Lesley?' he whispered.

She shrugged. 'She was always very naughty, even as a small child.'

'She wasn't. She was playful, funny.'

'She was different.' She laughed mirthlessly. 'Your fault, darling. Or some ancestor of yours who had a roving eye, a taste for a bit of—'

'That's offensive, Lesley.'

'It's realistic, darling. It's the world we live in. They have it under better control in South Africa.'

'She's not going to boarding school, I'm telling you absolutely. She comes back to Singapore with me.'

'With you? In the state you're in?'

'With me!' He stood up and nearly knocked her over as he left the room.

Sylvie dodged away just in time. She went to find her grandmother, who was in the washhouse sorting the clean clothes. 'What's wrong with me, Nana?'

'There's nothing wrong with you, pet. You are just about perfect. A brave, clever girl.'

'My mother hates me.'

Mrs Conrad took a long time to fold her sheet. 'That's her loss, pet. The fault's with her, not with you.'

'She says Dad's ancestor had a "roving eye" and that's why I'm so awful.'

'Did she now?' said Mrs Conrad. 'Well, Sylvie, your mother, silly as she is, is my only begotten, even beloved, daughter but she's *such* a fool. Now then, can you fold those pillow slips for me? If you smooth them straight away they take so much less ironing.'

# Chapter Forty

## Festive Meal

That night Mrs Conrad lit the fire in the dining room and threw a linen cloth on the long table. 'Tonight we're eating in style,' she announced.

She had Sylvie repolishing spotless glasses and Frank laying out the best silver. She had soup bubbling on the iron hotplate, lamb packed with rosemary in the oven, and bottled-plum tart on the cold shelf in the pantry. She pulled out the last bottle of her husband's port from the sitting-room cupboard.

'This is very grand, Nana,' said Sylvie. 'Is it a party?'

'Well, perhaps,' said Mrs Conrad. 'I suppose you might say parties are to mark changes in family life: births, deaths, marriages, christenings. I suppose this is to mark a change. Your daddy's rebirth; your courage. Something like that. We need our best bib and tucker to celebrate that tonight.'

'What's that? Best bib and tucker.'

'Fancy dress. Pearls. Whatever you want. Go and tell them it's best bib and tucker.'

Bo wore his new suit. Lesley wore a generously cut black dress she'd found on her way through London. Sylvie wore her mother's pearls and a new white blouse with her kilt. Frank wore a floppy green bow tie with white spots. Mrs Conrad wore her fitted wool frock with the lace collar.

Warmed up with a generous glass of port (and perhaps his own nervousness) Frank was unusually talkative. He told funny stories about his early teaching days. Bo told some tales from the old colony. Lesley talked of schoolgirl japes at The Mount. It was all very congenial.

When they had cleared away the last of the plum pie and all the dishes, Mrs Conrad served cups of tea and announced she had something to show them. She brought an old cigar box to the table, tipped out a pile of photographs and laid them out on the table as though she were laying out a hand of patience.

Sylvie recognised the picture of the little boy in a dress holding the Ayoshi doll called Mimi.

'I was struck by a coincidence,' said Mrs Conrad. 'That little doll that Maurice has in his hand is just like Sylvie's doll, Ayoshi.'

'Ayoshi,' Sylvie said to Feargal. 'I got her from my friend Virginia Chen.' Feargal looked out of the window away from her. It was as though she'd never spoken.

One by one Mrs Conrad turned over the other photos. They showed images from the last eighty or so years: men, women and children posing in front of cardboard scenery, frozen with the need to be still for a full minute.

'What's this?' said Lesley. 'I haven't seen these before. Why haven't I seen these before, Ma?'

'They're your father's family, Lesley. He liked to keep them tucked away. See, here's his parents – teachers, of course. Then here's his grandfather, who traded in silk across in Sunderland. A very handsome man. And here is *his* father, the image of your father, don't you think, Lesley? So fair and handsome. And,' she turned up the last card from under the pack, 'here is *his* wife.'

Lesley gasped. Bo murmured something under his breath. Sylvie stared at an image that was exactly like the one in Virginia's grandmother's room: a graceful young woman with black hair dressed high in combs, lounging very slightly to one side and smiling at whomever was taking the photograph. She was very clearly Japanese.

'Is this some kind of joke, Ma?' Lesley was near to tears.

'No joke, my dear. Just a little truth. This handsome man here simply fell in love with the daughter of a colleague, who worked in the silk trade out of Sunderland. There were quite a few Japanese people in that town at the time. Your father loved his great-grandma but he kept this picture tucked away.'

'He must have had a "roving eye",' said Sylvie.

Lesley stood up, smoothed the napkin on to the table beside her, then walked quickly from the room. Feargal waited a second then followed her. He was the only one around the table who had no idea at all about just what had happened.

Mrs Conrad pushed the photograph towards Sylvie. 'Would you like to keep that picture of your great-granny, love? I thought perhaps you might like to put it alongside your

Ayoshi. I have to say you have quite a look of her, in some lights.'

Sylvie took the photograph from her nana and ran her fingers over the fine-boned face, the very black hair. She thought she smelled magnolias.

Bo rubbed his hands together very hard as though clearing them of one final speck of dirt. 'Well then, Sylvie, did Miss Chen tell you which ship she'd booked to go home?'

Mrs Conrad put a hand on Sylvie's and squeezed it tight.

'No, she didn't. But it was next Tuesday, I think.'

'Not so hard to check. If we get our skates on we might travel together with Virginia and her Albert Taft. A little Eastern sun will do me a world of good.'

'Well, that's all right then,' said Sylvie, nestling into her grandmother's ample side. 'Now we can go home.'

# Epilogue

V. Chen: Her Book

November 1947

Hurrah! The deal on the bungalow is finally clinched and Albert and I will move there next week. Everyone (including Albert) has been very good about his living at the shophouse, but the time has come for us to be alone. There are new cousins in the shop helping Uncle Wo but, even so, I will go to the shophouse each day. I know I will miss my grandmother.

Albert's job at the docks is now permanent and I am enjoying my teaching at the girls' school. I see Sylvie most days although she is not in my classes. She fights now and then, but this is ignored. There is an understanding of what she has endured. There are others like her. She comes with me every week to see my grandmother.

Albert and I went to Hibiscus Lodge for tiffin on Sunday and had an interesting time. Mr Sambuck is at last fit and very well, and working down at the quay as hard as ever. Three of his Chinese colleagues and their wives were there for tiffin (sign of the times). He's getting involved in Singapore affairs much more than before. (These affairs are fraught now by the European 'returners' wanting things to be as before and the Singaporeans determined not to go back to old colonial ways. I think it will get worse before it gets better.)

Mrs Sambuck has put in for an English divorce. Sylvie says that she has a South African sweetheart whom she will marry. She knows about divorce from American films and does not seem too troubled. From my (and Sylvie's) point of view it is an easier house without Mrs Sambuck but I am sorry for Mr Sambuck. Then again, he seems to be delighted to be back in his 'own' country in the company of his beloved daughter.

The English nana is visiting for two months, rather crowing at missing the worst English winter in decades. She will not keep out of the kitchen, which is a source of great annoyance to Cookie. She spends a lot of the time 'chewing the fat' with Jamie Chase, who is still stationed here. Sylvie says her nana is taken with Jamie, not least because he is the son of an English lord from their district in Durham, England.

Jamie Chase is always at Hibiscus Lodge. It is charming to watch Sylvie with him. He helps her with her homework. They play tennis together a great deal, they swim, they picnic, they juggle and they go to the pictures. I know she is nearly fifteen now and he is more than twenty, but there is something about them when they are together. I cannot quite bring myself to cast them as Romeo and Juliet, as that would cast me in the role of 'nurse' and I think I am neither so old nor so decrepit. But . . .

I have had another letter from Simon at Cambridge. He is doing brilliantly in his studies but becomes more radical there even than he was here. He is obviously itching to be back here to join in the struggle for change. I think that is inevitable now and I embrace it. I have one great hope: that Syl Vee (and her father) will embrace the changes with me.

It seems that it will be so.

## Afternote

After much internal struggle with the British a constitution based on a legislative assembly was enacted in Singapore in 1955. In 1957 internal independence was achieved. In 1963 Singapore joined Malaya in an independent Federation of Malay States. Then in 1965 Singapore separated from the federation and became an independent country.

In present day Singapore 0.5 per cent of Singaporeans are Eurasian. After independence, a sprinkling of European 'returners' took out full Singaporean citizenship.

## Further reading

If you want to find out more about this fascinating period of world history you may like to read:

Allen, Charles (ed) *Tales from the South China Seas*, André Deutsch, 1983

Allen, Sheila *Diary of a Girl in Changi*, Kangaroo Press, 1994

Barber, Noel *Sinister Twilight*, Collins, 1968

Bloom, Freddy *Diary of Captivity, Changi. 1942–5*, Bodley Head, 1980

Elphick, Peter *Singapore: The Pregnable Fortress*, Hodder & Stoughton, 1995

Farrell, J. G. *The Singapore Grip*, Weidenfeld & Nicolson, 1978

Lee, Cecil *Sunset of the Raj: The Fall of Singapore*, Pentland Press, 1994

Gough, Richard *SOE Singapore 1941–2*, William Kimber, 1985

Hayter, John *Priest in Prison*, Tynron Press, 1991

Jeffreys, Betty *White Coolies*, George Mann Ltd, 1973

Kennedy, Joseph *When Singapore Fell. Evacuations and Escapes 1942*, Macmillan, 1989

Lim, Janet *Sold for Silver*, OUP, 1958

Murfett, M. H., Miksic, J. N., Farrell, B. P., Chiang Ming Shun *Between Two Oceans. A History of Singapore: From First Settlement to Final British Withdrawal*, OUP, 1999

Nelson, David *The Story of Changi*, Changi Publication Co., 1973

Tsuji Masanobu (Col.) *Japan's Greatest Victory, Britain's Worst Defeat. The Capture of Singapore 1942*, Spellmount Ltd, 1997

The Imperial War Museum has a comprehensive archive of unpublished material, especially internees' experiences. I looked closely at the diaries of Mrs E. Collet, Mrs E. Innes Kerr and Mrs P. M. Briggs.

# Kitty Rainbow

## Wendy Robertson

When the soft-hearted bare-knuckle fighter Ishmael Slaughter rescues an abandoned baby from the swirling River Wear, he knows that if he takes her home his employer will give her short shrift – or worse. So it is to Janine Druce, a draper woman with a dubious reputation but a child of her own, that he takes tiny Kitty Rainbow.

Kitty grows up wild, coping with Janine's bouts of drunkenness and her son's silent strangeness. And she is as fierce in her affections as she is in her hatreds, saving her greatest love for Ishmael, the ageing boxer who provides the only link with her parentage, a scrap of cloth she was wrapped in when he found her. Kitty realises that she cannot live her life wondering who her mother was, and in Ishmael she has father enough. And, when she finds herself pregnant, deprived of the livelihood on which she and the old man depended, she must worry about the future, not the past. But the past has a way of catching the present unawares . . .

'An intense and moving story set against the bitter squalor of the hunger-ridden thirties' *Today*

'A rich fruit cake of well-drawn characters . . .' *Northern Echo*

'Fans of big family stories must read Wendy Robertson' *Peterborough Evening Telegraph*

'A lovely book' *Woman's Realm*

0 7472 5183 5

**headline**

# The Jagged Window

## Wendy Robertson

Edward Maichin's eloquent sermons and blond good looks have ensured his popularity amongst his congregation in the small Welsh mining community where he and his family live. But at home, the dark side of Edward's character runs riot, and since his errant father ran away to America, his mother and younger siblings have been powerless to prevent Edward's cruelty which dominates their lives.

Only his younger sister Theo, a gifted writer haunted by her stillborn twin, is brave enough to defy Edward's hypocrisy. But her promising career as a journalist is cut short when the suspicious death of their grandmother's maid – rumoured to be bearing Edward's child – forces the Maichins to flee the valley for the pits of North-East England.

There, on the wild moors of Durham, Theo takes up the position of companion to an old lady who lives with her shambling bear of a son. Theo realises that she has found a family even more vulnerable and fractured than her own. But will the price of healing this family – and hers – be more than she is prepared to pay?

Praise for Wendy Robertson:

'A cross between the yarn-spinning style of Catherine Cookson and the powerful literary talent of Pat Barker' *Sunderland Echo*

'This wonderful historical saga has to be on your reading list' *Woman's Realm*

'A blend of accessibility and total sincerity' Pat Barker

'Wendy Robertson's characters are wonderful . . . quirky and interesting people, utterly believable . . . A triumph' *Northern Echo*

0 7472 5978 X

## headline

Now you can buy any of these other bestselling Headline books from your bookshop or *direct from the publisher*.

FREE P&P AND UK DELIVERY
(Overseas and Ireland £3.50 per book)

| | | |
|---|---|---|
| The House on Lonely Street | Lyn Andrews | £5.99 |
| A Glimpse of the Mersey | Anne Baker | £5.99 |
| The Whispering Years | Harry Bowling | £5.99 |
| The Stony Path | Rita Bradshaw | £5.99 |
| The Bird Flies High | Maggie Craig | £5.99 |
| Kate's Story | Billy Hopkins | £5.99 |
| Taking a Chance on Love | Joan Jonker | £5.99 |
| The Jarrow Lass | Janet MacLeod Trotter | £5.99 |
| All or Nothing | Lynda Page | £5.99 |
| A Perfect Stranger | Victor Pemberton | £5.99 |
| Where Hope Lives | Wendy Robertson | £5.99 |
| Better Days | June Tate | £6.99 |
| A Rare Ruby | Dee Williams | £5.99 |

TO ORDER SIMPLY CALL THIS NUMBER

**01235 400 414**

or visit our website: www.madaboutbooks.co.uk

Prices and availability subject to change without notice.